Don't Stop Till You Get Enough

(Book Three in the Stafford Brothers Series)

Chicki Brown

Please Note

This is a work of fiction. Names, characters, places, and incidents either are the product of the author's imagination or are used fictitiously, and any resemblance to actual persons, living or dead, business establishments, events or locales is entirely coincidental.

What readers are saying about the Stafford Brothers series...

"This family series is right up there with the likes of the Westmorelands (Brenda Jackson), the Graysons (The late Francis Ray) and the Wolf Pack (Maureen Smith). Get the first one and settle back, enjoy the ride from the ATL to Vegas to Nigeria." – Amazon review by Brenda #BRAB "Brenda L"

I absolutely loved the book. It is a beautiful love story about Marc and Gianne. It makes you wish that if you had to deal with a health crisis, you were blessed with a strong caring man like Marc Stafford. This book made me cry. I've already read the second book in the series and you will be just awed with the entire Stafford family. Can't wait for the third book. I've read every book that Chicki has written, and she truly has the gift to pull you into the book and the characters. Keep up the good work!!! – review of *A Woman's Worth* by Amazon Customer

"Brown lays out the flavor of Nigerian culture and politics, planting Charles and Adanna squarely in the middle looking for a solution that will satisfy both families and allow them to be together. Adanna wears her caring heart on her sleeve, causing Charles to fall for her that much more, and Charles shows himself to be as upstanding as he is a gifted surgeon, making Adanna a goner. The fast pace of the story makes it an easy, entertaining read, and Brown lays the groundwork for the next brother's saga in a manner that takes nothing away from this story--a juicy bone tossed to eager readers who will anxiously await the next Stafford installment." – Amazon review of *Till You Come Back to Me* by pwriter

Acknowledgments

I would like to express my thanks to all those who helped me with "insider information."

Patricia Balentine for coming up with the name for Greg's show.

Tashika Crawley for insight on therapy and counseling, even though I did the opposite of everything she told me.

ReShonda Tate-Billingsley for answering my questions about on-air TV personalities.

Jill Renee White for the New York subway info

M.J. Kane, Bettye Griffin, Natalie Owens; Zee Monodee, Ednah Walters, and Joanna Villalongo for giving me their input on the early chapters.

Estella Robinson for being my faithful beta reader.

And Karen McCollum Rodgers of Critique Editing Services, my new editor, for doing a tremendous job of fixing up my mess.

Chapter One

Greg Stafford slammed the door to his Upper East Side New York apartment, engaged both locks then dropped his head to the door and banged it several times—hoping the pain might snap him out of his nightmare. No such luck. He dragged his body to the sofa, slumped down and tried to concentrate on the tinkling sound of the floor-to-ceiling Asian fountain in the foyer. Even that did nothing to calm him. He'd just spent the past four hours at the local police precinct, waiting for his attorney to get him released. His arrest would surely be headline news. He wasn't a major star, but he had become a fixture on New York television and the markets in which the show was syndicated.

At a complete loss for what to do next, he picked up the remote for the TV and turned the channel to the network to which he'd been contracted for the past two years. Would they report his arrest? Or would they ignore it? Wishful thinking for sure. They couldn't ignore breaking news involving one of their own. Could they?

His co-host, Arianna Wolfe, with whom Greg shared the desk every day, said, *"A member of The Scoop family is off the air tonight, as authorities investigate indecency charges. He will not be at the desk until the investigation is complete. We will bring you up to date when new information becomes available."*

Thankful they had avoided the details, Greg changed the channel. Sadly, he knew the other stations wouldn't be as kind.

"In breaking news, the wife of New York Senator Carl

Price was arrested this weekend for having engaged in sexual relations in broad daylight in an alley not far from Barney's. The man has now been identified as Gregory Stafford, the host of the top-rated magazine show, The Scoop. Both were charged with indecent exposure and public lewdness and released on their own recognizance.

We contacted Senator Price's office, but received no response. Stafford has been unavailable for comment. Legal issues aside, these arrests raise questions about the stability of the popular senator's marriage, which has been under scrutiny for some time. Mrs. Price, who is twenty-five years younger than the senator, has been seen frequently on the New York club circuit alone. Stafford is single and is a well-known regular on the club scene."

The report hadn't ended more than two minutes before his phone started ringing. *His boss.* Then it rang in succession ten more times. He stared at the screen. *His publicist. The station manager. His co-anchor. His father. His mother. Charles. Marc. Vic. Jesse. Nick.* Coming from a big family could be a blessing, but it could also be a major curse. The Scoop was syndicated in most major markets, and inevitably, members of the family watched the show every night. Right now, he didn't want to speak to any of them. What could he say to explain the situation he'd put himself in? If he wanted to hang onto his job though, he had to respond to his boss and the station manager. He pressed his head between his hands as though he could squeeze the condemning voices out, then stood and walked into the kitchen. Vodka. Yes, vodka seemed appropriate right about now. Even though he wasn't a big drinker, he kept a bottle around for when he had guests. The freezer always held a bottle or two of Stoli. After he poured enough for three people into a water glass, he swallowed three times and picked up the phone. No, not yet. He had to think for a while before he spoke to anyone.

From puberty on, his sexual appetite had been what most people would consider normal. But in the past few years, he'd graduated from a serious relationship, to casual dating, to serial dating, to strictly sexual relationships, to one-night stands, then to online porn when he couldn't find a hook-up. He usually avoided thinking too deeply about the reasons why he'd gotten to this point. Normally, he didn't allow his mind to venture into that kind of introspection. His outlook tended to be more on the *don't cry over spilt milk* side. But recently he had begun to question his escalating sexual appetite, which had begun after he'd moved to New York.

Why couldn't he be more like his brothers? All five of them were committed to just one woman, and they all seemed happy. Not just happy, but satisfied. Marc and Gianne were always thirty seconds from jumping each other's bones, but they were newlyweds. Doing the wild thing seemed to be at the top of Cydney and Jesse's list of favorite pastimes, as evidenced by her perpetual pregnancies. Vic and Mona had been married for ten years; yet sometimes, the strong sex vibe between them could be sensed by anyone within ten feet. Even his single baby brother, Nick, boasted about his upcoming second anniversary with his girlfriend, Cherilyn.

What was wrong with him? No woman held his interest for more than a weekend or two. Hadn't they all been raised in the same home with the same lofty moral values? And what changed. He hadn't always been like this. The third oldest of the six, Greg had managed to keep his problem a secret from his family; although when Charles came to New York to stay with him not long ago, he'd taken his brother to a couple of his favorite clubs. When he invited two of the women they'd met back to his apartment for the night, Charles begged off. He obviously disagreed with Greg's lifestyle, even though he didn't come right out and say anything. His facial expressions, tone of voice, and early departure made it plain. Hopefully, he hadn't discussed his suppositions with the rest of the family. Not that it mattered now. Everyone would know within a matter of hours.

He gulped down the rest of his drink in an effort to fortify himself before he listened to the voicemail messages. *Might as well go in order.*

"This is Ken. I suppose you've already heard The Scoop had to put you on administrative leave for the immediate future. You, me and the people from Legal need to sit down and figure out where we go from here. Get back to me as soon as you get this message."

He forwarded to the next message. "Please pick up, Greg," his publicist, Jordyn, pleaded. "You know why I'm calling. I have to speak with you before I can figure out what kind of spin to put on this…*event*. Call me ASAP."

Next message. "Greg, it's John Hanke. It's imperative we speak as soon as possible. Your attorney informed us of the situation. Your arrest has raised some legal concerns, not for the station, but for you personally. I want to discuss them with you immediately. I'll be waiting to hear from you."

"Hi, Greg. It's Arianna. We tried to gloss over the details as best we could. Let me know how you're doing. I'm worried about my co-host. Please call me back."

"Gregory, this is your father. What the hell is going on up there? Your mother is frantic. She's been crying since we heard the report. Couldn't you at least have warned us? Why did we have to find out from the television? An explanation is in order, son. I expect a call tonight."

He forwarded to his mother's message. The tremor in her voice put a lump in his throat. "Sweetheart, I know Daddy called, but I wanted to talk to you myself. Are you all right? I hope your absence from the show isn't permanent. Let me know you're okay, please."

He couldn't face his father's reproach. Calling his mother would be less painful.

The calls from his brothers, except for Charles, were of

the WTF variety. Charles merely said, "You're out of control, man. It's time you thought about getting some help. If you want to talk, I'm here."

The cold empty glass in his hand mocked him. Icy and vacant. Like his life at the moment. He wandered back into the kitchen and refilled the depleted vessel with chilled liquid. Why couldn't *he* be filled? Why did he feel such a void?

What was I thinking? I recognized her, but I wanted her so badly, / I didn't care what the repercussions might be if we got caught. Why can't I control myself? He threw the glass across the room, and it shattered on the red wall over the black Chinese symbols for peace.

He had been on his way into the studio and stopped at Barney's to buy a new cologne at the men's fragrance counter when she appeared next to him and inclined her head exposing her long creamy neck. "What do you think of this fragrance?"

He leaned closer and inhaled. "Intoxicating."

She studied his eyes for a long moment, then breezed away leaving an enticing trail of expensive fragrance behind. He followed it like a cartoon character drifting on a visible ribbon of scent wrapped around his head. Her gaze locked with his as the elevator door opened and she stepped inside. Greg quickened his steps so he might enter the cab before the doors closed. They rode in silence for one floor.

"I know you," she said, giving him a blatant head-to-toe scan. "You host a TV show…The Story…The Chat…"

"The Scoop," Greg corrected her with a smile. "And you're Mrs. Carl Price."

"Melinda. You are an extremely good-looking man."

Greg couldn't believe what happened next. She pressed the stop button. The elevator halted its descent, and she took two steps toward him so there wasn't even an inch of daylight between them. When she put her palm against his chest and raised her chin so he felt her breath on his face, he curved his right arm around her back and pulled her body against his. "And you're a very beautiful woman."

"Are you on your way to an appointment?" she asked, her lips brushing his.

"I am now." With his free hand, Greg cupped her booty and pressed her hips against him. He backed her against the wall of the elevator and raised her dress around her hips.

"Not here," she said between raspy breaths and yanked the dress back down. The wife of the state's wildly popular junior senator pushed the button to restart the elevator. "Let's leave." When the door opened on the first floor, she strode out and headed for the main store entrance. Greg followed her like a starving dog panting after a rare steak.

Out in the sunshine on bustling Madison Avenue, she slipped her sunglasses down from the top of her head and quickened her pace until she shifted into a jog. Greg's heart thundered as she turned onto E. 61st Street and glanced over her shoulder to see if he still followed her. The suspense of where she might be going threatened to kill him. She turned the corner again and disappeared into an alley.

When he caught up with her, she had dropped her shopping bags to the ground and stood with her hands on her hips as though proposing a dare. Unable to slow his pace, he slammed her against the brick wall of the building. The way his head spun from the chase and the headiness of the challenge, he had to press his hands against the wall on either side of her head to get his balance.

"Hurry! We can't stay here long before someone sees us." She wriggled her dress up and stepped her feet apart. "Hurry!"

♥♥♥

Greg rubbed his eyes. He needed to start returning these

calls. The station manager wouldn't wait, and neither would Jordyn. She needed to know how to respond to the media. He started with John, who said he wanted them to meet first thing in the morning. Greg then called his publicist and asked her to meet him. He wanted to avoid speaking to his father for as long as humanly possible, so he dialed the house number instead. When his mother answered, he cleared his throat and simply said, "Hey, Mama."

"Is it true, Gregory?" she asked, sounding as though she were heartbroken.

He closed his eyes and dropped his head back so it thumped against the wall. "Yeah."

"I just have one other question." She exhaled a long sigh. "Why?"

The muscles in his throat constricted, and his eyes welled. "I don't know, Mama. I'm—I'm not like my brothers."

"I'm so worried about you, honey. We heard them say you'll be off camera for the time being."

"It's not a permanent decision. I'll find out the details tomorrow. Don't worry about me, Mama. I'll be all right."

"I'm not so sure, Gregory. Maybe you should talk to someone about this."

"I will. I promise. Sorry, I have to go now. Talk to you later." He clicked off the call overwhelmed by shame, his constant companion lately. Whenever he had a hook-up with someone, afterward he felt no elation or even sense of satisfaction. Just shame and emptiness, and hearing the disappointment in his mother's voice multiplied the shame ten-fold.

Greg didn't even go into his bedroom. Most of the night, he stayed awake with the television on but not really watching the screen. He'd sunk to his lowest level. Sex in broad daylight with a married woman—a married woman whose famous husband was adored by his constituency. Charles had been right. His sexual appetite had escalated to the point where it felt unmanageable. The press had been kind to Melinda Price since her husband's election as senator. The media had downplayed her fondness for the party life in favor of her involvement in many high-profile charitable causes. Greg didn't understand what the pretty thirty-year-old saw in the fifty-five-year-old politician, but to each his own.

He might have slept two hours, before the alarm clock startled him back to consciousness. Following a long, hot shower, he dressed, put on his shades, and one of his favorite duckbill caps. He put the lanyard, which held his studio ID, over his head then took the elevator down to the lobby where Roland, the doorman, hailed him a cab. Greg wondered if Roland knew what had happened to him. If he did, he hadn't let on.

When the taxi pulled in front of the towering building housing the studios of most of the network shows, he spotted two men outside the entrance who seemed out of place. One wore a gray vest, khaki pants, sunglasses, and running shoes. The other was dressed in jeans and sneakers, and a white shirt with the tails out—nothing out of the ordinary except for the cameras hanging around their necks. Paparazzi for sure. Greg paid the driver, pulled his cap down low on his forehead. It wasn't much of a disguise, but at least he didn't have to look them in the eye.

"Greg!" Khaki Pants yelled. "Can you tell us what's going to happen now that you've been taken off the air?"

"Have you spoken to Mrs. Price since your arrest? Will you two continue seeing each other?" the other one hollered as Greg rushed past them.

His automatic instinct was to punch them both, but he knew not to respond, give them more fuel for the fire. Greg bypassed the newspaper box, his normal stop on the way in through the revolving doors into an enormous lobby. Once he flashed his badge to the security officer at the main desk, he jumped on the first open elevator. Two other people followed him in before the doors closed, but he didn't bother to look at either of them. He pushed the button for the twenty-sixth floor and rode up feeling as though he'd swallowed one of the boulders from the fountain outside the iconic building. Hopefully, his attorney and his publicist had already arrived.

Greg mumbled good morning to the few people he passed in the hall on his way to the open door of the conference room. The aroma of coffee greeted him as he walked in.

"Morning, Greg," John said, sounding as if being pleasant were a struggle.

He removed his sunglasses and hat and nodded to the station manager, Thaddeus Jones, his attorney, and Ken Peterson, his immediate boss. "Morning."

"Fix yourself some coffee," John continued. "We're waiting for someone from Legal and your publicist to get here."

Thankful for the brief reprieve, he went to the table in the front corner of the room and poured two cups, mixed in cream and sugar and covered one with a plastic top. This morning, after all the vodka he'd downed last night, he needed the extra fortification. Before he found a seat at the long table, Jordyn entered. After Greg introduced her, she greeted the men, and headed right for the coffee cart, still carrying her portfolio and purse.

Greg didn't know the last person to enter the room and assumed he must be the legal eagle. John pointed to the coffee and waited until the man seated himself. "We all know why we're here. This situation not only gives The Scoop and the network a black eye, but it's also a breach of contract on your part," he said, pinning Greg with a hard stare. Confusion drew Greg's face into a frown, and John went on to explain further. "A morals clause is a standard inclusion in the contracts of all on-air personalities. Unfortunately, almost no one remembers reading the clause before they sign it." He slid the papers in front of Greg, and Thad picked them up before he had a chance to take a look.

"This is pretty cut and dried," Thad said after a few minutes. "To give you the short version, it's a provision in the contract which curtails, restrains, or forbids certain behavior. The clause is used as a means of holding you to a certain behavioral standard so as not to bring disrepute, contempt or scandal to the network and their interests."

"Breaking this clause is grounds for disciplinary action or termination," Ken added.

Always one to think ahead, Thad asked, "Does he have any recourse?"

John squinted. "What kind of recourse, Mr. Jones?"

"What if Mr. Stafford is willing to submit to counseling for a specified period of time?"

"Therapy would play well with the public," Jordyn chimed in. "Any kind of rehab does."

"Rehab?" Greg asked of no one in particular.

"There's rehab for everything these days—not just the big problems," she explained. "They have rehab for racism, homophobia, rudeness, stupidity—you name it." A chuckle echoed around the table.

"Would the network be willing to reinstate Mr. Stafford if he completed a mandated course of therapy with a reputable therapist?" Thad asked, directing his question to the station manager, who in turn glanced at the corporate legal guy.

"The decision would be up to you, John," the corporate

attorney said.

Greg had held his tongue long enough. "I don't get any input in all of this?"

John sent him a snide smirk. "Your gift for *inputting* got you into this mess, Greg. I'm afraid your judgment can't be trusted."

Humiliated, Greg averted his gaze and fiddled with his phone.

A tense silence hung over the room while the station manager contemplated Thad's proposition. After what seemed like an eternity to Greg, John replied, "Listen, Greg, until now I haven't been aware of transgressions on your part since you've been with The Scoop. I don't make it a habit of judging another man's personal life. Who you sleep with is your private business, but since this story broke, the rumors about you and staff members have become the number one topic of discussion in this building. From what I hear, there are even pools to guess the number of coworkers you've screwed. You have a problem, and you need to face it." He stopped and pushed his glasses up on his nose. "This mandated therapy has nothing to do with the women you've been involved with on the job. It's the result of your arrest only, but I have to warn you. Some of the women on staff will surely talk if TMZ or some other outlet offers them the right price. You'd better be prepared for more fallout. And," He slid a newspaper in Greg's direction. "it looks as if you have another complication."

Greg lifted the paper folded to the headline which read, *Senator Price makes an official statement*. He quickly read the text of the article then passed it to Thad. The senator accused Greg of pursuing his young wife.

"There's nothing he can do to you legally, Greg, but he's a powerful man, and he can make your life miserable. I don't want you to respond to him personally."

"But he's accusing me of being the aggressor, and I wasn't," Greg protested with his balled fists on the tabletop. "The whole thing was her idea."

"Let Jordyn create a statement addressing the station's decision to allow you to return to the air after finishing counseling."

Thad cleared his throat. "I know of an excellent therapist another one of my clients used. Is that acceptable?"

"I don't see why not," John answered tentatively, then said, "As long as he's certified and reputable."

"It's a woman. If you want to check her out, I can give you the link to her website," Thad offered.

"How does that sit with you, Greg? Will having a female therapist be a problem for you?" the station manager asked.

"No. No problem. I'll go along with whatever you decide." What else could he say? If he bucked against the idea, he'd appear problematic and not serious about his continued employment with the network. He had no other choice.

♥♥♥

Greg's apartment seemed quieter than usual when he returned. Once he kicked off his shoes and stretched out on the sofa, he focused his gaze on the fountain. One bamboo bowl filled with water, tipped and emptied its contents into the one below. The relaxing qualities of the repetitive motion only reminded him of how empty he felt at the moment. The Chinese symbol for peace he'd commissioned an artist to paint on the living room wall taunted him.

After being in Manhattan for a little over a year, he'd beat out ten other applicants to become the host of The

Scoop, one of the top nighttime entertainment magazine shows. The thirty percent salary increase over what he made at his former job as an Atlanta news anchor qualified him for the apartment in The Caldwell, one of the older upscale buildings on the Upper East Side. He had chosen the Upper East Side for its urbanity and sophistication. Staffords were raised to always consider respectability first. Sometimes he wished he could simply step out from his home onto the sidewalk and be in the midst of a party crowd, but if he would consider anything responsible for his current predicament, it would be getting involved in the New York party scene.

He still hadn't spoken to his father, and he didn't want to, but he needed to return Charles' call. Greg was closest to Charles, one of the twins, who'd arrived into the world only eighteen months after him. He needed to talk to someone, so he hit redial and waited for his brother to answer.

"I got your message, but I wasn't in the mood to talk."

"How're you doing?" Charles asked, with concern deepening his voice.

"I'm doing," he said, gazing down at his photo in the article in the newspaper he'd carried out of the conference room. "I just left a meeting with my boss, the station manager, and my attorney. The station decided if I voluntarily submit to therapy, they won't fire me, even though I broke the morals clause in my contract. At least I still have my job."

"They're making you go to therapy for an isolated incident?"

Greg hesitated. "Well…the decision wasn't just based on what happened yesterday."

"What do you mean?"

"Uh…once the word got out, some of the women in

the office started spilling their guts."

"What do they have to spill?"

"Nothing major." He groaned. "They were just…concerned about how many of them might have something to say."

"Damn, man! Were you popping every female on the staff?"

"No," Greg snickered. "But it amazes me how they are suddenly so willing to go public about a private affair."

"There's a bigger issue going on here, don't you think?" Charles said, sounding graver than Greg thought necessary. "I noticed it when I stayed with you. Maybe it's time you faced what's happening."

Greg ground his teeth at the censure in his brother's tone, and he immediately went on the defensive. "Lots of people do threesomes. Why is it a crime when I do it?"

"It's not a crime, but the way you seem to be taking risks, I wonder if it only happens every now and then or if it's become your lifestyle."

"My *lifestyle*? Seriously? You're talking as if I'm some kind of deviant. I like sex, and I don't care to be tied down to one woman."

"I know I sound like Mama and Daddy, but what's wrong with finding a nice girl and settling down? It's not as bad as you might think. In fact, it's not bad at all."

"What? Did you ever stop to think maybe it's just not in the cards for me?"

"Why would you think it isn't?"

"Because if it was, then one woman would grab my attention and hold it. It just hasn't happened. They *all* grab my attentionfor about twenty minutes."

"You're not eighteen anymore, man. There comes a time when you have to grow up."

This sage advice coming from his younger brother grated on his nerves. "So because I don't want a ball and chain around my ankle it makes me immature?"

"Just the fact that you see a good woman as a shackle shows how much growing up you need to do."

"I expected Daddy to chew me out, but not you. Look, I don't have time for this. I've gotta go."

"Yeah, right. You just don't want to hear the truth. Let me say this before you replace your voice with the dial tone. A year ago, I didn't think there was anyone special out there for me either, but I met Adanna and everything changed. Marc said the same thing about him and Gianne. We don't know what the future holds."

Part of him believed he could end up with a normal, respectable life like his brothers had, but another part reminded him it hadn't happened yet even though he was past thirty-five. "What if the future just holds more of the same for me?"

"You don't really believe that."

"I don't know what I believe anymore."

"Maybe going to therapy will help you figure it out. I'm glad you kept your job. Keep in touch, will you?"

"Yeah. Okay. Tell Adanna I said hello."

He ended the call, slipped his feet back into his shoes and took the elevator to the roof garden. Thankfully, no one else occupied the space. In early May, the pollution, which often choked the city air during the summer had not yet appeared. He stood at the wall and gazed out over the East River then he put on his sunglasses, stretched out on a chaise and thought about his brother's words. Could Charles be right? Had his enjoyment of physical pleasure turned destructive? From his early teens, he'd loved the fairer sex, but being honest with himself, he didn't feel the same way he had years ago. The women he met were different from the girls he knew as a younger man. Most of them didn't require anything of him. They were quite content with being in his company for the evening and nothing more. They only wanted sex, which didn't bother him in the least. But the blame didn't rest solely with them. In all honesty, he never went looking for women who wanted more, so naturally it seemed as though they were nothing more than jump-offs. Until today the thought had never crossed his mind.

Chapter Two

*R*hani Drake rearranged the chairs in her office in preparation for her new client. She always made sure there was plenty of personal space for both her and her client. The appointment with her first celebrity client had been made a few days ago by Thad Jones, a lawyer she'd met years ago at a networking event. He explained the particulars of his client's arrest, the mandated therapy, and the importance of confidentiality, as though a licensed therapist wouldn't already know.

She walked around the office giving the small room where she counseled her clients a critical scan. Rhani liked to think of it as cozy. When she'd opened the office two years ago, she had paid close attention to the décor and the feeling it might give those who came in. The addition of unlit scented candles, plush pillows and soft lighting helped to give the room a secure, intimate atmosphere. After she filled the carafe with cold water and placed it on the table in front of the sofa, she checked the tissue box on the end table then glanced at her watch again. His appointment was scheduled for 3:30 p.m.

Why did she feel so nervous? Greg Stafford wasn't a Hollywood movie star or anything. Quite possibly her jitters had to do with the fact that she watched The Scoop every night while she ate dinner. The show's unusually handsome host had a smile capable of melting the hardest woman's heart. But his looks were of no consequence. He was coming to her for help with a serious problem. She couldn't allow his celebrity or physical appearance to cause her to treat him any differently than she would any other client struggling with a sexual addiction.

At 3:25 p.m., Rhani turned the small shelf sound system to its normal, barely-audible volume. Soft instrumental music always helped clients to relax. Since Thad mentioned Mr. Stafford's therapy had been ordered by his employer, he might very well be there under duress.

The gentle chime on the front door sounded, and Rhani waited until her receptionist escorted him into the office. Before her stood one of the best looking men she had ever seen, which was quite an accomplishment in a city the size of New York.

"Mr. Stafford? Rhani Drake. Nice to meet you." They shook hands, and she mentally chastised herself for the prickling sensation running across her skin when their flesh touched. She had seen him numerous times on TV, yet meeting him in person was a jolt to her senses. The first thing she noticed was his height. He towered over her five-feet-six inches. His scent registered with her senses next. The cologne he wore had a luxurious, spicy fragrance—a mix of grass, cloves, jasmine and some other delicious scents. Dressed casually yet stylishly, his appearance came across as easy-going and self-confident.

Rhani glanced up just in time to catch his questioning expression.

"Is there something wrong?"

He removed his hat but kept the shades on. "No. It's just...I expected you to be older."

For some reason, hearing this pleased her. "Is my age a problem? I assure you I am well-qualified." Rhani pointed to her framed diplomas on the office wall then waved a hand toward the sofa. "Please have a seat."

He sat with his long legs open, his elbows on his knees

and studied the room for a long moment. "Nice office." The emotionless tone of his voice didn't convey his appreciation.

"Thank you." Once she settled into the chair at the end of the sofa, she crossed her legs and rested her notebook on one knee. "Tell me why you're here."

He flashed the dazzling smile she'd seen on the TV screen so many times. Her stomach flipped, and she wanted to slap herself. "You already know why. I'm sure Thad told you when he made the appointment."

Annoyed by her sensual reaction to his presence, Rhani purposely didn't return his smile. "He did, but I'd like to hear your take on the situation. And do you mind taking off the sunglasses? I like to make eye contact with my clients."

He poked out his lips, moved them from side to side then pulled off the shades and put them in his shirt pocket. "I got arrested for…having sex in public, which in addition to being against the law, also constitutes breaking the morals clause in my contract. In order to keep my job, I have to attend counseling for a minimum of three months."

"Is that the only reason you're here?"

"Excuse me?" He met her gaze for the first time since he'd arrived, and she had to look away. His light eyes were evident on television, but looking into them in person was a different story. They were hazel—an intriguing combination of several other colors including green and brown with less melanin than brown eyes, but more than blue. Why would she even be thinking about this at the moment? Rhani blinked, straightened and returned to her questioning. "Did you come to counseling to keep your job or to deal with the reason the therapy was ordered to begin with?"

A muscle ticked in his jaw, a square jaw covered by a smooth, neatly trimmed beard. "I *need* my job." His voice deepened in timbre and intensity.

"I think you've answered my question. You're saying you don't want to be here."

He gave an insolent shrug.

"Okay. I'd like to take a few minutes to tell you how I handle counseling appointments, what you can expect from me and what I expect from you." She always liked to address the important points right out of the gate. After a brief rundown on confidentiality, cancelled appointments, and financial responsibilities, Rhani asked if he had any questions. Greg shook his head. "Why don't you tell me about Melinda Price?"

He flinched. "There's nothing to tell. I don't know her."

"Can you explain? According to the news reports, she was the woman arrested with you."

Greg exhaled a long sigh as though he'd already run out of patience with her. "That's right, but I'd never met her in person until we ran into each other in Barney's."

Rhani didn't react to the revelation, but simply made a note on her pad. Many of her clients engaged in sexual liaisons with strangers, so she wasn't shocked. "I understand."

"I doubt it."

He seemed intent on provoking her, and she refused to allow their first session to start on a negative note. Clients who entered with an attitude needed her to be tough. "Mr. Stafford, you're not the first person this has happened to. Your situation is not uncommon. The only difference is you made the news."

"If we're going to do this, you might as well drop the *Mr. Stafford*. What should I call you?" He asked with another smile, which didn't reach his eyes this time.

"Ms. Drake, if you don't mind. I like to keep things

professional."

Greg rolled his shoulders then grunted, "Fine, *Ms. Drake.*"

This wasn't starting out well at all. She decided to lead from another angle. "You said your therapy was ordered by your employer. How do you feel about that?"

He leaned back in his chair, still refusing to look her in the eye. "I guess the station is within its rights. I did break the *morals clause* in my contract."

"You say it as though you think a morals clause is ridiculous."

"I'm a television host, not a preacher."

"You did agree to adhere to the stipulations of the contract, didn't you?"

"I signed it, if that's what you mean," he snapped. "My lawyer didn't go into detail about exactly what it meant." As was common among her clients, he tried to transfer responsibility from himself to someone else.

"I assume he felt it was self-explanatory. Most morals clauses generally say the employee agrees not to commit any act or do anything which might tend to bring himself into public disrepute, contempt, scandal, or ridicule, or which might reflect unfavorably on the network, or sponsors. It was your responsibility to read the contract."

Greg reared back in his seat and raised one eyebrow. "So you're a lawyer too?"

She would not allow him to take control of the session. Time to change direction. "Tell me about your family, Greg. Do you have any siblings?"

His loud bark of laughter startled her. "Do I! My parents have six sons."

"Wow, six boys. What number are you?"

"Three. The twins and the baby of the family are after me."

"Tell me about growing up in a large family with all male siblings?"

"It was good. Personally, I think there were too many of us, but nothing can be done to change it now, right?"

"I'm afraid not. How did you get along with your brothers?"

"We got along fine. I mean, we had the regular fights most siblings have. You know, the *he took my bike* kinda stuff until we got older, and it changed to the *he took my girlfriend* beat downs of epic proportions." He gave a humorless snort.

"Did your brothers ever take one of your girlfriends?"

"Vic and Jesse are older than me, so they were allowed more freedom than I had. They also got cars before I did." His audible sigh put a question in her mind. "And girls always liked the dudes with their own ride."

"So you're saying yes then?"

"Yes, it happened a time or two, but you get over that stuff and move on."

"Really?" Rhani made a note of this point then proceeded to the next question. "And your relationship with your parents?"

He immediately jumped to their defense. "I have great parents. When we were kids, my mother had her hands full with six boys. My father had a growing medical practice to deal with. They kept us out of trouble by making sure we stayed busy with school and church activities. Whatever issues I've got have nothing to do with them."

"Did you enjoy those activities?"

"Yeah, for the most part, but I've always leaned more toward the fun stuff rather than the educational or religious."

He scratched the whiskers on his chin, which for some reason looked incredibly soft rather than scratchy, and pondered the question for a moment. "Like...I would've rather spent the summer working at Six Flags than going to Space Camp, but my father said I didn't need the money as much as I needed the education."

"You went to Space Camp?" She tried hard not to sound impressed.

The way he nodded said he'd found the experience as stimulating as a warm glass of milk, although he was recalling this from the mind of a disgruntled tween and not a grown man. From what she knew, a week at the famous camp ran close to a thousand dollars, which probably exceeded all her father had spent on her all of the years she'd lived at home. Greg Stafford's childhood sounded like a stark contrast to hers. Judging by what he'd told her thus far, he and his brothers had lived with comforts and luxuries she had only dreamed about.

Rhani and her two brothers and one sister had existed barely above the poverty level all their lives. They had only survived because her mother did whatever work a high school dropout could find, and she applied for every city, county, state and federal program available. Her father floated from job to job never staying at one for more than a few months. Every time he got fired, he came home with an unbelievable story, which firmly placed the blame on someone else or even on the company itself. He collected unemployment benefits when he managed to stay on the job long enough. Otherwise, he lay around the apartment watching television until her mother badgered him into going out and searching for a new job. The cycle repeated itself year after year until Rhani graduated from high school and left for college.

"I meant what were your relationships with them individually?"

"My mother tried her best to divide her attention between each of us…"

"Do I hear a *but* there?"

Greg snickered. "When you have two older brothers and three younger, it's easy to get lost in the crowd."

"I can imagine. Did you ever find yourself doing things to get your parents' attention?"

His smile seemed to light the entire office. "All the time. My mother believes that's where my acting ability came from."

"What kinds of things did you do?"

"She says after the twins were born, I became a sofa diver. Then, when I got a bit older, and we had a pool, I was the stunt man."

This explained a lot. "We're going to stop right here, Greg. I think we've made a good start. See my receptionist to schedule your next session."

As soon as he left the office, Rhani closed her notebook and threw it into the tote bag she carried to hold her clothes for dance class. For the past six months she had been taking jazz classes at the Broadway Dance Center. She changed into her Skechers, turned off the copier, shut off the lights and locked the office. The walk over to West 45th Street provided the warm-up she required and also helped to clear her head. Meeting Greg Stafford had thrown her off kilter. Normally she maintained control of the sessions and directed them in the way she thought they should go. Yet, as much as she hated to admit it, despite his attitude, something about him was so appealing. She was a therapist, for God's sake. He'd come to her for help, albeit unwillingly.

During her walk, she wondered about the stories of the strangers she passed in the cool late afternoon weather. Greg had a story, and she'd need to work harder to get him to gradually reveal it. He clearly didn't want to open up to her. Her internal reaction to him bothered her most, though. His looks were striking, but they weren't what unsettled her. An undercurrent of raw sexuality like she had never experienced from a man ran just beneath the surface. He hadn't said anything even remotely sexual to her, but she sensed it radiating from him. As part of her training, she had learned how to disregard her personal feelings toward clients. As disinterested and detached as he appeared, the connection between them was unquestionable. There had to be a way to put her emotions, no matter how strong they were, aside. With her phone to her ear, she began her trek to the center while she convinced her best friend, Katandra, to meet for dinner after her class ended. Speeding taxis, joggers and bikers whizzing by her at the curb didn't intrude on her thoughts and before she knew it, she'd arrived at the dance center, her sanctuary. The girls behind the front desk greeted her as she signed in then made her way down the bright orange hall to the locker room. After she put her sneakers in the tote, stashed it in a locker and secured it with a combination lock, she headed for Studio 4 where the jazz class was held. Rhani joined the dancers already in the studio for the Assaf warm-up used by many of the teachers. Some of the dancers worked barefoot, but Rhani wore neoprene jazz booties with her footless tights and camisole bra top. They began the opening stretch by inhaling with their hands clasped under their chins then dropping their heads back and lifting their elbows to the sky. They raised their arms, waved them overhead, bent over at the waist and rose on their toes with the rhythm of the percussion music. By the time the dancers completed all seven sections of the warm-up, they were ready to do some real dancing.

One of the downsides of being a therapist was the amount of time she had to be still. All her life she had been a physically active person, and she'd had to train herself how to sit motionlessly during client sessions. These classes and sometimes a morning run helped to remind her to empty her head of all the clutter. Often she found it nearly impossible not to take to heart everything she heard from her clients. When she wasn't diligent, her own spirit suffered from constantly listening to the awful things people had done or had done to them. In the past couple of years, she'd learned how not to transfer her clients' fears and issues onto herself. Sometimes the financial responsibility of running her own practice, the constant ingestion of client problems often overflowed within her. Regardless of how much Rhani liked the workouts, they served as a sorry substitute for a long, sweaty workout between the sheets. But they would have to do, since she didn't have a man in her life. When she felt as though the issues would send her to the ceiling like a neglected pressure cooker, a dance class and a girls' night out were in order.

Over time, Rhani had learned how to shut off her mental processes and submit to the pure joy of physical movement. Unfortunately, tonight, once the ninety-minute class ended, Greg Stafford's handsome face reappeared, and so did reservations about her new client. After a quick, hot shower, she changed back into her office clothes and caught a cab to the restaurant where Kat waited for her.

"Girl, you look fantastic!" Kat said as Rhani approached her in the foyer. "All that dancing has that body looking tight."

Rhani greeted her with a hug. "It wouldn't hurt you to do some, you know. Your idea of exercise is dragging your sample case around all day." Rhani knew Kat got more physical exercise during her day than she did sitting and listening to clients, but she loved to tease her friend about her staunch resistance to formal workouts.

"I'm a pharmaceutical salesperson. Walking through hospitals and medical office complexes eight hours a day is enough exercise for me." Katandra gave her a dismissive wave. "J is on her way. She had to close tonight."

"Why can't you call her by her name? It's not impossible to pronounce."

"Oh, please!"

Rhani rolled her eyes. "It's French, Kat, and it means delight or gladness. I bet you don't have any problem saying citalopram hydrobromide when you want to make a sale. Her name might be spelled J-o-i-e, but it's pronounced *Zwa*. It offends her when you won't even bother to say it right."

The hostess finally said their table was ready, and the women followed her into the crowded restaurant. A few minutes later, Joie strutted in looking like her usual gorgeous self. Tonight she had her long natural hair braided and styled into a dramatic upsweep. The light from the overhead tracks glinted off of the oversized gold earrings dangling just above the shoulders of a loosely-constructed pants outfit. A pair of insanely high heels and a purse big enough to hide a small human inside finished off her fashionable look.

"Sorry I'm late. I had to close the boutique tonight and drop the day's receipts in the night deposit at the bank."

Once they placed their drink orders, Rhani leaned forward and said, "So how did everybody's day go?"

"Mine are usually the same. I did get to meet a very cute doctor at one of my stops. He's new, so I need to make a return visit to his office soon."

Joie chuckled. "Girl, you're always on the lookout."

"Better be. You think I'm joking when I tell you I'm going to marry a doctor. You wait and see," Katandra insisted.

"I believe you, but while you're husband hunting, this sister is working on establishing herself in the fashion world. Every month the boutique is doing better. We're starting to attract some well-known customers. Fifty Cent's girlfriend came in the other day and spent over twelve hundred dollars." She smiled proudly. "Come to think of it, you two haven't been in to visit in a while. I thought we vowed to support each other."

"We did, but we didn't know everything would be so expensive."

"*Everything* isn't expensive," Joie protested.

Rhani gave her the eye. "Come on, girl. The last time I came in, I had all intentions of buying something small like a pair of earrings. Even those were fifty dollars! You know I don't spend that kind of money on clothes unless it's a special occasion, and I haven't had one of those in a long time."

"We keep telling you that part of your life has to change. All work and no play makes Rhani a very dull girl. You need to do something out of the ordinary."

"Please, don't remind me, Kat." Rhani twisted a curly strand of hair around her index finger and waited while they placed their orders with the server. "Something definitely out of the ordinary happened to me today. I can't give you the details, but I had a client this afternoon who made me really uncomfortable."

"For real?" Katandra asked with wide, rounded eyes. "You, the sex therapist? I didn't think anything could shock you."

"I didn't say I was shocked. The uneasiness didn't come from what he said. It was *him*."

"Why? What did he do?"

"He didn't have to *do* anything. His mere presence caused the apprehension."

"What was wrong with the guy? Or can't you tell us?"

"Obviously he came to me because he has issues, but I found it difficult to concentrate on his words because of his…aura, for lack of a better word. When he walked into my office, the air changed."

Katandra snickered. "He must've been seriously funky."

"Kat!" Rhani glared at her. "I mean the *atmosphere* changed, and it wasn't just because he's make-you-drool fine. He had sex coming out of his pores. There are some men who don't have to say a word. All they have to do is stand there." She groaned. "I've had some male clients who *thought* they were raw sex on a stick, but this one really is. Nothing like this has ever happened to me on the job or off."

Joie studied her for a moment. "Uh oh. This guy really had an effect on you. You're wondering whether or not you should counsel him, aren't you?"

She sighed again. "Yes, I've never been so attracted to a man in my life, and this one came to me for help. It's so…unethical."

One corner of Katandra's mouth rose along with one eyebrow. "So, what's his problem?"

"Typical stuff. Multiple partners, dangerous behavior, etc. Knowing all that, how could I be attracted to him to begin with? What does it say about me?"

"It says you've been without a man for a loooong time, and you just ran into the one who shakes your tree. What are you going to do?"

"I'm not sure. He's scheduled to come twice a week for the next three months. If I'm going to do anything, I need to do it now."

The friends were silent for several minutes when their meals arrived. The moment the server left the table, Rhani continued. "The strange thing is he wasn't the least bit friendly. In fact, he seemed a bit hostile."

"What reason does he have to be hostile? Oh, wait," Joie

folded her hands under her chin and met Rhani's gaze. "He's not seeing you of his own free will, is he? Somebody else is making him get counseling. Am I getting warm?"

Rhani dropped her gaze. "Look, I've already said too much. What I need to do is consult with a colleague for advice on how to handle the situation. Let's eat and talk about something else, please."

During the rest of the meal, Rhani tried her best to be present in the conversation, but thoughts of the ill-tempered, hazel-eyed Greg Stafford monopolized her attention. She skipped dessert, promised to meet Kat and Joie for drinks on the weekend, and took a cab back to her apartment.

After she shed her street clothes and changed into her soft cotton pajamas, Rhani retrieved her phone from her purse and the client notebook from her tote bag. She lay across the bed, stared at the ceiling, then at the telephone and back to the ceiling. She thought about calling Dr. Albert Spruill, a colleague she'd met at the Executive Summit, the annual conference of the American Psychotherapy Association. She and Dr. Al had hit it off right away, and Rhani had often contacted him for advice when she had a particularly difficult client. But she already knew what his recommendation would be, and it would come with a stern warning. *Never mind.*

The reason why her notes from Greg's session were short and cryptic escaped her at the moment. Her typical session summaries tended to be quite thorough. For whatever reason, she hadn't gone into detail about how he presented himself or what he had said, although it was burned into her brain. Rhani reached into her tote bag for her iPad, pulled herself into a sitting position and propped two pillows behind her back. Since she kept her session comments on the iPad, she used codes for clients just in case; God forbid, she lost or someone stole the device. She typically used the date of their first visit.

Client 517, a college-educated, African-American male in his late thirties is a colleague referral. His employer ordered a minimum of ninety days' counseling as a result of his arrest for public indecency. Asked him questions about the woman with whom he'd been arrested, but he couldn't answer, because he doesn't know her personally.

Initially, he was reluctant to talk and hid behind his sunglasses until I asked him to remove them. Gradually he began to share. He wasn't hesitant to discuss his family relationships. From the little he said, it's apparent he loves and respects his parents and had a somewhat privileged upbringing. Need to inquire further into his relationship with his older brothers. Something of a middle child, with two older and three young brothers, he admitted to being the attention hound of the family during his childhood. He believes it's how he developed his on-air presence. Got the feeling he's used to charming women with his smile.

Rhani closed the file and logged into her e-mail account, but her mind still lingered on her intriguing client. Disconcerted by her attraction to him, she contemplated the reasons why she felt this way. She'd had good-looking male clients before, but never one with Greg Stafford's presence. His self-assurance made her skin tingle, and that set off warning bells. The ethical thing to do would be to refer him to a colleague, but a desire to know more about him burned in her chest. She wanted to know what made him tick and what had driven him to the point where he had been ordered to seek therapy. On the surface, a man like him had no need to seek out sexual liaisons. Women would come to him unbidden, which is exactly what happened the day of his arrest. Surely he wasn't used to women saying no to him, which tended to make men arrogant. She hadn't gotten that impression from him though. Instead, she'd sensed an underlying shame behind his words.

Chapter Three

What was that all about? Greg stalked down the block in search of a cab in his pseudo-disguise. Had Thad played a joke on him by scheduling his therapy session with the sexiest woman he'd met in months? Rhani Drake appeared to be the embodiment of what Greg considered the perfect woman. Downright tempting with thick, curly hair falling past her shoulders. A few errant tendrils dangled over her forehead, and he imagined coiling them around his fingers. As she interrogated him, he visualized how irresistible she would look beneath him with her wild mop spread out over the pillow. Not a great way to start therapy.

A taxi finally stopped for him. He got in, gave the driver his home address then dropped his head back on the seat and closed his eyes. Thankfully, he hadn't gotten one of those talkative drivers. He needed silence to think about what had just occurred. No way would he allow himself to be attracted to the woman who wanted to deconstruct him and put him back together the way she saw fit. Right away she'd started in on his family, and he wasn't having it. They had nothing to do with the reason he'd been sent to her. In fact, if he were more like them, he wouldn't be in this mess to begin with. But since he had to endure three months of scrutiny, discovering *why* he was so unlike them might make it worth the torture.

She hadn't asked about the actual incident, which seemed strange. After all, it's what brought him to her office. Every time he replayed the episode he became aroused, so he tried not to dwell on it, but often the scene appeared in his mind unbidden.

He'd been dizzy with exhilaration, ripped his belt open and yanked his zipper down to free himself. The alley hadn't been the place to take her panties down, so he reached between her thighs and pulled the narrow crotch of her delicate panties aside. Melinda Price was tall and the stilettos she wore made her even taller, so he only had to bend his knees a little to get into the right position. He didn't want to hurt her, but it also hadn't been the time or place for foreplay or rummaging through his wallet for a condom. Bareback time.

When he thrust into her, Melinda had taken his shoulders in a death grip. Her stiletto-clad feet came off the ground and hooked around his hips. The cry she uttered had him so drunk; he couldn't do anything but go for the goal. Nothing else mattered. He clasped his hands under her and pumped like a madman while the world around them faded away. She moaned and he growled through their climax. Once the blood returned to his head, Greg comprehended the voices shouting at them.

"NYPD! Release her and put your hands above your head!"

He steadied Melinda as her weak legs dropped to the ground. When he realized she wasn't going to fall, he shoved himself back into his underwear and zipped his pants.

The officer continued, "You are under arrest for public indecency and performing a lewd act under Section 245 of the New York Penal Code."

Arousal then shame. The story of what his life had become. How had he let himself get to this point? Greg rubbed his eyes in an effort to wipe away the scene then straightened his shoulders and told himself it would never happen again.

When the taxi stopped in front of his building, he paid the cabbie, scanned the area and sprinted toward the entrance where Roland stood sentry. He needed to explain his current situation to the doorman.

"Hey, Roland. Can I talk to you for a minute?"

"Of course, Mr. Stafford. What can I help you with?"

"What's going on with me right now is common knowledge, so I guess you've already heard. I just wanted to give you a warning about reporters and photographers. A couple of them were stalking me outside of the studio, and they might show up here. I can't avoid having my picture taken, but I'm not doing any interviews, and I'm not expecting any visitors."

Always professional and discreet, Roland nodded. "I understand, but legally they have a right to be anywhere on the sidewalk as long as they don't block the entrance."

"Gotcha. Thanks, man." He slapped his favorite doorman on the back and went inside. Once he'd locked the apartment door, he remembered he'd turned off his phone during the counseling session. When he took it out of his pocket, there were six new messages. He removed his shades and hat and checked the numbers. Four of the six were from his father. Knowing the old man's determination, Greg figured ignoring the calls would only result in more. He paced across the small foyer a few times, and then hit the return call button.

"I was wondering how many messages I'd have to leave before you called me back," his father said when he answered.

"Sorry, Daddy. I just wasn't in the right frame of mind to talk."

"What's going on with you, son? Your mother said you told her the story was true, so how do you explain this mess? None of you boys ever had a problem getting women, so what's wrong?"

Greg sat on the edge of his bed and rubbed the back of his neck where a knot of tension with his father's name on it twisted tighter by the second. "I can't explain it, but you'll be happy to know I didn't lose my job, and I started therapy today. Maybe it'll help me figure out why I…"

"Well, at least there's something to be thankful for." His father's next question burrowed under Greg's already sensitive skin. "How is this going to affect your reputation in the industry?" The man had always been more concerned about image than anything else, it seemed.

"I can't answer that, but like I told the therapist, I'm a television personality not a preacher." He chuckled.

"If that was supposed to be funny, you missed the mark," the older man grumbled.

Unlike some of his brothers, Greg had never been afraid to square off with his father. "Right now, all I can do is laugh. What good would it do to cry?"

"Kurt Vonnegut once said 'Laughter and tears are both responses to frustration and exhaustion.' So, which one are you fighting?"

His father rarely waxed philosophical, so Greg chose not to give a smart reply. "Both, I guess."

"Don't throw your life away for a new piece of tail, Gregory. It's never worth it."

It sounded as if the old man were speaking from experience, but if there had been indiscretions in his father's past, none of his sons knew anything about them. "Don't worry about me, Daddy. I'll work it out."

"Work hard, and if you need to hide out for a few weeks, you can always come here."

The offer surprised him, but then he assumed it actually came from his mother. "Thanks, but I have to stay in New York to complete my therapy. I appreciate the offer though."

"Keep in touch."

Now he felt more depressed than ever. Because he'd

expected a tirade, this compassion made him feel lower than pond scum. He would rather have faced a chewing out than listen to an expression of pity. Victor Stafford, Sr. commanded respect, and he had raised his sons to do the same. What Greg didn't understand was why he'd been so compassionate. After all, he'd had a major meltdown when Marc decided to quit medical school and go into fitness training and when Charles sold his plastic surgery practice and joined a medical volunteer organization. Why all this love, peace and hair grease over his arrest for something as mortifying as having your son literally caught with his pants down? Perhaps the family patriarch had undergone an emotional overhaul after all. Not long ago he'd worked out his running feud with Marc and had even flown all the way to London to help Charles' make an impression on his fiancé's parents. All the years they were growing up, there had been running battles between his brothers and their father. They all knew he was a decent man who loved and provided for his family, but his unrelenting stance on certain matters often drove a wedge between them. Now it appeared as though age had begun to soften the sharp edges that had frequently cut his sons deeply.

After that call, he needed a drink. The cold vodka in the freezer called his name. Already on a guilt trip of major proportions, Greg went into the kitchen asking himself why the alcohol seemed so alluring all of a sudden. Prior to this, the bottles would remain untouched for months unless he had company. Man, he was more screwed up than anyone knew.

With glass in hand, he grabbed the remote control and sank back into the thick padding inside the curved wicker chair resembling a jai alai basket. The womb-like shape of this seat had a comforting effect on him whenever he was disturbed. The news came on at six o'clock, so he sipped the chilled vodka and watched the commercials leading into the broadcast. The first three reports covered an international event, a domestic affairs announcement from the White House, and a triple murder in Queens. The newscaster prefaced the next block of commercials with a promise to return with Senator Price's latest statement on his wife's arrest. In spite of the alcohol's effect, Greg perked right up.

This time the senator lacked his famous smile. The reporters questioned him as he entered a summit on homelessness in the city, one of his pet projects.

"Senator," one reporter said, jumping right to the issue, "Do you have anything to say about the incident involving your wife and Greg Stafford?"

"There will always be men who prey on women for their own pleasure. Melinda is young and unfortunately not seasoned when it comes to dealing with predatory men. She is embarrassed at having been taken advantage of, and she would rather not speak to the media personally."

Greg nearly spit his vodka out at the screen. What the hell? If anyone were the predator, it was the seductive Mrs. Price, who was as well seasoned as the average street walker. The good senator had tried to paint her as an exploited innocent, and he obviously wanted to keep her from talking to reporters. Greg imagined this incident hadn't taken the senator by surprise. Melinda Price had been photographed dozens of times at nightclubs alone. Surely, he wasn't her only conquest.

"Are you saying Mr. Stafford forced himself on her?"

The senator gave the reporter a curious scowl. "All I have to say is she was influenced into acting against her better judgment. No more questions, please." He pushed through the crowd of reporters and disappeared inside the building. Greg dialed his publicist even before the network commentator returned to the screen to close out the story.

"Jordyn, it's Greg. Do you have a minute?"

"Sure, what's up?"

"It looks as though Senator Price is building a case against me. I just saw a story on Channel Four where he claimed I influenced the young, innocent Mrs. Price. I'm not claiming I'm blameless in this whole thing, but I do think I should defend myself. Can't we respond to this with some kind of statement? Keeping quiet makes me look guilty."

Jordyn groaned. "You *are* guilty. No matter what you do, it's not going to look any better, Greg. Even if she did come on to you, you should've refused her. You knew she was married, and you knew who she was married to." She sighed. "The least you could've done was gotten a hotel room. Let me get in touch with Thad and see how he thinks we should play this."

Everything she said was true, but it didn't temper his desire to fight. "Please do, and let me know what he says. Thanks."

Not used to being cooped up in the apartment, he wanted to get out, but he knew it would only subject him to public scrutiny. He really wanted to hit a few clubs and dance off his tension. Only he knew where it might lead.

An hour later, he sat at the bar in Bembe watching a group of girls dance together in a circle to the live bongos and congas. One of them, a brunette, who reminded him of Katy Perry, kept catching his eye. The way her long hair and perky breasts bounced in time to the rhythm drew him off the barstool onto the dance floor. He infiltrated the circle and used his best moves to get closer until their bodies were a few inches apart. When she smiled, he knew he wasn't risking a loud reprimand, and they finished out the song. During a lull in the music between songs, they introduced themselves then she told him her girlfriends' names. Greg bought a round of drinks for everyone, and for the rest of the evening the two of them became part of the writhing, sweaty crowd.

♥♥♥

Sunlight streaming through the bedroom windows woke Greg at seven o'clock. He groaned and pulled the sheet over his head. When he slid a hand across the mattress and it touched soft, warm flesh, he opened one eye and looked over his shoulder. The woman's long dark hair covered her face. Who was she? The several drinks he'd had before he left the club rendered his memory fuzzy. He remembered dancing with a woman who hadn't been the least bit shy about letting him know she was down with whatever he wanted to do next. Obviously this had been the last decision he'd made. A careless, stupid one. He slipped from under the sheet being careful not to wake his companion, whose name he couldn't even recall at the moment, and headed for the kitchen. After he threw a K-cup in the brewer, he leaned over the counter and massaged his temples.

I knew it was a mistake to go out last night. Why didn't I listen? I don't even trust myself. I can't stop even with my job in jeopardy. God, I do need help.

He needed to get this woman out of his apartmentnow. He vaguely remembered using a condom last night. As soon as the ready light came on the coffeemaker, he poured a cup, added cream and sugar to the hot liquid and popped another cup into the machine. If he were going to kick her to the curb, at least he could send her off with some caffeine. When he returned to the bedroom, he pulled the cord on the drapes, flooding the room with light. She didn't budge. He needed to rouse her, so he sat on the edge of the bed and gently nudged her shoulder. For the life of him, he couldn't recall her name.

"Hey, sleepyhead. I'm sorry to wake you, but I have an appointment this morning." He rose from the mattress. "I made you some coffee."

He considered brushing her hair back from her face with his hand, but he didn't want to touch her. Finally, she groaned and turned onto her back. "What time is it?" Her sleep-roughened voice might've sounded sexy to another man, but it just irritated him. He wanted her to get out of his apartment.

She stretched and reached out to him. "Come back to bed."

"No can do, baby. Time to get out of bed and get dressed. I need to leave in a few minutes, so I'll ask the doorman to get you a cab." He had nowhere to go, but what better way to get rid of her?

"Wow, this is some sendoff. Well…" She threw the sheet back exposing her nude body. "At least we had fun last night."

Greg averted his gaze from her as she swung one leg over onto the floor, giving him the money shot. His groin tightened and his Johnson kicked at the sight. He blinked, shook his head and left the room.

A few minutes later, she padded into the kitchen dressed and carrying her stilettos and purse. Without a word, he handed her the coffee in one of the disposable Styrofoam cups he took in the cab every morning.

"We did have fun last night." Greg looked at her from the corner of his eye while he stuffed some papers into his portfolio case and zipped it. "Do you go to Bembe often?"

"At least once a week."

"Maybe we'll run into each other again," he said, trying his best to make her understand that he wasn't about to ask for her phone number or give her his.

She glared at him then dropped her shoes to the floor and wriggled her feet into them. "Yeah, maybe we will. Call the doorman, please."

"I'll go downstairs with you. It's time for me to leave."

The silent ride down seventeen flights in the elevator couldn't end soon enough for Greg. He slipped a twenty-dollar bill into her hand. "This should cover the cab." When they reached the lobby, he dropped a fast kiss on her lips.

After he told Roland to hail a taxi for her, he made a fast scan of the street for any photogs then exited through the glass doors onto the street, leaving her with the doorman. The coffee shop down the block seemed like the best place to hang out until his overnight guest had left the neighborhood. He grabbed a newspaper from one of the boxes outside the restaurant and folded it under his arm. The only sunlight in the restaurant came from the front windows, but he maneuvered his way to the counter between the wooden chairs without removing his shades.

"I'd like a large coffee, light and sweet with a buttered hard roll, please," Greg told the woman before he took the last seat at the counter next to the wall and opened the newspaper. Not being on his way to work felt peculiar. For the first time in years, he wasn't among the working throng. At least he was still employed—technically, but he felt displaced not having a destination this morning. Working at The Scoop was the perfect job. He had a Master's degree in Communications, but he really wasn't convinced his education had helped him snag the anchor position as much as his personality and appearance. He loved the work, though. It wasn't difficult, and it made use of his talents. Over the years he'd been told how much the camera loved him, and the feeling was mutual. Every time he thought about his next counseling session, his shoulders tightened. The prospect of the lovely Ms. Drake prying into his personal life made him cringe, but he would do whatever he needed to in order to maintain his employment with the network.

The waitress placed the coffee and roll in front of him then stared at him for a few beats. "Don't I know you?"

Greg peered over his glasses knowing what she meant. "I live down the street, so I stop here a couple of times a week," he said, hoping it was enough to stop her from asking any more questions.

"I thought so. Enjoy your breakfast." She turned her attention to another customer.

He blew out a relieved breath and searched the morning paper for more statements from Senator Price. The only mention appeared in one of the gossip columns and no longer on the main news pages. *Thank God for small favors.* As he sipped his coffee, he read the scurrilous story, the first one to hint at Melinda Price's questionable social life. Rumor said the Senator had his eye on Gracie Mansion, and it questioned her suitability as a possible future First Lady of the great City of New York. He smiled. The general population had no idea what a freak Mrs. Price was. He raised his cup in the air to ask the waitress for a refill then thumbed through the rest of the paper.

What in the world would he do with the rest of the day? Like his brothers, Greg had inherited the Stafford work ethic, and he found it hard to occupy himself when he wasn't working. He'd wanted to read a couple of books, so he took the last bite of the roll, washed it down with the rest of his coffee and headed out the door toward Barnes & Noble on 86th and Lexington. When he left the store, he'd bought a celebrity autobiography, a suspense novel and a couple of magazines. His brother, Marc's mantra, "When in doubt, work out," echoed in his head. Marc claimed the endorphins released into your system would improve your mood, so Greg used the five-block walk back to his building as a warm-up then went directly upstairs to change into shorts, a tank and sneakers.

No one else occupied the small private gym when he arrived, so he had his choice of machines. He wasn't nearly as diligent about exercise as Marc. Fitness wasn't simply his brother's business, it was almost a religious conviction. Greg had considered the hours he spent on the dance floor and between the sheets to be his regular workouts, but this was the best he could do if he intended to maintain a low profile. After a forty-minute workout, he headed back upstairs sweaty and spent. On the way, the ringing of his phone filled the elevator.

"This is Greg."

"I just talked to Thad," Jordyn said. "He doesn't think you should make a statement right now. We both feel you should stay under the radar for a while."

"Fine," he grumbled. "I'll do whatever you two think is best, but I don't know how long I'll be able to live like my mug has been on *America's Most Wanted*."

"Nobody is saying you have to live like a hermit, Greg. Just keep your pretty face away from the cameras for a while."

"Right. Thanks, Jordyn."

During a quick shower, he considered where he might go and not be noticed, but he drew a blank. He snatched the bookstore bag he'd dumped on the kitchen counter, got back on the elevator and settled on the roof garden atop the building. It wasn't often that Greg took advantage of the open air sanctuary. Summer temperatures were too hot, and the winter months were out of the question. He preferred the peaceful oriental atmosphere of his apartment, which was a decent size for Manhattan. Today, though, he needed a respite from the walls that suddenly seemed to be closing in on him.

Pleased to see he was the only person who'd decided to take advantage of the warm weather and sunshine, Greg reclined on one of the chaises and thumbed through the magazines. Seeing photos of people he had interviewed and endless pictures of celebrities out on the town just reminded him of the new restrictions on his life. He stuffed the magazines back into the bag and opened the suspense novel. Maybe it would take his mind off of his own issues. The book started out with a bang, but it still wasn't enough to hold his attention. After about thirty minutes, he found himself staring out over the river and the city he had grown to love.

As an Atlanta boy transplanted to the Northeast three years ago, he had taken to New York right away. The perpetual motion of Manhattan spoke to his extroverted nature. The city never failed to provide something to do or somewhere to go no matter what time of the day or night. Coming from Atlanta, where everything shuts down at three in the morning, he loved the fact that in Manhattan he could step outside at three in the morning and get Greek food if he had a yearning for it. But wasn't the availability of everything he could want or need at any hour of the day or night part of his problem? Perhaps he should consider going home for the duration of his suspension. He could always get a referral from Ms. Drake for a qualified therapist in Atlanta. At least here he wouldn't have to hide. People knew him there, but not like they did in New York. But a few things disturbed him about the option: having to feel the disapproval of his father, having to witness the disappointment on his mother's face, and worst of all, not seeing the sexy Rhani Drake. The idea traveled around in his head as though it were on a rollercoaster with positive thoughts on the ascent and negative ones on the descent.

The sun had gradually moved to the west by the time Greg made his decision. He couldn't leave New York. He needed to stay so he might get to know her better. And so she might learn who he really was, although she hadn't expressed a nanosecond of interest in him. Greg always liked a challenge, and the very professional Ms. Drake presented an interesting challenge. Why she so fascinated him, he didn't understand. Normally, the personal details of the women he got involved with were the furthest thing from his mind. He didn't want to know about their family, their interests or their preferences unless they had something to do with sex. But for some reason, even though her prying into his personal life irritated him, he wanted to know all about Rhani Drake. It wouldn't be easy, since she was the only one who could ask the questions.

No one knew about last night's slip except him and…. he still couldn't remember her name. It wasn't necessary to confess to Ms. Drake what he'd done last night. His gaze followed the East River Ferry drifting past below. He'd never been a dishonest person, but this habit had caused him to start lying on a regular basis. He lied to the women, to himself, and now he even considered lying to his therapist. If his lifestyle were normal and socially acceptable, as he often tried to convince himself, then why did he feel the need to lie? He pressed a fist against his mouth and puffed out his cheeks. In spite of what his emotions told him, the next counseling session couldn't come soon enough.

Chapter Four

*T*he next afternoon, Greg Stafford sat in Rhani's office again. This time he removed his shades without her asking.

"How are you doing today?" she asked, purposely sounding cheerful despite his somber expression.

He hesitated for a long moment then said, "I need to apologize for my bad attitude in our last session. This is hard for me—talking to someone about myself."

She smiled at the unexpected apology. "I have a hard time believing it's difficult to talk about yourself. You're a television personality, but I understand why discussing the reason you're here might be."

Greg managed a faint smile in return. "I make my living talking about *other* people and their problems."

"What's it like having the tables turned?" She pointed to the newspaper on the table in front of the sofa, which she'd folded to the article. "I'm sure you saw Senator Price's latest statement."

"He's trying to take any responsibility for what happened off of his wife and dumping it all on me."

"How does that make you feel?"

He shrugged.

"You must have some feelings about what he said," she insisted, studying his neatly twisted hair, which appeared to be so clean and soft she wanted to reach out and touch it.

"I guess he doesn't have any other choice. His wife is a ho. He knew it when he married her, but now that everyone else knows it, he has to do his best to clean it up by saying I pursued her. Like I'm some sort of perv. I'm well aware it doesn't excuse my part in the incident, but she was the aggressor. I just went along with her program." His bitter laugh filled the quiet office.

"You could've said no to her, couldn't you?"

"No red-blooded, straight American male is going to say no to an offer of spontaneous sex with a beautiful woman and no strings attached, Ms. Drake."

"You tell yourself that to ease your guilt, but there are healthy, heterosexual men who say no all the time."

"Like who?"

"Like married men who love their wives and don't want to jeopardize their marriage. Or single men who are looking for something more than casual sex." Rhani figured this was a good place to ask him more about the reason for the mandated therapy. "Are you saying this was not typical behavior for you? I'm curious, because I find it a little strange that your employer would order therapy for a single incident. Did something else happen?"

A flush crept across his cheeks and his chin dipped down. He cleared his throat and paused before he answered. "When the story broke in the news, it primed the gossip mill and…every woman at the station I'd slept with suddenly had a story to tell."

This confirmed her suspicion of there being more to the story. "I see. Did any of them lodge a formal complaint against you?'

"No," he said, still unwilling to meet her gaze. "They're just doing a lot of talking."

"How many of your coworkers were you involved with?"

"I really don't know. I wasn't keeping a record or anything."

She sent him a skeptical glance. "Give me a ballpark number—five, twenty-five, two hundred-fifty?"

"Does it really matter?" His pinched expression told her his inner-office conquests were more than a handful.

"Yes, it does."

He fidgeted and tapped his foot, and the way his gaze roamed about the room, she assumed he was trying to recall. "Maybe twenty-five, thirty. I guess."

Based on her experience with clients, she knew the number exceeded what he claimed. "Did these women know about each other?"

"I have no idea. We're not talking about *relationships* here. I never pretended to want more than a hookup with any of them."

"Are all of your brothers married?"

"All except one, and he just graduated from medical school. Nick's not thinking about marriage right now. Marc's been married for almost a year. Charles and his lady are getting married in the fall."

"Do any of them have a history of cheating on their mate?"

"Nooo," he answered emphatically. "When they meet that special woman, it's almost like those girls put the whammy on them." He laughed, and then his expression turned rueful. "I've always been different from my brothers."

"You say it as though it's an indictment against you."

"I suppose it is. They're all good guys, and they love their women. Just like my dad and my mother."

"Your father never cheated on your mother?"

"Not to our knowledge. Old Vic is a straight arrow. Homey don't play that."

Rhani snickered at his humor. They were about the same age, and his reference to the pop culture figure they had both grown up watching on television made him seem more relatable. "Have you ever been in a serious, committed relationship with a woman?"

He turned away for a fraction of a second—long enough for her know the answer. His shoulders drooped ever so slightly, and his voice lowered to just above a whisper. "Once."

"Let's talk about it."

The way his body stiffened and his knuckles whitened as his hands tightened around the chair arms, Rhani thought he would bolt, but then he eased back. "I—I don't want to talk about her."

"Why?"

"Because she has nothing to do with this. It's ancient history."

"How ancient?"

He pressed his lips together. "Before I left Atlanta." His Adam's apple bobbed as he swallowed repeatedly.

"Have you ever talked to anyone about what happened with her?"

"It was none of anybody's business."

"Talking about the challenges in our lives often helps us to see them more clearly, Greg."

"I didn't come here to talk about *her*." The firmness in his voice warned her to move on.

Rhani folded her hands in her lap. "All right. Is there something else you want to talk about?"

He met her gaze for a fleeting second before he began talking. "The other night…I couldn't stay in my apartment. I mean—it's a good size place for Manhattan, but it felt as if the walls were closing in. I'm not used to being home a lot. I knew I shouldn't be out in public unless I wanted to end up in the tabloids, but I got so restless I was climbing the walls. All I wanted to do was hit the dance floor and work off my anxiety."

Rhani had the feeling the story coming would be a whopper. "What did you do?"

"I went to a club called Bembe."

"I've been to Bembe a few times. They play great world music with the live drummers."

She smiled when his eyes brightened with awareness. "Have you ever been there?"

"A time or two. So did you work off your anxiety?"

"Do you like to dance?" he asked, skirting her question.

"I do, yes, but we're talking about you." He suddenly sobered, and she realized he had more to tell. "What happened?"

"I danced for a while, had a couple of drinks and…I brought a woman home." He dropped his head back on the sofa and stared at the ceiling. "When I woke up in the morning, I couldn't even remember her name." He ran a hand over his hair. "She was in bed next to me, and I didn't even know her name."

"That's progress."

"What?" He frowned and his voice rose. "How can you call it progress? I did exactly what I knew I shouldn't have done. And I must really be a head case, if I can't even go out for one night without bringing home a stray."

"Before you were arrested would not knowing her name

have bothered you?"

Greg combed his beard with his fingers, which really wasn't much more than a five o'clock shadow. For the first time since he'd arrived, he looked directly into her eyes. "I didn't think about it like that. But I still woke up with a strange woman in my bed."

"Yes, and now you're looking at what you did in a different light. It's a step in the right direction. I'm going to end our session here, but I have one more question. What was her name?"

"I just said I couldn't remember her name."

"Not her. The woman you were serious about."

He swallowed again and his eyes darkened. "Ev. Her name was Evelyn."

After he left, Rhani made notes on the session until her next client arrived. They had made progress today. This time she'd seen vulnerability in him, which hadn't been evident in his initial visit. She didn't want to push him. Clients did better when they revealed information of their own accord, but once she learned Greg hadn't always been fast and loose, she had to ask.

The way he talked about his brothers and his father impressed her. More often than not, her clients had deep-seated conflicts with family, and in view of his favorable comments, she wondered about the real reason for his obsessive sexual behavior. Why would he, after having an almost idyllic childhood, with above-average looks, a good education, and an enviable career, succumb to actions which jeopardized not only his job but also his health? He obviously wasn't telling her everything, but this was only his second session.

She thought about her new client's privileged background with all its associated benefits, and her thoughts inevitably drifted to her own childhood. When people talked about poverty, they usually focused on Third World nations. Most of what you heard about poverty in this country dealt with people in areas like the remote Appalachian Mountains or the Mississippi Delta. They rarely talked about children right in the middle of the most famous city in the world who went to bed hungry many nights like she and her siblings had. Television commercials showed starving kids on the other side of the world, but neglected to show how, right in the shadow of the Empire State Building rats competed with children for something to eat.

The Drake family had endured that plight, and Rhani had been the first to break out of their generational misery. By the time she'd reached middle school, she had determined in her heart to escape from the hood. She studied fanatically, even by candlelight during those times when the electric had been cut off in their tenement apartment. Her father had no work ethic and couldn't keep a job. He got fired on a regular basis, and each time he had a dramatic story to tell about it being someone else's fault. Her mother's mantra had become, "He's doing the best he can, baby," and Rhani always thought if that was the best he could do, he wasn't of any use to their family. So many times over the years, she questioned why her mother refused to leave him. Since he had nothing to offer, she concluded her mother loved his trifling ass, as Kat would say. Her mother, who didn't even have a high school diploma, did everything within her power to feed her children and keep a roof over their heads. They survived on government assistance between whatever minimum wage jobs she found. Painful memories arose whenever she recalled how embarrassing it had been to be one of the girls who had to get her prom gown from the Salvation Army thrift shop, because her parents didn't have the money. Her mother and father still lived together, and at the age of fifty-eight, his financial standing was no better than it had been twenty-five years ago. Her mother wasn't old enough to collect Social Security yet, so she still waited tables at a small neighborhood greasy spoon.

Thankfully, her mother had constantly talked to her about the importance of education, and why Rhani needed to read as much as she could. When it came time to for her to graduate, she astounded her teachers with an SAT score just fourteen points short of perfect.

Her older brother had succumbed to the lure of the streets, started dealing drugs and was currently serving a twelve-year sentence at Riker's Island. Her twenty-year-old sister was mother to four kids under the age of eight, each with a different father. Rhani came to terms with the fact that she couldn't help them, with the exception of her baby brother. He had graduated with a high B average, and with her help, he'd scored several scholarships and been accepted into City College. When he'd moved into the dorm, she'd paid for everything he needed to make his room comfortable and given him a refillable RushCard to take care of incidental expenses. So far, he was doing well.

Every extra dollar she earned either went to him or to help the girls at the community center where she volunteered. Every now and then she would also send a gift card for one of the local department stores to her mother. Rhani knew better than to send cash, because her father always found a way to get his hands on it. Hospitals, doctors and other programs referred clients to her. Normally she didn't have to go out and scrounge for new clients on her own. Basically, her income remained steady, and she often extended her hours a couple of nights a week in order to accommodate new clients.

She closed the notebook, and made herself a cup of tea, contemplating Greg Stafford. Prior to her discovery of his fondness for dancing, she'd been under the impression he only did the club scene to pick up women. A brief mental video flashed before her of what he might look like moving his tall body to the music. Big men who could really dance were a joy to observe. When she realized how far her thoughts had digressed, she shook her head. Right now she had approximately twenty-two clients, but Greg seemed to monopolize her thoughts. According to her calendar, she had one more client, and then she could head to the community center to conduct tonight's workshop.

Rhani bought two sub sandwiches and took the train over to the recreation center in her old neighborhood of Hunts Point in the South Bronx. In the late 1800s and early 1900s, the area had been a residential and holiday retreat to the city's elite. The area changed after World War I, when apartment buildings replaced manor houses, streets replaced fields and Hunts Point turned into a fusion of New York's multitudes. Conditions worsened to the point where nearly two-thirds of the area's residents left the neighborhood during the 1970s. Hunt's Point was now part of the poorest congressional district in the country, with more than fifty percent of the population living below the poverty line. The neighborhood in the NYPD's 41st Precinct had so many prostitutes and sex-oriented businesses it was considered a red light district.

Rhani had spent countless hours hoping and dreaming her family would one day get out and move to a house in the suburbs. A real house with nobody living on the other side of the walls. With a yard. And maybe a dog. Even though her mother held no expectation of one day leaving the neighborhood, she had drilled into her youngest daughter's head that education would be her means of escape. It finally did happen when Rhani went away to college. She applied for every scholarship and grant she could find, and her 4.0 grade point average had garnered a full ride with room and board. And she had drilled the same anticipation into her younger brother, Wil.

Now she had a chance to give back to the young girls who were still trapped there. The demographics of the neighborhood had changed over the years, and seventy-five percent of the residents were now Hispanic. She walked the two blocks from her subway stop to the old converted fire station, which now served as the Halleck Street Community Center. The 1940s two-story brick structure had been remodeled in the late seventies, and everything had remained basically the same since. Each room had been painted a brilliant color, with the only décor being PSA posters, printed bulletins and announcements taped or fastened to the walls with pushpins.

Once a week, she taught workshops covering everything from improving study skills, to the correct way to complete a job application and dressing for a job interview. Working with inner-city girls proved to be both frustrating and rewarding. Rhani saw herself in each one of the girls' faces. Sometimes it broke her heart to hear their stories, many of which made hers seem tame. When she first started volunteering there, the center's director had warned her not to fall victim to requests for money, but counseling had given her a propensity for discerning the honest requests from the cons, and she found a way to circumvent the rules. Rather than giving cash, if one of the girls didn't have the proper clothes for an upcoming job interview, Rhani picked up the item at a discount store. She had even bought a couple of MP3 players for the girls who said their apartments were too noisy to study. Of course, the positive music she downloaded served as more than merely a noise blocker. Several of the young women in the program had become dear to her, and she loved them like they were her own sisters.

Usually, as few as a half-dozen girls participated in the workshops, but they were the ones bent on improving their lives.

"Rhani, guess what!" one of them called out on her way down the long hallway leading to the room where they met each week. "I got a letter! They want me to come in for an interview."

"For real? I'm so happy for you, Alida! And tonight's workshop is going to get you ready."

This evening they occupied the sky-blue room for a workshop on how to build a basic business wardrobe on a budget. Teaching the girls why multi-colored leggings, sparkled shoes and midriff tops were improper would probably spark a lively discussion, but she could handle whatever they might throw at her. The others arrived in the next few minutes, and they gathered around the folding table. A couple of them took exception to the pictures of simple business attire in the PowerPoint presentation she'd put together.

"A white shirt and a black skirt? Boring," Guadalupe, the most fashionably expressive one, said with an exaggerated eye roll.

Rhani laughed then explained. "It's not boring, Lupe. It's understated and professional. Businesses hire people to represent the company's image, not yours. As an employee, you're there to help promote the company."

"But I need to be free to express myself," Lupe insisted. "It's who I am."

"There are ways to express yourself without breaking a company dress code. Unless there are rules against it, you can always accessorize with your jewelry and shoes. You don't have to give up your personality, just tone it down a little." A collective giggle filled the room acknowledging Lupe's style, which rivaled Nicki Minaj's.

Rhani asked the girls to come to the next workshop dressed in their best representation of business outfits, then asked Alida to help her in the kitchen that had once served Hunts Point firemen. She filled an empty pitcher with water and powdered fruit punch mix while Alida cut the subs into individual servings. She knew many of the girls hadn't eaten anything since breakfast, which in some cases amounted to nothing more than a small bag of plantain chips. She opened Pandora on her iPad and set it for her playlist, music most of the girls had probably never heard. They sat around the folding table, talked, laughed and ate. Because the girls were aware of her profession as a sex therapist, they always asked questions about sex, but they also asked her opinion on everything from stories they'd heard on TV to problems with family members. Rhani always tried to be open, honest and not get too clinical with them; it created an atmosphere of trust and respect, which meant the world to her.

Even though she was born and raised in New York, Rhani knew taking the subway back after dark wasn't safe for a woman alone, or for anyone. At nine o'clock she called the cab company that took her home each week. They always arrived on time since her pickup was a regular call. The girls' questions stayed with her while she rode in the back seat of the musty-smelling taxi. She wished people knew how vivacious and full of dreams they were. So often the general public wrote off girls like them because they were non-white and poor. But Rhani knew them up close and personal, and she knew how their hearts hungered for the things many took for granted. Their dreams were the same as most American girlspretty clothes, a boyfriend who treated them as though they were precious, to go to parties and hang out at the beach during the summer. But these girls, her girls, also dreamed about not being hungry, not being abused, and being able to make a decent income in order to help their families. The burdens they bore would bend the backs of mature adults, and certainly were too heavy for a fifteen- or sixteen-year-old, so she made herself available to guide and advise them no matter what the situation.

Rhani thought of the people who had helped her over the years: the teachers, guidance counselors, community leaders, a neighborhood pastor, and others. She had no doubt that she wouldn't have made it out of the old neighborhood without their help and encouragement. It only seemed right to pay their kindnesses forward.

Whenever she got home from the workshops, it took a while to calm down and relax enough to be able to fall asleep. Once she removed her makeup and changed into her pajamas, she turned on her iPad and transcribed her notes from today's client sessions. Some of them had been coming to see her since she opened the practice. The newer ones required more work and attention. The females always seemed to take to therapy more readily than the males. After talking with them for months, she concluded that the men had been more brainwashed by the media, their peers, and society in general to believe they would actually die without sex. Most of them also believed having only one sexual partner went against their physiological and psychological makeup. It usually took twice as long to get her male clients to consider another paradigm as it did her female clients. In most cases, the women developed extreme sexual habits as a result of early experiences in their lives—molestation, rape or incest. Rhani discovered the men's obsessions often developed from exposure to pornography, prostitution or undue influence to participate in abnormal sexual behavior by family or friends.

At this point, it was too early to determine the cause of Greg Stafford's problems, but going by what he'd disclosed about his childhood, there were other causes for his behavior. She would need to dig deeper and work harder to get him to start talking. At the moment, even though she had several clients with the same issues, his case monopolized her thoughts. And so did the reasons why she looked forward to meeting with him more than her other clients.

Rhani often considered the irony of her profession. Five days a week she counseled men and women about their sexual problems when she hadn't been involved in a sexual relationship in what seemed like ages. She had been trained in her field, but her personal experience was fairly limited. During high school, when her friends' ultimate goal was to catch the eye of the finest boy in school or to gain the attention of one of the jocks, she'd had higher goals: to make honors, graduate with a 4.0 GPA, and get into the college of her choice. And it was exactly what she'd done. Her goals remained the same in college. While everyone attended the fraternity/sorority parties or went into Manhattan to party, she spent most of her time in the library. Rhani knew having a boyfriend would divert her attention from the needful things, and she didn't have time for it. Of course, she dated, but those relationships never turned into anything more, and she preferred it that way. Once she'd gotten older and settled in her profession, the need for male companionship had started taking up more of her thoughts. Kat and Joie constantly pushed her to get out more, hoping she might bump into Mr. Right or at least Mr. Right Now, but Rhani wanted more than just right now. The prospect of meeting the type of man she not only admired but was also attracted to in one of the city's dance clubs seemed far-fetched. She went to the clubs because she loved to dance, and nothing more. Serious men, those with their eyes on the prize, didn't spend their free time clubbing. Her new client totally contradicted this ideal. His good education and enviable profession didn't overcome the negatives in his life. Knowing all of this, why then did he appeal to her so much? Of one thing Rhani was certain; in the very near future, she intended to uncover more about his relationship with the elusive Evelyn.

Chapter Five

*B*ack in college, Greg had signed with an Atlanta modeling agency. His first job had been a magazine spread for a local fashion designer. Unlike many of the other models who'd started in the business in elementary school, the attention was new to him. Females and males alike gushed over his bone structure, sparkling eyes and golden complexion, and it fed a neglected part of his ego. In his family, good looks were as common as hot wings at the neighborhood store. Within the walls of their home, no one made a fuss, because all six brothers could've been models or actors. But his parents had done their best to steer their sons into professions in which they used their brains rather than their faces or bodies. Only he and Marc had strayed from the plan, and Marc's body ended up bringing him a lucrative income as a personal trainer. He had a bachelor's and a master's like the rest of them, but Greg knew very well that Marc's spectacular physique was responsible for his success. Only Marc really understood Greg's driving desire to have a career outside of the medical field. And, although they had never discussed it, most likely, Marc would be the only one to understand his sex life, since the youngest twin had been a true player before he married Gianne.

Spending so much time confined to his apartment trying to avoid reporters and photographers had begun to drive him crazy. How much time could he spend on the roof deck? The East River wasn't all that interesting. His mother's invitation to come home for a while had tempted him for about five minutes, but the idea of taking a trip to Las Vegas appealed to him much more. There, no one knew him, and the city offered plenty of ways to entertain himself.

Greg lifted his phone and scanned his Contacts list for Marc's number. He still hadn't returned his brother's call from the night he got out of jail.

"Hey, man, it's Greg," he said, when Marc answered. "Are you with a client right now?"

"No. It's about time you called me back. What's going on, man?"

"I'm sure you got the dirt from somebody in the family."

"Sure did. All these years everyone called me the renegade, while you were out there showing your ass— literally." Marc howled until he started coughing then cleared his throat and said, "Seriously, how are you doing?"

"I'm okay, I guess. Just sick and tired of having to lay low. These walls are closing in on me."

"Why don't you come out here for a while?"

"I'd love to, but I'm kind of on house arrest, since I'm required to see the therapist twice a week. Can't do it if I'm in Vegas."

"What if you schedule your sessions for Monday morning and Friday afternoon? You could leave for the airport on Monday, stay out here for the week and fly back Friday morning."

"That just might work. I'll have to check with my therapist when I go tomorrow. Are you sure it will be all right with Gianne?"

"Quite sure. Let me know what you decide. I've gotta run. My next client is here."

"Thanks for the offer, man. I'll get back to you."

The thought of hopping a plane and escaping the confines of his apartment and the invisible boundaries of the

Borough of Manhattan tempted him, but jeopardizing his job wasn't something Greg wanted to risk. If Ms. Drake thought it wasn't breaking the counseling agreement, though, he'd be on the next plane.

What she'd said about Bembe and dancing had taken him by surprise, and since then he couldn't erase the image of her moving to the Afro-Latin rhythms with her wild curly hair flying about. The picture seemed so contrary to her staid, serious business personality. The women who frequented Bembe were generally uninhibited and had no problem working up a sweat. Imagining her being so free brought an involuntary grin to his face.

In the middle of the phantasm, the phone rang again. He checked the displayVic calling from Atlanta. Both of his older brothers remained on his imaginary *to be called* list. He didn't talk to Vic, the oldest, too often. His new job kept him so busy, social phone calls were relegated to the bottom of his to-do list.

"Hey, man. What's up?" he answered with forced exuberance.

"I called you days ago to find out."

Greg snorted. "I know our family. They've already given you the gory details, and I've been the subject of dinner discussions for the past five days. Daddy is still griping to anyone who'll listen, and Mama is still crying when nobody's looking."

"That's about right. She said you've been ordered to go for therapy. Did you start yet?"

"Yeah. I've had a couple sessions so far, but," he paused. "I don't know how much help it'll be."

"Why? You don't believe in the value of therapy?"

"Not when the therapist is so sexy you can't concentrate on what she's saying."

Vic groaned. "Don't touch that woman, Greg. They sent you there to fix your problem not create new ones."

"I haven't done anything to her! Damn, man, can't you give me the benefit of the doubt?"

"Hey, I'm not in any position to judge. There's all kinds of hell going on in my life at the moment."

"Aww, what's the matter?" Greg asked in a teasing tone. "Has being chief of surgery of the biggest medical center in the South turned out to be tougher than you expected?"

"No, the job is the least of my problems. I love my work. It's women who make my head explode."

"Did Mona max out all your credit cards again, or is she looking for another new house?"

"She's always looking, but we're not talking about my problems, little brother. How's this arrest and suspension going to affect your career?"

"Like I told Daddy, I'm a TV personality not a preacher," Greg said, repeating what had become his new mantra. "The American public has a short memory, and there are lots of people who are way more famous than I am who've done things way more serious. Nobody even remembers."

"Who are you trying to convince, me or yourself?"

Vic sounded so much like their father; it set Greg's teeth on edge. Always concerned about their image. "I don't need to convince myself. It's just a fact. Think about R. Kelly and Rob Lowe. Their careers haven't suffered one bit. In fact, they're bigger stars now than they were before their sex scandals. Robert Downey, Jr. was a hardcore junkie. Now he's Ironman, and he topped the Forbes list of highest earning actors this year. I'm not worried."

"I hope you're right, man. You've worked hard to get where you are." A momentary silence lingered between them. "Listen, you should call Mama. She needs to know you're okay."

"What would I say to her? She'll never understand."

"None of us understand, but I think you're underestimating her. Mama is probably the most compassionate person I know. She loves you, and she wants to understand what's happening in your life. Daddy is another story."

"I talked to him the other day, and he was more sympathetic than I expected."

"Really? He didn't go ballistic on you?"

"No, just the opposite. Let me ask you something." Greg glanced around the room as if someone might be listening, although he was alone. "Do you know if Daddy ever cheated on Mama?"

"If he did, none of us ever found out about it, but if you ask me, I can't see him ever creeping on Mama. Doing the right thing is as much a part of his DNA as his blood type. He's always been no-nonsense to the bone. Why do you ask?"

"My therapist wanted to know. Honestly, I'd never even thought about it."

"Why would she ask?" Suspicion edged Vic's tone.

"I guess she's trying to determine whether or not my sexual tendencies are inherited." He snickered. "I wish I had someone to blame it on, but I don't."

"Well, I'm not trying to get into your business. Just checking on you, and if this thing has become a real problem, I'm glad you're getting help. And if you need to get away, you can always hang out here for a while. If there's one thing we have here, it's extra space."

Greg chuckled envisioning Vic's new home, which reminded him of a modern castle. "Thanks, man. Marc made me the same offer, but I have to figure out if I can make my therapy sessions and travel too. I'll let you know. Tell Mona I said behave."

"For all the good that would do," Vic mumbled. "Keep in touch, man."

Since his arrest, Greg hadn't thought about anything other than his own problems, but the anxiety in Vic's voice concerned him. One of the most emotionally stable people Greg knew, Vic never displayed Jesse's anger, or Marc's defiance or Charles' withdrawal into silence. All their lives, Vic could be relied on to be level-headed, the reason why he claimed the spot as their father's favorite. Vic's personality and surgical skill were responsible for him reaching the professional heights he'd aimed for before he'd even graduated from medical school. He had a great life— enviable career, a former beauty queen wife, a spectacular home, and handsome little sons. But it didn't take someone with Ms. Drake's skill to sense the rumblings of something unpleasant brewing in his life.

♥♥♥

Greg drummed his fingers on the wooden arms of his chair in Ms. Drake's outer office. Confused by his nervousness, he waited for her assistant to call him in with a premonition of what was about to happen in this session.

Today she wore tailored slacks topped by a pink blouse with ruffles that drew his gaze to where they cascaded between her breasts. He inhaled, taking her light fragrance into his nostrils. She asked how he was doing and how he'd handled the past few days then launched right into the session.

"Last time, we talked about your family you said something about not being like your brothers. What did you mean?"

"They've all bought tickets on the monogamy train and have been riding happy ever since. Sometimes I wonder why I'm the different one."

"Were they always one-woman men?"

He had to think for a moment. "No. None of them ever had a shortage of women, but when they met their wives, it was all over. Just like that." He snapped his fingers.

"And you've never experienced the same thing?"

He didn't answer.

"Not even with Evelyn?"

His gaze jumped to meet hers, and the heat of anger rose in his chest. "I told you I didn't want to talk about her."

"I think we need to, Greg."

He squirmed at the way she pinned him with her gaze. What was she trying to do? Weren't therapists supposed to help you? Why would she intentionally torture him? "What purpose would it serve?"

"You said you think you're so different from your brothers, but I don't believe you are. Tell me about her."

"My mama raised me to never speak bad about the dead."

The color drained from her face, and she drew in a sharp intake of air. "She passed away?"

Her question sent a wave of cold through his body. "As far as I'm concerned."

Rhani exhaled a sigh. "She must've hurt you deeply."

Greg focused on the opposite wall and studied the lithograph of Monet's water lilies. "Let's just say she taught me a valuable lesson."

"The lesson being…?"

"Never trust a woman."

She scribbled something on her notepad, and then refolded her hands. "Do you believe all women are untrustworthy, even your mother?"

He refocused on the Monet once again. "My mother is different. She's from a generation with different values."

"And you feel all women in your generation lack those values?"

"From what I've seen, yes," he answered, refusing to look at her.

"Where are these women you're talking about?"

From her tone of voice it sounded as though she didn't believe him. "Everywhere. It doesn't matter where I meet them. All they want is professional hookups, money or sex, so that's what I give them. Nothing more." Her pensive gaze, and the way she sat with her chin resting in her cupped palm once again made him fidget.

"What did Evelyn want from you?"

He crossed his arms, took a deep breath and held it for a few seconds. "Why are you pushing this?"

"I think it's important. Have you ever talked to anyone about your relationship with her?"

"You mean a professional?"

"Not necessarily. Have you ever shared what happened between you and her with *anyone*?"

"No reason to. When it was over, it was over."

"You needn't be concerned about telling me anything," she said, as though she'd sensed the reason behind his reluctance to answer. "Everything you disclose in our sessions is strictly confidential." She lifted the carafe on the end table next to her chair, poured a glass of water and set it on the table in front of him. "How did you meet her?"

He reached for it and took a sip. "She worked as a production assistant at the station where I worked in Atlanta." He peered into the glass and swirled the clear liquid around as though remembering something. "We met her first day on the job when she handed me a shot list for the show. The next time we met, the cast was preparing for a trip to L.A. to do an on-location shoot. She brought me my plane tickets. I introduced myself." Greg frowned, wondering why all of a sudden he was sharing details he hadn't even told his own brothers.

She wrote something in her notepad. "I don't know much about the television industry, but a production assistant is an entry-level position, is it not?"

"Sure is. They do a little bit of everything, including functioning as gofers to run around and do everyone else's bidding. It's basically a stepping stone to bigger and better things."

"Wasn't it considered inappropriate for you to have a relationship with her?"

"At that point it was just a professional association."

"How did it develop into more?"

"I asked her to have a drink with me one day when we finished filming."

"What attracted you to her?"

Greg pressed his lips together so tightly he thought his

teeth might pierce the skin. When he opened them, the words that came out surprised him. "She was gorgeous, but I wasn't just impressed by her appearance. I'd been watching how she handled herself on the set, and saw how she seemed to be able to think on her feet, and how friendly she seemed without acting like a silly fangirl the way some PAs do."

"Do the fangirls annoy you?"

"Yes, the ones who only take the job in order to meet celebrities. They're not interested in being there to help you with the work. They just want to get close to you. I've experienced it, and I'm not even a star."

"You said that once before. I think most people would consider you a TV star. Why don't you?"

"Because it's true, so I try to be rational about it. A true television star is Kerry Washington or Charlie Sheen or even NeNe Leakes, someone who's become a household name. I might be recognizable, but I'm not a star. I know most people just refer to me as *the light-skinned guy on The Scoop*." He chuckled.

"You have a good attitude about it. Too many celebrities allow their success to go to their heads. Did she accept your offer?" He nodded. "Did you two start dating right away?"

"The first time we went out after the show wrapped, we talked for three hours."

"What did you talk about?"

"Everything—the job, our families, music, food." A faint smile crossed his face, but a distant look filled his eyes.

"It sounds as though you connected right away."

He bit the inside of his bottom lip. "Yeah, we did."

"How would you describe your relationship—platonic, casual, romantic or strictly sexual?"

He didn't want to answer, but her soft voice and gentle

75

demeanor drew it out of him like a bucket from a deep well. "It started out casual…but it turned…romantic."

"In what period of time?"

"Not long. Maybe about a month."

She appeared to be surprised by his answer, but plowed ahead. "Were you two exclusive?"

He swallowed several times to keep his throat from closing up, "*I* was." The words left a bitter taste in his mouth.

"What do you mean?"

Greg glanced at his watch and bolted from his seat. "I can't do this."

"Our time isn't up yet."

"Yes, it is," he said, meeting her gaze directly. "There's one thing I need to know before I leave. I'm thinking of visiting one of my brothers in Las Vegas. Will it work for you if we have a session early on Monday morning and then late on Friday afternoon? I could use some time away from the City."

"Of course. You're not wearing an ankle bracelet," she said, as if she were trying to lighten the mood. "Schedule it with Sherylle on your way out."

He managed a weak smile. "Thanks." After he took two steps toward the door, and put on his shades and cap, he turned back to face her. "I'm not trying to be difficult…really, but…not today."

"I understand. We'll see each other on Monday then."

On his way out to the street after he'd scheduled the upcoming sessions, Greg shook his head. He hadn't expected Ms. Drake to dig into his past with Evelyn, but it was her job, wasn't it? It only made sense for her to ask about his past relationships, and he couldn't be mad at her for doing so. This therapy experience had turned out to be heavier than he'd anticipated. She had such a way about her, though. She made him *want* to tell her things. He didn't understand it, because he *never* revealed personal, intimate information to women. To confound him even more, he'd started to look forward to his sessions with her.

After he stopped to pick up dinner, Greg returned to the apartment, ate and went online to check flights to Las Vegas. He booked a 12:30 p.m. flight following his Monday session then called Marc and got his voicemail.

"I'm set for Monday. The flight should get to Vegas around 5:30 p.m., and I'm renting a car, so I should be at your place an hour or so later. Please tell Gianne not to go out of her way for me. I don't expect to be entertained. All I need is a place to chill. Thanks, man." He hung up the phone and packed a small suitcase with enough clothes and toiletries for a four-day stay.

The prospect of getting away from New York temporarily took his mind off the reality of spending another weekend alone. He hadn't had sex since he'd gone to Bembe last week, a record for him. Miraculously, he hadn't been dwelling on his physical satisfaction nearly as much since he'd started the therapy sessions.

Rhani gave him a curious glance when he appeared at her office on Monday morning carrying a suitcase. Since he planned to take a cab to the airport as soon as they were done, he had to bring it with him.

She invited him into the inner office. "Either you've decided to visit your brother or you've joined the ranks of the homeless," she said with a look that made him want to touch her cheek.

"I'm flying out as soon as I leave here, and I won't have time to go back home."

"You can put your bag over in the corner."

He sat in his usual spot with his elbows on his knees and his hands clasped together.

"What's on your mind?"

"I didn't go out this weekend. No clubs. No hookups."

"Really? What did you do instead?"

"Nothing much—went to the gym, slept, read a little bit, watched movies."

"Do you know the reason why?"

"I've been trying to figure it out, but I'm not sure. It could be…because I'm more conscious of my behavior, whereas I didn't really think about it before."

"What's the longest you've gone without sex within the last year?"

"Usually not more than two days," he answered, avoiding her direct gaze.

"So you're on your way to breaking a record. Good. It's important for you to always be conscious of your actions and the triggers which set off those actions." She studied him for a moment. "And with that in mind, I want to present you with a challenge."

Not one to ever turn down a dare, Greg looked up. "What kind of challenge?"

"Since you're going away for a few days, and have chosen to make your destination a place aptly called Sin City"—he gave an exaggerated eye roll—"I want to challenge you to not have any sexual contact of any kind while you're there."

Greg eyed her with a skeptical squint. "You don't think I can do it, do you?"

"I think you can do anything you set your mind to."

"When you say no sexual contact, I take it you mean no strip clubs."

"Not necessarily. If you believe you can go to a strip club and not have a lap dance or any other physical contact with the women, then go ahead. It's just my opinion, but I think you'd be setting yourself up for failure by merely putting yourself in that atmosphere, though."

He poked out his lips then eased into a wide smile. "What's my reward if I'm successful?"

"Your reward will be knowing you have the mental, emotional and physical strength to resist something that has been ruling you for more than two years."

Greg scratched his chin. "Can we make the reward even sweeter?"

"What do you mean?"

"If I succeed, you agree to have a cup of coffee with me at Starbuck's around the corner after our next session."

"I don't make wagers on my client's progress. It's unfair and unethical."

"Unfair to whom?"

"You and my other clients, who don't receive any tangible reward."

"But I work so much better when there's an incentive involved. It's just a cup of coffee, Ms. Drake."

Their gazes locked, and she tapped her pen on the arm of her chair. "All right, but you do understand that when you say you've met the challenge, I'll have no way of knowing whether or not you're telling me the truth."

"I swear I'll tell you the truth. Nobody has a bigger stake in this than I do."

"Good to hear. We have a deal, if you agree to answer my next questions."

"I knew there had to be a catch." Greg had the feeling he knew what she was about to say, but he agreed anyway. "Fine. Let's shake on it."

She gave a small sigh then extended her hand. Her skin was so soft to his touch; he held her hand a few seconds longer than he probably should have.

Ms. Drake gently extracted her hand from his. "Now…when we ended last time, I'd asked how serious your relationship with Evelyn had become."

He knew it. She refused to let this thing with Ev go. He glared at her for a few seconds then grumbled, "You get right to the point, don't you? I still don't understand why we're wasting time talking about Ev. She has nothing to do with the reason I'm here."

"I'm not so sure. This was your last exclusive relationship?"

"Damn right. I don't need to be burned twice to know fire is hot."

"How serious was it?"

"About as serious as it gets." His chin dropped to his chest. "We were engaged to be married in eight months."

Chapter Six

*T*his wasn't the answer Rhani had expected, and neither was the way his eyes had clouded over when he looked up. "What happened?"

A groan came from deep in his chest. "We...uh...we'd been together for about eight months when I gave her a ring and asked her to marry me on her birthday." He rubbed the back of his neck and blinked several times. "A few weeks later, my mother threw us an outrageous engagement party. We'd set a wedding date..." His voice wavered so much; she thought he might break down.

"It's all right. Take your time." The anguish he felt showed in the way he twisted his hands between his open knees. She sat still and waited for him to speak again, which took a while. "About two months after we got engaged," he finally said, "the station sent me to New Orleans to do a live two-day broadcast. We finished up sooner than expected, and I decided to take an earlier flight back to Atlanta. Rather than waste time going to my place to dump my luggage, I went straight to her condo." He kept his gaze on the floor between his feet. "We had keys to each other's apartments, so I let myself in." Greg's breathing suddenly escalated; his chest heaved, and he went silent again for a moment. "I'll spare you the painful details...but let's just say...what I saw when I walked into her living room..." He swallowed hard. "Is burned into my brain..."

Interrupting him would have drawn him out of the moment, so Rhani waited for him to get the words out.

"I found her bent over the dining room table with some dude banging her from behind. They didn't even hear me come in. I guess I stood there like a fool for a minute before I asked what the hell was going on." He swallowed again. "If they'd been in the bedroom, they could've at least covered up with the sheets, but the two of them just stood there naked and guilty. Neither one of them could say anything. I'd bought her a bunch of gifts from my trip. I remember throwing them at her, calling her a bitch, turning around and leaving."

To Rhani's shock, when Greg raised his head, tears dripped over his well-defined cheekbones and down into his beard. Rhani plucked a bunch of tissues from the box on the end table and pressed them into his hand. She really wanted to put a hand to his cheek and wipe them herself. He seemed so broken. She gave him time to compose himself, and once she saw that he had, she said, "I'm so sorry. You didn't deserve for that to happen to you."

He sniffed and nodded his thanks, but didn't say a word.

"You said you loved her."

"Of course I loved her. I wouldn't have asked her to marry me if I didn't."

"Did you ever see Evelyn again?"

"We *worked together*. I had no choice, and I couldn't stomach seeing her every day, so I started looking for another job outside of Atlanta. I sent her a text message telling her I wanted the ring back. She sent it by FedEx, and I resold it to the jeweler at a loss. When I was offered the position with The Scoop, I left Atlanta. Everyone wondered what happened, but it was none of their business." After he took a sip of water, he leaned back heavily into the leather couch. "Now you know. Are you happy?" The muscles in his jaw worked as though he were grinding his teeth.

"Why would I be happy about something so awful? I just

believe you needed to open up and talk about the situation. It's never healthy to hold traumatic incidents inside."

"So what did all of this gut spilling accomplish?" Vexation gave his voice a hard edge.

"We won't know until we talk about it."

"There's nothing more to talk about. She did what she did. Isn't it self-explanatory?"

"Her actions were; yes, but you haven't said how you felt when you walked in and saw them."

"How do you *think* I felt?" Greg snapped, his voice climbing several decibels. "Come on, Ms. Drake, you don't need a degree"he waved toward her diplomas"to figure out how a man would feel seeing the woman he loves having sex with another man, especially after she made him wait for months before she gave it up."

She straightened with interest at that disclosure. "You and Evelyn weren't intimate from the beginning of your relationship?"

"No," Greg answered with a snort. "She played coy with me, saying she wanted to wait until we were *really committed* to each other. I took more cold showers during the first six months than I could count. The bitch was playing a game."

"Do you really think it was a game, or the way she lived her life?"

"I have no idea. Before it happened, I believed she was a sweet, honest girl. It blindsided me, and I couldn't understand how I had missed seeing that side of her. They were probably screwing the whole time we were together, and it was the reason why she didn't need to sleep with me. If your woman is creeping, there's always some kind of signif you're paying attention."

"And you weren't?"

His bitter laugh echoed in the room. "I *loved* her. Love makes you stupid. It takes away your suspicion. You end up believing whatever they tell you."

Rhani sensed he had deep trust issues. "You hadn't even been with her for a year yet, right? It's not as though you'd known each other for years and had built trust based on your history together. Some people are experts at deception."

"You're damn right."

"I need to ask a very personal question," she said, treading lightly. "If you think I'm overstepping my bounds, please say so."

"Go ahead." He smirked. "I don't think it matters anymore."

"What is your favorite sexual position?"

He rested his chin in his palm and sent her a seductive smile. "Doggie style."

"Why?"

His brows rose. "Because it feels *so good.*"

She tried her best to ignore his sensual tone. "Are you sure?"

"Am I sure it feels good? You're messing with me, Ms. Drake."

"No, are you sure that's *why* it's your favorite position?"

Greg lifted his chin from his palm and met her gaze. "Yes, why else would it be? Do you think I have dom tendencies?"

"I don't know, Greg. You tell me."

He gave her a wordless frown.

"I think we'll end here today. Think about the question while you're away. I'll see you on Friday afternoon. Enjoy

Las Vegas, and remember my challenge."

"How could I forget?" He flashed a grin that curled her toes. "You're having coffee with me on Friday."

"We'll see. Have a safe trip." She gave a nonchalant wave then opened the office door.

For the rest of the day, the image of a single tear running down Greg's face remained fixed in Rhani's mind. She'd thought his relationship with Evelyn had been central to his sexual addiction simply because he'd been so resistant to talk about it, but she hadn't been prepared for his emotional response. She'd also thought this emotional side of him didn't exist. During his first session, he had come across as somewhat narcissistic and self-absorbed. Today, the wounded man beneath the façade emerged. She hadn't been counseling for decades like some of her colleagues, but the one thing she had discovered early in her practice was that every person on this earth has issues—even those who appear to have it all together.

Tonight her professional association held its monthly meeting, and she looked forward to sharing with colleagues. She could talk about her practice without having to tiptoe around the details. Because Dr. Spruill had become her mentor, she didn't feel comfortable disclosing her growing personal interest in Greg to him. Also, she would rather talk with another female. Throughout the day, she rehearsed how she might present her dilemma to someone else. Anything she confessed could be looked at as unethical behavior, so she had to be careful. She had worked too hard and overcome too many obstacles to risk losing what she'd built. Half of her colleagues didn't respect her chosen area of therapy. Many of them didn't believe sexual addiction to be a legitimate addiction, like drugs, alcohol or even gambling. Regardless of their education, the detractors tended to agree with the general public that all these people needed to do was keep their pants zipped and their legs closed, and the issue would take care of itself.

When Rhani thought of whom she might confide in about this sensitive and embarrassing situation, one particular woman, Dr. Alexandra Policastro, came to mind. Now in her early fifties, Alex had been a therapist for almost twenty-five years, and her kindness and compassion came across whenever she and Rhani talked.

At the end of the day, Rhani arrived early at the hotel. She helped herself to a cup of tea at the beverage table, and then greeted other arriving members while she meandered around the room. When Rhani saw Alex enter the room, she waited until the woman fixed her beverage before she approached her.

"Hello, Alex," she said with a smile. "How's everything with you?"

She returned Rhani's smile. "I'm great. Been really busy lately. How're things going with your practice?"

"They're going well. If you have a few minutes before the meeting gets started, I'd like to ask you a question. It's a private matter."

"Certainly. Let's sit over there away from the door." She preceded Rhani across the room and took a seat at one of the unoccupied tables. "What can I help you with?"

Rhani sat beside her then glanced around to make sure no one stood close enough to hear. "I have an ethical dilemma involving one of my male clients. He's coming to me as a result of employer-mandated therapy. This is his second week." She paused and then sighed, unsure if she should reveal the issue to her colleague. "He's a very interesting man—well-educated, vibrant and extremely handsome." Alexandra winced at her words as though she already knew what was coming. "Today he asked me to join him at Starbucks on Friday when he gets back from a short trip. Would it be completely unethical to have a cup of coffee with him?"

Dr. Policastro eyed her with a wary gaze and waited until she finished before she spoke. "You're obviously attracted to him, or the question would be moot."

"Yes, I am."

"He's been referred to you because he has sexual problems. Knowing this, why in heaven's name would you want to get involved with him? You said his therapy has been ordered by his employer. Did he commit some kind of criminal act?"

"Not really. He got arrested, but it wasn't for anything predatory in nature. I can't say anything more without revealing who he is."

A small gasp came out of the doctor's mouth. "Do I know him?"

"You probably know him by face if not by name. Alex, this has never happened since I began my practice. I find myself looking forward to his sessions, just so I can find out more about him and his family."

"Are you sure you're not just attracted to his position or social standing?"

"Definitely not. He doesn't have a powerful position. I just find him exciting."

"Is he married?"

"No. He's never been married."

"It sounds as if you're quite attracted to him, and if you are, Rhani, acting on your attraction would be setting yourself up for professional disaster. You know what the state rules are about fraternization with clients or patients. If you did act on this, and someone reported you to the Board, you could lose your license. I don't care how smart and handsome he is, is he worth taking the risk?"

Rhani felt the color rising in her cheeks. "My question is, could I be reported for merely having a cup of coffee with him?"

Alex threw the ball back into her court. "*My* question to you is, why would you even want to take the chance? Don't be foolish, Rhani. This city is full of good looking, interesting men who won't put your career on the line."

"Where? I've been alone for two years now. I do everything the *experts* recommend. My friends and I go out on a regular basis. I attend professional meetings and volunteer outside of my normal surroundings, yet I haven't met one single man who not only grabs my attention but who's also interested in me."

"I hate to say this, but how do you know you wouldn't just be another one of his conquests? This isn't my area of expertise, but don't sex addicts get immense pleasure from new conquests?"

Her words hit Rhani like a slap. "He hasn't said or done anything inappropriate."

Alex's tone hardened. "And neither should you." Movement at the front of the room indicated the meeting was about to begin. She hooked her arm through Rhani's, and led her back to the beverage table where she refreshed her coffee.

Rhani made another cup of tea then she and Alex choose seats at one of the empty, white-cloth-covered tables. Throughout the meeting, the speakers addressed topics which should have kept her riveted, but Alex's severe warnings kept repeating in her head. Did she really believe Greg Stafford was worth risking the professional status she had worked so hard to achieve? After foregoing the fun and foolishness of high school to concentrate on her GPA, she'd been accepted by all of the colleges to which she had applied. She had literally begged for scholarship money and grant funds to cover her tuition and worked tirelessly in every course, because she'd been desperate. Desperate to never go back to the old neighborhood and to be able to help her brother when he graduated. Was she willing to lose everything she'd accomplished for a romance that could be short-lived? All her life she'd pitied women who gave up their dreams for a man. Her mother had done it all her life and gotten nothing in return but a hard life that had aged her face and body twenty years. Rhani had sworn to herself she would never succumb to the same fate, whether the man happened to be rich or poor.

The meeting ended, and Rhani spent a good half hour chatting with other members before she said goodbye to Alex and went to the hotel entrance to hail a cab to take her home. Tomorrow night she had a dance class, and she looked forward to shedding her professional persona and losing herself in the joy of movement. But tonight she needed to go over her client files. A couple of them had made such great progress she considered ending their therapy. One of her female clients had turned out to be a real challenge, though. With the exception of Greg Stafford, she ranked as Rhani's toughest case. At every session, she stressed how much she wanted to overcome her negative sexual habits, but at each subsequent visit she confessed to backsliding. Rhani hoped Greg wouldn't return from Las Vegas with the same admission. But how would she know if he were being straightforward? Perhaps he only wanted to use the bet as a way to get personal with her. Now she wanted to kick herself for agreeing to a wager with a client. Her gorgeous client had her doing things she previously would never have done in a million years.

♥♥♥

The intense jazz class helped Rhani get her mind off her

clients for a while. She concentrated on learning the new choreography, which gave her mind a chance to concentrate on something other than her patients. When it ended, she showered, dressed and called Joie. They had made a tentative date to meet for dinner and drinks. Kat had a work-related meeting and couldn't join them at their favorite spot.

"Hey, girl!" Joie called and waved from the table where she waited with a drink in hand. "You're all rosy and glowing. Did you just leave your mystery client?"

"Joie! I should never have told you about him." She heaved a frustrated sigh.

"Why not? I don't even know who he is. Not saying I wouldn't love to." She laughed and sipped her cocktail.

"If I'm glowing, it's because I just left dance class," Rhani insisted. She lifted an index finger to get the server's attention and ordered a strawberry-lemon mojito.

"Aww, I thought maybe you shared the couch with Mr. Sexy Client."

Rhani rolled her eyes at Joie's devious smile and raised her palm. "Please! What I said about him before was just a fleeting thought, and a crazy one at that." No one else besides Alex needed to know what she was considering. For Greg's sake, she hoped he'd be able to resist any temptation he faced in Las Vegas, but for her sake, she hoped she didn't need to make good on their bet.

"I don't think it's crazy at all. When's the last time you had such a strong reaction to a man? In the few years we've known each other, I've never heard you talk about a man with so much interest," Joie insisted.

"No matter how he affects me, it isn't justification to act on it. I'm a professional, and I need to keep my interaction with clients professional."

"Umm hmm." Joie folded her arms and sent her a

skeptical glance. "You might just be missing out on the one man who can bake your biscuits, and your oven hasn't been warm in quite a while, girl."

Rhani slapped a hand over her mouth to stifle a loud laugh. "Can we not discuss my sex life, Joie?"

"You have to admit, it's pretty ironic, wouldn't you say? A sex therapist who isn't getting any."

"How many times do I need to explain what I do? My job has nothing to do with whether or not I'm sexually active. I counsel people who have out-of-control sexual urges or behaviors."

"I know, I'm just saying…"

"Well, do me a favor—don't."

Joie wouldn't let it go, and she leaned forward over the table and whispered, "But it isn't good to go without for so long, Rhani. It makes you tense, irritable and unable to function in your daily life."

"It makes *you* that way. Speak for yourself. My daily life is just fine, thank you!"

"All right. If you insist on living in denial, I'm not going to argue with you. I just hope you have a good supply of batteries." She winked, and they changed the subject. "We were supposed to figure out a date I can come and talk to your girls at the community center."

"Right." Rhani called up the calendar on her phone and studied it for a moment. "Could you possibly do the seventeenth, or is it too soon? Kat is coming on the twenty-fourth."

Joie also checked her calendar. "The seventeenth looks okay. Now exactly what do you want me to talk about?"

"Share with them a little bit about your background, what you went to school for, what you did before you opened the boutique and the steps you took to get the funds. I'm trying to expose them to successful minority women. Just don't come too dressed up. It might be discouraging to them."

Her eyes widened. "Now you know I can't show up anywhere and not be fabulous."

"Just be fabulously casual, please. These girls have little to no money, and if they think they have to be decked out in designer suits, it could be intimidating."

"Gotcha. I'll probably come to your office and share a cab with you."

"Great! I'd better head home. I still have client notes to transcribe." Rhani stood and dropped a kiss on her friend's cheek. "Love you, girl."

Rhani had gone over and over what Joie had said about Greg and her sex life on the ride back to her apartment. Actually, she often thought about her lack of sexual intimacy, particularly after she listened to the often titillating details of her clients' escapades.

Her thoughts returned to her two problem clients while she typed the details of their sessions into her iPad.

Client 517 appears to be willing to work on his issues, but the next few days will tell just how much progress he's made, if any. It seems he wants to change and to overcome his addiction, but he just isn't sure he has the intestinal fortitude to do it. At the root of it all is his belief that he is severely flawed, and his brothers are somehow perfect. From what he's told me about his father, the family patriarch is a successful surgeon who demanded excellence from his sons, but he doesn't seem to have a problem with the man. From what I can ascertain, the client had more of a problem trying to stand out among the crowd in his home growing up. Still, he doesn't blame his brothers, and from what he's said so far, it sounds as though he has good relationships with all of them. His former fiancee's name is the only name that evoked strong emotion in him. The bitterness he feels toward her was evident the first time he spoke of her. After insisting he tell me about what happened between them, he gave in and became extremely emotional. Infidelity, which he witnessed first-hand, ended their engagement.

He is going out of town to visit one of his brothers in Las Vegas for a few days. I challenged him to stay away from anything that might be a temptation and to have no sexual contact. He, in turn, challenged me that if he is able to maintain celibacy, as a reward I would agree to have a cup of coffee with him at Starbucks following his Friday session. I agreed only wanting to give him some kind of incentive, but in hindsight I believe it was a mistake. Allowing him to challenge me gives him the upper hand and undermines my authority.

She looked at the clock next to her bed. *Nine thirty.* He had to be in Las Vegas by now. Hopefully he went directly to his brother's house. If he started out his visit with a pit stop on The Strip, his chances of avoiding temptation would amount to zero.

Chapter Seven

Greg spent the majority of his flight to Vegas internally berating himself for his emotional breakdown during the session. *I didn't want to talk about Ev, but Ms. Drake pushed and pushed until I was crying like a little girl. I can imagine what she thinks of me now. She probably assumes I came here to have some kind of secret out-of-state orgy, and normally she'd be right. But I want to prove her wrong. And what the hell was the question about my favorite sexual position all about? Every man alive likes it doggie style. Why am I suspect because I do? She could've just been teasing me, or maybe it was some kind of therapist head game.*

Why Ms. Drake's opinion of him mattered so much eluded him. Sure, he wanted to succeed in therapy, but for some other reason, he wanted to impress her. He couldn't comprehend why, but he was drawn to her. But her beauty, her intelligence and toughness made her quite different from the women he usually ended up with. To spend time with him, they didn't need to be the brightest blub, and usually they were pretty compliant.

God, I'm thinking as though we're starting a love affair. She's my therapist, nothing more.

But the idea of being able to convince her to take their relationship beyond the therapist/client level kept intruding on his thoughts. Their coffee bet might be the catalyst to change their affiliation. How could he prove he hadn't gotten involved in anything sexual while he visited Las Vegas? He'd have to come up with something believable before he returned to New York.

His flight landed on time, and he took a shuttle to the car rental location where he picked up his ride for the next three days. Since he wasn't very familiar with the city, he had asked for a car with a GPS. Thankfully, it directed him right to Marc's studio. When he walked in, the energy in the place was off the charts. Marc and Lance, his other trainer, were both instructing clients on how to perform cardio exercises.

"Hey, you made it!" Marc yelled over the music. "If you have some workout clothes, you can join us." When Greg shook his head, Marc said, "Grab a seat then, we'll be done in about thirty minutes."

Greg marveled at Marc's physique. It seemed the older he got, the fitter he became. He had twice as much muscle as Charles, his twin. While he watched the training session, Greg made a mental note to increase his weight training once he returned to New York. As soon as Marc finished and saw his client out, he grabbed Greg around the shoulders and hugged him as though they were the only ones in the room. He couldn't explain the lump in his throat, but he surrendered to the embrace.

Marc finally released him. "I'm hungry. Let's go out and get some lunch." He turned to Lance. "We'll be back in an hour or so." Lance nodded then Greg followed Marc out the back door to his car. "How're you doing?"

"Better, now that I'm away from the reporters and photographers. I felt like I couldn't breathe. They were on my tail 24/7, and I believe Senator Price has a lot to do with it."

"Yeah, I read his last statement. Your name is at the top of his hit list."

"You know what he's saying is bullshit, right?"

"I'd hoped that was what you'd say. You've never needed to force yourself on a woman."

"Thanks. I appreciate your faith in me, man, but I do have a problem." Greg stared out the car window for a few moments.

"Gianne and ChiChi will be home part of the day," Marc said, lightening up the conversation. "But Gianne usually takes her to Gymboree or a Mommy and Me class. The pool's been cleaned, so you can swim, if you want. There's plenty of food in the refrigerator, but I don't know if you will want any of it."

"Probably not," Greg answered with a chuckle. "I can't do your gerbil diet, but I have a car, so I can go out to pick up something. How's Gianne adjusting to motherhood?"

"Like a duck to water, man. She's an incredible mom, but I knew she would be. We had to jump through all kinds of hoops to adopt ChiChi, but it was worth it. We had a good life together before, but having the baby in it has made it even better."

Greg listened to Marc and marveled at the change in him. Of all his brothers, Marc was the one he thought would never marry. From the time they were in middle school, he'd had an endless array of pretty girls, and until he met Gianne, he had seemed content with his life. Everything seemed to have happened so fast. Marc and Gianne met one night at an affair given to honor their brother, Vic. Gianne, his father's former oncology patient, mesmerized Marc, and within a year, they were married. Soon after, Charles took a job with a medical volunteer organization in Nigeria. He'd been assigned to a small village hospital where an orphaned baby became one of his patients. Charles immediately thought of Gianne, who'd been unable to have children as a result of the aggressive cancer treatment she had received. It had taken eight months of creative finagling, which skirted on the borders of being illegal, to arrange the adoption, but Adanna, the nurse who was now Charles' fiancée, had made Gianne and Marc's dream of becoming parents a reality.

"So, what are your plans while you're here?"

In Greg's opinion, their family was too large, too prone to be workaholics and too nosy, but they would give their lives to help one another. And he needed help. "My therapist challenged me to have a celibate visit and to avoid anything temptation, so it looks like I won't be doing much."

"I'm not saying this because Gianne and I aren't happy to have you, but why'd you come to Vegas, of all places?"

"Vegas is as far away from Manhattan as I could get, and it's the best place to test my willpower. Maybe it's too soon, but I want to go out and see if I'm man enough to stand up to temptation. I can't go alone, though."

Marc snickered. "Charles' favorite spot is Sapphire, one of the premiere gentlemen's clubs."

"Will Gianne be upset if you go with me?"

"She's cool with stuff like that—as long as I'm taking a house guest and not dropping in there every day on my lunch hour." They both laughed.

"Otherwise, I just want to use this time to get my head together. It's been a rough two weeks."

They talked about Marc's business, which appeared to be thriving. Thankfully, Marc refrained from asking him any personal questions. After lunch, Marc drove him back to the studio to get the rental car then called home to tell Gianne he was on his way.

Gianne opened the front door wearing a welcoming smile when he arrived. Before she even spoke, he looked behind her and couldn't believe his eyes as ChiChi toddled toward them chattering at the top of her lungs.

"Two of the most beautiful women in the world." Greg stepped inside, set his bags beside the door and hugged his sister-in-law. He hadn't seen her since last Christmas. "How are you ladies doing?"

ChiChi stretched her arms toward him with a verbal request only she understood.

"I told her when the doorbell rang you were coming to see her. She wants you to pick her up."

He shrunk back, unsure of what to do. "I don't know anything about babies."

"Just pick her up. You're not going to hurt her."

"I will if I drop her." He bent over and cautiously slid his hands under the toddler's raised arms.

"You won't drop her."

He lifted the baby off the floor and marveled at how much she weighed. "She's a knockout, Gianne. I don't know how it's possible, but she's starting to look more like you."

His sister-in-law beamed. "Other people have said the same thing. It's just confirmation that she was always supposed to be ours. Come in the kitchen. I'll get you something to drink."

As he followed her to the back of the house, ChiChi put a pudgy hand to his cheek and smiled.

Gianne must have noticed his reaction. "She likes you, and she likes your beard. All you Stafford men have hair on your faces. Honestly, I think she believes all of Marc's brothers are the same person." She giggled, went to the refrigerator and took out one of the beers Marc kept for when his buddies stopped by. She removed the cap and set the bottle on the table in front of him.

Before he could take a sip, ChiChi patted his twisted hair then wrapped her arms around his neck and rested her head on his shoulder as though she knew him and loved him. The completely foreign wave of emotion swept over him, he pulled the baby out of the embrace and almost threw her into Gianne's lap. Puzzled and overcome by the purity and innocence in the baby's response, he stuttered, "I—I think I'm gonna take a dip in the pool if you don't mind."

Gianne studied him for a moment. "Sure. There are beach towels in the hall linen closet and sunscreen in your bathroom. I know how you Stafford boys burn. I'm going to put her down for her nap. You know where the guest room is."

"Thanks, sweetheart." The idea of swimming outside in May, which he couldn't do in New York, agreed with him. Once he changed into his swim trunks and grabbed a towel from the closet, he exited the house through the back door. Marc's pool and patio felt like an oasis. The quiet of the Las Vegas desert was such a contrast to the constant clamor of Manhattan. The solitude and physical exertion were just what he needed to think about everything going on in his life. After he did a few laps, he stretched out on a chaise and closed his eyes. The warmth of the late afternoon sun helped him to relax, and he considered what had happened earlier with ChiChi. It had been a long time since anyone had touched him as though they loved him. Other than his mother, the only person who'd ever caressed his face like that had been Ev. Remembering his former fiancée's touch put a knot in his chest. Until Ms. Drake wheedled him into divulging what happened between them, he hadn't allowed memories of Ev to invade his thoughts. Now he couldn't seem to prevent the mental video from playing.

Among all the things bothering him at the moment, the idea of not seeing his therapist until Friday left him feeling a strange void. He didn't miss the prodding and questions. He missed *her*. He'd always prided himself on being immune to the tricks women used on men, but Rhani Drake was able to reach into his head and pull out whatever she wanted to know. On one hand, it annoyed him. On the other, her power fascinated him, and he had a sneaking suspicion his willingness to open up was due more to his growing attraction to her.

When Greg decided he'd had enough sun, he took a few final laps in the pool and headed back inside. The sound of Gianne's laughter drew him down the hall to the room she and Marc had converted from the second guest room to a frilly room complete with a pink canopy-covered crib. ChiChi and Gianne were sitting in the middle of the room playing with a toy when he entered the doorway. "What are you ladies up to?" Immediately, the baby stood and toddled over to him smiling and babbling.

"It looks as though you've made a friend for life," Gianne said, sounding pleased.

He squatted, kissed the baby's forehead and sat down cross-legged with them on the pink and white alphabet rug. "She's gonna be a heartbreaker."

Gianne shuddered and shook her platinum blond head. "I don't even want to think about stuff like that. The thought of her going to preschool is enough to make me catch a case. I know it's not possible, but after all we went through to adopt her, all I want to do is keep her close forever."

"Are you and Marc thinking about adopting more kids?" He picked ChiChi up and placed her in his lap where she seemed content to sit and listen to their conversation.

"We've talked about it, but we wouldn't do another foreign adoption. It was a nightmare, but there aren't a lot of newborns available for adoption these days in the U.S. between birth control, abortion and these little girls keeping their babies."

"I never really thought about it. Back in the day, most of the girls we knew who got knocked up gave away their babies. Times have changed."

"They sure have and not for the better. I work in the

school system, and I see how many girls drop out each year because they get pregnant. Nevada has one of the highest dropout rates in the country, and a good percentage of them are girls. Then they end up with a child and not even a high school diploma. If there's no family to help them financially, there's nothing left but public assistance."

Greg studied her for a moment. "Did you ever think you'd be here—you know, married with a baby and living in a desert mini-mansion?"

"Never. Three years ago, I was just trying to stay alive. After I got the cancer diagnosis, I thought my life was over. I was referred to your father for treatment. He saved my life, and Marc showed me it's worth living. It's amazing how things can change so drastically in such a short time."

"And you weren't even expecting it, were you?"

"I dreamed about it, but I can't say I *expected* all these wonderful things to happen. Sometimes when I'm alone, I think about it and just cry."

"So, maybe there's still hope for me, huh?"

"There's always hope, Greg. And if you want it bad enough, you start doing things that bring what you want into your life, whether you recognize you're doing them or not." Her expression softened with compassion. "I wasn't going to bring it up, and I don't know how you got this strung out, but as long as you're breathing, you are able to change."

"She's right, you know," Marc said from the doorway where he'd obviously been listening. "Just because you're facing a problem doesn't mean you can't overcome it."

"How long have you been standing there?" Greg asked.

The baby ran to Marc. He bent down, lifted her into his arms and planted kisses on both cheeks. He joined them on the rug. "Long enough to know you're at some kind of crossroads. If you handle it right, you might have a whole new life ahead of you. And on that note, are we going out tonight?"

"If Gianne doesn't mind."

She gave Marc a curious glance. "Why would I mind?"

"We're going to Sapphire."

"Oh." She rolled her eyes. "Greg, are you sure Sapphire is where you want to go?"

"Definitely. It'll be a test of my willpower. My therapist challenged me to avoid any sexual contact while I'm out here."

"I'm going to pretend like I understand, but I really don't." She turned to Marc and gave him a fierce stare. "Keep him out of trouble, okay?"

He pushed her back against the floor, straddled her body and whispered in her ear. "I'm gonna have something for you when I get back."

She laughed and hooked her arms around his neck. "I bet you will. Don't make me wait too long."

Marc teased her with a long, deep kiss as a preview of what was in store when he returned home, then he stood and told Greg, "Give me a few minutes to change, and I'll be ready to go."

Forty minutes later, the brothers walked between the red velvet ropes of Sapphire's garish entrance.

"Wow!" Greg's eyes widened as he scanned the interior of the largest club of its kind in the entire country. "This place gives Diamonds a run for its money. Lead the way, little brother." He followed Marc into the semi-darkened main room and chose a table.

"Let's get a drink then you can do your thing."

After Greg settled into one of the curved club chairs, he glanced around at the sheer number of dancers entertaining the customers and frowned.

"What's the matter?"

"Where are the sisters?"

Marc chuckled. "This isn't Atlanta, man. We only make up eleven percent of the Vegas population. There are more Latinas dancing here than black women. Does it really matter? They all have the same parts."

"Yeah, but not in the same proportions. I like big legs and butts."

"And you cannot lie, right?" Marc said with a smile then raised his eyebrows. "We're sitting in a five-star gentlemen's club, and you're complaining? Maybe therapy is already working."

Greg signaled the waitress and ordered a Ciroc Diddy. Marc asked her to bring him a Red Bull. As soon as she left their table, Greg said, "Speaking of my therapy, I've run into a problem. Maybe not a problem as much as a challenge."

"I didn't want to ask how it was going."

"It's going okay, but my therapist is a woman who is a little too fine for her own good."

Marc smirked. "For *her* own good or yours?"

"It might not be good for either of us. This morning, I bet her that I'd be able to be celibate while I was out here, and if I could, I asked if she'd go with me to Starbucks near her office for a cup of coffee on Friday as my reward."

The server returned with their drinks, and Marc waited for her to leave before he asked, "And how did she respond?"

"She said she didn't make wagers with her clients on their progress, because it wasn't fair to her other clients who didn't get rewards. But I talked her into it," he said, recalling his pleasure when she had agreed.

"It sounds like she might be feeling you a little bit too."

"I hope so." Greg sipped his drink and sucked in his cheeks at the tart flavor of the vodka and lemonade cocktail.

"Why?" Marc asked with deep frown lines forming between his eyes.

"Because she's a unique woman. Naturally, she's very intelligent, but she's also not afraid to stand up to me. And she's a dancer."

"How do you know?"

"I mentioned the name of one of my favorite clubs, and she said she and some of her friends have been there a few times. Hearing it kind of stunned me, since she doesn't seem like the club type. So I asked her if she liked to dance, and she said yes."

"Interesting, considering Mama always said you'd rather dance than eat."

"If she goes with me on Friday, I'm going to get her to go out dancing next."

"Pretty confident, aren't you?"

"I have to be. If I'm not, I'll never convince her to go on a real date with me."

"Isn't it considered improper on her part? I thought doctors aren't supposed to fraternize with their patients."

"She's not a doctor, and I'm not a patient. She's a counselor, and I'm her client."

"You're splitting hairs, man."

"Maybe, but the more I see her, the more I'm interested in her, even though she won't let up on me."

"Could be having someone hold your feet to the fire is what you need."

"You might be right. For some reason, I don't mind her digging into my private life. In fact, I want her to see how serious I am about overcoming my addiction."

"Good, but won't getting personally involved with her affect your therapy?"

"I look at it this way, if she already knows everything about me and still wants to spend time with me, then we're a step ahead of the game."

"You have a point. That awkward stage when you start revealing yourselves to each other can be pretty tricky. At least she'll already know everything about you, but what about her?"

Greg grinned. "I can get her to tell me what I want to know."

"She should be treating you for overconfidence." Marc shook his head. "Come on. See anything you like?"

Greg shrugged and scanned the room. "She's interesting," he said nodding toward a dancer with an olive complexion and long dark hair.

His brother rose, approached the dancer and spoke to her for a few minutes. When he returned, he said, "She'll be here in a minute. Keep your hands to yourself and let her do the touching. Okay, what's my job in this experiment?"

"I want you to record it on your phone, and if I look as if I can't handle it, you need to get me out of here."

His brother's condescending smile spurred him to explain further. "Ms. Drake understands just how much restraint it takes for me at this point. In fact, it might be a good idea to have you do an unrehearsed introduction."

"Are you crazy? I wouldn't know what to say."

"Say how you feel about doing this for me. Give me your phone."

Marc complied. "How do I do video?"

"Just click on the camera app. When it opens hit the video button."

"Okay. Tell her what you thought when I asked you to do this, and be honest, or she'll see right through it. Ready?"

His brother ran a hand over his wavy shoulder-length hair. "She's going to give you a lap dance." He looked directly at the phone, drew in a long annoyed breath, nodded and addressed the screen.

The door opened, and the bikini-clad, raven-haired beauty entered wearing a seductive smile. "Hi, Greg. Your brother tells me you'd like a lap dance."

His gaze ran the length of her body. Yes, definitely his type—curvy with a little more junk in the trunk than the other dancers he'd seen in the main room. "Why don't you have a drink with us first? What's your name?"

"Gemini. I only drink water when I'm working." She took a seat next to him and crossed a pair of legs that seemed to go on forever. "Are you visiting Vegas?"

He handed her Marc's unopened bottle of water, and she twisted off the top with nicely-manicured nails. "I'm here visiting my brother for a few days. He told me this is the place to come to see beautiful women, and you're definitely one of the finest women here."

"Thank you." Gemini sipped her water and smiled. "So, you've never been here before? In that case, I'll have to give you the best Sapphire has to offer." She took a long gulp from the bottle and when the first few drum/bass notes of

Usher's *Good Kisser* pumped through the speakers, set it on the table and stood. "Are you ready?"

He shot a quick glance Marc's way and smiled, but he wasn't as confident as he hoped he appeared. "More than ready, baby."

She strutted up to him and worked her way around his chair before she put her palms inside his knees and spread his legs. Greg leaned back and tried to relax, but his temperature was rising by the second. Gemini lifted one leg and then the other to straddle him and began to writhe against his groin to the music. In order to get the best dance, he needed to encourage her, and he did it with his eyes and his smile. The only words he spoke were, "You're gorgeous, and you smell like heaven."

Her hands traveled over his hard, tense body, and his erection grew with her every movement. When she turned around and pushed her perfect ass between his open thighs, he grabbed onto the sides of the chair with such force his hands shook and his knuckles turned white. It took every ounce of willpower to keep from climaxing right there, and judging by the look on his brother's face, Marc knew just how close he was to going over the edge and losing the bet with his therapist.

Marc kept a close eye on him while he recorded the dance. The moment the song ended, he stuffed the phone back into his pants pocket. They both complimented Gemini on her skills and showed their appreciation with tips that sent her out of the room beaming. Marc waited until she left the room before he asked, "You okay?"

He peered down at his crotch and laughed. "Do I look like I'm okay? Are you sure you got the whole thing?"

"It took two takes, but I got it. What are you going to do with it?"

"Use it as evidence when I go for my session on Friday."

"Seriously? Won't it just condemn you?"

"Not at all. She challenged me to have no sexual contact. I just let a beautiful woman grind all over me, and I never touched her. I'd say that's progress. Thanks, man. Let's get out of here."

♥♥♥

The next morning, Greg had breakfast with Gianne and the baby. She and Marc wouldn't be home until late in the evening, and she reminded him. They had been invited to a community event where he and Lance were doing some exercise demonstrations. He went to the studio for a workout. Following a quick shower, rather than return to the empty house, he left the car where he'd parked it behind the studio and decided to go inside the mall and do a little shopping, but soon discovered Village Square had more service businesses than retail stores. At a loss for something to fill his day, he turned the car in the direction of the strip. What harm could it do to hang out there in broad daylight? The last time he'd been there, he'd accompanied his mother to see Marc's house when he first purchased it a few years ago. He could waste a few hours seeing the new additions on the world-famous street.

After he parked the car near the Luxor, he headed north on foot rather than taking the monorail. Not much had changed since he'd walked the strip with his mother, with the exception of the addition of the new SLS Hotel and Casino. His stomach loudly demanded attention when he finally reached the hotel at nearly two o'clock. Since his suspension was paid, at least he had money in his bank account. Why not splurge on lunch in one of the casinos? One drawback to staying with Marc and Gianne was the absence of *normal* food. Being raw vegans, they didn't eat like everyone else. He deserved to treat himself at least once during his stay.

A sign in the window of Umami Beer Garden and Sports Book in the SLS Hotel boasting of their selection by GQ magazine for the best burger in Las Vegas convinced him to go inside. The spot seemed pretty well occupied for the middle of the day, so he took a seat at the bar, asked the bartender for a Corona and a menu. He studied it briefly, and ordered the Original Burger. The closest thing he'd get to a burger at his brother's house was a gray-looking patty made from soybeans.

A few minutes later, a very attractive brunette smiled as she wiggled up onto the stool beside him. "May I take a look at your menu?"

"Help yourself," he said, handing her the glossy list and taking notice of the shapely tanned legs. She wore a pair of khaki shorts and a crisp, white shirt opened to the third button. Gold hoop earrings, an assortment of thin gold chains and a right wrist full of bracelets tinkled and drew his attention every time she moved her hand. She looked like a well-dressed tourist.

"Have you ever eaten here before?" she asked with her gaze on the menu.

"No. This is my first time. They seem to have some pretty good choices, though."

"Umm, the Greenbird sounds like my kind of sandwich. Can't go wrong with turkey and avocado."

"At least you're not afraid of turkey."

"Pardon me?"

Greg chuckled. "Right now I'm staying with two raw vegans. It's...interesting."

"I could never be a vegan, and a raw vegan. Hell no!"

When he turned to face her, she treated him to a friendly,

open smile and extended a hand. "Kenzie Roberts."

"Greg Stafford." Before he released her small, soft hand, her gaze met his. The way she looked at him sent a wave of heat through his body, and at the same time, set off a warning alarm in his mind. That day at the perfume counter in Barney's, Melinda Price had given him the same look, like she wanted to possess him.

His meal arrived first, and he consciously focused on the burger with Parmesan frico, shiitake mushrooms, roasted tomatoes and caramelized onions with a side of sweet potato fries until Kenzie said, "Looks delicious. Can I try a bite?" Her voice lowered to an enticing timbre, and her shiny pink lips parted slightly to receive the sample she expected.

The small piece of burger and vegetables he cut rested on the tip of his fork, and he put his other hand beneath it so it wouldn't fall onto the bar. Kenzie opened her mouth and slowly closed her lips around the fork. Greg couldn't rip his gaze from the soft rise of her breasts under the open neck shirt as he watched her savor the food then lick her lips and smile.

"Umm, fabulous, and I'm not even a real beef eater. Do you want to try mine?"

"No, thanks. I'm not one of those people who believe avocado makes everything better."

They ate for the next several minutes in silence, and then she said, "How long will you be staying with the vegans?"

"Just until Friday. I have to get back to New York."

"Why? Do you have a wife or a girlfriend waiting for you?"

"Neither. I have an appointment on Friday afternoon."

"What kind of work do you do?"

He didn't feel like explaining his current status as an on-air personality who wasn't allowed on the air right now. It would just lead to more questions he didn't want to answer. "I'm between jobs right now."

"Ah, a job interview." Kenzie placed her hand atop his on the bar and gazed up into his eyes again. "I hope you get the job."

"Thanks. So do I." He slid his hand from beneath hers and busied it by tipping the Corona to his mouth. The long gulp he took failed to cool him off. What the hell? Testing himself was one thing, but now it seemed as though the universe conspired to get him to give in to his physical demands and lose the bet.

He admired Kenzie's body with a sidelong glance. It appeared as though she took very good care of herself—stylish haircut, tastefully manicured nails and a slim, agile-looking body. But she reminded him too much of the lovely, insistent Melinda Price.

"Do you have plans for tomorrow?" she asked with such an alluring look in her eyes, he had to look away.

"Yeah, I'm working with my brother at his fitness studio," he lied.

"Where is his studio?"

"Outside Village Square Mall, not far from Canyon Gate."

"Maybe," she said, caressing his forearm, "I could meet you there when you're done, and we could do something fun."

Greg chuckled and continued eating. "What kind of work do you do, Kenzie?"

"I'm in public relations."

Yes, I bet you are. "Do you enjoy your work?"

"I love it."

Suddenly he knew exactly what to say. "Kenzie, I don't mean to be abrupt, but I'm celibate."

She blinked, her jaw dropped, and her shoulders slumped. "You are?"

"Yes, *intentionally*."

"Oh, what a shame. A good-looking man like you."

"How I look has nothing to do with my sexuality." *Where was this coming from?*

"True. You just looked a little lonely sitting here at the bar all by yourself. I thought you could use some company."

Greg finished his beer and wiped his mouth with a napkin. She'd hit the bulls-eye. He *was* lonely. He had been ever since… "I need to get going. Are you done with your lunch?" He laughed to himself at her questioning expression.

"Yes."

He took both guest checks, handed them to the bartender along with his credit card and waited while he cashed out the checks and returned the card to him. "Nice talking with you, Kenzie." Greg stepped off the barstool, leaned in and kissed her squarely on the lips. "Have a great afternoon, sweetheart."

He left the restaurant wearing a self-satisfied smile. For whatever reason, having Ms. Drake be proud of him had become more important than quenching a sexual need. This was a first.

Chapter Eight

*R*hani saw Greg's face the second she opened her eyes on Tuesday morning. Yesterday he'd been insistent on proving to her that he could remain celibate during his time in Las Vegas. It seemed so important to him to prove he could do it, and she wanted him to, for his own benefit. He needed to comprehend the power he had to control his sexual urges. She didn't want to think about the wager. Having a cup of coffee together wasn't inherently evil, but Rhani understood it represented something more. Meeting at Starbucks would be his way of putting them on the same level—as male and female and not therapist and client. In addition, it would knock down the first brick in the wall she had carefully erected between herself and her clients. It might also represent the beginning of a personal relationship.

Never before had she felt compelled to call a client to check on his or her progress. She had developed a wonderful rapport with the majority of her clients, but even so she'd never once checked on any one of them. She and Greg didn't even get along that well, but the chemistry between them was undeniable.

Once she reviewed the office schedule with her assistant, Rhani went into her office, closed the door then took her phone and iPad from her tote bag. She tapped into the current listing of clients' phone numbers on the iPad, but before she dialed his cell number, Alex's warning returned loud and clear. *Acting on the attraction would be setting yourself up for professional disaster.* Almost as though it became too hot to touch, she threw both devices back into the bag and got ready for her first client of the day.

Less than two hours later, her assistant buzzed her. "Rhani, Greg Stafford is on the phone. He said he's calling from Las Vegas."

"Okay, thank you." Her hand rested on the receiver of the desk phone, and she stared at it for a few beats before she lifted it. "Hello, Greg. I'm surprised to hear from you. Is there a problem?" She held her breath and waited for his answer.

"Good morning. No problems at all, Ms. Drake. The reason I'm calling is to tell you I learned something about myself last night, and I just wanted to thank you. You had more faith in me than I did in myself."

Rhani smiled. "Good to hear. I assume that means you tested yourself?"

"I did, and I have proof. When I come in on Friday, I'll bring it with me."

She couldn't imagine what he meant. "O-kay."

"You're not going to ask what it is?"

"No. You can explain in our session on Friday," she replied, trying to keep it professional.

He gave a good-natured snicker. "All right. And you might start thinking about what kind of coffee you want."

"You sound quite pleased with yourself. Remember, you still have three more days out there, so if it worked, keep on doing whatever you did last night."

"I'm not going out tonight. Just hanging out with my brother, sister-in-law and the baby."

"Sounds nice. Get some family time in." What else could she say? "Enjoy yourself, and I'll see you on Friday afternoon."

"Will do. I'm looking forward to it. I'll be coming right from the airport, so if there's any flight delay, I'll call the office. Have a great week, Ms. Drake." He clicked off the call.

She stared at the phone. Why did his calling her Ms. Drake sound so formal this time? She didn't have the answer, but whatever the reason, she had to shake it off and get to work.

By lunchtime, Rhani had seen three clients and needed a break. Whenever the weather cooperated, she went out for a walk. Late spring in New York City was perfect—no longer cold, but not warm enough to make you sweat from minimal exertion. Usually, she stopped in the deli around the corner and picked up a sandwich and a bottle of water and walked to the small park a few blocks away. At lunchtime the benches were filled with people who wanted out of their hermetically-sealed offices for a breath of fresh air, so she felt safe. After she polished off her lunch, she dialed her brother's phone. He didn't have classes on Tuesday, and he knew to expect her call.

"Hey, Wil. Are you up?" He'd been named after their grandfather, Wilbert. He hated the name, so she always called him by his nickname. Rhani also despised her name, which was her mother's idea of a female version of Ronald, her father's name.

"I'm awake. How're you doing?"

"I'm good. How are things with you? Do you need anything?"

"No. You just sent me money, and classes end in two weeks."

His scholarships covered his tuition and room and board, but something might come up he couldn't cover. She knew he wouldn't ask her for cash. "I know, but I figured you might need to get some summer clothes or go out with friends or something."

"You worry about me too much. Most of my friends don't have *any* money, so they're not going too far." Wil's good-natured laugh brought a smile to her face. "Whatcha been up to since we talked last week?"

"Very busy, which is a good thing."

"Are you seeing anybody?"

"Where did that come from?"

"You need a life, sis. All you do is take care of people. If it's not me, it's Mom or your clients, or the girls at the center. When are you going to start taking care of Rhani?"

"I have a life, and it's not *all* I do," she protested, knowing he spoke the truth. "I go out with my girlfriends and I take dance classes. There's no time for anything else."

"My point exactly," he continued. "Why can't you make time? When's the last time you went out with a guy?"

"It hasn't been *that* long, if you must know. Actually, I'm calling to see if you made up your mind about staying with me for the summer. You don't need to go back to Mom's. I have enough room."

Wil gave a soft sigh. "Mom said she wants me to come home, since I'll be working right in the neighborhood." He worked at the Hunts Point Produce and Meat Distribution Center. A neighborhood man they had known since they were children worked as a supervisor there. He'd hired Wil three years ago, and he allowed Wil to work during holiday breaks and over the summer.

She groaned. "You know she only wants you there so she can hit you up for money. Don't let her use you."

"She needs the help," Wil insisted. "And holiday breaks and summer break are the only times I can do it."

"Mom shouldn't be relying on a sophomore in college

to take care of her."

"She took care of us the best she could, Rhani. Can't you give her a break?"

"You know I send her money every month."

"I'm not talking about sending her money. I'm talking about forgiving her for the wreck her life turned out to be."

"Look what it did to us. She put a no-good man before her own children. Her life is a wreck because she chose it to be."

"Wow! I hope you aren't so cold-hearted with your clients."

"Most of my clients come to me because they recognize they need help. Mom refuses to acknowledge her problems. Besides, I'm an unrelated third party to my clients. This is personal, and I can't keep my feelings separate. At least you'd be able to relax there when you get off from work. My apartment is cleaner, more comfortable and in a quieter neighborhood. I can rent a truck to pick up your stuff from the dorm. Please don't go back there, Wil. It's no good for your mental health. Please think about it, and call me when you decide. Okay?"

"Okay. I'll think about it."

They ended the call, she dropped the paper bag from her lunch into the nearest trash can, and she walked back to her office thinking about her brother. His feeling responsibility for their mother seemed ridiculous. She actually felt bad for playing the guilt game with him, and he was too sweet and good-hearted to tell her to kiss off. She needed to work harder to get him away from her and the old neighborhood. In addition, what he'd said about her really hit home. If anyone understood personality types, she did. Wil had clearly put her into the category of the nurturer. She cared deeply for others and was sensitive to their feelings, was a hard worker and a good listener. On the downside, she tended to leave her own feelings unexpressed, had a tendency to place others' needs above her own, and definitely had a hard time saying "no." Probably the reason she hadn't been able to refuse Greg's wager.

Wednesday and Thursday flew by with a full schedule of clients, dance class and an after-work meeting with Joie to decide what points she would cover in her talk with the girls at the center on Thursday night. This would be the first time she'd invited a guest to speak, and she wanted to make the evening special. Rather than the usual sandwiches, Rhani called a pizzeria and ordered pizza, soda and dessert to be delivered.

On Thursday evening, Joie arrived at the office dressed in skinny jeans beneath a Christian Siriano top with one bare shoulder and one long sleeve, skyscraper heels and her usual satchel-size handbag.

"Didn't I tell you not to get dressed up?"

Joie crossed her arms and scowled. "Please, girl! I have on jeans. This is as dressed down as I get."

"I guess I have to take what I can get when I'm dealing with free help."

"You got that right!" Joie said with a musical laugh. "Are you ready?"

"Yup. Just let me get my things." Rhani went into her office and re-emerged with her laptop bag, purse and tote bag.

"Are you carrying everything you own?"

She locked up and Joie followed her to the elevator. "I

always have things for the girls. They need so much, you know."

"It's so sad."

"It is, so I want you to encourage them to go after their dreams regardless of their current situations."

The elevator arrived and as soon as the two women entered, Joie asked, "How's Mr. Sexy Client doing?"

Rhani rolled her eyes. "I haven't seen him since Monday. He went to Las Vegas for a few days."

"He went to Vegas, and he has issues with sex?"

"I know, right? He didn't go to stay at a casino, though. His brother lives there. We'll have a session tomorrow when he gets back."

The two women exited the building, stood at the curb and watched the passing traffic for an unoccupied cab. Soon one of the goldenrod vehicles stopped for them, and Rhani gave him the address of the center.

"Do you know you've never talked this much about any of your clients before? You're really feeling him, aren't you?"

"He's an interesting man, and…" She paused, unsure of what she wanted to say.

"And what?"

"I don't know. I've never found myself in this position before. He asked me to have coffee with him at Starbucks tomorrow, but…"

"What harm can a cup of coffee do, girl?"

"It's not the coffee. It's the principle. He's a client, and ethically we're not supposed to fraternize. Besides, he's a player."

"Do you think he's playing you?"

Rhani shook her head. "He's pretty straightforward with me, then again, I don't have a lot of experience with men like him…or men in general. My player radar doesn't work."

Joie laughed. "Girl, you're a therapist. You should be able to see through any game he might run."

"You're talking professionally. When emotions are involved, it's a very different story."

"Are your emotions involved?" Rhani didn't answer. "All right, describe him to me. Not his physical description, because you already told Kat and me how fine he is. I mean, what kind of person is he?"

"He's highly social, friendly and outgoing. Under normal circumstances, I believe he's loads of fun to be around, because he thrives on excitement. You know, the fun-loving, spontaneous type. If he had a motto, it would probably be, *all the world's a stage* or *life is a party*.

Joie peered over her designer shades and studied her for a long moment before she spoke. "Oh, yeah. Your emotions are definitely involved. I'll tell you what. If you decide you're going to be Ms. Professional and not get involved, I'll take him. He sounds like my kind of man."

"Joie! You don't understand how serious this is."

She grinned at Rhani. "You're going to do what your heart tells you to do, and if I know you as well as I think I do, it'll be the right choice."

"Let's not talk about him anymore. I hope you're prepared for my girls. They can be a tough audience."

"I'm ready for whatever they have to throw at me."

Three hours later, they were on their way back into Manhattan. Joie had done a fantastic job telling the girls about her career in fashion and how she had gone about getting the finances to open her boutique. She won them over with her charm and wicked sense of humor. By the end of the meeting, they were bombarding her with questions on everything from what classes she took in school to where she'd bought her shoes.

"You did great! Thanks so much for talking to them." Rhani rested her head back on the seat, satisfied that she'd given her mentees another peek at what their lives could be outside of Hunts Point.

"It turned out to be more fun than I'd expected. I hope something I said helps one of them. Listen," she said, her voice softened, "I didn't mean to make light of the situation with your client. It's obvious you're worried about it. All I can say is, sometimes doing what's considered right is not what's right for you. Just be careful."

Friday's appointments seemed to drag by. Rhani hadn't heard from him by three, so she assumed his flight had departed from Las Vegas on time. She tried unsuccessfully to keep her mind off the fact that he would be her last appointment of the day. Before she knew it, her phone buzzed and Sherylle announced his arrival.

Rhani came out to the front desk. "You can go on home and get a jump on your weekend." Sherylle sent her a questioning glance.

"You don't have to tell me twice." Sherylle slipped off her shoes and grabbed her sneakers. "Have a good weekend."

Greg looked tanned, relaxed and happy. In fact, he appeared a little too happy when he dropped his luggage in the outer office.

"You certainly seem cheerful. I guess you enjoyed yourself out there."

He followed her into her office and sat in his regular spot on the sofa. "I did. I hadn't spent time with Marc and Gianne since they've been married or since they got the baby."

She questioned his choice of words. "*Got* the baby?"

"Yes. Gianne can't have kids, so they adopted a baby girl from Nigeria."

"How wonderful. I admire people who will take in a child," she said, wanting desperately to jump right into the matter hanging over their heads.

"It's a wild story. Remind me to tell it to you sometime."

"I will. So, you said on the phone you had something to show me."

"Right." He reached into his pants pocket and took out his phone. "My brother, Marc will explain." He tapped the screen a few times then handed it to her.

An extremely handsome man with wavy shoulder-length hair and a neatly-trimmed Van Dyke framing full lips spoke directly to her. "Ms. Drake, Greg told me about the challenge you gave him while he's out here in Vegas. Personally, I don't really feel what he's about to do will be beneficial, but he insists it'll help him learn to exercise restraint. So, let it be known that I'm just the videographer here."

"Just hit the video button, and it will advance to the next video," Greg said.

She followed his directions, and her jaw dropped when she realized what she was watching. The music started and a woman wearing a bikini approached Greg. "I don't need to see this." She handed the phone to him.

"Please. I insist."

Rhani viewed the recording, which stopped in the middle of the song, without comment.

"Tap the video button again, and it will continue," he said, studying her reaction to what she'd seen so far.

The remainder of the clip showed Greg grasping the arms of his chair yet maintaining control while the dancer proceeded to rub every part of her body against him. The video ended, and Rhani handed him the phone without comment.

"How did I do?" he asked, sounding so much like a child seeking approval she had to laugh.

"You were a model of restraint, but did you think it necessary to go to such an extreme?"

He threw an arm over the back of his seat and cocked his head to one side. "I guess...I needed to put myself out there to prove I could resist if I really wanted to." His gaze, which appeared an olive green color today, met hers. "And I *really* wanted to."

"Good, but *why* did you want it so badly?"

'I don't know. Maybe because you're the first person to say you believed I could. Everyone else looks at me like I'm the poor damaged guy who can't control himself."

Rhani studied his body language. Judging by what she'd learned over the years, his words were sincere. "How did resisting make you feel?"

"At first I thought I'd feel like a punk, you know, a man who's afraid to do what comes naturally. But then, I remembered you said you believed I could do whatever I set my mind to. You had faith in me."

Something in his voice touched her. "So, I guess I owe

you a cup of coffee, huh?" The way he scratched his jaw told her he wasn't expecting her to make good on the bet. "What? You didn't think I'd follow through on your wager?"

He chuckled. "Not really."

"I'm a woman of my word. Now, let's use the next hour to accomplish something productive. You haven't answered the last question I asked before you left for Las Vegas. Do you remember it?"

"Of course, and I answered you."

"You said 'because every man loves that position' and 'because it feels so good.' I want to present this to you. Is it possible every time you have sex with strange women in that position you're unconsciously punishing Evelyn? It's what you discovered her doing, wasn't it?"

He jerked his head back and shook it, voicing denial then stammered, "No—I don't…"

"I want you to think for a minute. Were you partial to having sex in this position before you met her?" His eyes narrowed and cut toward her but he didn't respond. "Did you and Evelyn have sex in this position most of the time?"

Greg stroked the arm of the chair while his gaze seemed to zero in on a spot on the floor, evidently searching his memory, so she waited. He shook his head repeatedly as if in disbelief. "How in the world did you know?"

"I didn't. I'm just good at my job." She smiled. "I need to ask one more question. What did you do after you left the strip club?"

"Marc and I went back to the house."

"I mean did you gratify yourself in another way?"

He smirked. "No. I watched television for a while and fell asleep."

"You've taken a major step, Greg."

The long, agonizing breath he exhaled signaled another story about to unfold. "Something else happened the next day, though."

Rhani cringed internally. "Tell me about it."

"The next day, I didn't want my brother and sister-in-law to feel like they had to babysit me, so I went out to dinner alone. I chose one of the new hotels on the strip, because I read they had the best burgers in Vegas. Marc and Gianne are raw vegans, and no way could I satisfy my inner carnivore at their house. I'd been sitting at the bar for a few minutes when a woman took the stool beside me and started up a conversation."

Suddenly, Rhani felt her belief in him start slipping away. "What happened?"

"She was very…outgoing and quite physical. She kept touching my hand or my arm. It took me right back to the day at Barney's with Melinda Price. I told her I had somewhere to be, but she was very insistent. She suggested we get together the next day." His snide laugh confused her. "I wanted to get rid of her, so I told her I was celibate."

"You did?"

"I didn't know what else to say, and I just blurted it out. Do you believe it?"

"As a matter of fact, I do," she said, laughing at his confused expression. "And the only thing that could possibly top that announcement is a grande Caramel Macchiato. Let me lock up, and we can leave."

In the few minutes it took her to turn off the fountain and the copier, Rhani's mind ran through every conceivable reason why she shouldn't go anywhere with him. Yet, as she turned the key in the lock, she came to the conclusion that she really didn't care.

The brisk walk around the corner to Starbucks gave her

time to shift from therapist to…what? Once they were seated at the table outside of the professional boundaries her office represented, how would they classify their relationship?

Greg ordered for both of them then asked where she wanted to sit. He probably assumed she wanted to sit in the back away from the windows and the front counter. "Anywhere is fine with me."

"Let's sit in the back. It's quieter back there."

She nodded in agreement, remembering he still wanted to dodge the photographers. "I wanted to ask you a question."

"It's your specialty." The barista called his name. "Hold that thought. I'll be right back."

He returned in a flash and handed her the cup. "Before you ask your question, is it okay if I call you Rhani since we're out of the office?"

"I don't see why not."

The upturned corners of his mouth reflected his pleasure. "Now, what's your question?"

"The video introduction was an interesting way to meet Marc. Are all your brothers so handsome?"

Greg laughed so loudly, he had to cover his mouth with his hand. "Wow! That sure wasn't the question I expected. Yeah, we all resemble each other, but there are differences. Most women would say Marc wins the beauty contest, even though he and Charles are identical twins. Nick has these Bahama blue eyes none of the rest of us have. Vic has a commanding presence. He can walk into a room dressed in one of his designer suits and all conversation stops. Jess is the only one with a round face. He looks more like my mother's brothers."

"Fascinating. What do they say about you?"

His eyes closed for a second before he answered. "They say I'm the one with the personality. My uncle Rod used to say I could charm the panties off a nun."

Rhani snickered thinking how right Uncle Rod was.

"What about your family?"

Rhani shrugged. "Nothing interesting to talk about there."

"Oh, it's like that, huh? You've gotten me to spill my guts, but you're not going to share anything with me?"

"Let's just say my family has always been challenged in a lot of ways. I grew up in the hood, and my youngest brother and I got out as soon as we were able. My parents and my other sister still live there. My oldest brother lives on Riker's Island."

Greg frowned sympathetically. "I'm sorry, but I'm glad you two made it out. Where does your baby brother live?"

"Right now at City College. I'm trying to convince him to stay with me for the summer rather than going back to the neighborhood. The atmosphere there isn't conducive to anything positive."

"You're a good big sister. I always wondered what it would be like to have a sister. Our house always suffered from testosterone overload. It's the reason my mother is so thrilled to have daughters-in-law. The way she carries on over them, you'd think she gave birth to them too."

"You're blessed to have such a good family."

"Judging by what I hear from a lot of people, I guess they are. We've had our issues with one another, but they eventually seem to work out."

"You're very fortunate. I'm a therapist, and I can't get my family to work anything out." She laughed, but when she looked up, his intense gaze caught her off guard. "What?"

"It's just nice to know you're not perfect, Miss I-have-the-answer-to-everything."

"Would you have come back for a second session if I'd said, 'Gee, I've never heard anything so wild in my life'?" She crossed her eyes and talked out of one side of her mouth. 'I don't think I can help you.'

He howled. "I guess not, when you put it that way."

Rhani checked her watch then swallowed the remainder of her coffee. "I need to get going. Thank you for the coffee."

"Can we do it again sometime? In fact, can we do something a little nicer?"

She hadn't anticipated him asking, but as she contemplated her answer the words came out. "I look forward to it." She rose and hooked her purse strap over her shoulder. "See you on Tuesday."

Greg grinned up at her. "Have a good weekend." He walked her out to the street and waited until a taxi stopped to pick her up.

In spite of the way the driver repeatedly glanced at her in his rearview mirror, Rhani couldn't stop smiling. All weekend the smile returned every time she thought about him.

On Monday, she stopped in Starbucks for her morning coffee and picked up the paper on the way into the office. She usually arrived at least a half hour before Sherylle, and she used the time to get her mind ready for the day ahead. Only this morning, when she opened the *The Post*, she spent her half hour in a much different way. Her smile faded in seconds. Splashed over the Page Six were four incriminating photos of Greg and a blonde woman with the caption, *Paid suspension in Vegas?* Rhani swallowed the bile in her throat. In the first one, the woman had her hand on his arm. In the second, their faces were inches apart and he wore a smile, and in the last and most incriminating one, he was kissing her.

Rhani's throat constricted. He'd lied to her, and she'd fallen for it.

Chapter Nine

*I*t had been ages since Greg had felt as optimistic as he did leaving the coffee shop. He and Rhani had actually engaged in a real conversation, and she'd shared a little bit about her family. In his mind, they'd taken a big step away from their strictly professional relationship, and she hadn't run away screaming at his suggestion of an actual date. Contemplating where he might take her kept him in a good mood all weekend. He hadn't had a serious attraction to a woman since he'd left Atlanta, and in all honesty, it was the last thing he'd wanted. Yet he couldn't deny Rhani's powerful allure. Granted, he still didn't have her personal phone number or any other way to contact her outside of the office, but he believed it would happen soon enough.

Monday morning, on his way to the coffee shop for his usual coffee and hard roll, he picked up *The Post* from one of the street boxes. With his food in hand, he found a spot toward the back of the shop. As had become his habit, he opened the paper to page six, but today he couldn't read with detached interest. Photos of him and that Kenzie woman grabbed him around the neck like a noose. "What the hell?" Greg studied each photo carefully. He had obviously been followed, but by whom? Of course, TMZ might have someone assigned to keep an eye on him, but this seemed spiteful, Harvey Levin's show wasn't malicious. The creator and executive producer was an attorney, and he was a stickler about just reporting the facts.

The more he studied the photos and thought about it, the more Senator Price came to mind. Immediately, Greg dialed Jordyn. "Did you see this morning's Post?" he asked when she answered.

"I'm looking at it right now. Did you know this woman?"

"Never saw her before in my life."

"Then why were you kissing her, Greg?"

Her sharp tone put him on defense. "You know me, Jordyn. I kiss everybody, and as hard as she came on to me, I knew she wanted me to."

"Oh, God! Don't let anyone else hear you say that."

"Will you let me tell you exactly what happened, please?"

"Okay, tell me."

Greg recounted the story to his publicist then said, "I'm used to women flirting with me, but the more I think about it, the more I'm starting to think the whole incident was orchestrated."

"Why?"

"She seemed too insistent. It reminded me so much of the afternoon with Melinda Price, I ended up telling her I was celibate."

Jordan laughed. "Are you kidding?"

"No, and she looked so disappointed, I thought a quick kiss was in order."

She snickered. "Yeah, you hate to let down your adoring public."

"This is no joke, Jordyn," he snarled, failing to see the humor in it.

"I'm sorry. You're thinking it's Senator Price, aren't you?"

"Yes. He's retaliating, and he wants to ruin me. I'm sure he has his own people tailing me."

"Maybe I should put a call in to Thad and see what he thinks."

"Tell him to call me after you two talk."

"Don't jump to conclusions. We don't know who's behind this yet, and until we do, it's best to keep quiet."

"Easy for you to say. You're not the one being maligned here."

"I understand how you feel, Greg, but you don't want to say anything out of turn and end up in a lawsuit. Don't make any comments to anyone, if you're contacted. Okay?"

He gave a disagreeable grumble. "Whatever you say." After he hung up, Greg studied the photos with a critical eye. Whoever had taken them must've been sitting close to them. He tried to recall who else had been in the restaurant bar, but he hadn't really been paying attention at the time.

Within the hour, Thad called. "Jordyn left me a long message and said you wanted me to hit you up. She told me what's going on, and now I'm starting to agree with you. I haven't seen the paper yet, but it might be time for you to speak up. The final decision is up to the network. Who should I contact over there, Ken Peterson or John Hanke?"

"John's the station manager, so he has final say-so on those decisions."

"If he green lights this, the four of us will need to get together to figure out what you should say. I'll put a call in to him now, and will let you know when I hear back from him."

Twenty-four hours passed, and Greg hadn't heard back from anyone, so the next day he returned to the coffee shop with the morning paper under his arm. He froze and slapped a hand over his mouth to keep the first bite of buttered roll and sip of coffee from coming back up. The gossip page had pictures of Rhani and him in Starbucks with the caption, *Now it's his therapist?* Cold fear settled in his heart. Had Rhani seen it? What would this mean for her professionally? Greg took out his phone but couldn't make himself dial her number. He stared at it for several minutes. If she hadn't seen the paper, he needed to warn her before someone else sprung it on her. This time he dialed her office.

"New Vision Counseling. This is Sherylle. How may I help you?"

"Good morning, Sherylle. It's Greg Stafford. I have an emergency, and I need to speak to Rha—Ms. Drake. It's urgent."

"I'm sorry, Mr. Stafford, but she's in a client session right now. I can have her return your call as soon as she's done."

He exhaled an anxious sigh. "Does she usually pick up the morning paper?"

"Umm…most days. Is there something you want me to tell her?"

"No, I need to speak to her before she goes out for lunch. Make sure she calls me as soon as her session ends, please."

"Are you all right, Mr. Stafford?"

"Yes, I'm fine, Sherylle. Thanks."

The early lunch crowd had begun to enter the restaurant. He asked the waitress to bring him a fresh cup of coffee, and then he changed his seat so his back faced the door. No telling who had seen the paper, and he wasn't in the mood to answer questions.

His phone rang, and he snatched it from the table

without checking the display. "Rhani?"

"No, it's Thad. How do you manage to get yourself into situations like this?"

Greg massaged the tension in his forehead. "It's not intentional, man. In fact, I believe there wouldn't be a situation right now if I hadn't been set up."

"Seriously?" Thad laughed aloud.

"I'm not BSing you, Thad. The more I go over what went down in the restaurant in Vegas, the more I'm starting to believe she was a plant."

"And you fell for it."

"Not really. I got rid of her as fast as I could, because I had the feeling something wasn't right. I brushed her off nicely, gave her a kiss and left."

"But you just *had* to kiss her, didn't you?"

"There was nothing to it, Thad!"

"Maybe not, but the picture makes it look otherwise. If you want this issue to go away, keep your lips, your hands, and everything else away from the females. Okay?"

"What do you mean *maybe not*? I'm telling you what happened, but there's another problem this morning."

"I already saw it. Why were you out with your therapist?"

"We weren't *out*. I finished my session, we left the office at the same time, and I asked her if she wanted a cup of coffee. What's so wrong with that?"

"Don't be naïve, man. This could play out very badly for her, and it makes you look like you're taking the network's decision as a joke."

"So what do you suggest I do, stay locked up in my apartment for three months? I wasn't ordered to stay away from women." The call waiting on his phone beeped, and he glanced at the display. "I have another call. It's my therapist. Let me get back to you."

He took a deep breath and clicked over. "Rhani, I'm glad you called."

"What is it, Greg?" Her words came out clipped and void of concern.

"I take it you already saw this morning's paper."

"I saw yesterday's paper, and I know you purposely deceived me."

"I didn't, but I think you should send Sherylle downstairs to get a copy before they're all gone."

"Why? Did you do something else newsworthy out in Las Vegas?"

"I didn't do anything, Rhani, in spite of what those pictures seem to say. But we have a more pressing issue right now."

"Oh, just tell me what you're talking about. I'm too busy to play games with you. And it's Ms. Drake."

Greg groaned. "Fine. Someone took pictures of us in Starbucks on Friday. They're on page six."

"Oh, my God. You've got to be kidding."

"I'm afraid not."

"This is awful," she murmured.

"I didn't want to get you in any trouble. Maybe we should cancel my session tomorrow...and...maybe you should refer me to another therapist. They're going to be watching us from now on. I'm sorry, Rhani. I'm really sorry, and I *did not* lie to you about Las Vegas. The pictures make it appear otherwise, but it happened just the way I told you."

"I'll see you tomorrow. We need to discuss this."

An hour later, Jordyn set up a conference call between Greg, Thad, the station manager and herself to discuss the latest developments. They decided Jordyn would make a statement to Arianna on next edition of The Scoop. They all agreed that the senator wouldn't be mentioned by name, since Greg had no proof he set up the photographs. The four of them brainstormed for fifteen minutes and agreed on a statement that satisfied him and the network.

The evening news showed reporters stopping Sen. Price as he left his office. One of them held a copy of the newspaper up to him and asked, "Senator, have you seen these photos of Greg Stafford?"

"Yes, I have," the senator answered, shaking his head with an exaggerated expression of disgust.

"Do you have any comment?"

"Greg Stafford is making a mockery of the disciplinary action handed down by his employer by publicly continuing to pursue women when he agreed to receive mandatory counseling for his problems. What is even more shocking is the woman he's obviously flirting with in Starbucks is his therapist. It just goes to show his lack of good judgment where women are concerned."

When he switched to The Scoop at seven o'clock, Greg had the surreal experience of watching his publicist sitting with his co-anchor talking about his life as though he were persona non grata. Arianna began the segment by saying, "Many of our viewers have asked about my co-anchor. His representative is here tonight to give us an update. How is Greg doing?"

Jordyn said, "He's doing well and continuing his therapy."

"Recent photos have raised questions on how serious he is about his counseling."

"We believe the photos were released by someone who has an axe to grind and wants it to appear as though Greg is disregarding his therapy. Nothing could be further from the truth. And the last time I checked, there is nothing immoral or illegal about having a cup of coffee with someone at a public restaurant. He is fully committed to completing his therapy as requested and should be back on the show soon."

Greg watched the segment wishing Arianna and Jordyn could call the senator out on his underhanded slander tactics, but he knew it was impossible. He had no proof.

In the morning, he arrived for his session anxious to explain to Rhani what his team believed to be going on. She looked beautiful, dressed in a salmon-colored outfit matching her lipstick. He had to push down the desire to press his mouth to her glossy lips. Judging by her solemn expression when he entered the inner office, she didn't seem very happy to see him.

"Good morning."

"Good morning," she said without looking up from the notebook in which she was writing.

Greg slumped down onto the sofa and removed his hat and sunglasses. "Are you going to let me explain?"

"It's your hour. Go ahead, explain." She twirled a corkscrew strand of hair around her index finger, a gesture he noticed she did whenever she was deep in thought.

"Someone is stalking me. It might be TMZ, or it might be someone hired by Senator Price. Whoever it is, they're documenting everything I do on film." She tilted her head as though she didn't give much credence to his theory. "Considering Sen. Price's comment, I believe he set me up. He's trying to destroy me."

"You're being paranoid. Nobody is trying to destroy you. You're trying to destroy yourself.

137

"Nothing happened with that woman in Vegas. We talked, she flirted, and I told her I was celibate then kissed her goodbye and left."

Rhani raised her eyebrows and just stared at him.

Greg puffed out his cheeks then released the air. "You don't believe me? I told you I wouldn't lie to you, and I didn't."

"You neglected to mention kissing her. The deal was no sexual contact."

"Come on. I hardly consider a two-second kiss to be *sexual contact*."

"Not the point, Greg. You had an urge to kiss her, and you acted on it to satisfy the urge."

"No. It meant *you're never going to see me again*."

"You conveniently omitted it to deceive me and win the bet." She raised her palms. "I had no business making a wager with a client in the first place. My bad, as they used to say."

It took him a moment to grasp that the look in her eyes was hurt rather than disappointment. Their relationship had turned a corner, and he forced himself not to smile. "Rhani, I would never do anything to intentionally deceive you. Other than my mother, you're probably the only person who believes I really want to overcome this problem, so I can have a normal relationship with a woman."

Her gaze moved from the notebook in her lap to his face. "I hope you're serious, Greg. If not, you're just wasting my time. You still have a lot of work to do before you get there."

When their gazes met, and she looked away, Greg knew she wasn't just talking about his therapy. "I know, and I'm willing to do whatever you ask." It wasn't just in his mind.

They were developing a personal connection, and for some reason, the thought didn't bother him. In fact, he rather liked it. "I'm sorry you got dragged into this."

"If it's anyone's fault, it's mine. I knew we could've been spotted together in such a public place, and I made a decision, and it turned out to be the wrong one." She shrugged, and he smiled. "How are you doing otherwise?"

"Good, I didn't go out anywhere over the weekend."

"What did you do instead?"

"I've been going downstairs to the gym a lot, which is good because I've also been lying on the sofa doing TV marathons and catching up on all the shows I've never seen that people have been raving about. This weekend I watched the complete seasons of *Orange is the New Black* and *Power*. Didn't know what I've been missing." He chuckled.

"*Power* is one of my favorites, but let me ask you this— how did you handle watching those graphic sex scenes. Did they bother you?"

"Not really. I can live vicariously, can't I?" He grinned.

"Were you able to do it without gratifying yourself?"

"Yes. I'm not as hopeless as you think I am."

Her voice softened. "I never thought you were hopeless, Greg." A quiver vibrated through his body then a momentary silence lingered between them. "Why don't we end here today?"

"Before I go, would you have dinner with me one night? I know a nice little place outside of the city where we could have some peace and quiet."

"Outside of the city where?

"Lindenhurst, Long Island."

The hint of a smile on her face encouraged him.

"Nobody is going to see us all the way out there. I think both of us could use a night out."

Rhani pursed her lips, tapped her pen on the arm of her chair and wound a long curl around her finger. "I don't know, Greg. It's seems like we'd be asking for trouble. Having coffee around the corner from the office can be explained away, but dinner? Maybe you don't need to be careful, but I do."

"Just think about it. I would really love to spend an evening with you."

"What if someone did recognize us? There would be no rational way to explain it the second time." He wondered if she were simply thinking out loud of if she were trying to convince herself.

"No, probably not. What matters is we do what *we* want to do. Do you want to have dinner with me, Rhani?"

"Go home, Greg," she said with a smirk. "Your session is over."

"Think about it, and let me know when I come on Thursday."

She shook her head then turned away and began writing in her notebook. In the quietness of the empty hallway and elevator he considered her response. When he exited the lobby and stepped onto the street, two photographers were waiting with cameras ready.

"Greg! No coffee today?" one asked.

He rolled his eyes and picked up his pace, moving away from the building.

"Are you and Rhani Drake dating?"

Those words stopped him in his tracks, and he whirled around. "No, we're not, but what difference does it make to you? Please leave her alone. She doesn't deserve to be harassed over something innocent." It had been his intention to catch a cab, but thought the walk might clear his head.

While he stalked down the street, his anger rose to the boiling point. Maybe if he went to visit Senator Price and tried to reason with him and explain that he never pursued Melinda, and it had been a mistake—a single, careless, unplanned mistake, the ambushes might stop. After all, he had screwed the man's wife. On second thought, if he showed up at his office and said anything at all, he might end up with a bullet to the brain. He tossed the crazy idea aside. The forty-block walk back to his apartment took more than an hour. Halfway there, his phone rang. Rhani's office number.

"Where are you?" Hearing Rhani's voice wiped out his insane thoughts and brought a smile to his face.

"I decided to walk today. I'm on Lexington almost at 62nd. What's up?"

"Since you left, I've been thinking. Dinner on Long Island sounds wonderful, if you think we can get out of the city without anyone seeing us."

Her agreement meant she knew about his background and the demons he was fighting, yet she considered him worthy of her time and attention as a man and not merely a client. "I'll be able to work it out. How's Friday? We could leave right after your last appointment—just not together."

"What do you mean?"

"If we don't want anyone following us, it might be best for you to meet me somewhere. Let me think about it and get back to you."

"Okay. I'm going to lunch in a little while," she said with tangible apprehension in her voice. He sensed her thoughts were on being approached by another photographer.

"Don't engage them, Rhani. Tell them you have nothing to say and keep walking. Those guys want to get you talking. They're experts at knowing how to get a rise out of people, and they want you to get angry and blurt out something you might not mean to say."

"Gotcha. I think I'll take Sherylle with me for moral support."

"Good idea. If anything happens, please call me back."

As Greg passed shops and restaurants, he concocted a way for them to meet and have a private dinner without being spotted by the vultures. The walk had energized him almost as much as Rhani's phone call. When he reached his building, he had a plan, and the first step was to arrange for a car service to pick them up. He called the private car service he often used.

"This is Greg Stafford. I'd like to reserve a car for Friday night." He gave the woman his phone number, which she used to pull up his information.

"Certainly, Mr. Stafford. Where and what time do you want to be picked up?"

"There will be two pickups in Manhattan, one at four o'clock and one at four-thirty. We'll be going out to 854 South Wellwood Avenue in Lindenhurst for dinner and will need a return pickup at ten o'clock. I'll have to call you back with the other addresses."

"Okay, I have you down for four o'clock on Friday night. Please call as soon as you have the exact stops."

He hung up dwelling on how they could pull this off without being spotted. He didn't want her to be embarrassed or humiliated, but he wanted desperately to show her that in spite of what she knew about him, he could be a gentleman who knew how to treat a lady.

Chapter Ten

*B*efore Rhani could finish making her notes on Greg's session, Sherylle buzzed her. "You have a call from a Dr. Alexandra Policastro on line one. She said you'd know what it's regarding."

She gazed up at the ceiling and didn't respond right away. Yes, she knew why Alex was calling, and she wished she could avoid the conversation.

"Rhani?"

"Yes, uh…I'll take it. Thanks." Rhani clicked off the intercom and pushed the blinking button. "Alex, how are you?" she asked, trying to sound extra cheerful.

"My dear, I believe I should be asking you that question. I see you made *The Post*." She waited for a response.

"Yes. It was nothing really, just an innocent cup of coffee."

"I think you need to come in and talk to me."

It took Rhani a few seconds for the suggestion to register, and she resented Alex's conclusion. "You mean as a *client*?"

"I mean as a friend. You're slipping, Rhani. We talked about this situation at the meeting, and you knew what seeing this man could do to your career, yet you went ahead and did it anyway. Perhaps we should talk about *why* you made that decision."

"I told you why. He's—"

"He's *what?* Good looking, charming, sexy?"

"All of the above."

"Those are very shallow reasons for putting the success you've worked so hard to achieve on the line. I have a few openings on my schedule."

"It's more than shallow reasons, Alex, and I don't need to talk about it. I haven't been drawn to a man like this in years. It's that simple."

"It's never that simple," Alex insisted. "So you have chemistry. *So what?* There are hundreds, maybe thousands of men in this city with whom you might have chemistry."

"I want to see where it goes. I'm not rushing into anything. Besides, I don't even know what kind of relationship he wants, if any."

Alex sighed. "You know I should report you for this."

"You have that option, but I don't believe you will." Rhani held her breath.

"How can you be so sure?"

"Because you're not just a colleague, you're my friend. And you know I'm not an impulsive person. What I see in this man goes much deeper than the pretty face and sexy voice, and I want to explore it."

"I hope you're right, because he'll have to support you once you're jobless or you'll be living on the street in a cardboard box. Be careful, Rhani. People already suspect there's a personal relationship between you and him. They're not going to let it drop. It's fodder for the tabloids."

"Thanks for caring about me, Alex. I appreciate it. I really do."

"Keep in touch, okay? Don't let me have to find out

what's going on from the gossip columns."

Rhani felt as though she couldn't breathe when she hung up. Was she making a huge mistake, and was she attributing traits to Greg he didn't possess? She needed to get out of the office and get some air. "Sherylle, can I treat you to lunch today?" she asked her assistant. "I don't want to go out by myself, because there are photographers waiting for me downstairs."

"Waiting for *you*?"

Rhani pressed her lips into a thin line before she answered. "They were following Greg Stafford. We had a cup of coffee together at Starbucks on Friday, and now they're following me."

Sherylle's eyes widened. "Oh, snap. That's why he called back?"

"Yes. It might've been a bad decision on my part. I assumed going for a cup of coffee was harmless, but then pictures of us showed up on the gossip page in *The Post* on Tuesday."

"Get out! I never read the paper, so I didn't have a clue. Can't say I blame you, though. He is one fine specimen."

Rhani's mouth fell open. "Sherylle!"

"I'm just speaking the truth." Sherylle took her purse from her bottom desk drawer. "We can leave through the service door at the back of the building. I know how to get there."

"Thanks, I need to get some fresh air. Let's go."

After they locked up the office, Rhani followed Sherylle down the stairs to the lower level of the building that housed the maintenance and electrical rooms. Once they reached the freight door, Sherylle pushed the heavy door open and squinted as she peered out and scanned the street.

"Nobody's out here. We can go around the corner to the Jewish deli. They have great sandwiches." Sherylle stepped out into the bright sunshine, grabbed Rhani by the hand and launched into a sprint. Their laughs filled the air as they dashed up the block looking over their shoulders to make sure they weren't being followed.

"I made a big mistake being seen with him in public," Rhani confessed to her assistant between bites of her corned beef Reuben. "No matter how innocent, the way the newspaper posted it with those awful headlines makes people think differently." She wiped a drip of Thousand Island dressing from the corner of her mouth.

"He seems to really like you, Rhani. I can tell by the way he talks about you."

"What has he said?"

"Nothing in particular. It's just the way he talks about you. With fondness in his voice, like you're very special to him. You know what I mean?"

"The media is trying to make it look like we're involved, and we're not. I could lose my license if someone says I'm in a personal relationship with a client."

Her assistant clasped her hands below her chin and looked her directly in the eye. "But you're thinking about it, right? Your interest in each other is obvious. You talk about him more than all of your other clients."

Rhani stared. Were her feelings for Greg so apparent? "I do?"

Sherylle nodded. "Not in a romantic way, but it's clear you care about him."

"But I care about all of my clients," she said, honestly trying to identify the difference in her behavior when she spoke to Sherylle about him. "I don't speak of them the same way? How so?"

"I don't know. Your tone of voice isn't the same. It's almost like when mothers talk about their babies. The voice is just different from when they talk about someone else's child. I guess the affection isn't there."

Affection. Oh, my God. Had Alex heard affection in her voice when she mentioned Greg at the meeting? Now that her assistant had pinpointed it, affection was exactly what she felt for Greg, along with a touch of desire. At the time, Rhani just wanted to get Alex's opinion on the Starbucks matter. If she couldn't mask her feelings for him at this point, what would she be like if they actually started seeing each other?

"I guess I am fond of him, but we're not seeing each other. And while we're talking about Greg, I don't know if those photographers know you're my assistant, but if they ask you any questions, please don't answer them in any way. Just ignore them. Greg said they're experts at tricking people into making comments."

"I saw them hanging out at the front door, but I just assumed they were following him. All of this interest is because you went to Starbuck's with him?"

"You know how those vultures are, they'll jump on anything they think might make a story. While we're here, I wanted to talk to you about something else. I've called my brother a couple of times, but I haven't heard from him. Today is his last day of school. I've asked him to move in with me for the summer, but he hasn't given me an answer. If he calls and I'm with a client, please interrupt me. If he's going to stay at my place, I need to rent a truck to move his stuff."

"Sure thing." Sherylle checked her watch. "We'd better get back. You have a 1:45."

Their leisurely walk to the office in the bright sunshine ended at the back doors of the building where Sherylle came to a dead stop. "Oh no. I didn't know these doors were exit only." They both stared at the smooth, hardware-free doors. Even if they banged on them, there might not be anyone on the inside to let them in. Sherylle tried anyway, pounding her fist a few times and calling out to anyone who might be on the other side. No response.

"There's no other entrance. We'll just have to go around front. Remember, if they are still there, don't say a word," Rhani warned as they rounded the corner.

The moment the two photographers saw them, they ran toward her. "Rhani! Are you and Greg Stafford a couple now? Did you make him an offer of more than coffee?"

She glared at them, wondering why they thought it okay to call her by her first name as though they knew her personally. What nerve.

"Does it bother you being Greg Stafford's latest booty call?"

If only she were able to spew a Godzilla-like death ray out of her mouth, she could incinerate them for being so offensive. Yet she held her tongue and walked faster, dragging Sherylle along by the hand, which she only let go of to push through the revolving door. With tears brimming beneath her eyelids and her blood boiling, she wondered how they dared to assume she was sleeping with a client, simply because they shared a caffeine fix in a public place. They weren't too far off, though. Hadn't her fantasies about him always been tinged with a sensual edge? What kind of problems did she have for wanting to be intimate with a man who'd admittedly had dozens if not hundreds of sexual encounters? Why didn't this disturbing fact turn her in the other direction?

When she and Sherylle finally re-entered the office, Rhani dragged in a few deep breaths in an effort to calm herself. Soon her next client would be arriving, and she needed to calm down first. "Hold any calls, except from

Wil," she told Sherylle. "I need a couple of minutes to get myself together." She poured herself a glass of water from the carafe Sherylle dutifully kept filled with ice water. Her hands shook so badly, the spout clanked against the rim of the glass and water spilled onto the table.

"Oh, crap!" She grabbed a handful of tissues from the box on the end table to soak up the mess, and then she dialed Greg's number on her cell.

He picked up without identifying himself, which strangely pleased her. Obviously, he had her number saved in his phone. "You're calling me back, so I guess something happened," he said.

"Yes. We snuck out the delivery entrance in the back of the building, but we couldn't get back in the same way, and we had to pass them at the front entrance. The questions they shouted at me were horrible."

"I'm sorry. You didn't talk to them, did you?"

"No. You said not to."

"Good, but I have to warn you, if they got any footage, it'll probably be on somewhere tonight."

She groaned. "I called hoping you'd say something to calm me down. Oh well. It seems to be the way this day is going. Earlier this morning, I got a harsh call from a colleague reprimanding me for my *lack of prudence*."

"For being seen with me." His despondent tone made her regret mentioning Alex's call. "I'm so sorry, Rhani. Maybe we should rethink dinner on Friday. The situation can only get worse for you if someone else sees us."

She hesitated for a long moment. "The media has already put it out there. Let people think what they want."

"Are you sure?"

"I am. Did you figure out how we can do this?"

"I did. If you take the Four or Five train from your office and get off at 86th Street, you'll see a Central Parking garage on the corner when you come up the stairs. It's where I park whenever I rent a car, and I'll pick you up there. The booth is manned around the clock. You'll be safe if you stand there and wait. I'll try to be there before you, but in case the car gets tied up in traffic, I'll tell the booth attendant to keep an eye out for you."

"Does this mean you're not coming for your Thursday session?"

"No. I'll be there. I thought it best not to discuss this in the office."

Rhani chuckled. "It's not like anybody's listening. Sherylle and I are the only ones here."

"I wouldn't be too sure."

Panic crept up on her. "Are you saying someone could've bugged my office?"

"Probably not, but anything is possible with those guys."

"Thanks a lot for planting that thought in my mind. I have a client in a couple of minutes, so I'd better go."

"Have a good afternoon, *Ms. Drake*," he said in a teasing tone.

"It's a virtual impossibility now. See you Thursday."

Later in the evening, Rhani ate Chinese takeout while she watched herself on TMZ trying to get away from the cameras at a near jog. Ten minutes later, Dr. Spruill called.

"Hello, Rhani. We haven't talked in a while. I see you've become a television star."

She tripped over her tongue to answer, shocked to hear her mentor even watched celebrity news shows. "I—um— I—they're after him not me."

"Interesting explanation. Why were you out with a client to begin with—one who has come to you for help with his sexual addiction?"

"Albert, please don't take this seriously. There's nothing going on between Greg Stafford and me. They just report what they see, then try to make mountains out of molehills."

"I hope that's the case. You've had a hard enough time getting some of your colleagues to take therapy for sex addiction seriously."

For the rest of the night, guilt nagged her for lying to the man who'd taught her so much. She paced through the apartment mumbling aloud. "Why couldn't I have met a man with no problems?" A laugh rose in her throat. *As if such a creature exists. What if Alex is right?* All kinds of negative thoughts assaulted her mind, and when she finally tired of pacing, she wandered into the bedroom, fell back across the bed and stared at the ceiling. It wasn't too late to back out on Greg's dinner invitation. Tomorrow he would be at the office for his second session of the week. She could cancel then.

Before she went to sleep, she called Wil once more. As with the last ten calls, it went directly to voicemail. "Wil, either there's something wrong with your phone or you're trying to avoid me. If you're avoiding me, it's because Ma is whispering in your ear. My offer still stands. Please call me."

When Sherylle ushered Greg into her office on Thursday, he had that cat that swallowed the canary expression as though he knew something no one else on earth did. Once Rhani closed the door, he sat and settled back on the sofa with his arm stretched across the back. "Have you ever been to

BayVue on Long Island?"

"No. Is that where you planned to take me?"

His eyes narrowed. "You said *planned*. Have you changed your mind?"

"After the two phone calls I received yesterday, I had considered it."

"Calls from who?"

"Two of my colleagues. Actually, one of them is my mentor. He was quite upset with me."

"For sitting in Starbucks with a client?"

"They see it as much more, and they're probably right."

"More much in what way?"

"They view it as a breach of ethics and poor decision-making on my part. Alex even asked me straight out why I would want to be involved with a man who's battling sex addiction."

His brows drew together in a frown. "Who is he?"

"She. Alexandra is a psychotherapist I consider a role model. She has a very successful practice on the Upper West Side."

"How did she know the reason for my therapy?"

"I told her. Since it's been all over the papers, it's not exactly a secret."

"True." He shrugged. "So, you're thinking about breaking our date because they questioned you?"

"Not because they questioned me. Their questions just made me rethink what I'm doing."

He pursed his lips and sent her a pointed glance. "You're not doing anything but allowing a man to take you to dinner at a public place. I could see if I'd invited you to my apartment. Don't back out on me, Rhani. The weather is supposed to be perfect tomorrow, and I know you'll love it."

The pleading in his voice changed her mind. How long had it been since a man seemed disappointed at the prospect of not being with her?

"The car is picking me up at 4 p.m.," he continued. "We'll drive over to the garage and wait for you to arrive."

She sighed. "Okay. I'll be there."

"Damn, don't make it sound as if you're being forced to do something you hate."

"I'm not. I'm just wondering what's going to happen next." She sighed again. "Let's get to work. We have some important things to cover today."

He smiled and relaxed. "I'm ready. Hit me."

And she did. "Your sexual behavior over the last couple of years has been dangerous to say the least. When's the last time you were tested for STDs?"

"I come from a medical family. My brothers and I don't have the same issues a lot of men have about seeing a doctor. I got an HIV test every three months, because I'd heard if you did contract something, six months is too long a stretch to wait."

Rhani noted his response in her notebook. "And you were negative?"

"Yes."

"Good. And the last time you went out to a club?"

"I told you about it. I haven't been out, and I haven't been with anyone since then."

"When you first started therapy, you said you hadn't gone without sex for more than two days in the past two years. It's been weeks now. How do you feel?"

"Not like I thought I would feel. Physically, I'm frustrated, but resisting the temptation has taught me something about myself. Before I started coming here, I'd talked myself into believing I had a normal sex life. Normal—for me. Now I understand I had no control over what I was doing."

"You should feel proud, Greg. You've made remarkable progress in a short time, but I'm still concerned about what happened in Las Vegas."

"Why? I explained what went down, and I'd be willing to bet it was a setup."

"You're probably right, but whether you were set up or not, your reaction to the woman is the issue."

His eyes narrowed. "What are you talking about? I thought I handled myself very well."

"We need to explore what your other options might've been. You seemed compelled to kiss her before you left. That means something, don't you think?"

Greg smoothed the neatly-trimmed hair around his mouth with his thumb and index finger and contemplated the question. "You have to understand something. I'm used to strange women talking to me. They do it everywhere I go and, because I'm on TV, I try my best to be approachable and polite. Nothing can kill a career faster than becoming known as being aloof to fans."

"Hmm," Rhani's eyebrows rose. "Are you saying because this woman appeared to want you to kiss her, you felt obligated?"

"I didn't feel obligated, but many times when you're dealing with the female public, a little peck goes a long way."

"A peck is on the cheek. You kissed her on the mouth."

When his face broke into a grin, Rhani almost asked

him why. But suddenly it dawned on her that her questions sounded more personal than therapeutic. The possibility of her sounding jealous horrified her, and she tried to clarify her intent. "The point I'm trying to make is you assume certain actions are meaningless because they're meaningless to you. We always have to take into account how the other person is receiving the action."

His smile widened. "I understand what you're saying, but I'm very good at reading women's signals. I was leaving the restaurant and knew I'd never see her again, so I figured it didn't matter."

"This isn't on the same level, of course, but you're using the old rapist's excuse—*I just gave her what she wanted.*"

His expression soured, and he leaned toward her. "You're comparing me to a rapist?"

"You know I'm not, Greg. I'm trying to make you see that by saying you did something because you believed a woman wanted it is just an excuse for doing what *you* wanted to begin with. Just because a woman smiles at you doesn't mean she wants to have physical contact with you."

He covered his mouth with a fisted hand and dropped his gaze to the floor. A few moments passed in silence before he glanced up at her once again. "You're right, of course, but she did more than just smile at me. My brothers and I had a conversation about this once. We're all used to women coming on to us. It happens so often, I guess I've considered it the norm and didn't think there will be times when a woman *isn't* sending me signals. Maybe she's just smiling." He paused. "But I'm convinced Senator Price or some media outlet sent Kenzie Roberts."

"It's probably true, but it doesn't have anything to do with how you respond to women."

Greg sucked in his cheeks and fixed her with a suspicious stare. "You still don't believe me."

"I believe you, but I still think you're putting too much of the responsibility for what happens in your life on someone else. You have to own up to your part, no matter who else was involved.

He contemplated what she said for a moment then said, "Because I have a problem with sexual boundaries, I need to be more diligent than the average guy when it comes to how I relate to women in general. I should've politely brushed her off."

"It's like what you told me about the paparazzi. Don't engage them at all."

Greg's face softened into a smile. "I understand, Ms. Drake, and I promise to do better next time."

Their session ended and he reminded her of their covert plan for Friday evening. For a while after he left her office, she questioned the wisdom, or lack of it, in going out to dinner with him.

♥♥♥

At the end of the day on Friday, Rhani said goodnight to Sherylle and locked the office door before she touched up her makeup, sprayed a spritz of fragrance mist into her cleavage and changed into the dress she'd brought from home. Miraculously, when she exited the building through the front entrance, no one with a camera hanging around his neck lurked there. As Greg instructed, she took the subway up to 86th Street and looked for the Central Parking garage when she reached street level. She crossed the street with her heart beating double time. Parking garages always gave her an eerie feeling, because she had seen too many movies where a murder took place in one. Luckily, she only needed to walk over to the attendant's booth not through the entire floor. The minute she reached the Plexiglass-enclosed cubicle and wiggled her fingers at the man inside, a car with dark tinted windows flashed its headlights and moved toward her. The back window opened and Greg called her name.

"Rhani Drake?"

"Yes, and you are?" she said, playing along.

He opened the rear door of the black Town Car and approached her with his hand extended. "Gregory Stafford. It's a pleasure to meet you."

"You too."

"I apologize for not picking you up at a nicer location, but it couldn't be helped. I hope you understand." Greg gestured toward the car door, and she got inside.

"The service said they offered privacy windows. Any extra barriers between us and the paps couldn't hurt. This is Javier," he said, gesturing in the direction of their driver.

"Hello, Ms. Drake. I explained to Mr. Stafford that our trip might take a little longer than expected, since this is Friday rush hour. So please relax and enjoy the trip."

Rhani took his advice, and while they rode, she told Greg her concerns about Wil.

He gave her the male point of view. "He most likely feels an obligation to your mother. She *is* his mother, no matter how poor a job she did. There's no other connection as deep as the one between a boy and his mother."

"Wil isn't a boy. He's almost twenty."

Greg sent her a patronizing look. "If my mother ever said she needed me for anything, I'd be there before she finished getting the words out, and so would my brothers. Lillian Stafford deserves anything and everything we can give her. She raised six boys basically by herself. My father was always at the hospital when we were young and at his practice when we got older, so the bulk of the daily discipline, encouragement, parent/teacher conferences, and everything else fell on her shoulders."

"But she was a *good* mother, Greg. Wil and I can't say the same, and yet she regularly guilts him into doing what she wants, which is usually to give her money."

"Where's your father now?"

"He's around, which is the reason why I send her a certain amount of money and no more. If she wants to stay with a man who won't support her, it's her problem. But if she keeps using my brother the way she does, he'll never be free. Wil is so smart and has so much going for him. He doesn't belong in the old neighborhood or around such bad influences."

"I can tell how much you love him, but Wil is a man, Rhani, even though you don't think of him as one. You can't dictate how or where he should live. It sounds as though he doesn't want to be found right now. The two of you have a good relationship; he'll get in touch with you when he's ready."

Her shoulders slumped, and she sent him a sad smile. "Did you ever think about becoming a therapist?"

Greg howled. "Never! I just grew up with five brothers and saw all of us go through our different changes. Wil is finding his way in the world, and he needs to do it on his own." He stroked the back of her hand with his thumb. The sensation sent prickles up her arm. "Don't worry about him. If he has a good head on his shoulders, he's not going to screw up."

Her worrisome thoughts eased, but thoughts of a different kind replaced them. Other than the handshakes they had shared at his first session and the one sealing the Vegas wager, this was the first time he'd really touched her.

Rhani glanced at their hands and for a fleeting second had the inclination to pull away. When she didn't, he gently squeezed her hand and held it while they rode.

Two hours later, Javier let them off at the entrance to BayVue, which literally sat on the water's edge of Long Island Sound. Greg instructed him to return at ten o'clock p.m., and Rhani watched the car disappear down the street. They went up to the rooftop lounge, and she let out a small gasp of pleasure when she saw the view.

At seven o'clock, the sun still reflected on the rippling water. "Oh, Greg, this is beautiful."

A waiter came and took their drink orders. He returned a few minutes later with her Little Blue Dress and his Bloody Mary and took their dinner orders. They silently sipped their drinks, listened to the jazz quartet and watched the boats bob up and down as they came and went in the marina.

Greg didn't say much until after the server delivered her seafood platter and his rib-eye steak. He appeared to be more comfortable talking when he had something to do with his hands. "I haven't asked how you felt about what happened to you and Sherylle. If this is causing problems for your practice, you might want to refer me to one of your colleagues to take some of the pressure off."

"They're restricted to the outside of the building. My practice isn't affected in any way. Since they don't know who my clients are, people going in and out of the building aren't being harassed. My issue is those guys aren't simply hanging out to get a few pictures. They are so rude. They asked me if I minded being your latest booty call."

He slammed his fork down on his plate with a loud clank, and other diners sitting close to them turned around. He lowered his head and pinched the bridge of his nose. "Oh, hell no!" The way his eyes took on a gold color that reflected his anger fascinated her. "I didn't know they were saying those kinds of things. They have no right to disrespect you, and you shouldn't have to defend yourself against something intended for me."

"Don't worry about me. I'm used to fending for myself. You weren't sitting in Starbucks having coffee by yourself, and you're not the only one who has to be responsible for his own actions."

He called the waiter over to their table and ordered another round of drinks.

Chapter Eleven

*D*o you mind if we stop talking about this and switch to something more pleasant?" He downed the rest of his Bloody Mary in one gulp.

"Gladly."

"The last time my co-host and I spoke, she said the fan mail has been steadily coming in for me. It seems as though many viewers feel my three-month suspension is overkill. She said the production assistants have been told to read every single e-mail and snail mail letter and make a note of the writer's opinion. As of last week, seventy-three percent of viewers who contacted the network feel my sex life is my private business, and they disagree with the morality clause in my contract. This whole so-called scandal might not be a career killer after all. In fact it might end up helping my career. Crazy, isn't it?"

"It's interesting the way the public views these incidents now. Years ago, their feelings would've been quite different."

What did she mean by that? "Are you saying they shouldn't be siding with me?"

"Of course not, but I am saying how they feel depends on who the celebrity is. What one gets excused for, another gets vilified for."

"The American public is fickle. They love you one minute and hate you the next."

She gazed at the setting sun as it colored the sky in vivid shades of pink, orange and purple. "I'm so happy my profession doesn't depend on my popularity."

"It's not a bad way to make a living, as long as you stay out of trouble. The hours are great, but sometimes I get really tired of representing the network at social and philanthropic events in the evenings and on weekends. It's not really like working though. I've worked jobs in the past that were like slave labor. In college I waited tables, did telemarketing, flipped burgers, you name it."

"But I thought you said your parents paid your college tuition."

The server cleared away their dishes and asked what they wanted for dessert. They made their choices, and when he left, Greg answered her question. "They did, but my father wouldn't give us money to blow. If we wanted to party on the weekends or go out of town with friends, we had to pay our own way."

"So, the doctor's son flipped burgers. Interesting."

Greg loved the way the breeze blew through her curls, and she had to keep pushing them away from her face. "Victor Stafford believed in teaching life lessons. Marc and I always loved to party, but my other brothers didn't. They had to keep their noses in the books because they were pre-med. Marc eventually switched from pre-med to exercise physiology and nutrition science, so his course load wasn't as intense as Vic's, Jesse's or Charles'."

She focused on his face and didn't look away until he finished speaking. It wasn't one of those dreamy *you are so fine* looks some women gave him. She appeared to be honestly interested in what he had to say, or maybe it was her therapist's training. They *had* to be good listeners.

"I didn't party at all in college," Rhani said. "I just wanted to make the dean's list and graduate with honors, and it's exactly what I did."

"So you were the bookish girl?"

"To the extreme. My roommate used to go so far as to bribe me to go out with her and her friends. Back then, it wasn't what I wanted to do. I have a better social life now than I ever did. My girlfriends and I try to do something together every week, even if we just go out for dinner."

"What kind of work do your girlfriends do?"

"Kat is a pharmaceutical salesperson, and Joie owns a fashion boutique."

"Zwa?"

"Yes, it's spelled J-O-I-E. It's French."

"Ahh, like joie de vivre. So her name is really Joy then."

"Exactly, and she is a joy. I wish you could meet her. You two would get along great."

Greg caught the faraway look in her eyes. "Why can't I meet her?"

Her expression sobered and she spoke in just above a whisper. "Greg, we can't start doing that. If we did, you might weather it, but I could lose my license. I can't take the chance."

He eyed her with a curious squint. "We're sitting in a public place for the whole world to see." He snickered and waved a hand toward the other diners. "Do you trust these strangers more than your own friends?"

Her gaze shifted from left to right. "They don't know us. Even if they recognized you, they have no idea who I am. It would be a totally different situation if our friends found out."

"Found out what?" He grinned.

"That we're…seeing each other."

"Is that what we're doing?" he asked with a smirk. "I've

never been to your place, and you've never been to mine."

"I didn't know residence visits were the only yardstick of a relationship," she said with a sarcastic edge. "We've had a cup of coffee and a very nice dinner together. Are we having a *relationship*?"

He found himself in unfamiliar territory. He'd spent years perfecting a convincing spiel explaining to women why he *wasn't* interested in anything distantly resembling a real relationship. Now he found himself about to tell her why he wanted the one thing he'd been running from for the past three years. He took her hand and stroked the soft skin beneath his fingers. "We have to start somewhere, if we want to be together. It's what I want. Do you?"

They stared at each other for a long moment. "It's what I want too, but I have to level with you, I refuse to be one of many." Conviction colored her voice.

"I'm not seeing anyone else, and I'm not interested in seeing any other women."

"I have no reason to believe it. Remember, I know your history."

"Right. I guess all I can ask you to do is give me the opportunity to show you."

"Getting involved with you will probably cause me some professional hassles, but something tells me you're worth it."

He couldn't help breaking into a wide smile. "You think so?"

"Yes, I do."

She thought he was worth it. He didn't deserve a woman like her. Greg raised her hand to his lips and pressed a kiss there. The anticipation of what the future might bring reverberated between them while they finished dessert.

Rhani reapplied her lipstick, and they exited the restaurant with their hands linked and waited by the water for Javier to return. After Rhani slipped into the back seat, Greg slipped an arm around her. When she rested her head on his shoulder, he inhaled the light floral scent of the mass of soft curls.

"Thank you for a wonderful night."

He gently brushed his knuckles across her cheek then fingered a long curl and tucked it behind her ear. "I'm glad you had a good time." Without thinking about the next move, he did what he had always tried to avoid with the women he dated. Since Ev he hadn't been big on kissing or cuddling. It was too personal. His relationships had been all about sex, not feelings or emotions, but at the moment there wasn't a single thing he wanted more than to hold Rhani in his arms. He drew her closer and kissed her forehead. Rhani closed her eyes. She wasn't going to resist. He closed the embrace and brought her soft curves against his chest wishing they weren't sitting so he could feel the length of her body against his. The past month had been a test of his will, and he desperately wanted to taste her. But he didn't want to seem like a hungry beast. Instead, he brushed his mouth lightly against hers, warning himself to take it slowly. She parted her lips inviting him to explore. A fire ignited inside him, and almost involuntarily, he thrust his tongue into the sweet warmth between her shiny pink lips. Her body tensed in his arms, and she uttered an almost imperceptible moan. Her fingers caressed his nape then worked their way into his hair pulling him even closer, and her other hand caressed his back in a soft, circular motion. Greg's blood coursed within him, hot and thick. The sweet caramel flavor of the crème brûlée she'd eaten for dessert lingered on her soft lips, and the gentle yet eager way her tongue met his made him wish the kiss could go on forever.

Well aware he was taking a chance at getting his face slapped, he rested a hand on her knee. When she didn't protest, he slipped it beneath the hem of her dress and stroked her outer thigh. She had a dancer's legs, firm and strong. He willed his hand to stay away from her inner thighs, because the hidden treasure between them was too tempting for him to stand. His erection twitched at the mere thought of those legs clamped around his back. Since the day they met, he'd fantasized about her touch. He closed his eyes and delighted in the sensation.

Suddenly he remembered they weren't in a limo, and the Town Car didn't offer privacy partitions. When he opened one eye and peered at the rearview mirror, he met Javier's curious gaze. Greg raised his index finger and pointed forward warning the driver to keep his eyes forward. The trip back to Manhattan would take nearly ninety minutes. He wanted to get beneath Rhani's dress more than he needed air at the moment. More importantly, though, he needed her to feel his desire yet also see the control he now exerted on himself—no matter how much it hurt. They spent the entire drive kissing and petting like teenagers. When Greg felt he couldn't take it any longer, he thought talking might distract him from the dangerous territory where his thoughts had wandered.

"I'd love to do this again. Can we have dinner together during the week or"—an idea came to him—"we could go out dancing." The spark lighting her eyes told him he'd hit the bull's-eye.

"I'd love to go dancing, but where?"

He considered her question for a second then said, "Bembe is always packed. We could just meet there. If we make sure we haven't been followed, it should be fine. Speaking of not being followed, I want Javier to take you home, but he needs your address."

"Yes, I suppose he does." She told him the location, and he relayed it to the driver.

"Drive by once and circle the block," he instructed Javier when the car reached her street, "so we can make sure there are no photographers still hanging outside." The driver complied. "You can pull over," Greg said once he saw no lurkers outside the entrance.

"I think we should say goodnight here, just in case someone is watching. Those guys are devious." Their lips met, and his pulse shot into a frantic rhythm. Momentarily forgetting all about Javier in the front seat, he tangled his fingers in her hair and deepened the kiss. "It's best if I don't walk you to the door."

"No problem. Thank you for a perfect evening. I had a wonderful time."

"Thank you for agreeing to come with me."

She reached into her purse, took out a business card and placed it into his hand. "My home number is on the back."

"I'll call you tomorrow. Javier," he said, leaning over the front seat, "will you see Ms. Drake to the door?" He had explained the paparazzi situation to the driver before they'd left his apartment.

Javier exited the car, opened the rear door and took her hand. As she stepped out, Greg scanned the street for any diehard photogs hiding in the entrances of any of the adjacent buildings. The driver waited until she unlocked the front entrance and entered the building then he got back behind the wheel.

Greg rested his head back against the seat and closed his eyes as the car pulled off. The night couldn't have gone better. Well, it might have if they'd been in a limo with a partition between them and the driver, but he couldn't be certain. Thinking about how enthusiastically she'd responded to his kisses put a smile on his face. Not acting on his impulse to initiate sex had been the hardest thing he'd probably ever done. In fact, he couldn't even remember the last time he had gotten so close to a woman and it didn't end with some headboard banging. But this was different. Kissing her had stirred up emotions in him different from the grope, bump and grind preliminaries he'd been used to. For reasons he did not yet understand, he needed to make love to Rhani, and he wanted to romance her. And he wanted her to know she was special. No woman had evoked that kind of emotion in him since Ev. The thought surprised him. But the sudden realization that he could think about Evelyn and it no longer felt as though someone was stabbing him in the chest surprised him even more.

Four days later, in his next session, Rhani began by saying, "I'd like to keep our conversation in sessions restricted to your therapy. Let's save anything personal for outside of the office."

"All right."

"How do you feel your therapy is going?"

He glanced up at her face, forcing his attention from her thighs and the memory of what it felt like to caress her there. "The other night, I discovered something. Before I started therapy, I couldn't even think about Ev and what happened between us without feeling like I was choking. Now it's not only possible for me to think about it, but I can talk"

Before he had a chance to finish answering, the phone beeped. Rhani reached over to her desk and pushed the intercom button. "Is something wrong, Sherylle?"

"Sorry to interrupt, but there's an urgent phone call from your brother on line one."

"Excuse me, Greg. I need to take this." She pushed the flashing button and put the call on speaker. "Hey, it's about time you returned my calls. What's so urgent?"

"Rhani, I don't have much time to talk. I need your help. I'm in jail."

The blood left her face, and she grabbed hold of the edge of the desk. "What! Are you all right? What happened?"

Greg listened and studied her horrified expression.

"I was sitting out in front of the building with some of my boys when the cops pulled up, jumped out and told all of us to put our hands behind our heads. We asked why, and they told us to shut up. They threw Raekwon down on the pavement. We tried to explain that we'd been sitting there for the past hour, but the cops didn't want to hear it. One of them said they'd had a report about a black man with long dreads and a baseball cap with two accomplices who just took part in a carjacking a few blocks away. They arrested all of us. We're at the precinct on Longwood Avenue."

"I'll be there as fast as soon as I can get a cab. Have they charged you with anything?"

"Not yet. Mookie says they can hold us for twenty-four hours regardless."

"Tell him not to say *anything* without an attorney present," Greg interrupted.

"I'm on my way. Don't answer any questions or make any statements until you get a lawyer, Wil." Her hands shook as she replaced the receiver and lines of worry creased her forehead. "I'm sorry, but I need to leave right now."

"Where's the Longwood Avenue precinct?"

"In the Hunts Point section of the Bronx."

"I'm going with you."

Her shoulders relaxed. "Would you?"

"Of course. I wouldn't let you go up there by yourself."

"It's where I'm from, Greg. I'm not afraid."

"I know, but you'll have to deal with the police. In case you've forgotten, I just went through this a few weeks ago."

"Right," she said with a tremulous smile. "Of course. Let's go then. Sherylle will just have to cancel the rest of my appointments for today."

After she explained the situation to her assistant, she and Greg headed to the street to catch a cab. A single diehard photographer still camped out at the building entrance.

"Greg! Rhani! Is this an early lunch date? All I need is one good shot. How about a smile?"

"Ignore him," Greg barked and pulled her by the hand toward the curb. The sound of the shutter snapping in rapid succession told him this predator had already gotten numerous shots.

Fortunately, a cab stopped for them, and they jumped in with the click-swish-click repeating behind them until Greg slammed the car door. "Take us to the Bronx. 1035 Longwood Avenue," he instructed the driver.

"He's never been arrested before, and with everything happening between young black men and the cops lately, I know he's scared to death."

"He has good reason to be. Do you have a lawyer?"

"No, just the one I used when I set up my practice, but she doesn't do criminal law."

Greg took out his phone, hit a button, put the phone on speaker and waited. "Thad, is it possible for you to meet me at the 41st precinct station in the Bronx?"

"What the hell did you do now, man?" his attorney barked.

Greg snickered. "It's not for me. Rhani's brother got arrested, and he doesn't have a lawyer."

"Hmm. Let me check my schedule." After a momentary silence, he said, "Is this serious?"

"I wouldn't be calling you if it wasn't."

"I think I can swing it. Give me thirty minutes or so to get there. I assume this is a criminal case."

"It could be." Greg gave Thad the pertinent facts as he knew them.

"Okay. Wait for me there. I'm on my way."

Rhani didn't seem as though she wanted to talk, so he held her hand and told her not to worry. He watched the scenery change as the cab took them from Manhattan to the Hunts Point section of the Bronx. In the three years since he'd lived in New York, he had never visited the Bronx once. The only thing that caught his attention in the dreary area was a spectacular block-long mural featuring colorful artwork along Garrison Ave.

They arrived at the precinct, an old brick building which reminded him of something straight out of one of those throwback TV cop shows. He paid the driver and accompanied Rhani inside. "Do you feel comfortable talking to them, or do you want me to?"

"I'm okay. Just jump in if I look like I need help, please." She gave him a weak smile and walked into the precinct entrance. The presence of computers, and other office equipment gave the interior of the building a slightly more modern appearance than the outside.

"I got a call from my brother, Wil Drake," she said when they approached the front desk. "He was brought in about two hours ago. I'd like to see him, if it's possible."

"The last name is Drake?" the uniformed desk sergeant

asked as he scanned his computer screen.

"Yes. What was he arrested for?"

"He's a carjacking suspect, but he—"

Greg squeezed her hand hard warning her not to speak.

"It will be a little while before you can see him. Can I see some identification?"

Rhani dug into her purse and produced her driver's license.

"Have a seat over there," the officer said in a disinterested tone after he examined her ID and pointed to a row of plastic chairs lining the wall.

The forty-five minutes they had to wait gave Thad time to get there. When he saw Greg and Rhani sitting together, he approached them wearing a confused expression.

Greg stood and they embraced. "Thanks for coming, man. I believe you already know Rhani."

"It's been a while." The long, admiring look Thad gave her irked Greg. "Good to see you again, Rhani." Thad reached for her hand and gave it a firm shake.

"Yes, it has. I really appreciate you being here. I haven't seen my brother yet. They told us to wait."

"I'll see what I can find out. What's his full name?"

"It's Wil—Wilbert Drake."

"Okay. Sit tight while I talk to the desk sergeant."

Rhani gave a nervous nod and sat beside Greg once again. "He'll get Wil released, if they haven't charged him with anything. Take a deep breath. We'll be out of here soon."

A moment later, Thad returned and sat in one of the hard plastic seats beside them. "An officer will be out to escort you to where they're holding your brother. I have to warn you not to ask him any questions, and don't let him talk about what happened. Tell him I'm willing to represent him, if it's what he wants. I'll go in to see him when you're done. I need to ask you a couple of questions."

"Anything."

"Does Wil have a record?"

"Oh God, no. He's an honor student at City College."

Thad offered her an understanding smile. "Has he ever been arrested before?"

"Never."

"If he's a student a City College, what was he doing at the location where the cops picked him up?"

"It's where our mother lives. He's home for the summer and was just hanging out in front of the building with some of his friends."

"Does he own or carry a weapon?"

"No. I don't think he's ever touched a gun in his life."

An officer came through a door on the far side of the room and called her name.

"Go with him, and remember to watch what you say," Greg warned before he patted her shoulder and watched her leave with the officer.

As soon as Rhani left, Thad turned to Greg. "So the papers were right. You are boning your therapist."

"It's not like that. We were in the middle of a session when she got a call from her brother. She seemed so upset; I couldn't let her come here by herself."

"Why? Do you two have more than a professional association? First it's coffee together, now this. What's going on, man?"

"She's a friend, Thad."

"Are you sure that's all it is?"

"For the time being, yes. What difference does it make to you?"

"As your attorney, I should know the facts," Thad said with a devious grin.

Greg mimicked his expression. "If you were defending me in court, I'd agree, but you're not. You're just trying to get into my business."

"Okay, don't bring her to me when she's brought up on ethics charges."

"Who would do that?"

"I don't know." He glanced up at the ceiling. "Her competition, a jealous friend, Senator Price." Thad folded his arms and eyeballed him. "Speaking of the good senator, have you heard from the lovely Mrs. Price?"

"No! I think he has her on lockdown. Besides, we don't even know each other."

"You're obviously not speaking in the biblical sense." Thad rubbed his shiny, bald head and chuckled. "I tell you the truth. You're my most interesting client. I never know what to expect when I get a call from you. It's a good thing we're friends."

"What do you mean?"

"If we weren't friends, I'd probably tell my assistant to block your calls." Both men laughed but stopped abruptly when Rhani reappeared in the waiting area red eyed and dejected.

Greg slipped an arm around her slumped shoulders. "You've been crying. How is he?"

"He's scared, and so am I. Can you talk to him now,

Thad? He said he wants you to represent him. You have to get him out of here."

"On my way." He approached the desk sergeant and this time identified himself as Wil Drake's attorney. An officer ushered him through the door leading to the holding area.

"At least one positive thing came out of this," she plopped into a chair. "He agreed to move in with me for the summer."

"Good. That should ease your mind."

Several minutes later, Thad returned to the desk and engaged in a lengthy conversation with the desk sergeant who promptly called another officer over. Greg strained to hear what they were saying, but their voices were hushed. The second officer left and returned a little while later with papers in his hand. Thad read and signed a paper then came to sit next to Greg again. "They didn't have anything on him. Either they had to produce some evidence or release him. He'll be out as soon as they process him."

"Really?" Rhani's face brightened. "Thank God!"

"They're mainly after the driver. He's the only one they have a good description of. Descriptions of the others guys with the driver were vague. You know how they do us. We all look alike to them. Wil seems like a good kid, but the way things are with the police lately, he needs to stay off the street."

"He's a great kid, and those were my exact words to him. My mother talked him into coming back to the neighborhood to stay with her, but it's the last place he should be. I hope he understands now."

Thad laughed. "I think he does. I can always tell the innocent ones, because they're scared shitless."

Rhani handed him her business card. "Please send your

bill to my office."

Greg snatched the card from his friend's hand. "No need. It's already taken care of." Rhani's eyes widened and Thad's narrowed. "I'm the one who dragged Thad out of his office in the middle of the morning."

"Works for me. Rhani, it's good to see you again. I need to get back to my office." He and Greg shook hands, and he left them.

"You didn't have to, Greg. I'm quite capable of paying my own bills."

"I know you are. Consider it a gift."

Rhani rolled her eyes. "Talk about ethics violations. Now I'm accepting monetary gifts from a client?"

"Only you, Thad and I know, and he wouldn't reveal private information to anyone."

"All I can say is thank you. I wouldn't have known what to do. Thad knew exactly what to do to get Wil released," she said with a grateful smile. "How long has he been your lawyer?"

"Since I came to New York. How did you two meet?"

"We were introduced at a networking event, and a few of us went out for drinks afterwards."

Greg didn't voice his suspicions, but he had a strong feeling from the way Thad had eyed her that he was attracted to her. The thought pleased him. A desirable, successful woman—just the kind of woman Thad liked—was his. His thoughts about her had changed since Friday night. Even though nothing physical had taken place between them yet, it amazed him how he'd begun to think of her as his woman.

Chapter Twelve

An hour passed before they officially released Wil. Rhani groaned internally when his eyes widened as he entered the room where she and Greg waited. He wasn't used to seeing her with a man, and he walked toward them with his gaze locked on Greg. Before she had a chance to speak, Greg stood and extended his hand.

"Greg Stafford. How're you doing, man?"

Wil grasped his hand. "Good to finally meet you. I saw you and my sister on TMZ the other night. So…I guess what they're saying on TV is true."

Rhani lowered her gaze to the worn floor and let Greg respond.

"I happened to be at her office when you called, and I thought she might need some moral support."

"Thanks for not letting her come by herself, man. Let's get out of here."

"I'll see if I can get a cab," Rhani said, heading toward the exit.

"She said you agreed to stay with her," Greg said as they walked down the hall toward the exit.

The moment they exited the building, the same photographer who had been outside her office shouted, "What's going on, Rhani? Did you have *another* client in jail?" Then he addressed Greg, "If you give me a statement and pose for one shot, I'll disappear."

"Who is he?" Wil asked.

"One of the paparazzi who's been stalking us," Greg replied. "Turn your backs to him and don't answer."

"Yeah, she's right about the neighborhood," Wil said, returning to their conversation. They stepped outside while Rhani called a cab.

"I'm glad you finally understand," she said. "If you want to go by Ma's and get a few things, we should do it now. On the weekend I'll rent a truck to get the rest. How did you get all your stuff home anyway?"

"A friend of mine was going home to Connecticut. He got one of those U-Haul trailers to pull behind his car, and he had extra space."

"Why didn't you just let him bring you to my place to begin with?"

"You know how Ma is. She kept calling asking when I'd be coming home. I didn't want to disappoint her."

"Hmph!" Rhani snorted. "You know as well as I do why she does it, Wil. You have to stop letting her use you."

"She needs the money, Rhan."

She and Greg shared a passing glance. "Isn't he there now?" she asked, referring to their father.

"He's there."

"Then she needs to get what she needs from her husband. If she wants to be with him so badly, then he should take care of her."

"You know that's not going to happen," Wil said without looking at her.

"Then it's not my problem, and it's not yours either."

The cab pulled up to the curb, and she gave the driver her mother's address.

"He'll probably follow us." Greg kept his eyes on the photographer through the rear window as the cab drove off. "I don't know how he did it, but he figured out a way to trail us to the precinct. Those guys are like leeches. Once they stick to your skin and start sucking your blood, it's hard to get them off."

They rode in silence until Greg asked, "How much stuff do you need to move, Wil?"

"What I had in my dorm room—clothes, stereo, laptop, microwave, a small refrigerator, a floor lamp and a couple of boxes."

"If you need help moving your things to Rhani's place, I could rent a van and bring you back up here. It would give me something useful to do, and your sister won't have to take time away from the office."

Her smile warmed his heart. "That would be wonderful. What do you think, Wil?"

"Sure, if it's not going to be an inconvenience."

"No inconvenience. All I've been doing since I've been on suspension is read, watch way too much TV and work out in the gym. It's kind of like being in jail." He snickered. "Get my number from Rhani, and call me tomorrow."

"Thanks, man." Wil reached across Rhani and gave Greg some dap.

When they reached her mother's building, she saw Greg glance around the neighborhood. He didn't comment and tried to be discreet, but she knew what he was thinking. Her presumption proved right when he asked, "You come up here twice a month to work at the community center?"

"Uh huh. Actually, it's gotten much better since I left after high school. Several active community groups are working to make it into a greener, safer area. There are some big projects, like the Bank Note Building, and The Crossings development. The shopping area over on Southern Boulevard has changed a lot too. The streets are cleaner, and they even put up Christmas lights now. I think within ten years and the addition of a few more developments and greenscapes, it could be a decent neighborhood."

When she looked up and saw Greg's smile, she burst out laughing. "I was trying too hard, huh?"

"Yeah." He chuckled. "A little bit."

The taxi stopped at the address she'd given the driver. Wil got out of the cab and looked back once as he started up the front steps toward the graffiti-marked entrance.

She closed her eyes for a second then rolled down the window. "Give this to her." She took out her checkbook and scribbled a check. "We'll wait for you here. Just don't tell her I'm outside, please." She had to respond to the questioning expression in his eyes. "No, Wil. I don't want to talk to her. Just grab what you need for a couple of days, and remember the meter is running, please."

"When's the last time you saw your mother?"

"Last year. Wil told her I volunteered at the community center. She showed up there one night to ask me for money."

"And your father lives with her?"

"If you want to use the word loosely. You remember the old Temptations song, *Papa Was a Rolling Stone*?"

"Yeah."

"Well, it's the story of his life, and she puts up with it."

He laughed.

"I don't think there's anything funny about it."

"Actually, I was thinking about my mother. She's as sweet as they come, but she doesn't take any crap from my

181

father. Lillian Stafford is one of the few people in this world who isn't intimidated by him. My brothers and I have seen her put him in his place, and he backs down like a Yorkie facing a Pit Bull." His gaze darted back and forth over the street as he spoke. "She always told us, 'Your father is the head, but I'm the neck, and I can turn the head any way I want.'"

She giggled. "What a good way to teach sons about how relationships *really* work. What do you keep looking at?"

"Just checking to see if we've been followed."

Her chest tightened at the possibility. "Do you see anyone?"

"I think we lost him this time."

Rhani blew out a long breath. "Thank goodness. They're leaning on my last good nerve, and it's getting harder and harder for me not to yell back at them. It's terrible the way they think they can say anything to you, no matter how foul, and you're supposed to just smile back and be cordial." She glanced up at the building entrance and cringed. "Especially when something like this happens."

Greg leaned over to peer out her window to see what she meant and saw Wil trying to maneuver through the door carrying two boxes. Their mother followed right behind him talking a mile a minute.

"But I *need* you here. I know she convinced you to leave. You have to stop letting her tell you what to do!" She looked at the taxi and saw Rhani in the back seat.

Rhani hit the window button, but her mother ran down the steps and reached the car before it closed.

"Why are you doing this to me? You know I need your brother here with me!" She waved a bony finger in her face.

"I'm not doing anything to *you*, Ma. I'm doing this *for*

Wil. For God's sake, he got arrested just for sitting outside on the steps! He doesn't belong here."

"All you've ever done is try to hurt me."

Rhani struggled to keep calm. She didn't want to look like a raving maniac in front of Greg. "You know that's not true, and everything isn't about you." She turned to the driver. "Can you pop the trunk, so he can put those boxes in please?" The driver complied, but didn't get out of the car to help, probably in fear of the escalating situation.

"You always thought you were better than everybody else. I don't know how I raised such a snobby little bitch!"

Rhani gritted her teeth and answered as calmly as she possibly could. "Don't flatter yourself, Ma. You didn't *raise* me. You were too busy chasing after the bum you married. My teachers and the people at the Boys & Girls Club raised me. Do you have anything else to go, Wil?"

"No. This is it for now." He went around to the rear of the taxi, closed the trunk then kissed their mother and joined the driver in the front seat. "Let's go."

"I'm sorry you had to witness that," she said to Greg with the heat of tears in her eyes as the driver pulled off, leaving her mother standing at the curb waving her arms and yelling.

"I'm a big boy. I can handle it." He put his arms around her and held her close until her labored breathing slowed. When he released her, she dropped her head to his shoulder and kept it there all the way back into Manhattan while Greg silently stroked her hair.

Finally, when they were close to her address, he said, "Why don't you two let me treat you to an early dinner? None of us had lunch."

"Thank you, but I'm just not in the mood for dodging the paparazzi. It's been a stressful day." She rubbed her forehead hoping to alleviate some of the remaining tension.

"All right then. How about we order in at your place?"

"Sounds great to me," Wil piped in.

She was outnumbered, and she really did appreciate Greg's offer. "That would be nice."

After she paid the driver, Wil retrieved his clothes from the trunk. He and Greg followed her into the building and took the elevator up to the fifth floor.

"You know the drill," Rhani said to Wil as she unlocked the door to her apartment. "Greg, please take off your shoes and leave them here at the door. She picked up an unopened package of men's white sport socks and put it in his hand.

"Yes, ma'am." He gave the living room a quick glance then bent down, untied his Jordans and set them next to the shoes she'd just slipped off. "This is just how I thought your apartment would look."

She wondered exactly what he'd expected. "How?"

Greg gave the room a thoughtful scan. "Cozy and comfortable with books everywhere. Nice."

"Thanks. Make yourself at home. The TV remote is on the table in front of the sofa. I'm going to help Wil get straight."

"Do you have any preference for dinner? How about Chinese?"

"There's a good place not far from here, and they deliver. The menu is up on the refrigerator. Let me see what Wil wants."

She stopped in the kitchen and took a can of Raid from under the sink then found him in the small bedroom at the back of the apartment. "Do you feel like Chinese for dinner? Greg's going to call somewhere."

"Fine with me." He took a few items of clothing out of one of the boxes and placed them in the empty chest of drawers.

"I know this room is small," she said by way of apology, "but it's quiet, and there are no roaches. By the way, examine your stuff to make sure you didn't bring any unwanted guests with you." She handed him the can of bug spray.

"This room is great. It's bigger than my dorm room, and I don't have to share it with anyone. Thanks, Rhan. I should've listened to you to begin with."

"It doesn't matter now. What should I tell Greg to order you?"

"Beef and Broccoli and a Pepsi are cool." He paused for a moment.

"Towels and washcloths are in the bathroom closet. The food should be here in about a half-hour."

"Thanks, Rhan."

She winked at him and returned to the living room where Greg was still perusing the take-out menu.

"How's he doing? I could tell he was torn about leaving your mother."

"Yeah, but it's only the guilt she uses to get him to do what she wants." She quickly changed the subject. "Did you decide what you want to eat? I'd like Sesame Shrimp and Crispy Green Beans. Wil wants Beef and Broccoli and a Pepsi."

"I'll call them now so we can eat, and I can get out of your way."

"There's no rush. It's still early."

He made the call, placed their orders and gave them his credit card number. When he finished, Rhani sat beside him on the sofa. She picked up the TV remote, pulled up the program guide and scanned the evening's offerings. "Something light is in order," she said, settling on *The Big Bang Theory*. "I love this show. I've seen the reruns several times, but it still cracks me up."

"I've never seen it."

"Are you kidding? It's won all kinds of Emmy awards for the past few years. The show is about a group friends— all brainiac physicists and engineers who are socially inept. It's hilarious."

Wil came up behind them. "Did he say he's never watched Big Bang?"

"Never," Greg confirmed.

The show began. Wil stretched out on the loveseat with his socked feet hanging over the arm and explained, "This is the one about Leonard and the football game."

"Do you mind if I put my feet up?" Greg asked, indicating the glass top table in front of the sofa.

"I said to make yourself at home."

The earlier tension from the drama of the day seemed to ease as they hooted over the antics of the sitcom's quirky characters. Rhani felt a strange stirring inside as she watched Greg. She liked seeing him so at ease in her surroundings, and she had the passing thought that he looked as if he belonged there. "I'll get it," she said when the door buzzed from downstairs. The visitor announced himself as the deliveryman from the restaurant. "Come on up."

Greg rose from his comfortable position and pulled a bill from his wallet. "I got this." He opened the door and peered down the hall for the deliveryman to get off the elevator.
When he appeared, Greg waved him into the apartment. "Mind if I check this before you leave?"

The man shook his head and stood silently while Greg unpacked the two large brown bags. "Looks like everything's here. Thanks, man."

"I hope everything is satisfactory," he said with a smile as he glanced down at the tip Greg handed him on his way out the door.

For the rest of the night, the three ate, shared small talk and watched sitcoms. "I'd better let you two turn in," Greg announced when the ten o'clock news began. He called a cab and told the dispatcher he would be waiting downstairs. "I really enjoyed this, Rhani. I've been alone too much these past few weeks."

"I'm glad. Next time I'll fix dinner."

"You can cook?"

"Oh, Rhani can burn," Wil chimed in.

"I'm going to take you up on that." Greg touched her cheek. "Don't forget to call me tomorrow about the truck, Wil."

The two men grasped hands and bumped shoulders. "Thanks again for going with me to the precinct and for calling Thad."

"Glad I could help." Greg turned to her. "Walk me to the elevator."

After they had been standing in front of the elevator for a few moments, Rhani realized he hadn't pushed the button to give them a few minutes alone. He put an arm around her waist and pulled her against him. "Let's go to Bembe this weekend."

She frowned and retreated a step. "I don't know. It'll be Wil's first weekend here. I'd hate to leave him alone with nothing to do."

"He'll be fine. For all you know, he might have plans of

his own."

"True. I'll let you know."

Greg closed the space between them and lifted her chin. Her knees weakened when he murmured, "Say yes," against her mouth.

"Let me talk to him and see what he has going on, and I'll let you know."

"You don't have to babysit him, Rhani. All you'll do is make him feel as if you're hovering. Wil's been away at school, and he's used to being on his own." He touched the tip of his tongue to her lips and teased them open, and a torturous heat pooled in her lower belly. She leaned into him until she felt his heart pounding against hers. He was a wonderful kisser, and when he sucked her bottom lip and gave it a little nip, she responded with enthusiasm.

Greg uttered a soft groan, slid his hands down and squeezed her booty then literally pushed her away. "You can't kiss me like that and then expect me to behave, Rhani." He shook his head, and pushed the elevator button with a fast peck on her cheek. "We'll talk tomorrow." The doors opened, and he left her with a smoldering glance as they closed.

They had a world-class conflict of interest going on. How in the world could she challenge him to remain celibate and then tempt him at the same time? It was unfair and just plain wrong, especially since she wanted nothing more than to find out what it would be like to make love with him. She needed to convince him to see another therapist if they were going to continue seeing each other.

After the elevator left her floor, she stood in the hallway for several minutes thinking about the royal mess she'd gotten herself into. For the past few years, work had been her top priority. Now it seemed as though her practice had taken an involuntary back seat in her mind. She cared about the business, but for the first time since she'd started the practice, she was in a real relationship. Being involved with a man had a way of monopolizing your thoughts.

Rhani knew she was a great therapist, and she'd helped numerous clients get their lives back on track after they had derailed because of extreme sexual behavior. Her relationship with Greg could put her success on the line. Her own mother had given up on her dreams and destroyed her life because of her twisted relationship with her father, a man who didn't care enough about her to even put clothes on her back. Already successful in his chosen field, Greg didn't have a problem with her career. The complete opposite of her lazy, irresponsible father, Greg wasn't the least bit stingy, loved his family and had already gone out of his way to help Wil, whom he'd never even met before today.

"I like him," Wil said when she came back into the living room and locked the front door. "Guess you can't believe what the media says, huh? They made him out to look like some kind of crazy perv."

"I know. He's a good man who's fighting some demons—just like the rest of us."

Wil gave her a sympathetic smile. "You know he must really like you, if he's willing to do this for me."

"He's not helping you because of me. Greg's a decent man, and he's very generous."

Wil's laugh filled the room. "Don't fool yourself, Rhan. He's feeling you."

"Yeah, I think he is." She couldn't stop the silly grin she felt creeping onto her face, and she quickly changed the subject. "What time do you need to leave for work in the morning?"

"About eight, I guess. It'll probably take me an hour to get there."

"I usually leave around the same time, because I like to have a few minutes to eat breakfast and look at the morning paper before Sherylle gets in. I'll wake you when I get out of the shower."

"Sounds like a plan." He clicked off the TV and set the remote on the table. "Thanks for doing this. Even though Ma got ticked off, it's the right thing for me to do."

Rhani smiled at him, thinking how much he looked like their father, who was a handsome man. At least Wil would have the benefit of good looks and a good education. "See you in the morning." She took off her makeup, changed into her favorite oversized t-shirt and crawled into bed thinking about the events of the day.

The next thing she knew, the high-pitched sound of her alarm clock filled the bedroom. She had obviously been more exhausted than she'd thought. Following her shower, she woke her brother, dressed and left him a note with her extra apartment key taped to the inside of the front door so he wouldn't miss it. She felt good this morning, as though she had tackled a major accomplishment by getting him to agree to stay for the summer. One less thing to worry about.

On her way to the office, she ran into the Starbucks around the corner and grabbed a crumb cake pastry and a grande Salted Caramel Mocha for breakfast. She convinced herself that after what she'd been through yesterday, she deserved a calorie-laden treat. On the way out of the coffeehouse, she pushed two quarters into one of the newspaper boxes outside, grabbed a copy of *The Post* and walked to the office with a new bounce in her step.

Much to her surprise, there wasn't a single photographer outside the revolving door. Today was going to be a good day. The happy thought lasted until she opened the paper and saw photos of her and Greg getting into the taxi, another of them entering the police precinct and another of the three of them exiting the building. She groaned when she read, "Therapist Rhani Drake served up some serious side eye as she entered the 41st precinct with temporarily benched TV host Greg Stafford." Somehow they had gotten Wil's name and the reason for his arrest, but at least they said he'd been released without being charged.

The next morning, before she left for work, Wil told her Greg would be picking him up to go back to the Bronx to get the rest of his belongings and put it all into storage until he returned to school in September. She'd given him her credit card and told him to pay for the whole three months.

That evening after her last client, she met Kat and Joie for dinner.

"There she is," Kat said as she approached the table where her two best friends sat with drinks in their hands. "The Page Six sistah!"

"You are not funny, Kat." Rhani pulled out a chair and dumped her tote and purse on the seat before she sat in the other empty spot at the table. "The past couple of weeks have been disturbing, to say the least."

"It's a shame we had to find out from TMZ who Mr. Sexy client is."

"Well, you didn't hear it from me." Rhani raised a finger in the air to get the server's attention. "I wasn't going to reveal his identity to you or anyone else. It's just played out this way, and now everyone knows. Please don't ask me any questions about him, okay?" She ordered a cocktail then turned her attention back to Joie who wore a frustrated frown.

"Not fair, Rhani," Joie protested. "You're seeing one of the finest brothers on television who also happens to be a sex addict, and we can't get any details?"

"You say it as though it's a good thing." Rhani shook

her head. "Being a sex addict is no different than being hooked on coke or alcohol. I can't tell you anything about his therapy, other than he's practicing celibacy now. But I *will* say he took me to dinner last week out on Long Island, and we had a great time."

"Are you saying the two of you won't be getting busy at all?"

"Exactly. Just because we're seeing each other doesn't mean I'm going to alter his therapy. In order for him to overcome his addiction, he needs to prove to himself that he won't die if he goes without."

"What about you? I know I couldn't be in close quarters with a man as sexy as Greg Stafford without jumping him."

"I look at it this way. I haven't been with anyone in a long time. A few more months won't kill me."

"So," Kat asked twisting her drink straw between her teeth. "how'd your dinner date go?"

"Believe me, it wasn't easy, but Greg figured out a way to throw the paparazzi off, and it worked. He told me to take the train up to a stop near his apartment and walk over to a parking garage to wait for him."

"You in a parking garage?" Joie exclaimed. "I know how you hate those places."

"He'd told the attendant to look out for me. I did what he said, and he was already there when I arrived, waiting in a Town Car with dark tinted windows. It took us out to Lindenhurst to a nice restaurant on Long Island Sound."

"Gee, sounds like something right out of a romantic suspense novel," Kat mused.

She giggled. "It was *different*."

"Did my boy kiss you goodnight, I mean considering

this was your first real date and all?" Joie fluttered her fake lashes.

Rhani lowered her gaze and her voice. "He didn't wait for us to say goodnight. In fact, he had to tell the driver to keep his eyes on the road."

"Oooh!" Joie's eyes rounded. "Look at you getting all tangled up. I said you'd do what your heart wanted, didn't I?"

Rhani rolled her eyes. "Yes, and it's a big risk to take when I don't even know if this is going to get any deeper."

"The only way to know," Kat said matter-of-factly, "is to stay in it until you're sure one way or another."

Rhani went on to describe the drama with Wil and her mother. "She acted like a fool and embarrassed me so bad, but Greg just brushed it off. I guess he figures my crazy mother is nothing compared to all of the mess he's been in lately."

"I have some news." Kat waggled her brows. "I paid another call to the doctor I told you about, and we're going out for drinks tomorrow night."

"Seriously?" Rhani brightened at hearing the news. "What did you do to get him to ask you?"

"I used my superpowers, and he couldn't resist."

"She slipped him one of those drugs she peddles," Joie said, making them all hoot with laughter, but the mirth died quickly when she asked Rhani, "What on earth would you do if they took your license?"

"I refuse to think about it, because I don't believe it'll happen." Secretly she believed the possibility was real. In fact, lately she'd been considering what she might do. She had even looked up a few psychology-related jobs that might interest her, but she loved counseling and didn't want to give it up.

"I hope you're right, girl," Kat said with a skeptical expression. "You wouldn't be happy doing anything else. Is this man worth giving up what you love doing?"

Joie laughed. "Oh, please! She can't cuddle up to her career at night. I'm a witness. If she has the man she loves, it'll be easy to find another job."

"The problem is I'm falling for him, but I don't know if he feels the same way. We've been together a lot, but we've only had one real date."

"Give it time," Joie encouraged her.

"A few things scare me. It's possible Greg just thinks he's attracted to me because of our client/therapist relationship. It happens more often than you'd imagine. Also, he might be doing what just comes naturally to him with women. Sex appeal and charm are built into his DNA. The other day one of those disgusting paparazzi asked if I minded being Greg's latest booty call."

"No he didn't!" Kat exclaimed, sounding offended for her.

"I would've slapped him into next week," Joie agreed.

"The way the laws are now, I'd get arrested for touching one of them. Even after Halle Berry and Jennifer Garner testified before a California Judiciary Committee about how those guys harassed them and their children, nothing changed. Look at how they stalk Kim and Kanye's baby."

Kat grunted. "Yeah, but they use the poor child as a way to get publicity. I don't think I've ever seen a picture of the baby smiling. It's almost as though she knows she's bait."

"North West is far from poor," Rhani grumbled.

"You know what I mean."

"We do, Kat, but what I need to know is if you're ready to come and talk to my girls at the center next week?" Rhani said, changing the conversation to a more pleasant subject.

"I am. Joie told me how much fun she had when she spoke to them. I'm looking forward to it."

After they finished their drinks, the friends parted with a promise to meet again next week.

Rhani called the pizzeria near her apartment and asked them to deliver a pie and a large salad to her address then she called Wil to let him know.

He was in the living room watching TV when she got home and started talking even before she took off her shoes.

"I want to talk to you about Greg."

A chill ran up her spine. "Did something happen today?"

"Nothing bad, if that's what you're thinking. He rented a van just like he said he would and picked me up at noon. We went up to Ma's, and he helped me bring everything down. After we put it all in storage, he bought lunch."

"Did she give you a hard time?"

"No harder than usual. She tried to explain why my reasons for leaving were ridiculous."

She shook her head and walked into the kitchen to wash her hands. "Of course she did."

"And she tried her best to talk Greg out of helping me."

"Oh, God. How did he handle it?"

"He definitely has a way with women." Wil chuckled.

"What do you mean? Tell me what he said to her."

195

"It wasn't what he said, but how he said it. I've never seen Ma act so giddy before."

"Okay, now you really have me wondering what happened." She poked a finger in his chest with an expression she hoped looked threatening. "Start at the beginning or you're not getting any pizza."

They both sat at the kitchen counter, and Wil described the scene earlier that afternoon. "I'd hoped she might be at work when we got there, but she was off today. He introduced himself, and she recognized him right away. I guess she didn't see him in the cab the other day. She kept trying to fix her hair and smooth her clothes like she was nervous."

"He has that effect on people," she said with a snicker. "Female people, that is."

"After he told her he was helping me put my things into storage, she apologized for the way she looked. He said there was no reason for her to apologize, because she was an attractive woman. From that point on, she was all grins and giggles. It freaked me out, and that's when I left the room to start taking my stuff downstairs. I did hear her ask if you two were living together."

"She did?"

"He said no, and told her he lived on the Upper East Side."

Then his tone changed. "He's a good man. I know he's had his problems and all, but at the core he's a decent dude. And he *really* likes you."

"How do you know?"

"Because of the way he talks about you—like you can do no wrong. He said you've done more to help him than anyone else in his life. What have you been doing for him?" His eyes narrowed to slits.

"He's just talking about his therapy." Rhani chuckled.

"Come on. Just admit you're seeing each other."

"We had one date, Wil. It's nothing to make a fuss about."

Chapter Thirteen

*D*uring the three weeks that passed, Greg spent more time at Rhani's apartment. He and Wil talked for hours and began developing a real friendship in spite of their age difference. Wil seemed to need a father image as much as Greg needed the camaraderie he'd had with his brothers before he moved from Atlanta. A couple of times, while Rhani worked on her laptop in the bedroom, he and Wil talked for several hours.

He continued his twice-a-week therapy visits. One day, as they finished the session, he said, "Since the paparazzi have backed off, it's a good time for us to go out dancing. How about we grab something to eat tomorrow night and then drop in at Bembe?"

"I'm up for it, if you are. Are we still doing the clandestine hide and seek thing?"

"Do you think it's still necessary? We haven't seen any photogs in two weeks. I think they've finally forgotten about us. I'll take a cab to your place and pick you up at seven."

The next evening he called from a cab to tell her they were a few blocks away. When the driver arrived at her address, she was waiting outside dressed in a pair of body hugging jeans, a bare-shouldered multi-colored top and big African-inspired earrings.

"You look great." He greeted her with a kiss when she joined him in the back seat.

"Thanks. Gotta have the *world look* to go with all the fabulous world music." She flipped the earrings so they jingled. "I hope you're ready to work up a sweat, Stafford, because other than my classes, I haven't been out dancing in months. I have a lot of energy to burn."

She made the statement quite innocently, but his mind zoomed to the other ways he'd rather help her work off the excess energy. Every cell in his body longed to know what making love with her might be like.

"Make no mistake. You've met your match on the dance floor. I guarantee it."

"We'll see," she teased him with an impish twinkle in her eyes.

After dinner at a restaurant near Bembe, they walked over to the club which sat beneath the Williamsburg Bridge. Even though the hour was still early, it was near capacity. He ordered drinks at the bar then, with glasses in hand, they found a spot on an antique-looking sofa in the downstairs lounge. As soon as they finished their cocktails, he led her back upstairs into the rollicking crowd filling the long, narrow room. As Rhani began to move to the music, he couldn't take his eyes off her. Since she said she took dance lessons, he anticipated she would be graceful, but he wasn't prepared for her to be so animated and energetic. She closed her eyes and worked her body to the Afro-Latin beat in wild, sexy movements that were hypnotic and almost dirty at the same time. At least in his mind they were. The serious therapist had completely disappeared, and had been replaced by a sultry, uninhibited woman who knew how to lose herself in the beat.

They danced non-stop for the next hour. Her skin glowed with a light sheen of perspiration, and when the DJ put on a down-tempo reggae tune, Greg moved closer, cupped his hands under her booty and pulled her against his body. They did a slow grind; he backed her against the brick wall and tried to satisfy himself with the heady feeling of her soft curves meeting his hard muscle. Rhani locked her hands behind his neck and seemed to give herself over to him. She smelled like a mixture of flowers and lemon. He snuggled his nose into her neck and breathed in deep, pressing the best or perhaps the worst erection he'd had in months between her open thighs. They swayed, rocked and moved their fused hips together to the beat. A couple minutes of that was all he could take.

"Let's go back to my place," he spoke into her ear so she could hear him above the music.

Rhani drew back and studied his face for a moment. "What do you have in mind?"

He locked his gaze with hers. "I want you to spend the night with me."

"I'd love to," she said before she hit him with something he never expected. "But I will never make love with you in a bed that has been occupied by dozens of other women."

His hips stopped moving and he froze. The thought had never even crossed his mind, and the reality instantly deflated his erection. "Uh…Oh, Rhani, I…" he stumbled over his words, at a loss for how to respond.

"I want it to be just you and me. No memories. No shadows."

The song ended, and he guided her toward the bar with his arm around her waist. They took their drinks back down to the lounge where it was relatively quiet. Unsure of what to say at first, Greg took a long sip of his watermelon juice and vodka before he spoke again.

"That was insensitive of me. I'm sorry. I understand what you're saying, and I can't blame you. Guess I needed the wake-up call." He sat silently for a while as she stared into her Caipirinha and stirred the limes around with the straw. The words that came out were what he'd been thinking, but he hadn't meant to say them aloud. "Every year my parents have a huge July 4th barbeque, and my brothers and I fly in for the weekend." His gaze zeroed in on her face. "Will you come with me next week?"

"Why?"

Rhani's questioning expression almost made him laugh. "Why? Because I want you to meet my family, and I want them to meet you."

"Thanks for inviting me, but are you sure it's what you want to do?"

Now he returned her curious expression. "Why wouldn't I? You'd like them, especially my sisters-in-law."

"Do you plan to tell them who I am?"

"If they've been watching TMZ, they already know who you are."

She bristled and rolled her shoulders. "Just a couple of weeks ago, I told you it wasn't a good idea for you to meet my friends. Now you want me to come out to your *family*? We might as well run a full-page ad in the *Times*."

"The paparazzi have finally backed off. I think it's a good time to *come out*, as you call it." He smirked.

"Everybody flies in just for a barbeque?"

"We're all financially able to do it now, and most of us only come home twice a year, July 4th weekend and Christmas."

"What are you going to tell them about us?"

"I'm not going to tell them anything. You'll be my guest for the weekend, and that's all we need to say."

"Come on, Greg. I know how nosy family can be. They're going to ask questions."

"My family isn't a problem. We'll have a great time. My

mother goes all out. Have you ever been to Atlanta?"

She exhaled a loud sigh. "Once, years ago."

"Well, this time you'll be visiting with a hometown boy. I'll take you for some real southern cooking, and I know Mama has an outing planned for the ladies."

"I can't just show up and barge in on their plans. They don't even know me."

"Believe me, baby, there's no such thing as barging in on a Stafford party. My mother lives to entertain, and she welcomes whoever shows up." He didn't verbalize it, but he knew his mother. If he brought Rhani home, she'd automatically be a special guest. As much as she denied it, his mother was a matchmaker at heart, and she wanted to see all of her sons happily married. "Will you come with me?"

"I have to think about it."

He waited for about sixty seconds. "Okay, you've thought about it long enough. Say yes."

She hung her head for a moment, but when she raised it, her cheeks puffed with a smile. "Okay. I haven't been anywhere out of state in a while. Are we driving or flying?"

"Driving? I don't do road trips. Can you leave the evening of the second?" She nodded. "Great. I'll check on flights when I get home. Are you ready to go?"

"Yes, I guess we should."

They stood outside the entrance of the club and waited for a cab to cruise by looking for passengers. One finally stopped, and Greg gave the driver her address. Both of them retreated into their thoughts with only the intermittent chatter of the dispatcher's radio filling the interior of the car. He wanted to say something else about her refusal to go home with him, but anything he said might offend her or make her angry, so he kept his mouth shut. A while later, back in Manhattan, he walked her to the building entrance and left a soft kiss on her lips.

After Greg got back to his apartment, he lay on the sofa for the next couple of hours half watching the television, plagued by the foolish mistake he'd made earlier. Rhani knew his sexual history, and she couldn't be fooled even if he wanted to deceive her. If their relationship was going any deeper, he needed to carefully think through his every move. She was too kind and too sweet for him to insult or hurt her. Sometimes he couldn't believe she even wanted to be with him. She had faith in him, and she didn't hold his mistakes against him. Rhani Drake was unique and special, and he loved her.

He bolted upright and clicked off the television as though he'd just heard the words aloud. *He loved her.*

When he'd left Atlanta, he'd been certain he would never be able to say those words about any woman again. The last time he'd loved someone, she'd destroyed him. His life had been an out-of-control, twisted mess ever since. This whole thing scared him to death.

Am I setting myself up for the same kind of destruction again? He knew beyond a shadow of a doubt if it happened again he wouldn't survive. Restless and feeling slightly claustrophobic, he paced around the apartment then locked the door and took the elevator up to the roof. At night the city appeared more serene, and the twinkling lights always relaxed him. A chaise facing the Manhattan Bridge offered the perfect view for his introspection.

Since he'd been in New York, Thad had been the only other man with whom he felt close enough to confide. He hung out with a couple of guys from work, but he didn't consider them friends. As nice a guy as Thad was, everything he thought and said seemed to be filtered through a legal screen. Right now Greg needed someone impartial, because he needed to talk about Rhani. Thad already knew her, and though it might have been Greg's imagination, he thought Thad seemed more than a little interested in her. He couldn't very well talk to Thad about his feelings for her.

Their counseling sessions were becoming increasingly more awkward. She knew he no longer fulfilled his sexual needs with strange women. He didn't want to lie to her, but he no longer felt comfortable confessing to her things like whether or not he masturbated. Not the kind of thing you shared with your lady. Damn. Exactly when did he start considering her *his lady*? Things were moving fast—inside his head. Yeah, he definitely needed to talk to someone.

♥♥♥

He called Rhani's office on Monday morning and told Sherylle he needed to change his Tuesday appointment from morning to the last one of the day. He knew if he were the final client, Rhani would send her assistant home.

Although he hadn't meant to, as soon as he sat on the sofa, he blurted out what had been on his mind. "I need to tell you something. After I got home Friday night, I couldn't sleep. I went up to the rooftop lounge. I can think better up there." He sat forward on the sofa; legs spread, and rested his elbows on his knees. "Something has changed between us. Changed for the better, in my opinion." Up until then, Rhani had been flipping through the notebook she used during their sessions. Those words made her stop. "Do you agree?" Their gazes met for a moment before she gave a silent nod. "If we're going to explore it, I can no longer be your client."

Rhani leaned back in her chair and folded her hands as she always did when she listened carefully. "But you're making such great progress. Stopping now might result in a setback. I'm not sure I'm comfortable with that."

He studied her face for anything which might reveal how she felt about what had happened between them, but her features remained blank. Time to change tactics. Rhani took her job seriously. The only way to make her understand would be to put all of his cards on the table.

"You're an incredible therapist, but I think we've become too close, and I'd prefer to see a man."

A muscle ticked in her jaw before she stood and walked behind the desk. "Actually, I've been thinking the same thing. It would be the best thing for both of us. There are a couple of people I can recommend." She took a business card file from the center drawer, flipped through a few pages, and removed two cards. "Let me make a copy of these for you. When you make an appointment, let me know so I can fax him your file and notify your job of the change."

When she stepped from behind the desk, he stood and met her at the doorway, blocking her path to the copier in the outer office. He held both hands up in front of her. "Not yet."

He had her full attention now, and he turned and twisted the doorknob, locking them inside her office together. With her assistant gone for the night, there would be no interruptions. Sensing his intentions, Rhani's mouth opened as if to protest, but closed quickly. Greg took a moment to explore her body with his eyes without touching her, a difficult task to say the least, because at this moment he wanted her more than he wanted to take his next breath. He hadn't experienced a feeling like this since he'd been with Ev.

His M.O. for the past few years would have been to bend her over the desk or hold her against the wall. Her clothes would've been hanging off, panties pushed to the side, and she'd be calling his name while he took his fill.

But that's not what he wanted from Rhani. Not now.

Not ever. His therapy with her had reminded him there was more to sex than just the act. He wasn't an idiot. Watching his brothers with their wives and the way his parents interacted with one another after years of marriage had taught him what was real. His sick, twisted mental revenge against Ev had destroyed his desire to ever show tenderness and vulnerability to a woman again.

But Rhani…she set something off inside of him. Made him want more. Made him want to be more. For her.

And after the kiss they'd shared, he knew that on some level, she felt the same. Or could it be she'd been turned on by his stories of having sex with women in random places and wanted a taste of her own?

He had no clue. But he was sure of one thing: she wanted him. She just didn't want to be with him at his place. And they couldn't go to her apartment, because her brother was there. So instead, he decided now, it would be here, in her office, where there were no excuses to be made and no interruptions, he would make love to her.

Greg took a step forward and placed his palm at the base of her throat. The accelerated rhythm of her heart sent ripples of electricity through him. He slid his hand up and cupped the side of her face. She responded by leaning into his palm, gripping his wrist, and closing her eyes. Taking advantage of the exposed flesh, he dipped his head and placed a kiss below her ear. He inhaled the scent of her flowery perfume and slid his tongue out for a quick sample. They moaned at the same time. Encouraged by her response, he kissed his way up to her chin and then to her mouth. He moved closer so her hips were against the edge of the desk. Hating the loss of contact, he released the control he had by holding her head in his hands and instead, planted his palms on the desk on either side of her hips, successfully hemming her in.

Rhani didn't seem to mind. While he kept her in place,

she took control of the kiss by gripping his head in her soft hands. Her fingers slid around his neck, up into his hair, and down across his shoulders. The shivers her simple touch sent through his body were more of a turn on than some random unknown woman shoving her hands down his pants.

Wanting more, he leaned forward and teased the corners of her mouth with the tip of his tongue. Rhani opened to him, returning the kiss with such passion it took him by surprise. Unable to resist, he released his hold on the desk and threaded his fingers into her hair, taking charge again, then leaned her back just enough to give him a better angle to explore every corner of her mouth.

She inhaled in surprise when he lifted her onto the edge of the desk and positioned himself between those firm, shapely dancer's thighs. She wore a skirt, and her legs were bare. The only thing that stood between him and ecstasy was a pair of panties. The thought made his head swim, but he made up his mind not to rush.

But tease? Oh yeah, he was about to do that for sure. Greg went into forbidden territory and pushed against her core introducing her to the erection threatening to burst through his jeans. She moaned her pleasure, her hands now snaking down past his shoulders, pulling him closer. He trailed kisses down her neck until he reached the opening at the top of the tailored white shirt which revealed the sweetest, softest flesh he'd ever touched. With one hand, he worked the buttons until the shirt opened and exposed her satiny black bra. He covered one of her breasts and reveled in the fact that it filled his hand completely.

And he had big hands.

Rhani was perfect. After he pulled the shirt down over her shoulders, he yanked it from the waistband of her skirt then stood back for a moment to appreciate the woman before him, something else he'd never done before. "You're beautiful."

"So are you." She tilted her head to the side, and a slow, sexy smile spread on her face as something wicked flashed in her eyes. Not breaking eye contact, Greg gasped as she reached between them, ran her hand between his legs, and explored his tormenting bulge. She unbuckled his belt and unsnapped the front of his jeans. He closed his eyes and his pulse kicked into overdrive. He hadn't expected her to slip both hands into his briefs, so when she cupped him and gently squeezed, he nearly lost it.

"Does that feel good?" she asked in a voice so sexy it sounded unfamiliar. After all the conversations and sessions they'd had, she'd never spoken to him like this. Talk about an aphrodisiac.

"Better than good," he managed between raspy breaths. When he managed to regain some semblance of control and opened his eyes again, he met her gaze and returned the favor by sliding his hands beneath her skirt and testing what he searched for. Rhani gasped, and her response was all he needed. He gripped the thin edges of her panties, snatched them over her hips and down her thighs then sank to the floor before her, slipped them off over her ankles and the heels she wore. For a moment he spun them around on his finger, which made her laugh, then he tossed them to the floor.

"Lay back for me." When she did, he parted her knees and kissed his way up her inner thighs. Propped with her palms spread on the desk behind her, she raised her legs onto his shoulders; an invitation to have his way with her. He wanted to shout.

The way she writhed, he had to hold her hips in place in order to concentrate on the spot that would give her the ecstasy he wanted her to experience. By the time he finished nibbling and sucking, Rhani's back was flush with the desktop, and she reached her pinnacle calling out his name.

Greg couldn't remember when he'd spent so much time

in foreplay. It hadn't seemed important during his clothes-ripping, goal-oriented sessions with nameless women. This was something completely different. He held her trembling body until it calmed then picked her up and carried her to the chaise. End of Round One.

Time for Round Two. He laid her on her back, removed her skirt, and once again, took the time to appreciate the gift she offered him. The only article of clothing left was her bra. With her full breasts, round hips and thick, curly mane spread behind her head, he couldn't imagine a sexier picture. The way she gazed up at him with longing in her brown eyes tempted him to forego any more preliminaries and just go for the finish line. Only he didn't want to do that. He wanted to take his time, to sample, and explore. He wanted to know Rhani's body in a way he'd never known another women's before.

She parted her thighs wordlessly asking him to fill the open space. He did, but not before he took a moment to pull his own shirt over his head, tossing it somewhere in the realm of where her panties had landed. Next came finishing the job she'd started of removing his jeans.

Greg with pride at her reaction when she filled her hands with him. Once again, a wicked smile spread on her face as one of her knees swayed back and forth. He had no idea his therapist could be so…uninhibited. In the beginning, he thought she would be reserved, even prudish, when it came to sex. But she'd proven him wrong, and in some ways, he wondered if she were his match. Just the type of lover to tame him.

Naked, Greg nearly forgot to retrieve the condoms from his wallet before it got lost in the pile of clothes. After starting his sessions, she'd encouraged him to stop carrying protection in order to avoid the excuse for having random sex with strangers. He'd followed her advice. But hoping things would go the way he wanted in the office today, he'd made sure to grab a few to be on the safe side.

Settling between her legs, he leaned down, unhooked her bra, and took her breasts in his hands. He fondled them gently before giving attention to each one with his mouth. Her nipples hardened at the contact. She seemed to be enjoying this as much as he was, so he took his time. Rhani murmured an appreciative sound and reached out to touch him again. His mouth busy, he basked in the feel of her hands over every part of his body she could reach. His head, his shoulders, his back, and try as she might, she didn't succeed, but very nearly reached down to his butt. What she couldn't touch with her hands, she grasped with her thighs as she arched up beneath him, wrapping her legs around his waist and moving against him. She obviously wanted him to do more.

Calling on every bit of restraint to keep from plunging into her, he sat up, pulling her legs free, and explored her folds that were slippery and swollen from his mouth's attention. Rhani dropped her head back and spread her legs wider. The sounds escaping from between her open lips filled the office and only made him more eager.

Slow down. Slow down, he kept repeating in his head. This was killing him, but he was determined to give Rhani every ounce of pleasure he could. Instead of thinking about his own impending release, he concentrated on her as she moved to meet his rhythm. When he thought she couldn't take it any longer, he replaced his fingers with what her body really craved.

Rhani gasped then murmured something incoherent. Greg closed his eyes and maneuvered both hands beneath her hips so he could immerse himself fully into the paradise he'd fantasized about for months. She grabbed his shoulders and sunk her fingernails into his skin letting him know how much she was enjoying him.

They moved so perfectly together, like the beat of an

old Sade song. He could practically hear it playing in his head. For the first time in years, he found himself focusing on the journey rather than the goal. The tightness of her body around him reminded him of what she'd said about not having been with a man for quite some time.

For a moment, he lost his focus and his rhythm slowed. He had become so used to being with women who did nightclub bathroom hookups; he wasn't sure of what to say to her. Should he say something? Dirty talk had become second nature when he had sex, but it seemed wildly inappropriate with her. He risked a peek. Rhani had her eyes closed and her back arched as she moved to meet him. She seemed to be so far gone she didn't need to hear words. So he did what he did best and let his body do the talking.

He slowed for a moment, taking his time. Her response had been to slow down as well, but it didn't last long. She gripped him, holding on as she worked against him, demanding he increase the pace until the passionate sounds of their moans and damp skin slapping filled the room.

Rhani's breath came faster. She tightened her arms around his back and her hips moved furiously. He sensed that she had only seconds until she reached her climax. Being inside her felt so intense; he had to fight to hold off until she broke out into a scream that sent him right into the stratosphere. They rocked together until their bodies calmed. He rolled onto his side, pulling her with him, hooked a leg over her hip, and silently stroked her hair.

For the first time in years, he didn't feel the urge to run or break their contact; instead he felt comfort. He reached for the crocheted throw she kept hanging over the arm of the sofa beside them, covered them and closed his eyes.

Chapter Fourteen

*R*hani lay in his arms watching how his chest gently rose and fell after he'd drifted off to sleep. *I've lost my mind. I just had sex with a client and now I'm lying stark naked with him on the same chaise where I've counseled him for the past few months. I'm going to hell. Me, the girl who's always followed the rules and done the right thing, just helped a man break the celibacy I'd convinced him was crucial to his recovery. Oh, I'm going to hell.*

They had just crossed a line and there was no going back. But making love with him had surpassed everything she'd imagined. Greg had not only been passionate, but attentive, gentle, and considerate—a complete contrast to the way he described his liaisons with women in the past. She didn't understand why he'd been so quiet. He was a talker—always very animated. Even though he hadn't said much, it seemed as though he'd really enjoyed himself, and the way he'd demonstrated his concern for her pleasure had made her head spin.

What would happen now? If he were leaving her as a client, the sexual tension between them in sessions would be eliminated. But even though she knew it was the best move, the thought of not seeing him every Tuesday and Thursday dismayed her. His therapy had been ordered for a minimum of ninety days, but he needed to continue beyond the required deadline in order to maintain control over his old habits. She hoped he would contact one of the male therapists she'd recommended, but she couldn't force him.

She closed her eyes. *Relax and just savor the moment. Don't let crazy questions ruin this.* Once she did, she smiled at how truly scandalous the past hour had been. Now she understood where most of Greg's body mass was hidden, and the discovery had taken her breath away. He was tall and slender, not big and muscular like his brother she'd seen on the videotape, so she'd never expected him to be so well-endowed.

She hadn't experienced the sensation of warm skin against hers in ages. None of her recent relationships had developed to the point where she felt comfortable moving to a sexual level. They had been nice men with decent looks and decent jobs, but she hadn't felt the spark she'd felt the first time she met Greg. The initial, primal attraction was crucial for her. She couldn't understand women who said they didn't need a deep sexual attraction to their man. Of course, other qualities were essential, but if she didn't feel a thrill at the prospect of sex with him, why bother?

Greg stirred and released a sigh when she caressed his chest. "I guess I fell asleep. I'm sorry."

"Why? I like sleeping with you."

He pulled her closer on the armless chaise and placed a kiss on her forehead. "I do too, but it's a wonder we didn't fall off onto the floor."

"I didn't buy it with the intention of it being used in this way, you know," she said with a giggle.

"It certainly did serve the purpose, though." He gazed down at her, smiled and then asked, "You haven't changed your mind about our trip, have you?"

"No. I'm looking forward to it."

"So am I. I haven't been home since Christmas, and then I only stayed overnight. Being there the whole weekend will be nice."

♥♥♥

The day before the barbeque, they arrived in Atlanta. On the way to the house from the airport in the car he'd rented to get them around the city, Rhani retreated inside her thoughts. She still wondered how much they should tell his family about their relationship. He had given her the choice of staying in a guest room at his parents' house or getting a hotel room together. After he explained the house rules, she decided to try her best to make a good first impression and stay at the house. When he called to let his mother know, she asked them to come by for drinks and hors d'oeuvres at 6 o'clock p.m.

"It'll take less than a half-hour to drive to their house," Greg explained. "They live on the west side, which used to be the exclusive part of town for blacks. My father is a real traditionalist, so he's refused to leave the area, even though other areas have become new enclaves for us. This is their second house. Only Nick grew up there. The house where the rest of us were raised is about ten minutes away."

"It's only two-fifteen. We're *very* early."

"There's no arrival time at our house. Mama just wanted us to know when everybody would be coming for drinks tonight. You don't need to be concerned. Until then, we all just sit around and talk."

"Even that makes me nervous."

"Why?"

"I'll be the stranger, and I'll be in the midst of a roomful of doctors."

Greg laughed. "You deal with doctors all the time. Don't the majority of your clients come from doctor referrals?"

"Yes, but that's different. Those are professional relationships. I didn't grow up around professional people, and I don't have a clue what they talk about in an informal social setting."

"The same stupid stuff other families talk about when they get together—the latest gossip, the grandkids, vacations, television, books, who's screwed up since the last time we all got together." He paused and smirked. "I guess I'll get the prize for that one this year. Mama has a rule. She says, 'At family gatherings, no one is a doctor,'" and she means it. If my father or brothers start talking shop, she puts a quick end to it. If they want to do it, they have to go into Daddy's office."

"Do you think they're going to pick on you?"

"Probably, but they'll dial it back a bit since you'll be there."

"It sounds as though Mama doesn't play."

"She doesn't, but she reprimands you in such a sweet way, you don't even know you're being chastised." He laughed again.

"What do your brothers' wives do? Do they all work?"

He gave her a little background on the sisters-in-law as he drove. "Mona, Vic's wife, is married to medicine, and she doesn't believe in working, but she's very involved with all kinds of charity activities. Cydney is a homemaker. Her and Jesse's kids are little, so she's busy at home. Gianne, Mark's wife, is a school librarian or media specialist, as she prefers to be called. Charles' fiancée, Adanna, is a nurse, and she's started a foundation she and Charles created to raise money for the hospital in Nigeria where she used to work. They both work at the Atlanta children's hospital."

"How do you plan to answer questions about us?"

"Like what?"

215

"Like, aren't we breaking some kinds of rules by dating each other?"

"I'll say, yes we probably are, but we're having too much fun together to worry about it."

All she could do was shake her head.

"By the way, I made an appointment for next Tuesday with Steven Bolling. You can send him my file."

"Good. I'll call Sherylle and tell her to do it today."

"Here we are," he said, a few minutes later, as he turned into the entrance of the Guilford Forest subdivision.

"These homes are incredible." Rhani didn't take her gaze from the passenger window for a second as they wound their way through the quiet residential area. "I'm a New York native, and I'm not used to seeing empty streets, especially in the middle of the summer."

"You see more of that in the city itself. We're in the suburbs, and it's too hot here to hang outside. Everybody's inside with the air on." He turned into the driveway and parked behind a car with a rental sticker on the back. "Looks like Marc's here already. Besides us and my aunts and uncles, he and Gianne are the only ones coming in from out of town." He exited the car and went around and opened her door. "You're gonna turn blue if you don't take a breath," he said, taking her hand. "There's nothing to be nervous about. Let's go see who's here."

They walked up the long sidewalk to the front door of the traditional-style brick house. He rang the bell, turned the antique brass knob and then stepped inside with a shout. "Hey, where is everybody?"

"That can't be anybody but Greg and his big mouth," a deep male voice responded.

His brother came around the corner with a ready smile.

"Ma, the New Yorkers are here!" He grabbed Greg into a hug. "Good to see you, man."

"This is my brother, Marc. You kind of met him already," Greg said, referring to the Las Vegas phone video. "This is Rhani Drake."

Marc didn't look surprised to see her, which meant their mother had already told him Greg was bringing a female companion. "It's a pleasure, Rhani."

"When did you get here?" Greg asked. "And where's Gianne?"

"She's in the kitchen with Mama. We got here about two hours ago."

Greg took her hand, and she followed him down a hall, dreading what might happen once they reached the kitchen.

"Hey, Mama! We're here," Greg announced as they entered a kitchen probably five times the size of the one in her apartment. Rhani saw the woman with platinum blond hair first. *Oh, God, she's stunning.* So this was Marc's wife. Her trendy hairstyle contrasted with her mocha complexion and instantly made Rhani feel like the ugly stepsister, but she smiled nevertheless.

"Gregory!" The slender older woman rested a chocolate-covered spatula on top of the cake she was icing and rushed to meet them. "And this must be Rhani. I'm so happy you're both here."

"This is my mother, Lillian, and Marc's wife, Gianne. Ladies, this is Rhani Drake."

"Please, pull up a stool and join us, Rhani. I take it you two had a good flight."

"Yeah, it was uneventful, which is always good when you're flying," Greg answered then turned to his tow-headed sister-in-law. "What's new with you, girl? Still enjoying married life?"

Gianne's light brown eyes twinkled. "You know it."

"Where's the baby?" he asked, peering into the family room.

"In the library taking a nap," his mother answered. "I didn't want to put her all the way upstairs, because we might not hear her when she wakes up. Do you two want some sweet tea? It's hot out there."

Rhani knew she'd feel more comfortable keeping her hands occupied. "Yes, thank you."

"I'll get it," Greg said, crossed the room and opened the refrigerator.

"How long will you and Rhani be staying?" His mother sent him a hopeful glance as she positioned the second layer and spooned the rest of the rich-looking chocolate icing over it.

"Since the holiday falls on Friday this time, we can stay until Sunday evening."

Mrs. Stafford looked pleased. "Good. When you came home for Christmas, you ran in and out so fast we weren't sure you were actually there. Did you bring your luggage in?"

"No. It's still in the car."

"Well, when you do, you can put Rhani's in the blue bedroom. She'll be rooming with Adanna. You and Charles can share the tan room. Uncle Rod and Aunt Velma should be pulling in sometime soon, and I'm putting them in the gray room."

"Gee, Mama. Charles and Adanna are engaged. Don't you think they can share a room?"

She gave him the side eye. "They're not married *yet*, Gregory."

Hearing all of this talk about accommodations played right into Rhani's curiosity. "How many bedrooms do you have?"

"Six including the master," she said shaking her head. "When we bought this house, most of the boys were in high school or college, but they still came home for holidays and summer break. It only made sense to have enough room for everyone. Now we have grandchildren who spend the night." She turned her palms up and shrugged. "Gregory, show her around when you bring your bags in. Our home is your home, so don't be shy. If you can't find something, just ask."

"She stocks this house like a hotel," Gianne said with a chuckle. "Wait until you see the guest bathrooms. The Intercontinental Hotel doesn't do as good a job."

Mrs. Stafford gave them a proud yet reserved smile. "I always want our guests to feel comfortable."

"This is a gorgeous house," Rhani said, giving the European-style kitchen and the family room's stone fireplace and wall of windows an admiring scan. "I've lived in apartments all my life, so having an entire house is like a fantasy."

Her comment seemed to spark his mother's interest. "Did you grow up in Manhattan, Rhani?"

"No, the Bronx. I live in Manhattan now, and the apartments there are notorious for being small. I have a girlfriend whose apartment is less than nine hundred square feet."

The older woman's eyes widened. "Lord have mercy! How in the world does she manage?"

Marc let out a howl. "Mama can't imagine that. Her closet is probably nine hundred square feet."

"Stop exaggerating, Marcus! I have a nice closet, but it's

nowhere near that big."

"Well," Rhani explained. "She lives alone, and she's a whiz at organization and space conservation. Actually, her place is cute, but she just can't throw any parties there."

"My daughter-in-law, Mona has the most extravagant closet I've ever seen." She removed two bowls from the refrigerator and removed the plastic wrap from two golden cake layers.

"Yeah," Greg mumbled. "You could park a couple of cars inside that sucker. I remember Vic gave us the tour when they were building the house. I thought I'd walked into another bedroom."

Rhani gaped at him. "Seriously? I'd love to see it."

"Don't listen to them. These boys exaggerate everything."

"Tell the truth, Mama." Marc grinned.

"Yes…Mona's closet is quite large." She spread whipped cream over the first cake layer then topped it with fresh strawberries. Rhani noticed a disturbing note in her voice and wondered how well Mrs. Stafford got along with Mona.

Greg rose from the table. "I'm going out to get our bags. Be right back."

"I'll help you," Marc stood and followed him toward the front door.

Rhani's gaze zeroed in on the well-defined muscles under Marc's tight t-shirt. He was an exquisite model of male perfection. She shook her head and hoped Gianne hadn't noticed her admiration. Just in case she had, Rhani said, "Mrs. Stafford, are all your sons so good-looking?"

"I'm afraid so. You have no idea how hard Victor and I worked when they were growing up to get them to understand that they were more than their looks, but those little girls made my job twice as hard. I'm so glad they are all finally settling down."

"Just wait until you see them all together," Gianne said with a giggle. "It's a beautiful sight."

Rhani already liked her. Marc's wife seemed to be warm and friendly and down to earth. A few seconds later, she got to see the third of the six brothers. Greg and Marc returned with the suitcases followed by a gorgeous dark-skinned woman and a man who resembled Marc without the bulk and long hair.

"Look what the wind just blew in!" Marc said with his arm hooked around his brother's shoulder. "They were pulling up when we walked outside."

"That's Charles and Adanna. He's Marc's twin," Gianne said, offering commentary Rhani appreciated.

Mrs. Stafford wiped her hands on a kitchen towel and met the couple with hugs. "I'm surprised you're here early. Weren't you working today?"

"No, I was on call, but things were slow. They'll pick up tomorrow with all of the fireworks and barbeque injuries."

Greg came up behind her and circled his arms around her waist. "I want you to meet Rhani Drake. This is Charles and his fiancée, Adanna."

"Hello, Rhani," she said with a British accent Rhani wasn't expecting to hear. "We didn't know you were joining us. It's great to have a little more estrogen in the mix."

"It's great to meet you." Rhani studied them for a fraction of a second. Another beautiful woman, only she and Charles were a study in contrasts. She was short and curvy with ebony skin and eyes and closely-cropped natural hair; while tall, golden skinned, green-eyed Charles towered above her. A beautiful couple.

"Me too," Charles said, shooting Greg a confused look before he turned to Rhani. "I hope you're prepared to have fun this weekend."

"I certainly am. It's a treat just to be around such a big family. It's just my brother and me."

"Us too," Gianne said, pointing to Adanna and herself.

"Really? It's hard for me to imagine what it would be like growing up in such a large family."

Adanna nodded in agreement. "I love being around them when the whole tribe gets together. In my country, there are many very large families, and I always envied them, so I look forward to these family celebrations."

"Your accent is marvelous," Rhani said. "It sounds so regal compared to American English."

"Thank you. I'm still getting used to the way people talk here in Atlanta. Charles and I haven't been here a year yet, and sometimes I feel as though I need a translator."

"Ah. bless your heart, shawty. Ain't nothin' so different about da A. We dirty South to the bone," Charles said, pouring on the southern accent and mixing it with Atlanta slang."

Adanna swatted him. "See what I mean?"

"Greg told me you adopted your daughter from Nigeria," Rhani said to Gianne when everyone finished laughing. "That's wonderful. I can't wait to meet her."

"She's not much of a baby anymore. In a few months she'll be two, and she talks non-stop. We just can't figure out if she's speaking English or Yoruba," Gianne said with a smile that spoke of her love for her adopted daughter.

"Whatever it is," Mrs. Stafford said. "It's adorable.

"Do you have any kids?" Gianne asked her.

"Me? No. I've never been married, and I've put all of my time and energy into my job for the past couple of years."

"You're a therapist, right?"

Rhani sent Greg a fleeting glance. "Yes."

"Do you like your work?" his mother asked.

"Very much."

"I taught school before I had this army of boys. Back then, I loved being in the classroom, but I don't know if I could do it now. This is a whole different generation of children."

"They're a little more world-wise, but all of them aren't bad the way some people think," Gianne said. "I love my kids. Most of them are eager to learn, and since what I do involves technology, they're more interested than they might be in other subjects."

"You're a media specialist, aren't you?"

Her heart-shaped face broke into an appreciative smile. "Yes, and you got it right! Most people outside of the school system still call us *librarians*."

"I made that mistake when we first met," Marc chimed in. "She looked at me like I was missing a couple of screws and swiftly corrected me."

"Where's Daddy?"

"You know your father, Greg. He's at the office, and he promised to be home before everyone gets here tonight. Vic is working today too."

The next brother to arrive entered the family room alone. A few inches shorter than the others with a five o'clock shadow and sparkling aqua eyes, Rhani thought he was downright adorable. Greg introduced him as Nick, the youngest of the brood, and then he asked, "Where's Cherilyn?"

"I have no idea," Nick answered leaving the family exchanging questioning glances.

Greg voiced everyone's internal question. "You have no idea? Last time I came home, you two were joined at the hip. What's going on, man?"

Nick shrugged nonchalantly. "She said she needs to take a break, because it was getting too serious."

Mrs. Stafford whirled around looking shocked by his disclosure. "What? When did she come to that conclusion?"

"A couple of weeks ago." Judging by the way he refused to look anyone in the eye, Nick seemed embarrassed.

Gianne leaned over and whispered in Rhani's ear. "Wow, we all thought Nick and Cherilyn's would be the next wedding."

"I'm so sorry to hear that, Nicholas. Cherilyn is a sweet girl. Is there any hope you two will get back together?"

"I don't know, Mama. We'll see what happens."

Luckily, for his sake, the doorbell rang, and a statuesque woman with long, thick hair swept over one shoulder entered with two older boys.

"Hey, Mona!" a collective greeting rang out.

"She's Vic's wife, right?" Rhani asked Adanna.

"Yes. Isn't she beautiful? She's a former Miss Georgia."

Gianne laughed. "She's so tall; she makes me feel like a midget."

They watched with interest as Ramona warned her sons about their behavior. After they said hello to the adults, she shooed them off to the downstairs theater where Greg said the kids usually hung out. She handed the foil-covered pan she carried to Mrs. Stafford. "I had Maite make three dozen of those empanadas everybody likes so much."

"Who is Maite?" Rhani asked. "I never heard Greg mention her."

Adanna snickered. "Because she's Mona's live-in housekeeper."

"Oh, lucky her. I've never lived in a place big enough to warrant hiring someone to clean it."

"Make sure Greg takes you to see Vic and Mona's house while you're here. It's like a mini-castle, the most beautiful house I've ever seen, and there are some spectacular ones in Vegas."

That piqued Rhani's curiosity. "Does everyone live in huge houses like this?"

"When we relocated here, Charles said having a large home is kind of expected of Atlanta doctors," Adanna chimed in. "A housekeeper or at least a cleaning service is necessary, especially if the wife has her own career. I'm staying with relatives right now, but once Charles and I get married we're going to live in the high-rise condo he owned before he came to Nigeria. He uses a service. So do Marc and Gianne. Mona is the only one who has a live-in."

"We should go see if Mama needs any help," Gianne suggested. "Honey, listen for ChiChi, please," she said to Marc as the three women rose and filed into the kitchen, where Ramona and Mrs. Stafford were chatting.

"What time should we expect Vic?"

"I'm the last person you should ask," Mona grumbled. "He doesn't even bother to give me an ETA anymore. It's pointless."

Her mother-in-law sent her a sympathetic glance. "I

remember those days. If I hadn't had a houseful of boys to keep me occupied, I probably would've gone crazy. For the first few years I taught school, but by the third baby, I just couldn't handle the job and everything else."

"I hate being left alone all the time, Mama. I *really* despise it."

"We came to see if you need any assistance," Adanna said.

Mona poured herself a glass of wine and watched Mrs. Stafford arrange several cookie sheets on the center island.

"Thank you, girls. There isn't much to do. I don't cook like I used to. There are too many of us now. I ordered the appetizers yesterday. They only have to be reheated. The cold ones are in the refrigerator. They just need to be put into the chafing pans or on platters. Wash your hands, and I'll give you each an apron so you don't ruin your clothes. Wine is on the counter. Help yourselves. If you want something stronger, it's on the bar."

They followed her directions, but Mona remained on her stool in the corner. She didn't look like the apron type anyway.

The chiming of the doorbell and ensuing commotion in the foyer announced another arrival. "That must be Cydney and the munchkins." Mrs. Stafford walked toward the hall leading to the front of the house. "We're in the kitchen, Cydney," she called out over the noise. "Bring the baby in here. The girls can go downstairs with the rest of the children."

"I haven't seen the new baby yet," Gianne said. "It looks like Jess and Cyd are trying to break your record, Mama."

"How are the wedding plans coming along, Adanna?" Mona took a long sip of wine.

"Everything is almost done. The bridesmaid's dresses have been completed. And the dressmaker also made matching hats and vests for the groomsmen."

"Rhani, Adanna and Charles are having a multi-cultural ceremony," Gianne explained.

"Many Nigerian brides have two ceremonies—a traditional one and what's often called a white wedding." Adanna described further. "We didn't want to do both, so we decided to combine them. We'll have a combination of Nigerian and American attire, food and music." She chuckled. "It should keep everyone happy."

"What a great idea. I hope it all goes well."

"Well, I hope you will be there. Perhaps you don't know this, but bringing a woman home to a family celebration is how the Stafford brothers always introduce them before they propose."

Feminine laughter erupted in the kitchen when Rhani's eyes bugged. "Is that true?" She looked to Mrs. Stafford for an answer.

"Let's just say my sons never bring women home to meet Victor and me unless they are *very* serious."

Charles appeared at the pass-through window between the kitchen and family room. "What's so funny?"

"Oh, we were just telling Rhani to beware now that she's been introduced to the family," Mona explained. "We all know a wedding isn't far behind."

Rhani felt heat rush into her face, and she stuttered, "I—I don't think we're anywhere near—that. In fact, I was surprised when he invited me."

"Maybe so," Mona continued with a sneaky smile on her stunning face, "but we're just telling you the way it's always gone. These brothers always have a plan, and they don't deviate from it."

"She's right, Rhani," Charles whispered, and Rhani assumed he didn't want Greg to hear his confirmation of Mona's declaration. It is the way things go in this family. Look at her. She's blushing!"

"Honestly," she insisted. "We just met a few months ago."

"What difference does that make? I knew I was going to marry Adanna the first time I saw her." He winked at his fiancée. "And Marc said the same thing about the night he met Gianne."

Mortified now, Rhani dropped her gaze and busied herself with placing the hors d'oeuvres on the baking sheet.

"You all leave Rhani alone," Mrs. Stafford admonished her tittering family. "We'll just have to wait and see. Charles, go back with your brothers and leave the girl talk to us."

"Move out of the way, Charles," an attractive woman carrying a baby on her hip who reminded Rhani of actress Nia Long pushed him aside with a bump of her other hip. "Let me get in on the girl talk."

"Okay, I can take a hint. I'm going." He retreated to the family room where the men were watching television.

"Rhani, this is my other daughter-in-law, Cydney. She's married to Jesse. Rhani is Greg's guest this weekend," Mrs. Stafford said, obviously unsure of what to call her.

"Nice to meet you, Rhani." She set the infant carrier on the upholstered bench in the breakfast nook. She washed her hands then walked over to one of the kitchen drawers and tied on an apron which read *Kiss My Grits*. "Mama, you have enough aprons here for every student at Le Cordon Bleu." She squeezed in at the island next to Rhani and fell right in with the assembly line.

Mrs. Stafford went right to the baby, bent down and kissed the sleeping infant's face. "I've received most of them as gifts. Everyone knows how I love to entertain. The funny thing is I don't cook much anymore. Tomorrow our feast is coming from This is It."

"What's that?" Rhani asked, thinking about how expensive the mountains of appetizers must have been, and Mrs. Stafford was talking about having an entire barbeque catered the very next day.

"One of Atlanta's best soul food caterers," Greg's mother said. "This family has tripled in the past ten years, so no more cooking for me."

"Their food is wonderful," Mona added. "Vic and I used to go there all the time before he got so…" She downed the rest of her wine. All of the women shared a questioning glance, but no one said a word.

For the next hour, Rhani felt right at home sipping wine and helping to reheat the finger foods. At one point, Greg peeked through the window as though he were checking to see she was getting along with the female battalion. He winked. She smiled and raised her glass.

Greg's father and brother, Jesse came through the front door together just as Greg lit the first flames beneath the chafing pans. "Right on time, Daddy. What's up, Jess?"

"Listen to that New York accent," the dignified, gray-haired man said. He was a dead-ringer for General Colin Powell, and Rhani understood how he and his wife had created such handsome sons. He met Greg and Marc with enthusiastic hugs. Their love for each other was so apparent, and it touched Rhani's heart yet saddened her at the same time. If only her family had the same kind of affection for each other. But then it served no purpose to dwell on what might have been. This was a night for fun, not dwelling on unfulfilled dreams. She left the kitchen in response to Greg's beckoning finger.

"Daddy, Jess, I'd like you to meet Rhani Drake." He slipped an arm around her waist. "This is my Dad and my second oldest brother."

"Hello, Rhani. I see Lillian has already put you to work," his father said, glancing at her French maid's apron. "Well, you are certainly welcome here." He seemed to be studying her as he spoke, not in a critical way but as if he'd seen her before.

Of course he had seen her before—on television— running from the cameras. Rhani pushed the thought to the back of her mind and returned his scrutiny, amazed at how Greg was an intriguing mixture of both parents. "Thank you. I'm having a great time already."

She wasn't sure how to act when Jesse bent down and kissed her cheek. "Tomorrow is when all the fun happens. Mama even hired a DJ. I hope you like to dance."

Her eyes widened. "Are you serious?"

Greg grinned. "He sure is. We're going to show these folks how to turn it up New York style."

Before they arrived, she'd had a mental image of them sitting around sharing polite conversation, but it looked like the day might be more promising than she expected. She couldn't wait.

A distressed cry moved Gianne from her seat. "There's ChiChi."

"I'll get her," Marc volunteered. "Enjoy your wine," he said with a smirk. Gianne grunted. "He's such a pain in the butt. I'm not as staunch a raw vegan as he is. He doesn't drink fermented beverages.

A few minutes passed, and Marc returned to his seat next to Greg with the toddler in his arms.

"Hey, Little Bit," Greg said with a smile. "You're even prettier than the last time I saw you."

Rhani and the rest of the family watched in fascination when ChiChi stared at Greg for a long moment then reached her arms out in his direction. He took her from Marc, and she studied him again then spoke to him in what her parents had dubbed, *Engoruba*, a combination of English and Yoruba.

"No joke? Seriously, girl?" He kissed her pudgy cheek. "If I'd known, I would've been here sooner."

ChiChi giggled and took his face between her little hands.

"She remembers you. At first I believed she thought all of you brothers were the same person, but you have such an amazing effect on her. ChiChi doesn't respond that way to anybody but Marc."

"It's incredible," he observed. "The longer she's with you, the more she looks like you and Marc."

The way Greg smiled at the baby put a lump in Rhani's throat, an expression she'd never seen from him and showed a side of him she previously didn't believe existed. Every hour she learned something about him she'd never have seen back in New York.

Chapter Fifteen

"She fits right in, man," Jesse said, as he and Greg watched Rhani make trips in and out of the kitchen with the other women to fill the chafing pans with all kinds of great smelling food.

Greg grinned at the notion that she seemed to hit it off with his mother and sisters-in-law. "Yeah, she looks like she's having a good time."

"And you're happy about it." Jesse phrased it as a statement not a question and eyed him with a smirk.

"Yeah, I am."

"Do you have something to tell us, man?" Charles asked.

Greg shook his head. "Not yet."

"Did you hear him? He said *yet*," Nick pointed out, eliciting a laugh from his brothers.

Their mother called to Mona from the food table. "Mona, since Vic isn't here yet, do you want to fix him a plate?"

He and his brothers all wore shocked expressions and the women appeared uncomfortable when Mona swept her hair over her shoulder and said, "No. He'll just say he already ate. I've stopped saving dinner for him at night, because I just end up throwing it in the trash."

What was going on between Vic and his beautiful wife? He and Mona had been married for almost twelve years and, even though they weren't openly demonstrative with their affection, their deep love for each other had always been evident. This was the first time they'd heard her speak negatively about Vic.

His father interrupted the uneasy silence that followed when he stood and said, "Let's say the blessing."

After the mothers fixed the children's plates, called them upstairs and situated them at a card table in the family room, Mona and Cydney introduced them to Rhani. The adults served themselves, then the couples paired off and jockeyed for seats. Maite's empanadas turned out to be the biggest hit of the evening.

"How does she make these?" Charles asked after he went for his second helping.

"I've never watched her," Mona answered. "But she says they're made with brisket, garlic crema, pico de gallo, and feta cheese. Divine, aren't they?"

"You don't know what you're missing," Nick taunted Marc and Gianne, who were raw vegans and had their plates filled with salad, fruit, raw almonds and other things his mother knew the couple ate.

"Yes we do," Marc fired back. "But I'm not going to ruin everyone's appetite with the facts."

"Thank you, Marcus," his father jumped in before the usual nutrition debate began. "Rhani, tell us about yourself."

Greg held his breath. Her shocked expression told him she wasn't ready to be the center of attention, and he hoped nobody asked her anything embarrassing. "Daddy, can she eat before you give her the third degree?"

His father frowned and ignored his objection. "Tomorrow will be organized chaos, so I'd like to get to know her before the crowd descends on us."

"It's all right," she said after she swallowed and dabbed her mouth with a napkin. "There isn't a lot to tell. I was born and raised in New York in the Bronx. I got my undergrad degree from Fordham and my Masters in psychology from NYU. I worked for a couple of years with a non-profit behavioral health organization before starting my own practice a few years ago."

"Do you have any family?" his mother asked.

"My parents still live in the Bronx, and right now my brother is staying with me while he's home for the summer from City College."

"What do you like to do when you're not working?" It didn't sound as if his mother was being nosy, just a sincere interest in the woman he'd invited home to meet the family.

"I *love* to dance," Her face lit up at the mention of her favorite pastime. "And I take jazz and hip-hop classes at the Broadway Dance Center twice a week."

"Another amazing thing she does is mentor teenage girls," Greg added with pride. "She goes back to her old neighborhood a couple of times a month and talks to them about life and what it takes to be successful."

Cydney's face brightened. "Really, Rhani? I'd love to do the same thing, but I don't have a career, so I don't know how much I could tell them."

"You don't have to be a professional woman to mentor girls. Many of them don't know proper etiquette, or correct child care or how to take care of a home. It's not like back in the day when the older women taught the younger ones about those things. Now these girls just have to figure it out on their own."

His father gave her an approving smile. "Impressive. Giving back is an important component of success. You sound like a busy woman, Rhani."

"Sometimes too busy. Thank you."

"We've all read about what's going on with you and Greg and seen the news stories. Since you're his therapist, aren't you afraid of what might happen if someone wants to make an issue about you having a *personal relationship* with a client?" A collective groan echoed in the room when Ramona asked the one question everyone else had so far avoided.

"Honestly, I have thought about it, but I don't know of anyone who's out to get me." Rhani chuckled, but Greg could hear the anxiety in her voice.

Nick said what Greg knew the others were thinking. "But there *are* people out to get Greg."

Time for him to jump in, so alternating his gaze between Mona and Nick, Greg answered them. "We don't want to talk about it today. We're here to have a good time and get away from all of scrutiny and"

Before he could finish, Vic came through the front door and walked into the family room looking more haggard than Greg had ever seen him look.

"Hi, Daddy!" His sons greeted him with big smiles, obviously happy to see him.

He walked over to the card table where they were seated and gave both some dap. "Sorry I'm so late. It couldn't be helped."

Mona snorted, and his mother quickly tried to cover. "There's plenty of food on the table, and the wine is in the pass-through window."

"If you want a real drink, everything's on the bar," his father offered, probably assuming Vic needed the extra fortification.

Of all his brothers, Vic was the most serious, and he

had a more austere appearance. Greg noticed he also looked thinner than he had last Christmas. The stress of his job as chief of surgery seemed to be taking its toll. Once Vic fixed himself a heaping plate and poured a Scotch and soda, Greg introduced him to Rhani.

"It's a pleasure, Rhani," he said with a weary smile then glanced around the room. "It's good to see everybody. Gianne, Adanna, it's been a while. You two are looking beautiful, as usual." He grabbed a spot on the sofa and dug into his overflowing plate. "Wow, I'm hungry. I didn't eat, because I knew Mama would have a feast even if it's only appetizers."

"God forbid Mama has to throw any food away," Mona grumbled.

He glowered at her. "What are you bitching about now? Don't start. I'm not in the mood."

"So what else is new?" She snapped back with a sneer. "You haven't been in the mood for three months."

With that, everyone in the room concentrated on their plates, afraid to look at the feuding couple.

"This should be a private conversation," his mother warned in a tone that left no question about her seriousness. "Either take it to another room or take it home."

The Queen had spoken, and if Greg didn't think he'd be slapped, he would've laughed aloud at the way the family devoured the rest of their food at light speed. The women returned to the kitchen, the children went back down to the theater, and the men retreated to the television.

"You can have my chair," his father offered as Vic refilled his glass. "Looks like you need it."

Vic gratefully flopped into the recliner and picked up the remote control. After he took two long drags of his Scotch, he rested his head back and hit the massage button.

Greg sat at the end of the sofa next to him and leaned in close. "Was Mona serious when she said you two haven't rocked the mattress in three months?"

"I don't know. Yeah, I guess so."

"No wonder she's all bent out of shape."

Marc joined them in the corner. "You and Mona have always been my role models for how to get it right. What's going on, man?"

"She's hostile all the time now. When I got promoted to chief of surgery, she was thrilled, because it meant she'd have more money to shop. Now it's almost as though she's jealous of my job. Mona's an intelligent woman. Why doesn't she understand that the position came with more responsibility than I had as a staff doctor? There's nothing I can do about it."

"So you're just brushing it off?" Greg scowled. "Mona is a beautiful woman, and if you're not taking care of business, somebody else will."

Vic looked at Greg as though he'd taken leave of his senses. "Are you volunteering your services, Mr. Bang 'em in the Alley? She's not that kind of woman."

"What kind of woman, Vic?" Marc asked. "Beautiful? Vibrant? Sexy? You can't ask her to put aside her sexual desires because you're *busy*."

Greg continued. "I know I'm not married, and maybe I shouldn't even say this, considering the issues I've had, but you're a *doctor*. You know women's sex drives can be as strong as ours, even stronger at times. If you don't take care of this situation, you're going to have real trouble on your hands."

Vic's heavy brows drew together as he scowled at his younger brother. "Like you said, you're not married, so you're hardly an expert on the subject," Vic snarled.

Greg threw up his hands in surrender. "Fine, don't come crying to us when you go home one night and find somebody else doing her in your bed." The second the words left his mouth, a flash of Evelyn and her lover momentarily obscured his vision, but he was able to blink it away. He left his brothers with a dismissive wave and went to find Rhani.

He found her seated on one of the tall stools at the kitchen island. He inched up behind her, wrapped his arms around her waist, moved her hair aside and kissed her neck. Rhani looked over her shoulder and puckered her lips for a kiss. The other women smiled with approval.

"I saw you in that huddle. What were you guys talking about?"

"You don't want to know, believe me." He gave Mona a fleeting glance and noticed she was the only one who still had a wine glass in her hand. "Mama, do you mind if I steal Rhani for a few? I want to show her around the house."

"Go ahead. We're winding down anyway."

Rhani hopped down from the stool when he took her hand and followed him into the hall. "I wanted to look around, but I didn't want to seem nosy."

He turned left into the great room at the front of the house. "This is really the living room, but nobody ever uses it. We're always in the family room." They crossed the room, and he took her into another room. "This is my father's office. He rarely uses it anymore either. As he's gotten older, he prefers his recliner in front of the big screen."

Rhani scanned the built-in bookshelves filled with medical books, classics and family photos. "Nice room. It says a lot about him."

From there, he took her to the lower level. Her eyes widened when they entered a large room with a regulation-size pool table in the center. The walls were lined with framed photos from his and his brothers' school days, award ceremonies, graduations, and other events. She admired them and asked questions about each one. Chatter drew them into the theater where the kids were watching a popular animated movie.

"I'd kill for a room like this," she whispered glancing at the overstuffed recliners and wall-sized screen. "I love watching movies."

I guess I'll have to make sure we have a theater in our house then. What the...? *Being home around all these married couples must be affecting my mind.* He shook it off and addressed his nieces and nephews. "Hey, guys! What are you watching?"

"*Big Hero Six*," Trey, Vic's oldest son answered.

"I wanted to watch *Frozen*," Jesse's four-year-old daughter whined. "But they wouldn't let me."

"Why?" Greg asked, totally oblivious to the difference between the features.

"Frozen is for *girls*," her cousin said with a turned-up nose.

"Well, Aria should get to see what she wants too, so when this is over, she gets to watch *Frozen*. Okay?"

The boys groaned, and Aria, who was Cydney's spitting image, grinned and hugged his leg. "Thank you, Uncle..."

"Greg." He patted her head. "Don't mention it, baby."

"My, how very diplomatic of you. Who knew you were so good with kids."

"If there's one thing we always have a surplus of in this family, it's children. There were six of us, and now three of the six have kids of their own. My mother is in her glory."

"Yes, she seems to love being a grandmother."

"Don't let my father fool you. He gets as stupid over the grandkids as Mama does, but he just doesn't show it. You wouldn't believe how they go overboard for those kids at Christmas."

"That's sweet."

"Let's go up to the second floor. I'll show you your bedroom."

On their way through the main floor, they saw Ramona's back going out the front door. She'd left the boys there with Vic, who was now buzzed from the Scotch and sodas.

"Looks like either somebody will be driving Vic and the boys home or they're staying the night."

"That was a pretty uncomfortable scene. I'm sorry they're having problems."

"All couples have problems. Don't they, Madame Therapist?"

"Yes, but the determining factor is how they choose to work them out. It doesn't look as though Vic and Mona have gotten to the point where they're ready to resolve theirs yet."

When they reached the upper level, he showed her to the room his mother had assigned to her and Adanna. "I hope this room is okay for you. It has twin beds, so it might give you flashbacks of your dorm days."

"Are you kidding? It's great." She actually looked happy to be sharing a room with a woman she'd just met.

"You'd rather sleep in a twin bed here than with me in a king-sized bed at a hotel?"

"I didn't say that. I'd love to sleep with you tonight, but I wanted to stay here at the house. And in view of your parents' rules, I think it's best for me to stay on their good side." She stood on her tiptoes and kissed him.

"After what we did in your office the other day, it's *really* unfair of you to do this to me." He pushed the door closed with his foot, backed her against it and teased her lips open with his tongue. Her passionate response put his body on high alert, and he reached behind her to maneuver the lock.

"You're *not* going to talk me into this," she murmured against his chest.

His hands traveled over her curves, and she whimpered when he tilted his hips, cupped her bottom in both hands and grinded against her.

"Greg, are you in there?" Nick said from the other side of the door. "Uncle Rod and Aunt Velma are here. They want to meet Rhani."

With a groan, Greg dropped his forehead against the door and exhaled a long sigh. "Yeah, okay. Tell them we'll be right down."

Rhani giggled. "See, the universe is trying to tell you this can't happen. Let's go downstairs so I can meet your aunt and uncle."

Greg glanced down at his zipper. "Give me a couple of minutes. I can't go down there like this. Are you going to make me suffer the whole weekend?"

She cupped his face between her hands and kissed him. "I probably shouldn't say this, but learning to control your body is part of your therapy."

He lowered his head until their foreheads touched. "I hate you." He kissed the tip of her nose. "I really do."

"Yes, I can feel it." She wiggled against him, pushed him away and opened the door with a laugh. "We don't want to give anyone the wrong idea. I'll be in my room."

He rolled his eyes. "Of course not. We might as well go downstairs, so Uncle Rod can cross-examine me. Some people say women are nosy, but Rod could win an award for his interrogation skills."

A few minutes later, he and Rhani rejoined the family on the first floor. After the introductions were made, his father's brother embarked on his usual fact-finding mission.

"Are you back to work yet, Greg?"

"Not yet. I have another month to go on my suspension."

"What have you been doing? I mean, a man can't sit around and do nothing all day."

"It's only for ninety days, Uncle Rod. I look at it as an extended vacation." He gave Rhani a quick glance. "I've been catching up on all the things I haven't had time to do, like reading and working out."

Marc came to his rescue. "I've been meaning to ask how you're doing with the upper body routine I gave you. It looks like you've bulked up a bit."

"I'm up to four sets of each exercise," Greg said, thankful his brother disrupted their uncle's interrogation. "And I've upped the weight ten pounds. Still can't get into cardio other than the treadmill, though."

"Great. The treadmill is sufficient, as long as you push yourself and you're not just strolling and watching TV."

Rhani seemed to notice his dilemma, and joined in on the conversation hoping to effectively keep his uncle from continuing. "Since you're talking about exercise, what do you recommend for someone who sits still all day? I take dance classes twice a week, but that's all."

"Dance is an excellent full-body workout. Do you also belong to a gym?"

"No, my dance classes cost enough."

"If you don't have access to a treadmill, try to get in a thirty-minute walk on the days you don't have class. You already have a great body, so all you need to do is keep your heart in good working order."

Apparently bored with the conversation, Uncle Rod left them and joined Greg's father on the other side of the room.

"Thanks," Greg said with a grateful smile. "I love the dude, but he's a pain in the ass." He took Rhani's hand. "I want to show you something out back before it gets too dark." She frowned at the secretive grin he and Marc shared.

They exited the door leading to the back yard from the kitchen. She took in the manicured lawn and shrubbery. "What a nice yard. I've never lived anywhere that had one."

"My father's always been a real stickler for having a perfect lawn, but this yard also has a surprise at the back." She followed him down a path of stone pavers lined with flowering crape myrtle trees in alternating shades of pink, lavender, white and fuchsia. When they reached the rear of the property, her eyes widened.

"A lake! Oh, Greg, this is so pretty." She literally ran ahead of him to the water's edge. "Why did Marc give you that look when you said we were coming out here?"

He chuckled, caught up with her and waved toward a stone bench. "My mom and dad call this the *kissing bench*."

"Brought a lot of girls out here, have you?" she asked with a sidelong glance.

"I'm not the only one. By the time Mama and Daddy bought this house, most of us were in high school. It was the only place we could get some privacy when we brought a date home."

"Can we sit for a while?"

He brushed off the bench with his hand and sat then pulled her down to join him. "Why do you think I brought you out here?"

"It's so peaceful," she said, resting her head on his shoulder and admiring the sunset and the homes on the opposite side of the water. "Such a nice change from the city."

"If you like the suburbs so much, we need to get away from the city more often." He drew her into his side and pressed his cheek against her hair. "Would you ever leave Manhattan?"

Rhani looked up at him with a longing in her eyes as though she were seeing something invisible. "All my life I've dreamed about living in the suburbs in a real house with a yard, but I'm not convinced I'd be happy there. The pace is so much slower and everything isn't as accessible."

"What's nice about Atlanta is, even though it's much smaller than Manhattan, it offers many of the same things you'd find there: music, dining, nightlife, sports. Only they're easier to get to. Mass transit isn't on the same scale as the MTA, and it doesn't cover the entire suburbs. If you live outside of the city, you need to own a car."

"I imagine it must be annoying to have to drive everywhere." Something in her voice didn't sound quite convincing.

"If you did try living in the 'burbs, where would it be?" He gently wound one of her curls around his index finger.

"Probably somewhere across the river in Jersey like Cliffside Park or Palisades Park where I could still see the Manhattan skyline."

'It sounds like you've been doing a little research."

"I did a couple of years ago, before I started my practice, but I put the idea on the shelf." She caressed his chest with her open palm. "Thanks for bringing me to meet your family. I'm having such a nice time."

"The fun hasn't even started yet, but I'm happy you're enjoying yourself. You're going to have an even better time tomorrow."

"I thought it was just a barbeque."

"It's one of my mother's barbeques. The guys will be here at the crack of dawn to put up the tent and lay the dance floor."

She sat up straight and her jaw dropped. "You're kidding."

"No, we're talking about Lillian Stafford here. She doesn't believe in throwing a grill in the middle of the yard and surrounding it with folding lawn chairs. It's bigger than our Christmas weekend, because so many other people come. My father always invites some of his colleagues and even a few of the neighbors."

"They certainly have enough property to hold them all. This should be something."

He gave a throaty laugh. "It's something all right. The mosquitos will eat us alive if we stay out here now that it's getting dark, but before we go back inside, I have to kiss you. The bench requires it."

"Oh, the bench requires it, huh?"

"Yes, ma'am. Whoever sits here *has* to kiss." He slipped one arm behind her back and moved her hair to the side so he could access her neck.

Everything about the moment—the warm breeze, the fragrance of the flowers, the shadows from the setting sun, and the feel of his lips against her skin—was perfect. He would've been happy to stay right there all night. He trailed soft kisses across her cheek until he reached her mouth.

With one hand on her thigh he smiled to himself when she squeezed her thighs together and opened her lips to his seeking tongue. She eagerly returned his kisses and caressed his neck with her fingers. All he could think of was repeating the episode in her office, but it wasn't possible. They had to go back into a house filled with family, and she was sharing a room with Adanna.

She grabbed his shoulders and gave them a gentle shove. "Greg, they're expecting us back inside."

"So?" The sun had already set, and she couldn't see his devious smirk.

"So let's go in the house."

Greg groaned and rested his chin on the top of her head. "Are you trying to kill me? Okay, give me a minute."

When they re-entered the house, most of the family had gone back to their own homes. His father's other brother, Clifford and his wife, Betty had arrived from Birmingham.

"Your brothers said they didn't want to disturb you," his mother said with a smirk after Greg had introduced Rhani and they talked for a few minutes. "They said they'd see you tomorrow afternoon. Rhani, on Saturday I'm taking all of the girls out for a spa day, so please don't let Gregory talk you into going anywhere else."

"Sounds fabulous. Thank you."

"On Sunday we all go to church together. I hope you'll join us."

Greg hadn't mentioned church to her. They'd never talked about their beliefs, and since he didn't attend church in New York, he figured it would be a conversation to be had at a later date. They said goodnight to the remaining family and climbed the stairs to the second floor.

"Charles and Adanna must already be in our rooms, so

I guess I have to kiss you at the door like we're back in high school." His lips gently met hers and she sighed at the contact. "I'm glad you're here with me. Sleep well."

He walked to his room cursing himself for not talking her into getting a hotel room.

Chapter Sixteen

*R*hani opened the bedroom door and nearly floated inside. She quickly regained her composure when Adanna glanced up from where she was sitting on the bed smoothing a fragrant cream onto her arms and legs.

"Hello, roomie. I'm finished in the shower if you want to use it."

"Thanks. Usually I shower in the morning, but I want to check out the bathroom. Gianne told me about how Mrs. Stafford stocks the guestrooms."

Adanna chuckled. "Yes, take a gander. If you can't find it in there, it probably doesn't exist. Look at this basket." She pointed to a wicker basket containing both sweet and salty snacks, an Atlanta guidebook, bottles of spring water, and a TV Guide.

"She's a wonderful hostess. My apartment is microscopic, so I'm not used to having houseguests. I could learn a lot from her."

"We all could. You have no idea how gracious she is. I have to tell you about what she did for all the girls at Christmas."

Rhani sat on the side of the other bed and leaned forward, anxious to hear the story and discover more about this family she liked more with every passing hour.

"The family has a tradition of the husbands giving their wives a day to Christmas shop for themselves. From what I understand, in past years they had a limit, but last year they gave us their credit cards and said there was no limit. Rhani, I was stupefied, because I'm not even a wife yet. Charles had just proposed to me on Christmas morning," Adanna said with wonder in her voice. "A saloon came to pick us up, and it had a bar with mimosas already made for us."

"A saloon?" Rhani asked, confused by her terminology.

"I'm sorry. I keep forgetting you call them limousines here. We went to two malls and bought whatever we wanted then had lunch at one of her favorite restaurants where the staff treated us like royalty. Mama talked to us about being the daughters she never had because, as she says, 'Victor can only make boys.'" Her big, dark eyes sparkled as she spoke. "It was the most glorious day I've ever had in my life."

"Really? Greg never told me about all of that."

"So I guess he didn't tell you about his parents going to London to meet mine?"

Rhani blinked. "He sure didn't."

Adanna recounted the story of how her father and brother had been against her marrying Charles, not because he was American, but because he wasn't of the Igbo tribe. Rhani's mouth hung open while Adanna told her about the kidnapping and how Mrs. Stafford convinced Dr. Stafford to visit her parents two days after Christmas. "She's an amazing woman, and now she's also my wedding planner."

"Honestly, Adanna, I feel as though I've stepped into some kind of fairy tale. My family is so far opposite the Staffords it isn't even funny."

"It's the same with Gianne, Cydney and myself. I think because of our family backgrounds, we're attracted to men who have such strong family ties."

"But I didn't even know about Greg's family when I first met him. In fact, I wrongly assumed he came from a family with serious issues."

"Oh, you mean because of his *problem*?"

Rhani nodded. "Your family is okay with your marriage plans now?"

"More than okay. Let's just say Lillian and Victor went to London and charmed their undies off."

"That's awesome. I didn't get much of a chance to talk to Dr. Stafford today, and actually I'm kind of glad."

"Why?"

"Greg talks about his mother a lot. He clearly adores her, but he doesn't say too much about his father."

"I think they get along pretty well. Marc and Daddy were the ones who had the problem, but they seem to have worked it out."

"You have to tell me about it, but I want to take off this makeup, wash my face and brush my teeth first." Rhani rose, opened her suitcase, took out her pajamas, and then headed into the attached bathroom.

"Well, everything you could possibly need is on the counter."

"Oh, my God!" Rhani exclaimed, dumbstruck at the collection of toothbrushes, shampoos, conditioners, dental floss, and makeup remover wipes in one basket. At the other end of the vanity counter another basket contained body washes, lotions, baby powder, tampons, eye drops and pain relievers. "I feel like I'm in the cosmetics aisle at Duane Reade!"

After she finished her nightly routine and changed into her PJs, Rhani sat cross-legged on the bed and braided her hair. "Adanna, did you mean what you said earlier about when the brothers bring a woman home?"

"Yes. It's their pattern. Charles explained it like this: Over the years, he and his brothers avoided bringing girls they dated home to meet their parents, because Mama said it always upset her when she got to like them, and then a few weeks or months later, they disappeared because her sons had ended the relationship."

"So when they do, it means the relationship is serious," Rhani said, more to herself than to Adanna.

"That's right. Congratulations."

"Tell me about Marc and their father." Rhani lay on her stomach and propped a pillow under her chin.

Adanna went into detail about Marc changing his college major from pre-med to exercise physiology and Dr. Stafford's reaction to his decision. She explained their continuing conflict the way Charles had described it to her. "They had been at each other's throats for years until recently."

"So many parents want to plan out their children's lives, and they mean well, but it never works out. Marc seems to love Gianne and ChiChi very much, and she's not even his child. Greg told me they adopted her from Nigeria."

"Actually, I adopted her first." Rhani listened in amazement as Adanna unfolded the story of how the baby became a part of the Stafford family. "She was born at the hospital where I used to work, and her mother abandoned her because she had a severe cleft lip and palate. From the beginning I knew there was a reason why she came into my life, and I couldn't allow her to go into a children's home. Little did I know that on the other side of the world, Charles' brother and his wife couldn't conceive and were considering adoption. ChiChi became my patient after Charles operated on her. To make a very long story short, we brought her here to meet Marc and Gianne, and they fell in love with her. Once the Nigerian government approved my adoption, I moved here to the U.S. and we did a private adoption."

After they said goodnight, Rhani wiggled beneath the sheet and pulled it over her head. She couldn't question Greg about the purpose of this visit without putting him on the spot and perhaps setting herself up for possible humiliation. Tomorrow would surely be an interesting day.

Rhani awoke to the sound of an engine, a loud clattering outside the bedroom window and the aroma of coffee drifting upstairs from the kitchen. From the empty bed and the open bathroom door, she assumed Adanna had already gone downstairs. She peered out into the back yard where a large truck had backed up to the edge of the yard, and a crew of men were unloading metal poles and sections of what looked like a parquet floor. She showered, combed out her braids and pulled her hair into a ponytail, then dressed in a pair of shorts and a t-shirt. When it came time for the barbeque, she planned to change into a different outfit.

When she got downstairs, what appeared to be the normal separation was already in effect with the men in the family room and women in the kitchen. Everyone held a mug in their hands except for ChiChi, who happily sucked on a sippy cup.

"Good morning. Am I the only one who slept late?"

"No, Uncle Rod and Aunt Velma aren't down yet," Greg answered. "Do you want coffee? We have Mocha Swirl and Caramel Vanilla Cream." He pointed to the Keurig machine in the corner of the kitchen counter.

She grinned. "You know I do."

Mrs. Stafford came through the back door. "Everybody's up? I'm sorry about all the noise, but I scheduled the tent delivery for eight o'clock. No breakfast this morning. We'll be eating all day long. I bought six boxes of cereal and three gallons of milk. Bowls and spoons are on the counter. Help yourselves, and put your dishes into the dishwasher when you're done. We need to keep the kitchen clear for when they deliver the food at noon. Until then, you have the morning to do whatever you want."

"Yes, ma'am," all of her sons said in unison before she went back out into the yard.

Greg left the men and joined Rhani in the kitchen while she fixed her coffee. "We have the morning free. What do you want to do?"

"I want to see the house you grew up in. Can you take me there?" she asked as they both poured their choice of cereal into bowls.

"Okay, but that'll only take a few minutes."

"What do your brothers have planned?"

"What are you guys doing until barbeque time?" he called to the twins through the pass-through window.

"Nothing special, Charles answered.

"I have an idea," Marc said. "Why don't we go to the parade? I haven't been in years."

Rhani wrinkled her nose. "I've never cared much for parades."

"You've never been to one like this," Greg said with a laugh. "It's crazy. Step teams, choirs, and you know there's nothing like a black southern marching band. They have several each year."

"Really?"

Gianne nodded. "Really. It's a lot of fun unless it's too hot out."

Mr. Stafford chimed in. "If it gets really hot, the fire engines spray everyone along the parade route."

"I'll go, but I'm telling you one thing"—Gianne put a hand on her hip—"if they get my hair wet, there's going to be a showdown between me and some firemen."

Charles laughed. "Okay, we need to take lawn chairs and get a spot on Peachtree before eleven. The parade kicks off at noon. If we stay for an hour or so, we can be back here by two, so Mama doesn't develop an aneurysm."

Marc lifted ChiChi from her high chair. "Punkin, you'll love this. There are balloons and floats and music and dancing."

"Everybody'd better grab a bottle of water and a hat," Gianne suggested. "Honey, do you think your mother has any sunscreen around here?"

All of the brothers burst out laughing.

Gianne shrugged. "Yeah, I guess that was a dumb question. I'm going outside to ask her where it is and see if she needs us to do anything around here before we leave."

"Okay, it's settled then," Greg agreed. "As soon as everybody's ready, we can head out. I want to ride by the old house on the way. Rhani wants to see where we grew up."

The three women exited the back door where the workmen were busy setting up metal poles for the tent. Two others were snapping wooden sections together for the dance floor on the other side of the yard. Clearly in her element, Greg's mother directed the crew. When they approached and asked her what she needed them to do, she waved them away. "Velma and Betty will be here, if I need any help. You kids go and have fun, and make sure you're back by two."

She told Gianne where to find the sunscreen, and they all went upstairs to get ready for the parade.

Adanna and Charles rode with Rhani and Greg. Marc, Gianne and ChiChi followed them in their rental car. When they drove up to the hilly Niskey Lake area, Greg parked in front of a brick bi-level house.

He looked up at the property bordered with pine and old oak trees and smiled. "This is it. The house where we grew up."

Rhani scanned the 1960s-style traditional home. "It's nice, but it's hard to imagine all of you living there."

"It had quite a few rooms, but they were small. It didn't matter when we were little, but once we all got into high school it felt like we were bumping into each other at every turn."

The men immediately got out of the cars, left the engines running, so the women wouldn't suffocate from the heat. Rhani and Adanna watched as they stood together and studied the house that held nearly two decades of memories.

"Look at their faces," Adanna said. "They look as if they've just stepped back in time in their minds."

"Yes," Rhani dug in her purse for her phone. "And I have to get a picture of this." She rolled down the window and snapped a few shots of the brothers while they stood talking and laughing among themselves. "I don't think I've ever seen three such good-looking men. Later today I need to get some shots of all six of them together."

Gianne exited the other car, said something to Marc and joined Adanna in the back seat. "We might be here for a little while. ChiChi is napping, and the guys are telling stories. I just caught the tail end of one about Greg falling out of that big tree and breaking his collarbone."

"He told me he was the sofa diver and the stunt man when they were young."

"Yes," Adanna agreed. "There's no question he is the one with the charisma. What confused me was the conflict between Marc and Daddy. Greg was the first one to go against the family tradition and choose a non-medical career."

"Daddy says he always knew Greg would do something out of the ordinary, because he was a performer from birth. He finally admitted he believed Marc was the most brilliant one of his sons, and he would've made a world-class surgeon. I think Marc disappointed him the most," Gianne said with a touch of sadness. "They're still working on restoring their relationship, but it's much better than it used to be."

Rhani listened with interest. "Greg never told me."

Gianne eyed her with curiosity. "I assumed you knew everything about him, considering you're his therapist."

"He's no longer seeing me professionally. We both felt it best since we're personally involved now."

"I imagine that could prove to be sticky. Charles told me about the last time he visited Greg in New York right before he came to work in Nigeria. It really disturbed him."

She raised her eyebrows. "He never told me about that either." Hearing these things for the first time, Rhani wondered what else Greg had never shared with her.

"He felt Greg was out of control. He didn't confront him about it at the time, but he did call Greg the night he was released from jail and didn't bite his tongue about Greg's behavior."

"Well, it looks as though he's doing much better. Marc said Mama was thrilled when she found out you were coming home with him. Greg hasn't done that in a very long time."

Adanna cleared her throat. "They're coming back."

"Enough reminiscing," Greg said when he opened the car door and the heat rushed in. "Marc said ChiChi's awake, G."

"So much for my break." She chuckled and exited the

car. "See you downtown."

Charles returned and took Gianne's spot next to Adanna in the back seat. "I haven't been here in years. Brings back memories."

"Good ones, I hope," Rhani said.

"Very good. We had some great times there."

"Sure did." Greg gave the house a lingering glance before he put the car in gear and pulled off.

"One of these days you have to tell me the story about the tree."

"Okay." He grinned and headed toward downtown Atlanta.

The men carried folding chairs and found a place for them to sit at the curb in the shade of the Georgia-Pacific building on Peachtree Street. The parade turned out to be more fun than Greg had described. For the next hour, they enjoyed an eclectic mix of parade participants, moved to the beat of high school marching bands, sang along with the choirs and took pictures of celebrities riding on the backs of convertibles waving at the crowds along the route.

By the time they returned to the house, several cars were parked in the driveway and on the street. Rhani couldn't believe the transformation the yard had undergone while they were downtown. A white tent covered a large portion of the yard and a shiny wooden dance floor filled the rest. Tables laid end-to-end now held dozens of chafing pans. A bartender dressed in the standard black and white, organized bottles, cups and utensils behind a portable bar which also seemingly appeared out of nowhere. "It's amazing what can happen in a couple of hours," Rhani said, watching a disc jockey busy setting up his equipment.

Greg studied the food tables. "I told you Mama knows how to do it. Come on, I'm starving. Let's see what we can swipe before everybody gets here."

"It's so hot. I need to freshen up and change my clothes first. This isn't what I planned to wear to the barbeque."

Gianne took the toddler from her car seat. "I'll come with you, so I can change ChiChi's diaper."

"I'll go see if Mama needs any help," Adanna said, scanning the yard for her future mother-in-law.

By the time Rhani changed her clothes and pulled her hair up into a ponytail, a van from the catering company had arrived. Greg, Marc and Charles helped the driver unload, and Rhani watched them carry dozens of roasting pan-sized containers to the tables. Mrs. Stafford told them where she wanted the items, and once they were done, she tipped the delivery man and sent him on his way. She then recruited Nick, and her husband to light the Sterno cans and Velma and Betty to arrange the dessert table. Her two sisters-in-law had done the baking and transported all kinds of cakes, pies and cobblers from home. With the set-up done, she instructed the DJ to start playing while the guests trickled in.

The family dynamic fed Rhani's interest in human nature, and she studied everything they did with fascination. Greg had been so right about his parents. His father might have been the head of the house, but his mother was definitely the neck. She ran a tight ship, and everything operated like clockwork. He didn't question her authority as the directress, and when he spoke, she didn't usurp his. Rhani loved the way they functioned perfectly together, and something in the back of her mind wondered if their relationship developed further, could she and Greg could operate as well.

Gradually the yard filled with guests, and the brothers spent considerable time introducing their significant others to people they hadn't seen in years. Jesse, Cydney and the kids pulled up in their Lexus SUV and joined the rest of his brothers in their corner of the tent. Not long after their arrival, Mona arrived in a beautiful new Bentley which Greg and Marc had not yet seen. They approached the car before she even exited. When she opened the door and stepped out, all conversation came to a halt. Rhani wasn't sure why until Ramona stood to her full height.

"What in the world is she wearing?" Cydney whispered.

Gianne punched Marc in his bicep when he said, "I don't know, but she sure looks hot!"

They all stared. The midriff top she wore bared her tight abs and a pair of boy shorts showed off her long legs. At forty years old, Ramona's five-foot-nine frame was in better condition than many twenty-five year olds, thanks to her personal trainer, Pilates classes and regular massages. Her boys jumped out of the back, fetched fishing poles from the trunk and shouted a passing hello to the family as they ran across the yard toward the lake. "You two know the rules," Mona called toward their retreating backs. "Stay out of the water. If you need help, come and ask one of your uncles!"

Mrs. Stafford made her way through the guests at a fast clip as though she wanted to reach them before Ramona did. "You guys behave, please," she said with a smile as though she were merely making small talk about the weather. "If you make a fuss over Ramona's outfit, you'll have to deal with me."

Rhani held in a laugh as they all obediently responded, "Yes, ma'am." She leaned in to whisper in Greg's ear. "What's wrong with her outfit? I think she looks fabulous."

"Nothing per se," he said under his breath. "It's just totally out of character for her. She's known for her good taste and designer suits. I don't think we've seen Mona show so much skin since the pool party few years ago."

A few seconds later, Ramona strutted into the tent.

"Hey, folks! How's everyone doing?"

"Great," Cydney said, looking as if she were trying hard not to gaze at her sister-in-law's tiny shorts. "Where's Vic?"

"He was taking too long, so we left. He'll be here eventually."

Not long after their arrival, Mr. Stafford went down to the lake and retrieved his grandsons then called everyone into the tent. A man Greg identified as his parents' pastor blessed the food. As soon as he said "Amen," the covers came off pans of ribs, chicken, macaroni and cheese, fried fish, collard greens, potato salad and numerous other dishes, and the crowd settled in to eat at the rows of tables.

Vic strolled into the tent a few minutes later, fixed himself a plate and took a seat at the opposite end of the table from Ramona.

The consummate hostess, Greg's mother made sure the DJ had a plate before she joined the family. She, Vic Sr., the aunts and uncles, their pastor and his wife all occupied one table. Several times during the meal, Rhani glanced over and saw his father watching them.

"Your father keeps staring at us."

"I noticed. If you're finished eating, why don't we christen the dance floor and really give him something to stare at?" He winked.

She grinned and took his hand. "Let's go, Twinkle Toes."

Greg spoke to the DJ as they passed, and by the time they stepped onto the wood, the first three "Ohs!" of the Wobble filled the humid air. Within seconds, all of the brothers except Vic joined them. Mona sent Vic a challenging glare then grabbed Nick by the hand and dragged him onto the floor. Greg led her to the front of the group, and everyone followed them. He jumped forward then backward, bent over at the waist and moved his hips to the beat of the dance that had become a tradition at black weddings and other events. At least twenty-five people danced in synchronized movement throwing their hands in the air and doing the cha-cha step.

Women often say men dance the same way they have sex, and it was certainly true where Greg was concerned. His movements were so free and sensual; she couldn't take her eyes off him. The way he moved his body stirred up more in her than just the desire to dance. She couldn't think of anything but how his hips worked beneath her hands as they made love just a few days ago. She wanted nothing more than to replay the whole delicious event.

The opening notes of Frankie Beverly's *Before I Let Go* snapped her out of her thoughts. Greg's parents and the aunts and uncles squeezed in among the bobbing heads and did their thing to a song they finally recognized. By the time it got to the chorus of the old-school classic, everyone in the yard was singing along. "Y'all sound *so* good!" the DJ said before he cut the music for a few seconds and let their combined voices sing the, *I will never, never, never, never, never, never, never let you go* refrain.

Greg wrapped his arms around her waist and swayed to the music. "I can't remember the last time I had so much fun," she said looking up at him with a contented smile.

He kissed her neck and when he spun her around to face him, she saw Mr. Stafford's intense gaze locked in on them again. "Has your father said anything to you about us?"

"Not yet, but I feel it coming."

The younger guests, including the kids, stampeded the floor when the DJ went right into the snare drum riff of Lil Jon's *Turn Down for What*. The dance changed from a choreographed routine to a jumping frenzy, and only two couples had been able to keep up. All of the dancers had moved away from the center of the parquet leaving Ramona and Nick alone in the center. The whole family, including her two sons, appeared dumbstruck when Mona turned her back to Nick, bent over with her hands on her knees and performed a twenty-second twerk.

Vic came to the edge of the dance floor to check out the commotion. "Where did you learn to do that?" he screamed at her over the music with fire in his hazel eyes.

She yelled back. "If you ever went out somewhere other than the hospital, you'd know. Everybody is doing it."

"Not everybody! What the hell is wrong with you?" He asked in red-faced anger. He threw his beer bottle into the metal trash can with a clanging crash and stormed out of the yard with Jesse on his heels.

Mrs. Stafford met Ramona as she left the floor when the song ended, looped her arm through Mona's and steered her daughter-in-law away from the gawking guests and whisked her through the back door into the kitchen.

"Ooh, somebody is in *trou*-ble," Greg said in a sing-song voice as Gianne, Marc, Charles, Adanna and Cydney joined them in a corner of the yard.

"Think we should go check on Vic?" Charles asked.

Marc shook his head. "Jess's got him. He doesn't need all of us asking questions."

Cydney appeared stunned. "I've never seen Mona act so wild. She's always so poised. Something's definitely going on with her."

Greg raised his eyebrows and crossed his arms. "What do you say, Ms. Therapist?"

"Oh, I couldn't say without knowing her personally. It wouldn't be fair."

"Just give us your take off the top of your head," Nick

insisted. "Why would she pick me to show out with?"

Rhani sighed. "This is just a guess, but it looks like she's trying to get Vic's attention, and she chose you because you're the only single unattached brother."

"To tell you the truth," Marc said with a chuckle. "I never would've guessed Mona knew how to back that thing up."

Gianne rolled her eyes and slapped his arm.

Jesse and Vic returned to the yard, and Vic went directly to the bar. Jesse saw his brothers huddled together and he joined them.

"What's the deal with them?" Charles asked.

"I know he and Mona have been arguing non-stop, but he doesn't want to talk about it."

"Mama has her in the house right now. She'll get to the bottom of things. In the meantime, I'm going to dance." Greg grabbed Rhani's hand and pulled her back to the dance floor. "Give me something good, DJ!"

They danced non-stop to a mix of the top tunes, and one-by-one others returned to the floor. Eventually Mona and Greg's mother came back outside as though nothing had happened. Mrs. Stafford flitted around the yard with a smile and spent a few minutes talking to each of their guests. Mona found a seat under the tent and stayed to herself until the crowd thinned, the music slowed, and her mother-in-law called Rhani and her daughters-in-law together.

"Tomorrow morning the car will be here at eleven o'clock to pick us up for our spa day. Dress comfortably and get ready to be pampered. This is my treat, so you don't need to bring anything but your beautiful selves. Plan to be out the whole day. After the spa, we're going to lunch. Mona and Cydney, we'll stop by to pick you up."

The day had turned out to be more revealing than Rhani had expected, and she eagerly anticipated spending time with the women alone. Hopefully, this would be her chance to find out more about Greg from the woman who raised him.

Chapter Seventeen

When the barbeque ended around seven, the brothers helped fold the tables and chairs and stacked them for pickup in the morning. Nick, Vic and Jesse went home and promised their father they would return at eleven to visit with him while the women spent the day at the spa.

"You coming up, man?" Marc asked Greg, leaving the rest of them standing in the kitchen.

"I guess so. Unlike you, Charles and I don't have something soft and pretty in bed next to us. I have to look at this clown all night." He pointed to Charles. "And I'm a night owl. This is too early for me to turn in."

Greg considered how the interaction between the brothers had changed since half of them were now married or engaged. In the past, when they came home for a family event, he and his brothers would stay up half the night talking. Even Nick had his own apartment now, and he didn't stay the night.

He found Charles stretched out on the twin bed closest to the window when he entered the bedroom they were sharing. "I was concerned about you after I came up to visit. I'm glad you decided to get some help."

"I didn't really decide." Greg sat on the other bed and removed his shoes. "I had no choice, but now I know the network forcing me into therapy was the best thing that could've happened. I've discovered things about myself I wasn't willing to face before."

"Rhani seems like a nice girl, but do you really care about her."

Greg sent him a suspicious glance. "What?"

"Do you really *care* about her?"

Greg tamped down his annoyance, remembering everything Charles had seen when he came to visit in New York, and it had admittedly been his lowest point. "She saved my life, man."

"That's what concerns me. I've had patients who convinced themselves they were in love with me. And I was just their plastic surgeon. Is it possible you've mistaken her concern and attention for love?"

He stared at his brother and suddenly wanted to punch him dead in his face. "Do you think I'm that stupid?"

"I don't know. You're not the same guy who left Atlanta three years ago. I didn't even recognize you when I came to New York. Now you're telling me you've done a one eighty since then?"

Greg sat on the edge of the other twin bed and looked his brother in the eye. "That's exactly what I'm telling you."

Charles shook his head. "Forgive me, but that's a little hard to believe. You never even told me why you just packed up and left Atlanta—and Evelyn. You were *engaged* to her. How could you just up and leave her?"

"I couldn't talk about it before."

Charles pulled himself up against the headboard. "Why? What happened, man?"

"Besides Rhani, you're the only person I've told this to." Greg swallowed hard. "I didn't leave Ev. I left *because* of her."

"Come on, you're not making any sense. I was at the engagement party, remember?"

"How can I forget? *Everybody* was at the engagement party. That's why there wasn't anyone I could tell."

"Tell what? I can't imagine Ev doing anything bad enough to make you..." His gaze met Greg's and a look of comprehension suddenly changed his expression. "She cheated on you."

Greg met his brother's gaze but didn't say anything.

"Oh, damn. I'm sorry, man."

"It wasn't just that she cheated on me six months before the wedding. I walked in on her and saw it with my own eyes. She wasn't even able to deny it. We worked together, and I couldn't go to the station every day and see her face."

"Why didn't you tell us? You left town like your ass was on fire. It had us all wondering what happened. We thought you'd gotten cold feet about the wedding and run out on her."

Greg leaned forward, clasped his hands together between his knees and fixed his gaze on the floor. "I know what it looked like, but I couldn't even say her name until Rhani got me to face the reality of what happened. I ran, because I didn't know what else to do. I wanted to get as far away from Ev as possible. The New York network had just approached me about a spot on their team. Originally, I'd refused them, because Ev and I wanted to stay in Atlanta. But after everything went down, I contacted them and said I'd reconsidered. They wanted to know how soon I could be there, and that was all I needed to hear."

"You should've told somebody, man."

"I couldn't. I'd never been so humiliated in my life. Going to New York was the right decision at the time, and starting a new job was exactly what I needed. Learning about their format monopolized my thoughts, and the process of getting settled in a new city didn't give me much time to dwell on what happened."

Charles pressed his lips together in a tight line and then asked, "How did you get involved with all those women?"

"I started going out to clubs with some coworkers at the station. The opportunities presented themselves, and I took advantage of them. It happened so gradually, I didn't even recognize how extreme I'd gotten. To tell you the truth, I never felt like it was obsessive, but I also never enjoyed it. Now I understand it was a subconscious way to punish Ev, of saying, 'I can have sex with whoever I want just like you, Evelyn.'"

"Wow, that's deep. Well, I'm glad you figured out what was going on."

"If I hadn't been arrested and required to get therapy, I might never have grasped what was happening with me. My therapy with Rhani was the reason. She knows her stuff."

"She seems like a good woman."

"She is, and she knows all about me and still wants to be with me."

"You don't think you're worthy of her?"

His gaze returned to the floor. "Sometimes I don't. Rhani is such a decent person."

"You're a decent person, Greg. Don't condemn yourself because of one mistake."

"That's just it. It was hundreds of mistakes, not just one."

"Rhani obviously doesn't seem to hold it against you. If she forgives you, then you need to forgive yourself."

"You're right, but I don't know how. I'm changing therapists so I can talk about her."

In the morning after breakfast, the women got ready for their outing. Greg listened in wonder as Gianne gave Marc his instructions for ChiChi. It amazed him how much all of his brothers had changed. Even Charles, who wasn't married yet, seemed to be so willing to do whatever pleased Adanna. They definitely weren't whipped or anything. They just wanted their women to be happy, and he'd begun to feel the same way.

The limo arrived promptly at eleven o'clock, and his mother, Adanna, Gianne and Rhani left chattering in anticipation and promising to return around four o'clock.

Marc brought ChiChi down dressed in her Doc McStuffin's scrubs and clutching her Lambie. He placed the contents of her medical bag, which was a gift from his parents, on a blanket in the middle of the family room.

Vic and Jesse arrived with their kids in tow, and Vic sent his boys directly downstairs to the theater with orders. "Trey's the oldest, so he's in charge of the movies. He knows how to work the DVD. Behave," he added in a stern voice and everyone snickered. Jesse's two oldest joined the others, and he carried the baby into the family room and set her car seat on the floor near ChiChi who was concentrating on taking Lambie's vitals.

"I told your mother that was the perfect gift for her," his father said with a proud smile. "This girl's going to be the first female doctor in the family."

"Don't push it, Daddy," Marc protested. "She might want to become a fashion designer or a physicist or a media specialist like her mom."

Their father chuckled. "Look at her bedside manner, Marcus. She's a natural." They all cracked up as ChiChi patted Lambie's head and murmured something comforting in Engoruba before she put the stethoscope to its chest and listened. "She knows what to do with each instrument. Who showed her how to do that?"

"I did," Marc grumbled.

All of the men stared at each other when ChiChi took a reflex hammer out of her bag and tapped the stuffed toy's legs.

"You might be right," Marc conceded.

"Who's cooking lunch? I'm starving," Nick called out as he came through the front door.

"Nobody," their father answered. "We have a load of food left from yesterday. All we need to do is reheat it in the microwave. In the meantime, there's coffee, and we have a couple of movies to watch." He handed the DVDs to Nick and headed into the kitchen where Vic and Greg were filling their mugs. "Let's talk, Vic," he said, coming up behind them. "Meet me in my office."

Vic rolled his eyes behind their father's back as he left the room. "Okay."

"Maybe you should add a shot to your coffee," Greg suggested with a snicker.

Vic snorted a less than humorous laugh. "No, then he'll have something to say about that too." He turned and trudged toward the office.

The rest of them had settled in front of the TV and seemed to be riveted to the movie about a thief who steals corporate secrets from sleeping minds. Greg flopped down on the sofa, but couldn't focus on the story unfolding on the screen. In a few minutes, he would probably be sitting in the hot seat currently occupied by his oldest brother. Why did facing his father still make him feel like a ten year old? He was a grown man, for crying out loud. Thankfully, he'd never been held to the same ridiculously high standards his siblings were. His mother said she and his father had always known he was as gifted as his brothers but in a different way. They had always given him the freedom to explore his talent, but the one standard his parents never backed off from had to do with their reputation. Greg could still hear them saying, "Don't embarrass us. Carry yourself like a Stafford and don't shame the family." And embarrass them he did—in the worst way. Whatever his father had to say, Greg wasn't ready for it. He rubbed the back of his neck. When he glanced up, Marc was frowning at him.

"What's wrong with you?"

"Nothing."

Marc's eyes narrowed. "You look pretty tense for somebody who's just watching a movie."

"Daddy just called Vic into his office, and I'm probably next."

"That explains why you seem so uptight."

"Is that funny to you?" Greg asked, annoyed by Marc's smile.

"I'm just glad for once I'm not the one who's on the spot."

Greg picked up a magazine from the end table and tossed it at Marc's head. "Thanks a lot, man. You make me feel so much better."

He ducked and stood. "I'd better feed ChiChi, so I can put her down for a nap."

"Out of all of us, I never thought you'd end up being Mr. Mom."

"The right woman can make a brother do all kinds of things he never thought he'd do. I'm not a househusband. I *do* have a career, but I don't have any problem feeding, changing or bathing my little girl. For your information, I even do her hair." Marc grinned.

"For real?" Greg's eyes widened.

"Why do you think it's so strange?'"

"I don't."

Marc studied him for a few beats. "You're wondering if you could do it, huh?"

Greg raised his hands. "Hey! We're not at that level yet."

"Yet," Charles added, making it clear he'd been listening to their conversation. "You *did* bring her home to get everyone's opinion of her, didn't you?"

Jesse hit the mute button on the remote and turned to face them. "Come on, man, tell us the truth."

"We're all wondering," Nick chimed in. "Doesn't it feel weird being with your therapist?"

"I've never felt as comfortable with any woman as I do with her."

Charles tilted his head. "Why?"

"Because I don't have any secrets from her."

"None?" Jesse gave him an incredulous look.

"None."

"So she knows things about you we don't even know."

"Yeah. Something about her makes me spill my guts whenever I get on the couch."

"I bet it's not the only thing you two have done on the couch," Marc said with a wicked glint in his green eyes.

An instant flashback of their office escapade appeared before his eyes, and even though he tried, he couldn't avoid breaking into a grin.

Nick jumped up and pointed a finger at him. "Look at his face!" All the brothers whooped at his inability to keep the truth from showing on his face.

"I didn't say anything!"

"You didn't have to," Marc said. "I never would've guessed Ms. Rhani had a little freak in her, but she'd have to in order to be with him."

"She sure can dance," Jesse chimed in. "And you know what they say about the way a woman dances. Are they right, man?"

"I'm not telling you."

"Yeah, he's in love," Vic said from the doorway. "If he wasn't, he'd give us *all* the inside details."

None of them had seen their oldest brother reappear, but he didn't look angry or upset, so Greg assumed the talk with their father had gone well.

"I think you're right," Charles agreed. "Do we have another wedding to put on the calendar?"

Greg smiled. "How about we get *you* down the aisle first, then we can talk about me and Rhani."

"You're trying to avoid answering," Nick pointed out.

"All right. I'm looking at this realistically. Rhani and I have only known each other for a few months. We need to give it time and get to know each other better."

Their father appeared in the doorway behind Vic. "That's wise, son. Don't rush into anything. If she loves you, she's not going anywhere."

Vic snorted. "Being together for a long time isn't a guarantee. You can still be blindsided."

A nervous glance passed around the room, but nobody dared ask what he meant. It would come out sooner or later.

Jesse interrupted their uncomfortable silence. "It's time to feed the kids. Vic, give me a hand so we can get this over with. You guys can eat after we get them straight."

"I need to talk to Greg for a minute," his father finally said with a *leave us alone* expression. "We haven't had a chance to catch up since he got home. Go ahead and feed the kids." Marc, Vic and Jesse retreated into the kitchen. "Make yourself a drink or a cup of coffee and come into the family room."

This calls for something stronger than coffee. He poured himself some orange juice from the refrigerator, went into the family room and topped it off with vodka then made his way to the room where all serious discussions between father and sons had taken place for two decades.

"How're you doing, son?" he asked after Greg sat in one of the cushy leather chairs facing the desk.

Greg took a sip of his screwdriver then answered, "Better than I've been in years."

He gave Greg a long, scrutinizing glance. "It's only been two months since you got arrested, so I take it Miss Rhani is responsible for the change?"

"Completely. She's the one who got me to understand why I'd developed such extreme behavior. Rhani is a special woman, Daddy."

"You seem to be very proud of her. Is this something serious?"

Greg swirled his screwdriver around in the glass. "I ask myself that question every day. I think it could be, yeah."

"I figured it must be. You haven't brought a woman here since Evelyn." Greg winced at her name. "She's very pretty. I hope it's not the only reason you're attracted to her. Do you love her?" His father had always been direct and didn't waste time or words.

He pressed his lips together and nodded. "Yes. She's bright; she cares about other people, and she works hard—too hard sometimes."

"If a man loves a woman's soul, he'll end up loving one woman. If he just loves a woman's body or face, all the women in the world won't satisfy him."

Greg stared at him in disbelief. When had the physician become a philosopher? "Why are you telling me this?"

"Because if you love her, I can't understand how you can put the career she loves in jeopardy. It's one thing for you to be in the spotlight, but you've dragged her into it with you. Do you think that's fair?"

"Daddy," Greg began trying to disguise his impatience. "Rhani and I have talked about this. She doesn't have any enemies, and she doesn't believe there's anyone who'd try to take her license."

"It doesn't have to be an enemy, Gregory. Rhani might have colleagues who consider her behavior unprofessional. She *is* breaking ethical standards by having a personal relationship with a patient. There's no way around it."

"Client, not patient." His gaze roamed over the shelves of medical books filling the shelves. "And she's not my therapist anymore. Next week I start seeing someone else—a man."

"Good move, but it probably won't make a difference. She wouldn't be able to deny her involvement with you, since you two have been in the newspapers and on television together." The older man sat back in his chair and drew a deep breath. "Are you prepared to take care of her if she loses her license because of you?"

The possibility hadn't crossed his mind, and he took a gulp of his drink before he looked his father in the eye. "I am. She wouldn't like hearing it put that way, though."

"Of course she wouldn't. She's an independent woman, but you can't leave her hanging if the worst happens."

"I'd never do that."

"Glad to hear it. If she's been as good to you as you say, then she deserves everything you can do for her. Stafford men take care of their women."

"Yes, sir. That's exactly what I intend to do, no matter what happens. My suspension ends in a few weeks, and hopefully things will go back to normal."

"Your normal hasn't exactly been normal." His father peered over top his glasses. "Would you be able to stay faithful to her?"

"You're talking about my old life. I've started creating a new life for myself, and I want her to be part of it."

"I've got to be honest. I didn't expect you to say that. It's good to see such a change in you. When I look at how Marc has matured since he married Gianne, it almost seems like a miracle, but a good woman will change a man." He rose from the recliner and slapped Greg on the back.

"You're mellowing out in your old age, Daddy."

"Not really. I still wish you'd do something with that hair."

His father had a thing about hair. Over the years, he'd stayed on Marc's back for wearing his long. Since Greg had the kinkiest hair of all the brothers, he'd chosen to go with a more ethnic style, which also made the old man crazy. He laughed, patted his twisted hair and finished his drink then returned to the family room where his brothers had refocused on the movie.

Charles looked him up and down. "You survived. I guess Daddy didn't thrash you."

"No, and he surprised me. He seemed more concerned about Rhani than anything."

"He's changed a lot in the past few years. After what he did for Adanna and me last year, nothing he does would surprise me now."

"You know that was all Mama's doing."

"Yeah, but he didn't have to go along with it."

Greg sank down onto the sofa beside Charles and chuckled. "He did if he wanted to stay married to Mama."

"So, how's your therapy going?"

"Great, but I'm starting with a new therapist next week. We decided it was the best course for us to take."

"I don't know how you handled it once you realized you were attracted to her. How could you tell her your deep, dark secrets?"

"She has a way that makes you want to open up. Besides, I'd already told her the heavy stuff in the first couple of visits before I recognized how I felt about her."

"I wonder what the ladies are up to," their father said when he re-entered the room, after he dismissed Jesse from his massage chair with a wave.

"Probably sipping champagne and gossiping." Jesse laughed.

"Rhani couldn't get over the invitation. She's not used to family events, so she's really having a good time."

"She doesn't have any brothers or sisters?" Nick asked as though he couldn't imagine it.

"Two brothers and one sister, but they're not close. She only has a relationship with her baby brother. In fact, he's staying with her for the summer while he's home from school."

"Why didn't he go home to his parents?" his father asked.

"They have some issues, and they live in a rough neighborhood in the Bronx. A couple of weeks ago, he got arrested just sitting outside in front of the building, so Rhani talked him into spending the summer at her place in Manhattan."

"That's too bad," his father mused. "I hope he wasn't charged."

"No. You know how the cops are. They were looking for some carjacking suspects. Wil and his friends loosely fit the descriptions even though they weren't anywhere in the vicinity of the crime. My lawyer took care of it."

"Your lawyer?" Marc asked with raised eyebrows. "See that! Now I *know* he's in love. He had his attorney represent her brother."

Laughter and warmth filled the room and reminded Greg of their younger days when they returned home from school and sat in the kitchen telling their mother about their day. He missed the unique togetherness that existed between blood brothers. Living alone in New York had once been his dream, and even though he loved the exhilaration of the Big Apple, the lack of closeness with his brothers left a void nothing else seemed to fill. Since he started therapy, he'd been thinking a lot about the condition of his life. At times he thought if he had never fled from Atlanta and the closeness with his family, he probably wouldn't have ended up addicted and incarcerated.

Jesse and Vic worked together reheating chicken, macaroni and cheese and corn on the cob for the children. They'd become used to cooperating in their father's practice for years before Vic got promoted to chief of surgery. He and Vic both had kids and were closer to each other than any of the other brothers.

After the older kids had their plates, Jesse warmed a bottle and fed the baby. Marc cut a chicken breast into tiny pieces and fanned a bowl of mac and cheese to cool it off for ChiChi, to whom they didn't feed a raw vegan diet.

During the past three years he'd been in New York, Greg had never seen this side of his brothers. Neither of them seemed the least bit self-conscious. The sight of two of the top surgeons in Atlanta doing kitchen duty spoke volumes. Watching how expertly Marc took care of the little girl's needs, including changing diapers, seemed so contrary to his rippling muscles and super-masculine appearance. ChiChi loved his attention, and he seemed proud of his new domestic skill. In fact, he lit up like a neon sign every time she called him Da-Da. Greg wondered what that felt like.

The scene playing before him was confirmation of the hollowness of his life since he moved to New York. Without a doubt, he made an excellent salary, had a busy social life and had received VIP status in his favorite clubs. Sadly, he hardly enjoyed the great apartment he'd spent a small fortune decorating. He'd been accompanied in bed by nameless, faceless women whom he quickly dismissed when the sun rose. While he observed the love, devotion and commitment his brothers had for their families, Greg realized he hadn't seen what was happening to his life before he went into therapy. No matter how some people tried to disparage the power and effectiveness of therapy, he knew it worked.

After the men disposed of the paper plates and cups, Jesse and Marc left the room to put the babies down for their naps. The movie ended, and Nick put on the second feature, a story about an Olympic runner who finds himself in a Japanese POW camp during World War II.

During the film Greg noticed the other men sneaking sidelong glances at Vic. They all seemed to notice how quiet he'd been for the rest of the afternoon, but no one dared bring up the subject.

Right after four o'clock, the door opened and the women returned looking stress-free and blissful. "We're back!" his mother sang as she preceded Rhani, Gianne,

Cydney and Adanna into the foyer.

"Did you ladies have a good time?" His father asked, rising to kiss his wife.

"It was absolutely wonderful!"

"Where's Mona?" Vic asked in a dry tone.

"We dropped her off at the house on the way back. Well, at least my house is still standing."

"Mama, we're old pros at this stuff now," Jesse insisted. "Everyone's fed, rested, dry and entertained."

"Yeah," Marc added. "We can do this thing as well as you ladies can."

"Huh! Give me a break," Cydney said with a laugh. "You can do it for one afternoon. Talk to me after you've done it every day, year round for five years."

Greg stood and walked over to Rhani. "You're glowing."

She grinned. "We got massages, body scrubs, facials, manicures, pedicures, and had a fabulous lunch. I'm all smooth and shiny." When he bent down to kiss her, she whispered in his ear. "I love your mother."

"We all do. She's one of a kind. Let's go upstairs, and you can tell me all about it." He loved the look of contentment on her face. Even though they had only been gone five hours, he'd missed her. What would he do if he couldn't see her for days or weeks? He had to make sure that didn't happen.

Chapter Eighteen

"**W**e had such a wonderful time!" Rhani gushed when they sat together on the bed in his room.

"I'm glad, but I knew you would." He moved closer, ran a finger down her cheek then kissed her.

"Oh, you did?" she asked, breaking the kiss and rearing back to look into his eyes.

"Yes, and it's why I brought you home with me. I needed to see you with them and them with you."

"And…do you like what you see?"

His golden eyes seemed to look right into her soul. "Very much."

She smiled and wanted to ask him exactly what that meant to their relationship, but decided against it. She knew opening up like that was a major step for him, and she didn't want to push him.

"I like going out with my girlfriends, but this was something special. Even though I hadn't met any of the women in your family before this week, I feel like I've known them for years," she babbled, still on a high from all the pampering and champagne cocktails. "I've never had a body scrub before. It makes your skin feel like satin."

His brows drew closer together. "I guess I have to take your word for it, since I'm not able to find out for myself." The languid scan he gave her body made her tingle all over.

"Why are you looking at me like that?"

"Because I missed you."

"We were only gone for a few hours."

"I know, but I missed you."

"How did you guys make out? It's hard for me to imagine you babysitting."

"I wasn't babysitting. I watched Marc, Jesse and Vic babysit. Those guys really surprised me. They're all so good with their kids. They probably don't do things the way their wives would, but they took care of business and the kids were happy."

"It's different when you're taking care of your own kids."

"I guess you're right. Did Mama ask you about my therapy?"

"Yes, but I told her I wasn't at liberty to share anything. I did reassure her your issues had nothing to do with your upbringing, because I had the feeling the possibility concerned her."

"Really? How could she think that?"

"Parents always feel responsible for their children's issues, no matter how old they are. I think it comes with the territory. She really loves you, Greg."

"I know, and I hated humiliating her."

"She didn't seem the least bit humiliated. She's just concerned about you. I told her you're doing much better and overcoming the causes of your past behavior."

"Did she believe you?"

"I think so."

He nodded. "How did Mona seem?"

"I don't know how she normally acts, so to me she

seemed fine. A little introspective, maybe."

"Did she say anything about her and Vic?"

"Not really."

"Vic isn't talking either. Something's obviously going on with them, but nobody knows what it's all about. Neither one of them is talking."

"How long have they been married?"

"Almost twelve years."

"She talked with your mother for a long time while we were at the spa, but I don't know what they discussed."

"Mona is spoiled rotten. Vic has given her everything she ever wanted. She doesn't work, and she spends money like he's the World Bank. I can't imagine what she'd have to complain about."

Typical man. Rhani gave him an indulgent smile. "Perhaps it has nothing to do with money. A lot of men make that mistake. They believe money covers a multitude of sins, but it doesn't."

He considered what she said for a moment. "True. If they get any advice from Mama, it'll be sound."

"I hope things work out for them. They've invested a lot of time in each other. It would be a shame for all those years to go down the drain."

"Enough about Vic and Mona. What are we doing tonight?"

"I'll leave it up to you."

"How about we go out to dinner alone? No family, just us, and then we can go somewhere to dance."

"I'd love it. Where are you taking me?"

"My favorite steakhouse. I know you're not a beef

eater, but they have great seafood too. You'll like it."

She studied his handsome face for a long moment then leaned in and kissed him. "I'm sure I will." When he moved his lips from her mouth to her neck, she dropped her head.

"I have plans for you, you know."

"Really?"

"Really. I love you, girl." Greg kissed his way back to her lips, this time with more fervor.

She hadn't expected to hear those words, and they went right to her heart. Her pulse raced, and suddenly she found it hard to breathe. Instead of questioning him, she circled his neck with her arms and told him the truth. "I love you too. It scares the hell out of me, but I do."

"I guess I am high risk, but I promise I won't disappoint you."

Her tentative gaze met his. "So what does this make us now?"

"I guess we're officially an exclusive couple, if that's all right with you."

"It's quite all right."

Their tongues met in a leisurely, enticing glide, sending a jolt of electricity out to her fingertips. But when he flicked the tip around the edge of her ear, she uttered a defenseless breath of desire. Greg leaned her back onto the bed and deepened the kiss. God, she loved the taste of him, and she wanted more. She hooked her leg behind his and tightened her grip around his neck.

Marc put a swift end to the passionate interlude when he walked past the door, stopped and said, "You could close the door, you know."

"Only if I want Mama to hang me. You know leaving the door open has been the rule since we were in middle school. How about you mind your business and go see about your own woman, man."

Marc laughed and kept walking.

Rhani sat up, smoothed her clothes then rested her head on his shoulder and closed her eyes. "This isn't right. I should go change my clothes and fix my hair. What time do you want to leave?" She felt uncomfortable getting too cozy in his parents' house, but she was also still reeling over his declaration.

He pressed a light kiss on her forehead. "How about seven?"

Rhani crossed the hall and entered the guest room she shared with Adanna. She assumed her roommate was still downstairs with Charles, so she stretched out on the bed and considered what had just happened between her and Greg. This hadn't been a frivolous decision on his part. He'd brought her home to see how well she fit in with his family, which to her was major. How major she still didn't know.

Later that night they had a quiet dinner alone at Bones, a top-rated steakhouse in Atlanta then to Prive nightclub to work off everything they'd eaten on the dance floor. Rhani loved the club's blue/purple-lit interior, and she'd never seen a club with the non-VIP in the center and the wall elevated for VIP. There were seven very different areas to explore, but Greg found seats in the outdoor sky lounge overlooking Spring Street. He went to the bar to get drinks, which took a long time, so she entertained herself by watching the incoming crowd.

"Is that who I think it is?" she whispered to him excitedly after he returned with their drinks and a couple of well-known entertainers and their entourages made their way past them.

"Sure is. Looks like there's a private party going on in VIP. One of my coworkers suggested we check this place out. He came to the grand opening last year."

Greg took advantage of the semi-empty balcony to get close, which they hadn't been able to do at the house. They kissed and took in the view of the Atlanta skyline then danced until Greg reminded her they had to get up early for church.

Early in the morning, they got up to attend service with the family at his parents' church. Since she hadn't been to church in years, Rhani wasn't sure what to expect. Her parents hadn't exactly been the church-going types, and she'd only gone to worship services a few times during her middle and high school years with friends. During her college years, a couple of her friends had been active in a campus ministry, and they had invited her to come to a few of their services. The lively, youth-oriented ministry appealed to her, and she had attended them on a regular basis. But after graduation, when she looked around for a church with a similar atmosphere, and found nothing, she stopped searching. Now her Sunday mornings consisted of a large coffee, a bagel with cream cheese and the Sunday Times.

"Vic and Mona and the boys won't be coming this morning," Mrs. Stafford said once the family had assembled in the kitchen for coffee.

"Maybe it's for the best, Mama." Charles stirred some cream into a cup of tea and handed it to Adanna. "There's no telling what might set those two off. It would be pretty ugly if we had to break up a fight in the sanctuary."

Adanna glared at him. "Oh, Charles, that's not funny."

"I wasn't joking, sweetheart."

"Listenall— of you," Mrs. Stafford said in her *I'm not playing* voice. "Vic and Ramona are having a tough time right now, and they need your support not teasing. And you newlyweds and pre-newlyweds need to say a prayer for them this morning, because your time is coming."

"Mama! Why would you say something like that?" Marc's hand froze in mid-air as he fed ChiChi her breakfast.

"Because I've lived long enough to know all relationships go in cycles. There are good times and bad times in the best of marriages, and the sooner you understand that the better off you'll be. The good marriages aren't the ones in which a couple never fights. They're the ones where the couple has their problems and figures out ways to solve them and still be happy together. Isn't that right, Rhani?"

"Definitely. I'm not a marriage counselor, but I think it applies to all relationships. It's learning to love each other in spite of your differences."

Mrs. Stafford smiled at her. "If everyone's had their coffee, we should get moving. We don't want to disrupt the service by bringing this whole caravan down the aisle late. Gianne, make sure you bring extra diapers for ChiChi, because we won't be coming back to the house until after dinner."

The convoy rolled up before the eleven o'clock service began at *Bourgie Baptist*, as the brothers secretly called it. The family waited in the vestibule while Cydney and Gianne took the kids to the children's ministry. When they returned, Greg took her hand and the entire Stafford clan, minus Vic and his bunch, filed in behind their parents.

"Mama loves this," he whispered in her ear. "Look at how she's cheesin'."

"She's proud of her family, and she should be."

Mr. and Mrs. Stafford wore proud smiles as they led the procession down the center aisle to the front left side of the sanctuary where Greg said his mother and father sat every Sunday for the last twenty years.

He didn't release her hand once they were seated in the

pew until he started to clap to the choir's rousing opening number.

Rhani loved the music, and even the pastor's message. Since the July 4th holiday was a big family reunion weekend, he talked about family. As he spoke, she considered what it might be like to be part of Greg's family. The two things her childhood had lacked—money and a close-knit family—the Staffords possessed in abundance. She had always thought if she ever had children, she would want them to be raised in an extended family just like this. But over the years she also scolded herself for fantasizing about marriage and children. Perhaps it wasn't in the cards for her.

When the pastor briefly mentioned the scripture, "He who finds a wife finds a good thing." Greg's lips twitched as though he was trying not to smile. Was he really thinking about marriage? It had only been months since his extreme lifestyle had landed him in jail. She knew very well jumping from that existence into a serious relationship in such a short time wasn't wise. But she couldn't voice her thoughts to him on the subject unless he brought it up. Right now she just wanted to be in his company.

At the end of the service, everyone filed out of the pews and shook the pastor's hand as he and his wife stood in the vestibule. She and Greg approached, and he asked, "You're Gregory's wife?"

Rhani kept silent when Greg answered, "Not yet, Pastor. Soon, I hope."

Not knowing what else to do, she smiled and told him how much she enjoyed the service and quickly moved on.

"Did he make you uncomfortable?" Greg asked with a hint of laughter in his voice as they made their way down the front steps.

"Yes."

"Why?"

Adanna and Charles were right behind them. "Can we talk about this later?" She inclined her head in the direction of the other couple.

He chuckled. "All right."

"Did you like the service, Rhani?" Mr. Stafford asked once he joined them on the sidewalk in front of the enormous brick edifice.

"I did. Your pastor is an excellent speaker."

"Yes, he is, and now that he's fed us spiritually, let's go and get some natural food." He put an arm around her shoulders and walked her toward the parking lot. "Most Sundays, we go to my favorite soul food restaurant for dinner. It's not fancy, but the food is superb. I hope you're hungry, girl."

"I'm starving." She couldn't help but notice Greg's contented smile, and she warned herself not to get all emotional and mushy over all of this warmth and acceptance. Perhaps his family treated all of their houseguests this way, it would be better to avoid deceiving herself into believing this treatment was anything special. Tonight she and Greg were going back to New York. She would no longer be inside this cocoon of affection and cordiality which had lulled her into the false reality that all was right with the world.

But I can bask in it for the next few hours…

Dinner at the restaurant wasn't at all what she had expected. The Atlanta landmark presented the food cafeteria-style. Every dish she chose was delicious, and the staff, who knew Greg's parents by name, treated everyone as though they were special guests. She had intended to forego dessert until Mr. Stafford convinced her to get a piece of the famous pink cake. Greg chose banana pudding and they shared.

She and Greg said goodbye to Jesse, Cydney and Nick in the parking lot. Each of them left her with a long hug and voiced their hopes that she would return, even though they all knew it depended on whether or not their relationship survived.

Back at the house, Gianne put ChiChi down for a nap then she and Adanna joined her in the bedroom while she finished packing.

Gianne sat crossed-legged on the bed and watched her for a moment before she said, "We know what you're feeling right now," Gianne started. "I don't know Greg well, but I've been watching him all weekend, and I'm convinced he's totally, completely in love with you, Rhani."

"There's no doubt about it," Adanna agreed. "If you want to be part of this family, let him know how you feel."

"But we aren't even engaged. We've only known each other for a very short time. What if I'm making a mistake?"

Gianne smiled. "It doesn't take long to know whether or not you're in love, Rhani. It doesn't mean you have to rush into anything. Take your time and be certain Greg is what you want."

"We would love to have you as our sister-in-law," Adanna added.

An unexpected tear trickled down Rhani's cheek. "You two are so sweet, and I know you understand. The Staffords are *so* different from my family. I wouldn't mind living with them even if I didn't marry one of their sons." She sniffed and then giggled.

Greg's mother peeked in the doorway. "Am I interrupting something?"

Rhani quickly wiped her face. "No, we were just saying

our goodbyes."

"Are you all right, dear?"

"Yes. Just a little emotional."

"Can you girls excuse us?" the older woman asked.

"We'll see you before you go," Gianne said as she and Adanna scurried out of the room.

Mrs. Stafford closed the door and sat beside Rhani on the bed. "This weekend has been so busy; we didn't get a chance to really talk. All I want to say is Victor and I loved having you with us." She took Rhani's hand and held it. "This is just between you and me, okay?" Rhani nodded. "You said Gregory told you about Evelyn. He never told me or his father what happened between them, but all I know is when it did, something broke inside him, and he's been broken until now. A different man came home this weekend. I believe you're the cause of his healing, and I thank you so much. I also believe his healing is due to more than therapy. You need to be certain, though."

Rhani answered with tears that flowed freely now. "It's true Greg has had problems, but he is an exceptional man. I've never had such strong feelings for anyone. Never."

Mrs. Stafford took Rhani in her arms. "Oh, don't cry, sweetheart. Gregory is my impulsive child. Always has been, but if he loves you like I think he does, everything is going to work out just fine. Don't let him rush you. Get to know him well, and don't make a move until you're sure you are ready."

A knock on the door interrupted them. "May I come in?"

Rhani grabbed some tissues from the nightstand and rushed to dry her face before he noticed. "Yes. Come in."

He froze on the threshold and stared at the ball of tissues in her hand. "What's going on, Mama? What did you say to make her cry?"

His mother smiled at the protective edge in his voice.

"She didn't say anything, Greg. We're fine."

He stepped into the room, knelt beside the bed and raised Rhani's chin so he could look directly into her eyes. "Are you okay?"

Mrs. Stafford rose from the bed. "I'll see you downstairs." She left the room and, much to their surprise, closed the door behind her.

"I guess I'm just a little emotional about leaving, and because your mother is so sweet."

His shoulders relaxed. "I thought she said something to upset you." He leaned in and rested his head against her breasts. Rhani loved the feel of his body heat, and she let her fingertips caress the soft, shiny twists covering his head.

"Not at all. Just the opposite."

Greg straightened. "So I guess you had a good time?"

"Better than good." She smiled down at him and took his smooth face between her hands then lowered her head. When their lips met, the warmth of his mouth sent a current through her. The scene in her office when he'd made love to her on her client couch played behind her closed eyelids. He slid his hands beneath her dress, up her outer thighs and back down. "The family is waiting for us downstairs," she murmured against his mouth, even though she didn't want to end their contact.

"They can wait. I haven't been able to touch you since we've been here." He gave her a gentle push back onto the bed and pulled himself up so his body rested between her legs.

Instinctively, Rhani wrapped a leg around him and arched her back. "I want to make love again, but not here.

She ground her hips against him. "We'll be back home in six hours. I can wait. Can't you?"

"I don't want to, but if you promise we can get a hotel room out by the airport for the night, I'll let you go."

Rhani didn't need to think long. She wriggled against him again. "Okay. I'll call Wil once we land and let him know I won't be back until tomorrow."

His cheeks dimpled and he released her. "I guess we should say farewell." He got to his feet and pulled her up from the bed by both hands. "You can go ahead. I'll be there in a minute."

Rhani felt guilty for getting him all worked up with no outlet for his frustration, but it couldn't be helped. She went downstairs where everyone waited in the family room. "Greg will be down in a minute."

"What time is your flight?" Mr. Stafford asked.

"Seven-thirty. We need to leave in a little while, but I wanted to tell you what a wonderful time I had. Now I understand what people mean about southern hospitality."

He patted her hand. "Darling, you're welcome here anytime."

"Yes," his mother agreed. "If you're important to Gregory, you're important to us."

Rhani swallowed the lump forming in her throat. "Thank you." She turned to Gianne who had ChiChi on her lap. "May I kiss her goodbye?"

"Heck, you can take her with you, if you want," Marc joked.

Greg came into the room as she lifted ChiChi into her arms and gave her a long squeeze and a kiss on her plump cheek. He took the baby from her and did the same. "Bye, sweetie. Next time I see you, I'm expecting to hear some

English." She babbled something and put both hands on his face, as had become her habit with him. He grinned, and Rhani didn't miss the approving looks on the faces of the women.

She and Greg hugged everyone, and he said, "We'll see you all at the wedding."

"We'd better. You're my best man." Charles pulled him into a brotherly embrace then he helped Greg take their suitcases out to the car. The family followed behind them and stood at the curb waving until they drove out of sight.

"I really hate to leave. Atlanta is so nice, and your family is too." She sighed and pulled her phone from her purse. "I need to call Wil and tell him I won't be back tonight."

Greg's seductive smile when they landed in New York reminded her of why they weren't going directly home. The goose bumps jumped up on her arms, and they had nothing to do with the air conditioning inside the rental car. It had been just a week since they had made love in her office, and she was as hungry as he seemed to be for a reprise.

"Hi, it's me," she said when her brother answered. "How'd you make out over the weekend?"

"Fine," he said with a laugh. "This isn't the first time I've lived alone, Rhani."

"I'm calling to tell you we won't be back until tomorrow, and I'm going right into the office."

"Okay, no problem. How'd it go?"

"Fantastic. I'll tell you all about it when I get home from work."

"Great. Have a good flight. Tell Greg I say hi, and I'll see you tomorrow."

♥ ♥ ♥

The flight landed at LaGuardia, and Greg checked them into the Airport Marriott. "Sorry I couldn't get somewhere a little nicer, but there's not much available in the area," he said after he set their bags inside the door.

She really didn't understand why he apologized. The room had a view of the airport. It looked and smelled clean and provided a spacious desk with an office-style chair, easy chair and a king-size bed. He obviously was used to more upscale accommodations, but it didn't matter to her. She just wanted to be alone with him.

He picked up the room service menu. "It's late, but why don't we see if they're still delivering. We'll probably be hungry later," he added with a teasing smile.

Once they perused the menu and ordered sandwiches and dessert, he pulled his t-shirt over his head and tossed it on the bed. "I want to take a fast shower before they get here. Will you join me?"

She placed her open palm on his bare chest and slid it over his stomach and let it rest on the waistband of his jeans for a second before she popped open the snap .Greg unfastened the buttons of her top and pulled down his jeans with one hand while he peeled off her top with the other. Amazed by his ability to accomplish both tasks at once, she remembered he'd had considerable practice. She blinked, forced the thought away and reached behind her back to unhook her bra.

"Don't," he said, covering her hands with his. "Let me."

His soft lips glided over hers, and she tasted the flavor of his cherry ChapStick. His fingers gently followed the lacy trim of her bra before their eyes met and she saw desire in them that made her weak.

Greg unhooked the bra, and tossed it. Her nipples peaked from the coolness of the air in the room and her expectation. His warm hands covered both breasts and he caressed them as though he were touching something rare, valuable and fragile. He kissed his way down her neck, over her shoulder and then took one nipple between his lips. Rhani whimpered at the warmth and wetness of his tongue. He groaned in response then undid the button on her pants. She wriggled them down to the floor and kicked them off, anxious to feel his body against her.

The atmosphere in the room suddenly changed and Rhani could have sworn she heard the sizzle of flames. She uttered a little squeal when he picked her up and carried her into the bathroom. In a blink her panties and his briefs were gone. Her knees threatened to buckle at the beautiful rear view when he reached inside the shower to turn on the water. They soaped each other's bodies at such a hurried pace, there was nothing arousing about it. But then they didn't need any more encouragement. They rinsed off, and he dried her with a towel before rubbing his own body down as though he were trying to break some kind of record. As soon as they stepped out of the bathroom, a knock sounded on the door.

"Room service," a voice called out.

Not wanting to be seen in her disheveled state, she stepped back into the bathroom and watched Greg wrap a towel around his waist before she closed the door. He took care of the food, opened the bathroom door and led her by the hand to the bed. She sat on the edge for a moment then lay back feeling a bit self-conscious when he stood over her and let his gaze run over her body. He positioned himself above her then pressed his body into hers, all rigid insistence. She loved the way his weight felt on top of her.

He slipped both hands under her booty, urging her

against the hard, inviting heaviness of his erection and moved in a slow precise rhythm kissing her the whole time. Rhani heard herself panting, and when he kissed her, she moaned into his mouth. Finally, when Greg's fingers attended to the throbbing between her thighs, she could no longer think. She couldn't even see straight. Every time she opened her eyes, the room seemed to be spinning.

"Condom," he said between unsteady breaths. He deftly removed the foil packet from his wallet with one hand and tore it with his teeth. When had he removed it from his pants pocket and placed it on the bedside table? The moment he covered his straining member, he palmed his erection and, with one piercing plunge that made them both cry out.

This was different from what happened in her office. Rhani became more aware of every movement, sound and scent surrounding them. Her entire body throbbed from the forceful pounding he delivered this time, almost as though he were testing her to see if she could keep up. And she did until her body pitched against him with such force she thought her heart might give out. She jerked, twitched and shivered as her climax hit like a semi meeting a Smart car. Greg prolonged the pleasure by lifting her hips and bringing himself to completion. She whimpered, melted in a white-hot afterglow and wilted against him. Both completely sated, sleep pulled them under.

Sometime later Rhani's growling stomach woke her, and her movement woke Greg. "I'm starving."

"So am I. Let's eat." He got up and rolled the cart next to the bed where they devoured the light snack in a matter of minutes, brushed the crumbs from the sheets and went back to sleep in each other's arms.

The digital clock on the night table read nine-eighteen when Rhani opened her eyes, and she sat up with a start. Greg had awakened her before dawn and enticed her into a replay of last night, and they dozed off once again.

"Oh no! Greg, wake up. I'm late." Rhani shook his arm then, for reasons she didn't understand, pulled the sheet up to cover her breasts. "I'd better call Sherylle." She reached for her purse behind the clock and snatched out her phone. "Luckily I didn't schedule any sessions until eleven."

She told her assistant they were at the airport and were taking a taxi into Manhattan. Sherylle didn't need to know the details.

"I thought about calling you on Friday," Sherylle said, "But I figured you'd be back today anyway. I signed for a registered letter for you from the State Office of the Professions. Do you want me to open it?"

"There's no one in the waiting room with you, is there?"

"Not yet."

"Yes, please."

Sherylle began reading, "The New York State Office of Professions has received a complaint. We have investigated this grievance and found evidence to support the claims made. You are requested to appear before the Board of Regents on Wednesday, July 15th at ten-forty-five a.m."

Rhani's blood went cold. "Oh, my God. This can't be happening. Is that all it says?"

Greg rubbed his eyes. "What's the matter?"

"It does say if you have any questions or need further information, to call this number."

"Please put it in my chair, Sherylle. I'll be there as soon as I can get a cab." She hung up, and covered her face with her hands.

Greg pushed himself up against the headboard. "What did she say?"

"The worst thing to end a perfect weekend. I'm being called before the Board of Regents for professional misconduct."

Chapter Nineteen

Greg's eyes widened then he shut them tight for a long moment and groaned. "No."

"Who would do this to me?" Rhani's voice trembled.

He shook his head. "Thad said anyone might have a reason to report you—your competition, a jealous friend, a colleague who feels like you need to be held to the same standard he or she is, or even Senator Price."

She stared at him as though she couldn't believe the possibility. "Senator Price doesn't even know me."

"But he might see it as a way of getting back at me. Will they tell you who lodged the complaint?"

"I don't know. Sherylle said the letter is pretty cut and dried, but it did have a number to call with questions. I'll do it when I get to the office."

He rubbed her bare back in comforting circles. "Does it say anything about having an attorney?" She shook her head. "Let me call Thad and see what he recommends."

"I need to go." She climbed out of bed, and walked into the bathroom as if she were in a daze.

The sight of her nude body instantly took his thoughts away from the issue at hand. Her smooth, mocha skin, tight, round booty and thick dancer's legs made it next to impossible to concentrate, and he watched her until she closed the bathroom door. They had just spent most of the night and part of the morning satisfying each other, but the sight of her made him want her as badly as if he hadn't gotten any at all.

Oh, yeah—Thad. I was supposed to be calling Thad.

He got past the receptionist, spoke to Thad's assistant and was holding for him to pick up.

"Good morning. *Please* tell me you're not calling for yourself."

"Good morning," Greg finally sat up and threw his legs over the side of the bed. "No, man, it's not me. It's Rhani."

"What happened to her?" The way the timbre of Thad's voice rose answered Greg's lingering question about his friend's interest in her. *Wow.*

"She got a request to appear before the Board of Regents next Wednesday to answer charges of unprofessional conduct. Does she need to have a lawyer present?"

"Oh, damn. Because of her involvement with you? I don't know. I'd have to get my assistant to research it."

"It doesn't say specifically. We assume so. They sent her a registered letter while we were in Atlanta this weekend."

"You took her home?" Thad sounded dumbfounded.

"Yes. I took her home."

"This must be more serious than I assumed. If you want an opinion off the top of my head, I'd say she doesn't have a prayer. The two of you have been seen all over the city together. There's no way she can say she went home with you for counseling purposes, unless she's created *therapy on the town* or something." He snickered.

"This isn't funny, man. And we haven't been seen *all over the city*. We tried to be discreet. Can you have your assistant find out what Rhani needs to do? If she has to have legal representation, are you available next Wednesday morning?"

A loud whoosh of frustration came through the phone. "Let me check my calendar. Hold on a minute." Rhani came out of the bathroom just as Thad said, "You're one lucky S.O.B. I don't have to be in court next Wednesday. I'll get Candice on it right now and get back to you. Man, I tell you, after all you've put that girl through you'd better do right by her."

"What are you, her father? Don't worry about what I plan to do with Rhani," Greg said with a snide laugh. "I'll be waiting for your call. Thanks, Thad."

"What'd he say?" Rhani rummaged through her suitcase for a clean bra and panties and slipped into them.

He stood and stretched. "Nothing. Offhand he doesn't know how those proceedings go, so he's having his paralegal check into it."

She jumped into a fresh set of clothes like a model changing between walks on the runway, threw her old clothes into the suitcase then pulled a brush through her hair. After she scanned his body from head to toe, she said, "Last night and this morning were marvelous. I hate to leave you here—all naked and everything—but I have to go."

Greg put his arms around her and pulled her against his exposed skin. "Leave your suitcase. I'll bring it later today, and I'll call you as soon as I hear anything from Thad." He dropped soft kisses on each eyelid, the tip of her nose and finally a deep kiss he hoped spoke what he wasn't able to say. "I love you."

"I love you too."

He should've been happy hearing those words, but her half-hearted smile and the sadness in her eyes stole every bit of the joy he'd felt earlier while he'd gotten lost inside her.

She grabbed her purse and left him standing there naked and alone.

After he showered and changed clothes, Greg went to the hotel restaurant, bought an extra-large coffee and called a taxi. By the time he arrived at his apartment, a little after eleven o'clock, Rhani called him again.

"Have you heard from Thad?"

"Not yet. His assistant needs some time to research the issue."

"This isn't an *issue*, Greg! This is my life!" She sounded frantic, which was so unlike her.

He did his best to calm her. "Rhani, you need to pull yourself together before you start seeing clients. They count on you to be the calm one."

She sighed. "You're right. I called the number on the letter, but they wouldn't tell me who filed the complaint. Please let me know as soon as Thad tells you anything."

"I'll tell him to call you at the office."

"Thank you…and I'm sorry for yelling at you."

"I can take it." He chuckled. "Try not to freak out before you know anything definite, okay?"

"I'll try."

"Rhani, whatever happens, I have your back."

"I know."

He ended the call dead set on finding out who registered the complaint against her. The thought of Senator Price hating him so much he would try to destroy Rhani filled Greg with anger so white-hot it actually scared him. His frayed nerves prevented him from doing anything more than pacing around the apartment. If he were going to keep his wits about him, he needed to do something to take his

303

mind off of the awful possibilities facing Rhani because of him. He knew exactly what to do.

After he locked the apartment, he hoofed it over to Urban Green, the furniture store on East 78th Street. Rhani had made no bones about never sleeping with him in the bed he now owned, and he had to admit her feelings were justified. If the situation had been reversed, he knew he couldn't handle the idea of making love to her in the same spot where she'd had sex with dozens of other men.

For nearly an hour, he walked around the store where he'd bought his Asian-style living room set a few years ago. His bedroom could handle a king-size bed, but it wouldn't leave much floor space in the room for a dresser or chest. He decided on a twelve-drawer storage bed then made arrangements for delivery in three days.

During his walk back to the apartment, Thad returned his call. "From what Candice could uncover, it doesn't look good. I'm getting ready to call Rhani now. Since she can't very well deny any of it, my advice is for her to take her punishment and keep quiet."

Greg's footsteps slowed to a stop. "What if the punishment is revoking her license?"

"There may not be any way around it. The rules are strict, and sexual involvement with a client or patient is considered one of the most serious infractions. I need to study it further, but the only possibility I can foresee is Rhani fighting for a temporary suspension rather than a revocation."

"I need to know if I'd be allowed to speak on her behalf. See if you can find out, but don't mention it to her. Also, I need to know if there's a way to find out who filed the complaint."

"I'll put Candice back on it, but if the senator is responsible, he most likely covered his tracks well. Look, I have to be in court in a few, but I'll call Rhani now. Talk to you tonight."

"Thanks, man. Later."

Before he arrived back home, Rhani called. "I just spoke to Thad. He didn't sound very positive."

"Yeah, I know. Why don't you come here for dinner tonight?"

"I really don't feel like eating, Greg." Her voice lacked its usual verve.

"So just come by for a drink, so we can talk about what happens next."

"What's there to talk about?"

"There's plenty. Come on, you shouldn't be alone right now."

"I don't want to spend the money for a cab. From now on I need to watch every penny. God only knows how long it'll be before I find work."

"Rhani, you're talking yourself into something that hasn't even happened yet. I'll take care of the cab. Just come here for a while. Please."

She sighed as though she didn't have enough energy to answer. "Why don't you come here?"

"Because I have something to show you."

"All right. You know I don't have the address."

Greg grimaced, realizing she was right. "It's 1520 York Avenue, apartment 1705."

"I'll be there in the next hour." She clicked off without saying goodbye.

He gave the apartment a quick scan. The cleaning service had been there before they'd left for Atlanta, so everything was still tight. After he called the Italian restaurant a few blocks away and placed an order for delivery, he turned down the lights and turned on the sound system and the fountain. She didn't sound good, and he wanted to do everything in his power to make her feel better, if he could.

The food arrived before Rhani did. He put the containers in the kitchen next to the microwave. When the buzzer sounded a second time, Greg dragged in a deep breath, walked over to the intercom and pushed the button.

"Mr. Stafford," the night doorman announced. "A Ms. Drake is here to see you."

"Thank you. Send her up."

He stood outside the elevator doors on the seventeenth floor waiting for them to open. When they did, he immediately saw the strain on her face and drew her into a hug. She offered him a weak smile.

"Hi. I'm glad you decided to come."

"This is a nice building. I wasn't expecting a doorman and all."

"I'm down the hall." He put a hand on the small of her back and steered her toward his apartment.

Rhani stopped on the threshold after he opened the door, took off her shoes and scanned his living room. "This is definitely you, What does that writing mean?" she asked, pointing at the red wall where he'd had a Chinese symbol painted in bold black strokes above the big flat screen TV.

"Peace."

Her gaze shifted to the ceiling-to-floor fountain. "It is very peaceful." She rested her purse on the arm of the low black sofa and strolled over to the bookcase to peruse the titles in his book and music collections.

"Can I make you a screwdriver?" He moved toward the kitchen. "All I have is vodka and orange juice."

"Yes, *please*."

"You can look around. There isn't much more to see."

She took his suggestion and padded across the diagonal slats in the dark wood floor into the bathroom then across the hall and stopped in the doorway to his bedroom as though she were afraid to enter.

He came up behind her and circled her waist, planting a kiss on her cheek. "This is what I wanted to show you. I bought new bedroom furniture this afternoon. It'll be delivered in the next couple of days."

Rhani looked up at him over her shoulder. "You did?" Her voice overflowed with more emotion than he felt the situation warranted. She seemed a little off kilter.

"Yes. I understood what you meant about staying here with me."

"Thank you."

"We need to talk about what's getting ready to happen, baby."

She followed him back into the living room, cuddled against him on the sofa and tucked her feet up.

"I want to go with you to the hearing. If you have to go through this because of me, the least I can do is be there to speak to the Board for myself."

"I appreciate that so much, but I don't know if it would help or hurt. The Board is going to rely on the studies done on matters like this. Most of the studies suggest ninety percent of patients who get involved in a sexual relationship with their therapist are harmed. Some have ended up being hospitalized and others have even committed suicide."

His eyes rounded. "Well, that's not the case with us. It's not as though you *took advantage* of me. Our getting together was a mutual decision between two consenting adults."

"We know it, but the Board members won't see it that way. It's even been recommended that any therapist who becomes sexually involved with a client should be charged with rape."

"Our situation is very different."

"What if it isn't different? And what I *did* influence you merely by not putting my foot down the first time you flirted with me?"

"You did nothing to coerce or influence me, Rhani."

"You came to me for help with your sexual issues, and I, in essence, encouraged you by allowing you to seduce me."

"That's ridiculous. We had a normal male/female attraction to each other."

"Not normal in the eyes of the Board. It's considered abnormal because I'm your therapist, Greg. There is something therapists call *erotic transference* where the client develops romantic feelings for the therapist. It happens more often than you might imagine. Perhaps I remind you of Evelyn."

"What!" He jumped up from the sofa and paced a few steps. "No. No. I can't even explain how different you are from Ev."

"My saying that clearly upset you. Why?"

"Because it's crazy, that's why!"

"As a rule of thumb, the more baggage we carry around, the more likely transference alters our views and limits our idea of the world. The brain forms our awareness to make it easier for us to endure circumstances that are too devastating for our consciousness to handle. It's a way to cope."

He frowned, folded his arms and stared at her. "So, you're suggesting I might not be in love with you at all. It's just a figment of my imagination?"

"Not a figment of your imagination. It goes deeper than that, but if it *is* the case, do you see how damaging it might be to a client's mental health if the transference isn't worked through properly. And it's not something easily handled by the client *and* the therapist. You *really* need to address this with your new therapist."

He sat beside her again. "I wanted to talk to you about him. My first session is tomorrow. How much should I tell him?"

"Everything. The Board has already decided to censure me, so it won't make much difference."

"Are you sure?"

She nodded. "We need to stop seeing each other while you're counseling with him."

"You can't mean that." He took her hands, held them and looked directly into her eyes. "I don't want to stop seeing you."

"Me either, but it's best for you right now.

Suddenly, he knew what might be going on. "Is it best for me, or do you want to distance yourself from me in case the Board puts you on a temporary suspension?"

Her mouth dropped open. "I'm thinking about what's best for you, Greg, not me."

"Oh really?" He rose, went back to the kitchen and made himself another drink. The possibility Rhani might be willing to sacrifice him in order to retain her license put a knot in his chest. On the other hand, was it considerate or even rational of him to expect her to give up the profession she loved for him? He leaned against the refrigerator and dropped his head back against the door. Could this whole situation be retribution for all of the twisted things he'd done in the past? Whatever it was, he refused to allow it to take Rhani away from him. After a few minutes of reflection, he straightened and called out to her. "Do you feel like eating something? I got stuffed shells, Chicken Marsala and salad."

"No. I think I should leave now."

"You're just going to drop this on me and walk out? We're not even going to discuss it?"

She reached for her purse and refused to look at him. "What is there to discuss? This is the best thing for both of us." Her voice overflowed with emotion.

"Maybe for you, but not for me. I love you, Rhani, and I can't give you up just like that."

"You've made so much progress, and you need to talk to your new therapist about what happened between us."

"Happened? You say it like you've made up your mind it's over. You're not even willing to fight for us."

Rhani stood, yanked her purse strap over her shoulder with tears filling her eyes. He grabbed her shoulders and tried to hold her, but she jerked out of his grasp. When she pulled the door open, she didn't look back as she ran down the hall to the elevator.

Stunned, Greg stood staring at the open door. He couldn't make himself go after her. How could she change her mind so easily? Had she come to the conclusion she didn't love him after all? He felt as though he'd been stabbed in the chest and his life was leaking out.

For hours after he closed the door and sat on the sofa, he stared at the wall wondering how this could be happening. Thankfully, his first session with his new therapist was scheduled for the next day.

♥♥♥

He arrived at Steven Bolling's office unsure of how he felt about talking to a stranger about his relationship with Rhani. While he waited in the lobby, he tried to concentrate on reading an article in one of the magazines, but his nerves wouldn't allow it. After several minutes, the therapist, who appeared to be in his mid-forties, opened the door and asked him to come in. He introduced himself and gave Greg a rundown of the basics the same way Rhani had.

"Ms. Drake faxed me your file. She told me she's going before the Board of Regents next week. Therefore, she doesn't want you to hold anything back in our sessions. I take it from those two statements she isn't denying the charges, so I find myself in a unique situation here. She is a colleague, and one whom I like personally, but I can't side with her in this matter. I have to treat you as I would any other client."

"Understood," Greg said, observing the other man's studious, conservative appearance. "I decided to find another therapist because of the feelings I have for her, but those feelings haven't changed. It had gotten to the point where I felt I needed to talk to another man about her. She told me to ask you about transference, because she said it's possible I might have some kind of transference issue going on."

He peered at Greg over his glasses. "Do you think she's right?"

"Absolutely not."

"Why do you feel it's not the case?"

"We didn't get into it in depth, but she explained that it had to do with me taking my feelings about someone else and transferring them to her. She suggested it might be my former fiancé."

"How do you feel about her theory?"

"I think it's insane, because I despise Evelyn. Rhani is everything Ev wasn't."

"How so?"

"Even though they're both beautiful and sexy, Evelyn was self-centered and deceitful. Rhani is giving and honest. There's nothing at all similar about them."

The therapist questioned him extensively about his feelings for Rhani, and took copious notes. Even though it annoyed Greg, he answered as honestly as possible, then Greg asked, "Can you give me your honest opinion about her chances at this Board hearing?"

"Truthfully, the Board could decide in one of a variety of ways. Ms. Drake could simply be censured and reprimanded. She could be fined up to $10,000 for each violation. Or the Board could suspend her license and impose probationary terms. If this is deemed a severe case of misconduct, the Regents may revoke her professional's license permanently."

"What's your opinion?"

"I don't have one, but her willingness to be seen with you publicly might be seen as a blatant disregard for the rules of the profession."

Greg lowered his head and massaged his temples in an attempt to alleviate the throbbing behind his eyelids. "I never meant for this to happen to her. Last night she said she didn't want us to see each other anymore."

"How did that make you feel?" Mr. Bolling asked with his chin in his hand.

"Like maybe she's willing to put our relationship to the

side in order to protect her career. I'm not willing to lose her."

"Even at the expense of her career? You don't think that's selfish on your part?"

His father's words echoed in his head. *Stafford men take care of their women.* He grunted. "Yes, I suppose it is, but if the damage has already been done, I guess I'll just have to convince her to marry me." Greg scowled hearing himself make this admission to someone outside of his family.

The other man pinned him with his intense gaze. "Our time is up, but I want to leave you with one last thought. You said you've only known Ms. Drake for a few months. Talking about marriage at this stage is pretty impulsive."

"I'm not rushing to the altar. A one-year engagement would be fine with me." An involuntary smile came to his face as he grasped what his heart really wanted. "Write that down." He stood and left the office.

Chapter Twenty

Wil had arrived home before Rhani came in from the office. She knew she had to tell him what was going on, but she didn't want to just jump into the details. "How was your weekend? What'd you do while I was gone?"

"The only thing I did was go with a couple of friends to the South Street Seaport to watch the fireworks, and then I just hung out here. You look tired, so the trip must've been good."

She kicked off her shoes and sank down onto the sofa. "Greg's family is wonderful. Everything went well until we got back." She went on to tell him about the letter from the Board of Regents. "I have to appear before them next Wednesday."

Wil sat beside her. "What does that mean?"

"It means they've been investigating me for the past couple of months and decided they have enough evidence to bring me before the Board on charges of improper behavior. It's my fault. I knew from the beginning it could happen, but I didn't think anyone would care enough to report me. I guess I was wrong."

"You mean charges like they can punish you in some way?"

"Yes, anything from a reprimand to a huge fine to suspension or worse. Greg asked Thad to check into it for me. He's going with me to the hearing just in case I need a lawyer."

"I'm sorry, Rhan. Is there anything I can do?"

"I wish. Just keep good thoughts." She curled up on the pillow at the end of the sofa and pulled her feet up beneath her. "Let's watch some TV."

The good thoughts lasted all of three minutes after Wil picked up the remote and turned on the television. Like a sign from the universe, the end of TMZ appeared on the screen. The free-flowing group of reporters were finishing up the previous story when one of them said, "I have a follow-up to the Greg Stafford story. It looks like his therapist is being charged with misconduct. She has to go before the New York Board of Regents next week. So he's getting his job back and she might be losing hers. This guy must really have something going for him, the way these women take risks to be with him." The crew laughed, and Rhani covered her head with the pillow.

Naturally, once TMZ reported a story, other local outlets jumped to report on it. Only two days went by before she got calls from Alex Policastro and Dr. Spruill. Alex made it clear she wasn't the source of the Board's charges, but she also didn't fail to remind Rhani of her warning of the possibility. Dr. Spruill voiced his disappointment, yet wished her luck with the hearing. Greg called her no less than ten times. She missed hearing his voice. Normally, they talked to each other at least twice every day, and the lack of communication left her feeling empty.

The next day, when she escorted her nine-thirty appointment out of the inner office, Greg was sitting in the waiting room facing the door where she wouldn't miss him when she opened the door. He rose and walked right past them into her office before she had a chance to say goodbye to the departing client.

Rhani didn't speak until she had closed the door. "Is something wrong?" she asked with a suspicious glance.

"Is *something wrong?*" he asked, his tone intentionally sarcastic. "Rhani, you have to be kidding me. I've called you a dozen times, and you refused to return my calls. You didn't give me any choice but to come here. We need to talk."

"You shouldn't be here, Greg. The photographers are back since TMZ did an update the other night. I have to appear before the Board on Wednesday, and you're making it look as though we're still seeing each other."

"This is your office, and it's not like I haven't been here plenty of times. They don't know you're not my therapist anymore. All they want is some pictures."

Her shoulders drooped. "You're probably right, but there's nothing to talk about."

"So, it was all a lie then. All of that 'I love you, Greg' was just bullshit?"

She shook her head so vehemently her hair whipped across her face. "No, I wasn't lying, but—"

"But what? You thought you loved me, but you misjudged your feelings? Or did you change your mind?"

"I do love you," she said with her gaze glued to the floor. "But we made a mistake."

He grabbed her shoulders and forced her to look at him. "Rhani, if you really love me, you'll let me stand with you when you face the Board. And if you really love me, it won't make a difference what they decide."

"You can say that, because you still have your career. What am I going to do if they take my license?"

"We'll figure it out. You're a smart woman, and you can do anything you set your mind to."

"This is what I trained for, and I spent every cent I had setting up my practice. There's not even enough money left for me to open up a lemonade stand."

He lifted her chin, and when she looked into his eyes she saw something she'd never seen before. "I have money saved, and I have money invested, Rhani. I'll help you do whatever you want to do."

Speechless, she couldn't come up with anything to say that didn't sound desperate and pitiful. She hadn't known him long, but in nearly twenty sessions she had learned how to tell whether he was being truthful or trying to skirt the issue. She didn't detect even a hint of deception in his voice or body language.

When she didn't respond, he moved closer, circled his arms around her, and put his lips to her ear. "Let me love you, Rhani. No matter what happens; just let me love you." A tear slipped down her cheek, and he wiped it away with his fingers. "Give me the address for the hearing. I won't speak unless you want me to."

All she could do at the moment was hold him with her face nestled against his neck. How could she get him to understand no matter what he said, the Board members would only take his words as those of a vulnerable, exploited client? And when the accusing thoughts came to her, she replayed every word they had said to each other during his initial sessions.

Who was she kidding? No matter how much she insisted they stay away from each other, she knew not seeing him for twenty-four hours seemed like twenty-four days. "Honestly, I don't think it will make any difference. They might not even allow you to speak, but thank you. Your being there for support will be enough."

"You sound like you've already conceded defeat. I don't hear any fight in you."

"How can I fight it? We both know the charges aren't being manufactured. I'm guilty, Greg." She went to the desk and scribbled the address of the hearing on a sticky note and put it in his hand. "Thad said he'd meet me there, even though I don't think his presence is necessary either."

"You don't know that. We'll both be there regardless."

"You're a good man, Mr. Stafford. I'd better not keep my client waiting." She took a compact from her desk, checked her face then ran the puff over the tear streaks.

Greg reached for her hands when she stepped from behind the desk. "Are we good?"

She smiled. "We're good. Now get out of here, and let me go back to work."

He pecked her on the lips, opened the door and left. Sherylle sent her a curious squint but didn't dare ask questions in front of the waiting client. Rhani had explained what the letter from the Board could mean for her and said she would understand if Sherylle started job hunting. Her assistant, whom she'd hired for her cheerful, positive attitude, said she would wait until the Board made their decision. Even though only a week remained until the hearing, she still appreciated Sherylle's loyalty. Rhani found it impossible to be as optimistic. She hadn't experienced anything distressing in her life since before she lived at home in the midst of her mother's dysfunction. Fortunately, or perhaps unfortunately, applying the principles she shared with clients every day just wasn't working for her.

In the days leading up to the hearing, Rhani felt herself slipping into depression at the thought of having to close her office and possibly move from her apartment. Those thoughts monopolized her waking hours and invaded her sleep with frightening dreams in which she was living on the street with no visible means of support. Two nights in a row she woke up sweating after dreaming of standing on a busy street corner begging for change. When she talked to Greg on the phone, she didn't mention the disturbing nocturnal visions.

She did ask him about his first session with his new therapist. "What did you think of him?"

"He was cool, but he made it clear just because he'd accepted me as a client didn't mean he agreed with what we've done."

"It's his job to remain neutral. Are you going back to see him?"

"My next session is on Thursday." His silence spoke volumes. It would be the day after the hearing. Surely he'd have lots to talk about in that session.

"Good. Just be completely honest with him. He needs to know what you're really feeling."

"Are you sure you don't want to have dinner tonight or tomorrow? I need to see you before we walk into the hearing room."

"No, I don't think so. Let's just wait until the Board makes its decision."

"Are you saying the future of our relationship depends on what a panel of strangers decides?"

"That's not what I'm saying, but I just can't make any decisions with this hanging over my head. Please try to understand. My feelings for you keep me from thinking clearly. I need to walk into the hearing without being emotional."

"I make you emotional?" he asked with a touch of laughter.

"Very."

"So, you *do* love me?"

"Too much."

"That's impossible, but it sure is nice to hear. I'll talk to you tomorrow."

The day of the hearing, Rhani woke up to a dark, rainy, late July day. Worry over what the morning might bring had kept her awake most of the night; she hadn't slept more than a couple of hours. A cab delivered her to The Office of Professional Discipline on 125th Street in Harlem. The intermittent lightning and thunder only served to dampen her already somber mood. She hoped the air in the hearing room was in top-notch working order. Thanks to the ninety-eight percent humidity and her jangled nerves, her blouse was already soaking wet beneath her suit jacket. She had dressed in her most conservative suit, because she wanted to appear as serious as possible.

Despite the stormy weather, a couple of paparazzi waited with their cameras outside the building beneath big umbrellas. They called out to her as she hurried past them inside where she discovered Greg and Sherylle waiting inside the front entrance.

"They're not allowed inside," Greg said as soon as she closed her umbrella and shook the water off onto the carpet mat.

"Thank goodness. The letter said the hearing is in Room 209." She scanned the first floor for an elevator. The last thing her moist suit needed was a climb up a flight of stairs.

"We shouldn't all arrive together. Let me go in alone," she said, once she'd located the elevator. "I have to find a bathroom first. See you upstairs."

"Rhani." Greg put a hand to her cheek and looked into her eyes. "Don't worry. Everything is going to work out."

She put her hand atop his for a moment then headed

for the elevator. As soon as the doors closed, she leaned against the wall and took a couple of deep breaths. No matter how much she tried to convince herself otherwise, Greg Stafford, with all of his secrets and past history, had taken possession of her heart, and she would love him no matter what happened inside the hearing room.

After she located the ladies' room on the second floor, she wet a few paper towels with cold water and pressed them to her face and neck. Contrary to what she'd envisioned, the room didn't have a courtroom feel. Instead, it had been set up meeting style with a long table and chairs at the front. Her hand shook with trepidation as she opened the door. Greg and Sherylle sat in the second row facing the table, so she sat on the opposite side of the room and didn't acknowledge them. One-by-one others entered the room, and Thad was among them.

He nodded to Greg then sat beside Rhani. "How're you doing?" he said in her ear so no one else might hear.

"Scared to death."

"I don't know if you even need me here. I've never represented anyone in a matter like this."

"Thank you for being here anyway. I hope this won't take longer than an hour."

"Don't concern yourself. Greg said he's taking care of my fee."

She sighed. "He's unbelievable."

Thad shook his head in a way that neither agreed nor disagreed with her. "I don't have any advice for you other than to listen carefully, answer honestly and stay calm. If something is said with which you take issue, just lean over and whisper it to me. I'll address it with the Board. Since you chose not to contest the charges, there isn't much you can say."

"Okay. What about Greg? He wants to speak on my behalf."

He frowned. "Did he tell you what he had in mind?"

"No, but he won't say anything crazy."

His brows rose for a fraction of a second, but he didn't comment. "If they allow witnesses, I'm sure someone will announce when they can speak."

The Board members filed in and took their places at the table. One of them, a middle-aged white man, announced the case then asked, "Is Ms. Drake present?"

Thad glanced at her indicating she should answer.

"Yes, I am."

"Will you please move to a seat directly in front of the table, Ms. Drake?"

"My attorney is also present," she informed him, glancing at Thad.

"He may join you. Introduce yourself, please."

She and Thad moved to the front, and Thad gave what she assumed was a standard courtroom introduction. Another member of the Board, an older black woman who looked like a kindly grandmother, gave him the hearing procedures, told him to just speak up if he wanted to make a point, and then she read the details of the complaint against Rhani.

Thad immediately asked if she were allowed to know who filed the complaint. The woman responded by saying the information was sealed to protect the anonymity of the complainant.

The only thirtyish member of the panel, a Latino man, read the charges against her, and shocked her when he said the Board had photographs of her in private social settings with Greg. He asked her to respond.

Before she could answer, Thad asked to see the photographs. He thumbed through the images then passed the folder to her. "Have you seen these?"

Shocked to see photos taken as recently as her and Greg's trip to Atlanta and one taken of them with his arm around her as they waited for their flight, she shook her head.

They asked several questions, most dealing with Greg's therapy and finally the older man said, "Ms. Drake, since you have chosen not to contest the complaint, would you like to make a statement before we begin our deliberation?"

She cleared her throat, thankful she didn't have to stand, because her legs shook visibly. "Yes, sir, I would. I am not here to deny the charges, but I would like to address my motivations. When Mr. Stafford started counseling, he came to my office twice a week. After a month of sessions, he asked me out for coffee. Of course, I should have declined, but I wouldn't allow myself to ignore the attraction between us—two unmarried, consenting adults. Although I regret breaking the rules of my profession, I will never regret meeting this wonderful man. I ask for leniency in your decision."

When Greg stood and asked if he could speak, Rhani turned in her seat. He waited for one of the Board members to acknowledge him.

"I'm Greg Stafford, and I would like to speak on Ms. Drake's behalf. It seems strange to me that no one questioned me, since I am the client involved. This decision is being made based solely on media reports. None of this is her fault. I pursued her and wouldn't take no for an answer. There was no undue influence on her part. Ms. Drake is a kind, caring woman who's spent the past few years of her life helping people get their lives back on track. Please don't take the work she loves away from her. Thank you."

"Thank you, Mr. Stafford," the older man said, "but you and Ms. Drake thumbed your noses at the established standards and chose to have your relationship play out in the media. The photographs the Board has in its possession were taken by our own investigator. Is there anyone else present who wishes to make a statement?" When no one spoke up, he announced they were taking a one-hour recess and would return with their decision." He and the other members left the hearing room through a side door.

"Are you okay?" Greg asked Rhani when he and Sherylle met her and Thad in the hall.

"I've had better days." She tried to smile, but her face couldn't handle the task.

Sherylle patted her back. "I wish I could've said something to help."

"It's all right. I just appreciate you being here." She introduced her assistant to Thad, who greeted her, then checked his watch.

"I guess I can hang around until they come back with the decision. Why don't we go and grab something to eat?"

Greg agreed. "I saw a few places up the block within walking distance. I'm sure you probably didn't eat any breakfast."

She shook her head and kept pace with his stride as they took the stairs down to the first floor. He hooked his arm through hers and popped open his golf umbrella when they stepped out onto the sidewalk. Relieved to be out of the building, Rhani took a deep breath of the sultry air even though the rain hadn't stopped and the temperature was in the eighties. She had no desire to eat, but Greg convinced her to get a small salad and some juice once they were seated in the small sandwich shop. They ate and promptly returned to the hearing room, this time all four of them sitting together.

The Board still wasn't back yet, and the additional wait only prolonged her agony. Twice Greg reached for her hand and stopped her from twisting her hair around her index finger. After they waited for an additional ten minutes, the somber-faced Board members returned. The woman asked Rhani to again sit in the seat in front of their table. Thad accompanied her.

"Ms. Drake, we have come to a decision. In view of the severity of these charges of having an intimate personal relationship with a client," She paused and peered through her glasses at the papers in front of her on the table. "Your license to practice in the state of New York will be suspended for a period of two years. You must appear before this Board again, at which time, you will be eligible for reinstatement."

All of the air rushed from Rhani's lungs, and she hung her head for a moment. As soon as she got her bearings, she said, "Thank you for your time and your leniency." She sat with an unfocused gaze and her hand over her mouth until Greg came and embraced her from behind.

"It's over, baby. Let's go."

She stared up at him for a long moment. "What am I going to do?"

"We'll figure it out. Come on, we need to leave now." He took her hand, and she stood as the reality of the decision set in. The first person she thought about was Sherylle, and she went directly over to her. "I'm so sorry, Sherylle. I'm going to have to close the office before another month's rent is due. Could you do one more thing for me, though?"

"Whatever you need." Sherylle appeared on the verge of tears.

"Thank you. We have to cancel all appointments, and I'll need to send letters to the clients letting them know the office is closing and giving them a couple of referrals."

"No problem. I can start working on it now."

"It could've been much worse—permanent revocation along with a heavy fine," Thad pointed out. "At least they're giving you an opportunity to get your license back."

"A suspended license is the death of a therapy practice," she whispered more to herself than to those with her.

Greg seemed to sense the numbness settling on her, so he hooked an arm around her waist and pulled her close. "I'm taking you home."

"I have to go to the office and start—"

Greg interrupted her. "Sherylle, can you handle whatever needs to be done at the office right now?"

"Sure. I'll draft the letter and cancel all appointments. Rhani, go home, get yourself together, and I'll see you in the morning."

Rhani's shoulders sagged and she sighed. She'd lost her last bit of fight. "I guess it doesn't make much difference. Okay."

Greg steered her toward the curb where he tried to hail a cab. When one eventually stopped, he put her inside and climbed in next to her. He spoke to the driver, but even though she watched his lips moving, she didn't hear a single word he said. All of a sudden she asked, "Where's Thad?"

"He had an appointment and left right after they handed down the decision."

"Oh, I didn't thank him for coming," she mumbled, finding it hard to focus. As though fireworks were going off in her head, Rhani's mind exploded in a hundred different directions at once.

"I did, and he said he'd call you tomorrow."

Don't Stop Till You Get Enough

"I'll probably lose the security deposit for breaking my lease, and—" she said with her thoughts racing. "And I need to call Wil."

"Baby, you don't need to do anything right now, but calm down and relax for a few hours. We'll tackle those things one at a time."

"Relax? You can't be serious."

"I'm very serious. If you don't calm down, you won't be able to think straight. I know. I just went through the same thing."

She glowered at him. "It wasn't the same thing, Greg. You were temporarily suspended for three months, and you were still getting a check."

"I meant when it happened, I had to get my head together and figure out what I was going to do," he tried to clarify what he meant.

She stared at him with her mouth open. "All you had to figure out was how you'd spend your paid vacation," she snapped. Hurt flashed in his eyes, and she regretted letting the words come out.

"You know what? I'm going to pretend you didn't say that." He gazed out of the window as though he didn't want to look her in the face.

"Sorry." She closed her eyes. "I'm just so scared."

He hugged her tight and rocked her back and forth for a moment. "Don't be afraid. I told you, I've got this."

She gazed up at his face and studied his thoughtful expression. "You're not responsible for me, Greg."

"Maybe that's exactly what I want to be," he said with his lips against her ear.

"I can't let you do that."

"Why not? Can't you let go of the Miss Independent role even for a minute?"

"Two years is a very long minute."

"Not when you understand it's only a fraction of forty or fifty years."

Rhani momentarily stopped breathing. "What are you saying?" she asked cautiously.

The taxi pulled to the curb in front of his building. "We're here. Let's talk about it when we get upstairs."

She glanced up and blinked. She'd been in such a daze, she hadn't noticed the cab wasn't going to her apartment.

Greg paid the driver, and the doorman approached the passenger door just as Greg opened it. "Good evening, Mr. Stafford, Miss," he said greeting them with a warm smile.

He stepped out of the taxi. "Hey, Roland. This is Rhani Drake." He caught how Roland's brows rose almost imperceptibly. Over the past few years, he'd seen Greg come home with scores of different women, but not once had he introduced any of them.

"Good afternoon, Ms. Drake." He reached in, took her hand and helped her out of the car. "It's a pleasure to meet you."

"You too, Roland. Greg speaks very highly of you."

The doorman beamed and escorted her into the building. Once she and Greg entered the elevator, she leaned against him with her head on his chest. They rode to the seventeenth floor in silence.

"I need to make a couple of phone calls," he said, once he'd opened the door to the apartment and flicked on the ceiling light. "While I'm doing that, I want you to stretch out right here on the sofa."

"Do you have anything for a headache?" she asked after

she removed her shoes.

"Yeah. Be right back."

In his absence, Rhani stared out at the dreary view of the East River through the rain-streaked window, going over all that had happened since she'd gotten out of bed this morning. It felt as if she were trying to recall the details of a dream.

"Oh, no." Greg's voice drew her back to the present. "Oh, God, baby, don't cry. Please don't cry." He knelt down in front of her and held her hands. Until that moment, she hadn't known she was crying. "Here, take these. They'll help your headache." He placed two pills into the palm of her hand and a glass of water in the other. "I brought you a sheet. It's a little cool in here. Just lie down and close your eyes for a few minutes. I'll be out as soon as I make these calls." He turned off the overhead light and turned on the fountain.

She swallowed the pills, reclined on the sofa then pulled the sheet over her body, listening to the sound of the water trickling down the rock wall. When she closed her eyes, hoping to stem the pain in her head, her mind replayed an argument she'd had with her mother almost a decade ago. During the altercation, Rhani had accused her of being a fool for a man. "You put your own life on hold for him and never did the things you wanted," she remembered screaming. Hadn't she just done the same thing? Is this what it felt like to be so in love with someone you ended up doing insane things? If it weren't the case, she would've done everything possible to protect her business, and she hadn't.

Rhani listened to Greg's muffled voice coming from the bedroom for a little while, but she couldn't make out his words. The next thing she knew, he was waking her up.

"It's seven o'clock. Do you want to go back to your place or stay here? I called Wil to let him know where you are."

She sat up and ran her hands over her face, forgetting about the makeup she had applied that morning for the hearing. "Did you tell him what happened?"

"Yeah. He sounded worried, so you might want to call him and let him know whether or not you're coming back tonight."

"Maybe later." When she glanced toward the bedroom, he answered her unspoken question. "My new bed came yesterday." One corner of his mouth turned up.

"What did you mean when you said two years is only a fraction of forty or fifty years?"

"I have a few thoughts to share with you, but only if you feel like talking about it now."

"Now is as good a time as any."

"Okay, just hear me out before you say anything." He pressed his lips together in a tight line. I'm not talking about next week or next month, but I already know I want us to be permanent. If you don't find another job right away, you might have to give up your apartment. You said you liked this place. Would you like to live here?"

"Are you asking me to move in with you?"

He finally treated her to a wide, open smile. "Yes. And then we can take our time deciding the next step to take."

"Oh, Greg, I don't know. I've never lived with a man before."

"And I've never lived with a woman before."

She thought about it for a long moment then said, "It would be a solution to my financial problem, but we shouldn't live together just to solve my money issues."

"I love you, Rhani, and it's probably the only way I'll

get you here." He chuckled. "I'm not trying to rush you, though. Think about it."

Rhani gazed into his eyes and tried to determine what emotion she saw in them. Honesty and caring reflected back at her. "It's a big decision to make. I need some time." She needed to talk to another woman before she made such a major decision.

"I'm a patient man. I'll wait. Now, are you staying the night or do I need to get you a cab?"

She gave him a tremulous smile. "I'll stay, but we're not breaking in the bed tonight."

"No," he agreed. "I want to do that when you're happier."

Would she ever be happier? The life she had trained and prepared for had just come crashing down in a couple of hours. Now she had to come up with a way to rebuild it.

As though Greg read her mind, he said, "Besides counseling what is the one thing you love doing most?"

"Mentoring my girls," she answered, knowing where he was leading. "But it's volunteer work."

"It doesn't have to be. Have you ever considered starting a non-profit organization that could help ten or twenty times the number of girls you work with now?"

"Yes, but I can't say I've given it any serious thought."

"This is just off the top of my head, but you might want to talk to Adanna and my mother about starting a non-profit corporation and going for grant money and contributions. It's what Adanna is doing for her hospital in Nigeria. Mama helped her get started with the research. It would keep your mind occupied if you're not working temporarily."

"That's an interesting idea, but I need to find a *job*."

"Why? You don't think I make enough money to take

care of both of us?"

She knew he meant well, but just hearing him say it got under her skin. "I don't need to be taken care of. I'm not helpless."

"I'm well aware of that, Rhani, but what's so wrong with taking some time off to investigate other options? It wouldn't be forever, just until you find another way to use your talent not requiring a therapist's license. Let me play therapist here for a minute, because I have the feeling I know what's bothering you."

She reared back and crossed her arms. "All right, go ahead."

"Baby, you are not your mother, and I'm not your father. With your gifts and talents you'll never have to wait tables in some greasy spoon. And I wasn't raised to be a man who'll run out on you."

The disturbing reality that she wanted him more than she wanted her career slapped her like an offended reality show housewife. She'd bought into the school of thought that her career should come before her romantic life, and since her last few relationships hadn't amounted to anything, she'd allowed work to take precedence over everything else. Yes, her practice was important, but if she was honest with herself, she had to admit she also wanted a committed relationship with a man who loved her.

"It *is* an interesting idea, and—"

"And you're going to take it into consideration?" His deep, coaxing gaze pulled the answer out of her.

"Yes…I'll think about it."

Chapter Twenty-One

*F*or the first time in three years, Greg slept in the same bed with a woman without anything sexual happening. It didn't take much—the scent of her perfume or the slightest caress of her soft skin—to make him want her, but Rhani seemed so fragile. He knew how important it was for her to know he wouldn't take advantage of her vulnerability, so after he'd kissed her goodnight, he didn't do more than stroke her hair.

For a while, he lay awake studying the empty space between them in his new bed. He wanted to spoon with her, but he didn't want her to wake up thinking he was trying to get some. Six months ago, he wouldn't have believed he'd not only be able to control himself, but actually be content doing it. Just the fact that she slept beside him was enough. Amazing.

Tomorrow their faces would be in the news again, but at least the uncertainty had ended. The decision hadn't been favorable, but it could've been worse. Tomorrow was a new day. He had a second session with the new therapist scheduled for ten-thirty. Rhani would start taking the necessary steps to close her practice, and he had to be there to support her. He went to sleep knowing when the sun rose they would be starting a new chapter in their lives. And they'd be doing it together.

He arrived at the therapy session early, strangely anxious to talk about the hearing and everything that had transpired yesterday. Greg left Steven's office feeling unusually positive. It wasn't brought about by anything the therapist said to him, but more what he had worked through in his head as they talked. Wasn't that what therapy was supposed to do? Greg laughed to himself while he waited for the bus that would take him to Rhani's office. One of his revelations was about becoming more aware of how he spent his money. The Scoop paid him an excellent salary, and he wasn't a big spender across the board. But he'd never paid much attention to the cost of his on-air suits or what he spent on food, drink and entertainment. Time to make some changes.

No one could ever have called him a fan of public transit, but it was much cheaper than taking cabs everywhere. When the bus stopped for him, he boarded completely unaware of the need for either exact change or a MetroCard. He fumbled through his pockets while the driver impatiently told him the box didn't take dollar bills for the $2.50 fare. A couple of the passengers sitting in the front offered him change for a dollar, and he finally deposited the necessary amount.

He stopped at Starbucks and bought extra-large coffees for Rhani, Sherylle and himself thinking it might be wiser to invest in a Keurig brewer. His mind was occupied with being able to provide for her, and the prospect agreed with him. He had grown up seeing the women in his family never lack anything, whether or not they had their own careers, and he wanted to be able to do the same for Rhani.

She was unusually quiet and introspective when he arrived at her office, and she just said she'd spoken with the management office about breaking her lease. They told her the company would indeed be keeping the two-thousand-dollar security deposit she'd paid when she signed the lease.

"What can I help you do?"

Rhani offered him a weak smile. "Sherylle cancelled all of my appointments and told each client to expect a letter with referral suggestions. She could use some help packing up the files."

The three of them worked in near silence with just the music from the small shelf system in the inner office playing in the background. About an hour in, she asked, "How did your session go?"

"Very well. I feel comfortable with Steven. By the way, he sent his regards and said he hopes everything works out for you."

"That was nice of him, even though I know he thinks I've gone off the deep end."

Greg wanted to correct her, because from what he'd seen, the men who knew her personally liked her more than they might be willing to admit. She had an underlying sexiness without being blatant, and he imagined most men found the softness of her appearance and speech irresistible. He certainly did.

"I believe he meant it."

The trio worked for about two hours before he asked, "How about I take you ladies to lunch?"

"Thanks, but I'm not hungry. You two can go ahead." Rhani absentmindedly rummaged through her desk.

"We're not going out without you," he insisted. "You can take a break, even if you don't feel like eating."

"I don't feel like going out." Her words held more emphasis this time.

"Okay. We'll walk over to the deli and get takeout."

Rhani shrugged. "Just lock the door on your way out."

Once he and Sherylle entered the elevator, he said, "Have you ever seen her like this?"

"No. I'm worried about her, Greg. This whole thing seems to be wearing her down. I really think she needs to talk to someone and get her feelings out."

"Do you know of anyone she'd be willing to talk with?"

"Yes, her name is Alex Policastro. Rhani really admires her, and they were pretty close."

"Could you give me her number when we get back?" He asked as the doors opened to the lobby.

Sherylle smiled. "Of course. You really love her, don't you?"

"She's going to marry me. She just doesn't know it yet."

"I understand about all the rules and stuff, but I like you two together."

"Thanks. There aren't many people who'd agree with you."

The instant they walked out of the building, someone called his name. "Greg! Greg, what do you plan to do to help Rhani Drake now that she's lost her license?"

He stopped for a second and drew in a long, fortifying breath then glowered at the man pointing a camera in his face before he took Sherylle's arm and continued walking.

"I thought you were going to clock him," she squeaked breathlessly.

He laughed. "That was my first thought, but dealing with these guys has taught me a whole lot about self-control. They try to goad you into saying or doing something you'll regret so they can splash it all over."

A couple of minutes later, they got in line at the busy deli. Greg ordered a sandwich for himself and Rhani and told Sherylle to order what she wanted. After they took beverages from the cooler, grabbed a couple of bags of chips, and he paid for everything, they headed back to the office. The photogs assailed them with different questions on the way back into the building.

"Have you found a new therapist yet, Greg? Is she as

pretty as Rhani Drake?" Greg ground his teeth and rushed toward the building entrance.

One of them pointed his camera at Sherylle. "You're Ms. Drake's assistant, right? What are you going to do for a job now?"

"Don't respond." Greg literally pushed her through the revolving door.

"Whew! They won't let up, even when you don't answer."

"What *are* you going to do, Sherylle?"

"I'm only twenty, and I still live with my parents, so I won't be homeless. Maybe I'll take my time, collect unemployment and look for another job. It'll be hard finding another boss as great as Rhani though."

"If you're interested in working in television, I can give you the names of a few people to contact."

"Thanks, Greg. I appreciate it."

When Sherylle unlocked the door to the office, Rhani was still sitting motionless behind her desk.

Greg set the bag on the table between the sofa and the chaise. "I got you a sandwich and some juice."

The way she spun her chair away from him so quickly, it was clear something was wrong. He put both hands on the high back of the executive chair and turned her to face him. Her red eyes and nose gave her away. She'd waited until he and Sherylle had left to breakdown. He grabbed the chair arms and bent forward so he spoke directly into her face. "Talk to me, baby."

"I can't do this. I can't just give up everything I've worked so hard for."

"You don't have any choice, Rhani. What you should do is jump right into something else. You've probably counseled lots of people about not giving in to depression. Think about what you told them. The same advice is just as good for you as it was for them. I know I'm responsible for this mess, but I refuse to let you wallow in self-pity." He took his phone from his pocket, dialed and put the call on speaker.

Rhani eyed him with a suspicious squint. "Who are you calling?"

"Hey, Adanna, it's Greg. I hoped you'd answer, so I wouldn't have to leave a voicemail. I know you're busy, but I need to ask a huge favor. I'm on speaker with Rhani."

"Hello, Rhani. I'm so sorry to hear about what happened."

"Hi, Adanna," Rhani responded unenthusiastically. "Thank you."

"Ask away, brother-in-law."

"She needs a crash course on setting up a non-profit corporation and who she needs to address her grant requests to. I was hoping you two might be able to do it between video chat and e-mail. Would that be possible in the next week or so?"

"Yes, but this is news. What kind of program?"

"Mentoring teens and young women. She's been doing it for a couple of years as a volunteer."

"That's wonderful! I'll do whatever I can to help, and I know Mama will also. Let me figure out what day will be best, and I'll ring you back."

"Let me give you Rhani's cell number, so you can call her directly."

"Thanks, Adanna," Rhani said when he finished giving her the digits. "We'll talk soon." She scowled at him as soon as he cut the call. "I could've done that myself."

"You needed a little push." He grinned, thinking she'd really be annoyed at his next call.

After they worked for another hour, Rhani sent her assistant home. Greg sat with her on the sofa looking at the stacks of files, pictures they had taken off the walls and accessories from the shelves. "Looks like you'll need a dozen boxes or maybe more. I can pick them up at U-Haul in the morning. How about you eat lunch now? It is almost four o'clock." He opened the bag and handed her the sandwich then twisted the top off the juice.

She opened the paper wrapping and stared for a moment at the turkey and avocado sandwich, her favorite. After a few minutes, she took a bite and followed it with a swig of orange mango juice. She took another bite and a smile momentarily broke through her sadness.

"That's the first smile I've seen from you all day."

"You take such good care of me," she said with a thoughtful expression.

"I'm trying." He took her hand and entwined his fingers with hers. "Wil and one of his boys said they'd help me move everything as soon as you're ready."

"The sooner the better. I want to get this over with as quickly as possible."

"Okay. I'll call around." He searched Google on his phone for truck rental companies while Rhani dallied over her lunch. She only managed to consume half of the sandwich, re-wrapped the other half and put it into the small refrigerator in the supply closet, locked up the office and they left the building with no specific destination in mind.

"Where are we going now?" he asked. She raised her shoulders with a blank expression. "It's too hot to be walking around. I picked up two MetroCards on my way over this morning." He reached into his pocket and handed her one of the blue and gold cards. "This'll save us some money on transportation. Let's hop the bus to your place and chill for a while. I need to talk to Wil." He pulled the MTA site up on his phone and searched for the right bus to take them to her apartment.

After a fifteen-minute wait, they boarded the bus. He noticed the curious glances and shared whispers of certain passengers as they moved toward two empty seats in the middle of the bus. "They recognize us," he said against her ear.

"Great."

A young brother sitting a few seats in front of them turned around, pointed his finger and asked loudly, "Hey, man. Aren't you the guy they been showing on TMZ?"

Greg chuckled. "I don't think so. You've got me mixed up with someone else."

"No, it's you," he insisted, his voice got louder as he spoke, causing everyone on the bus to turn around. "I watch it every night. You the one who got busted for tapping the senator's wife! Whatchu doin' ridin' the bus, man?"

Rhani groaned and turned her face to the window visibly mortified by his loud declaration.

Greg neither confirmed nor denied his identity and just said, "Same thing you're doing, man. Trying to get home."

The man sat back down and excitedly explained to his buddy who Greg was.

Greg turned to Rhani. "I'm sorry. Just when you think nobody knows who you are, some fool proves you wrong."

She mumbled, "One more reason why I despise public transportation."

The big-mouthed guy and his friend waved to him when they got off two stops later. Greg gave them a nod and breathed a sigh of relief. He and Rhani rode for another ten minutes before the bus reached their stop where they exited and walked three blocks to her building.

After riding the bus and walking in the heat, Rhani immediately went to take a shower. Wil hadn't gotten in from work yet, so as soon as Greg heard the water running, he dialed the number Sherylle had given him for Alex Policastro. "This is Greg Stafford," he said when she answered. "I got your number from Rhani Drake's assistant. Do you have a moment to talk?"

"Yes, Mr. Stafford, I do. How can I help you?"

"Rhani, would kill me if she knew I'd called you. The Board suspended her license yesterday. We spent today packing up her office, and she's not handling it well. I know she admires and respects you, and I think she needs to talk about all of this with someone besides me. Could you call her, and see if you can get her to open up? She hasn't been sleeping or eating well, and I'm worried about her."

"Yes, of course I will. Does she have any plans for the immediate future?" Dr. Policastro asked.

"I'm trying to get her to investigate setting up a non-profit girls mentoring program; I hope that's something she'll discuss with you."

"What kind of shape is she in financially?"

"She doesn't have to worry about that, and I told her so."

"Oh, okay," she responded with skepticism oozing from her words.

"I know what you're probably thinking, but I love Rhani, and I'm going to do everything in my power to help her, believe me. I can't talk long because she'll be coming back in a couple of minutes. Do you have her cell number?"

"Yes. Thanks for calling me, Mr. Stafford."

"It's Greg, and thank you for being her friend, Dr. Policastro."

"It's Alex. I'll call her later tonight."

He rested the phone on the table and hit the power button on the TV remote. A few minutes after the water stopped running, he heard Rhani talking to someone on her phone.

"Adanna just called," she said when she rejoined him in the living room with a towel wrapped around her head, a bottle of olive oil moisturizer, a wire brush and a large tooth comb in her hand. "We're going to do a video chat on Sunday afternoon."

"Great. When I spoke with her last, she said things are going well with her foundation so far."

Rhani removed the towel from her hair and patted it dry. He watched her part the kinky corkscrews into sections and start applying the oil and massaging it into her scalp. He took the bottle from her hand. "Here, let me do it."

She glanced at him and a flicker of a smile crossed her face before she scooted from the sofa onto the floor between his knees and put the towel around her shoulders.

"How much should I put?"

"Just a little squirt, then work it into the hair like this." She demonstrated then put the bottle back into his hand.

Her hair was the first thing he had admired about her in his initial session, and he'd since had the joy of putting his hands in it. Most black women had issues about people touching their hair, but not Rhani. Her natural mane seemed to call out for his touch. He parted the hair into sections, anointed each one with the fragrant oil then gently massaged it into the springy coils and brushed it through with the wire brush. Gradually she relaxed and uttered small sounds of pleasure at how good it felt. If they hadn't been at the end of such a miserable day, he would have escalated this moment into something truly intimate. But not tonight. Tonight she needed non-sexual comfort, and he wanted to show her that he could provide it.

"I've been thinking about the apartment. I need to stay here through Labor Day. Then Wil can move right back to the dorm. There's no reason for him to move twice."

Just then her brother came through the front door.

"Hey, man, we were just talking about you," he greeted Wil.

"What'd I do?"

"Nothing," Rhani answered with a laugh that sounded as though she had to struggle to get it to come out. "Sit down, so I can tell you what I'm going to do."

He left his shoes at the door and sat across from them. She told him about the immediate closing of the office, and her decision to remain in the apartment until he went back to school.

"Don't spend any extra money because of me, Rhan. I hate that you have to move, but if you need to leave here sooner, don't worry about me."

"I can't see myself getting it together and packing this place up in less than a month."

"Where are you moving to?" he asked innocently.

The grin on Greg's face must have answered his question.

"You guys are moving in together?"

Rhani voiced her decision aloud for the first time. "Yes, we're together all of the time anyway. It just makes sense at this point."

Greg scrunched up his face. "Damn, that *really* sounds romantic. She's the pragmatic one." He wanted to jump up and do an end zone dance at the moment.

"I didn't mean it like that. I'm excited about moving in with you, but right now I'm so worn down, it's hard to show it." She leaned her head back and puckered her lips. He leaned forward and obliged.

They talked about what to do with her office furniture and decided paying for a large storage unit wasn't cost effective, considering she had no way of knowing how long it would be before she'd have need of another office. She decided to take photos and post it on Craig's List right away.

He ordered Chinese and, even though Rhani said she still had no appetite, he convinced her to eat some vegetable lo mein and drink a couple of cups of tea. In the middle of their meal, her phone rang. When she said, "Hi, Alex," it was time for him to check out. He kissed her neck, gave Wil some dap, and headed to the bus stop.

The wait for the next bus and the ride back over to the East Side gave him time to think about what he needed to do to make Rhani's transition easier. Even though she'd never admit it, all of the upheaval in her life had to be painful and scary. It was a daunting prospect for him too. The idea of living with a woman 24/7 sent a chill up his spine. A chill that was simultaneously good and bad.

Would being in close confines change how they reacted to each other, or would it bring them closer? There wasn't a lot of room at his place, but he wanted her to have her own space—a spot where she could go to be by herself. Both of them were used to living alone, so sharing the apartment would be a major adjustment. He considered the pros and cons, and the pros won when he pictured Rhani walking around the apartment in nothing but a bra and panties.

First thing in the morning, he got a call from the station

manager's assistant requesting his presence at a meeting on the following Monday morning to discuss his reinstatement to The Scoop. As soon as he hung up, he dialed Jordyn, his publicist and asked her to attend, then he called Rhani.

"Good morning. What are you up to today?"

"Sherylle and I are going to finish packing, and I want to take pictures of the furniture so she can post it on Craig's List."

"Do you need me to do anything?"

"Mmm, I don't think so. We got a lot done yesterday. Do you have something on your schedule?"

He planned to spend the day moving things around in his place to make room for her. "There are a few things I need to take care of today, but tomorrow I can be there for you, if you plan on working on a Saturday. On Monday I have a meeting with the station manager at nine-thirty."

Her voice perked up. "You do? That's good news, right?"

"I guess. If they decided they didn't want me back, one of the network attorneys would've sent a registered letter or something formal like that. I think they just want to reiterate the station standards and give me a definite return date."

"I'm sure that's all it is."

"If you get any responses from Craig's List, I want to be there when they come to look at the furniture. Too many crazy incidents have happened with that site. It's not safe for you to meet strangers there alone."

"It's not necessary," she insisted. "Sherylle will be there with me."

"Rhani, be reasonable, please."

"Okay, okay. Just make sure you're available."

"I'm always available for you." In spite of the fact that she was an educated woman who helped other people get over their pasts, the only male role model in hers had been a sad example. She needed to know she could count on him.

Greg sat in his living room for the next hour trying to figure out what could be removed or rearranged to make room for whatever things Rhani might bring. She also had contemporary furniture, so if she wanted to merge their things, it wouldn't be a hot mess. Since he had an extra bedroom, he'd already decided to turn it into an office/sitting room where she could read, study or chat with friends without having to be in the living room or bedroom. It already had a futon which provided seating, but it needed a workspace and some accessories. Hopefully, she had whatever the room lacked.

Since he didn't have anyone to help him, it took most of the morning to complete the job, but he felt satisfied with the results when he finished. After he showered and dressed, he headed over to Lexington Avenue to take care of the most important task before his meeting with the station tomorrow. The single-minded determination with which he walked into Zales fizzled once he saw the displays. This wasn't going to be as easy as he'd thought. The salesman must have seen how overwhelmed he appeared by the sheer number of diamond rings in the showcases, and with a sympathetic smile asked if he could help. Greg wasn't certain he should even be doing this right now, and his heart beat like a marching band bass drum.

"I'm looking for an engagement ring. Solitaire. White gold. About two carats."

The salesman described what they had available and gave him a short spiel about the difference in diamond quality.

"I don't even know her ring size."

"Not a problem. We can give you a medium size, and it can be resized once you present it to her."

Greg exhaled a long breath and began his search for a stone and setting he knew she would love. After nearly two hours of the jeweler showing him different stones in various settings, he chose one and paid with his American Express black card. In the forty-eight hours it would take to create the ring, he would know the network's decision about his future position with, The Scoop. All he'd have to do then was figure out the perfect time to give it to her.

♥♥♥

He arrived at network headquarters Monday morning a little early, but not so much so that he looked desperate. John Hanke, the station manager, Ken, his immediate boss, one of the legal eagles, a woman from the station's public relations department, Arianna, his co-anchor and Jordyn, his publicist were all in attendance. They each gave him a pleasant greeting, but none of them said anything as definite as *welcome back.* He made himself a cup of coffee and sat beside Jordyn.

As the senior executive in the room, John opened. "Good to see you, Greg. It looks like everyone is here, so we might as well get started. The purpose of this meeting is to establish the ground rules for your return as co-anchor of The Scoop. I received a letter from your former therapist informing us that you had terminated counseling with her and selected another therapist." He cleared his throat. "Look, Greg, I'm going to drop the formality here and just be candid. "Your arrest threw us for a loop, and I believe we handled it the right way, but we weren't prepared for the subsequent publicity when *The Post* and *TMZ* reported you were involved with your therapist." He shook his head.

"Then last week it comes out that she had her license suspended as a result of all this. Do you have anything else to tell us before we make a decision about your return?"

Greg had made up his mind on the way into the conference room not to speak unless spoken to. It was his turn now. "Yes, I do. Rhani Drake and I have decided to move in together." He couldn't help but notice the mutual eye roll among those at the table. "I plan to ask her to marry me, but we will be having a nice, long engagement."

John's brows rose, and so did Jordyn's. John glanced at Ken, who wore an amused smile. "Ken, do you have any comments?"

"None of this has hurt the show. In fact, it's resulted in more e-mail, tweets and Facebook comments than we've ever received, the majority of it supporting Greg. I believe the fans will eat up a Scoop wedding."

"None of this is public knowledge yet, and I don't want it to get out prematurely," Greg warned. "When it's official, I've have Jordyn put out an announcement."

"Okay," the station manager continued, "We want you to sign an amended contract which contains a revised morality clause." He glanced at the attorney.

The lawyer explained. "This morality clause is a bit more specific than the original, and there is no option for suspension in the event of an infringement. "Any violation will result in immediate termination." He slid the contract across the table so Greg could peruse it.

Greg felt like a scolded child, but he knew he deserved it. "Are there any other changes?"

"No."

"If you don't mind, I'd like to fax a copy to my attorney. He wasn't able to be here today."

"Of course," John said. "Once the Legal department has the signed, revised contract, you and Ken can work out a return date."

"As far as your making any kind of statement your first day back on air, you should work it out between our PR department and your rep. You can stay here and get that out now if everyone has the time. If there's nothing further, I guess we're done." John stood, walked around to Greg and extended his hand. "Welcome back."

"Thank you." Greg smiled, gave his hand a firm shake then watched him leave the room.

Jordyn wrote down Thad's fax number for the attorney, and he also exited the conference room. The rest of them stayed behind and worked on the statement Greg would deliver his first day back on the show.

An hour later, he left to meet Rhani. She'd been so quiet lately and hadn't said much of anything other than she had arranged two appointments that afternoon from her Craig's List ad. He wanted to make sure she didn't meet them alone.

Chapter Twenty-Two

While Greg went to his meeting at the network's headquarters, Rhani took a cab to Alex Policastro's office. She felt guilty about spending the extra money, but in her frame of mind she couldn't deal with people on the bus or subway. She and Alex had talked for nearly an hour when she'd called the other evening. During the call, Alex insisted Rhani come to talk to her about everything going on in her life. After much hemming and hawing on Rhani's part, Alex convinced her.

Alex offered her a cup of coffee, and after Rhani stirred in cream and sugar, she sat in the spot reserved for clients.

"How are you, Rhani? I mean how are you *really*?"

She looked into her friend and mentor's face and sighed. "I'm scared, Alex. I'm in love. I'm jobless, and I'm soon to be homeless."

"Homeless?"

"I can't afford to keep my apartment if I'm not working. Greg asked me to move in with him, so after Labor Day, I'll be relocating to his place on the Upper East Side."

Alex silently studied her for a long moment. "Are you sure you want to do this, or are you merely acting out of fear of the possible financial situation?"

She didn't answer right away. "I love him, Alex, and I have to confess I'm nervous about moving in, but I *want* to live with him."

"Do you believe he's ready for such a commitment? Only a few months ago, he was deep in his addiction."

"He experienced a breakthrough that changed his entire outlook."

"Tell me about it." Alex crossed her legs, folded her hands and waited.

"His sexual addiction wasn't the result of childhood abuse or any of the textbook causes. She recounted Greg's history before, during and after his relationship with Evelyn. "Once he acknowledged and accepted his anger and hurt over what happened between them, he had a major breakthrough. He's a different man, Alex."

The long, penetrating look Alex gave her when she leaned back in her chair warned Rhani of an oncoming lecture. "I'm glad to hear he had a breakthrough, but you know as well as I do that he has a long way to go. He needs to deal with the challenges which will inevitably come against him. Have you asked yourself how it would affect you if he messes up?"

Rhani didn't have an answer, because she really didn't want to talk about the chance that it might happen.

"You're looking at him as though his issues are over and done with simply because he's crossed two hurdles. It's an accomplishment for sure, but what happens if he doesn't clear hurdle number three? Would you be able to forgive him for having sex with someone else?"

"I understand what you're saying, but every woman faces the possibility that her man might cheat on her. I believe Greg is no longer fighting those demons."

Alex shook her head as though she were speaking to a moron. "All right, Rhani. Let's consider his side. How do you think it will affect him if he disappoints you? The guilt he'll experience will be double, and he might not be able to bear it."

"You still don't understand what I'm saying. This is not an infatuation. I love this man, and I'm willing to stand by him and help him through anything he might face."

"Is he still in therapy?"

"Yes. He started with Steven Bolling."

"I don't know him, but it's good he's willing to continue counseling.

Rhani looked at her friend eye-to-eye. "I want to continue therapy too, but only if you promise not to keep insisting Greg is going to backslide. I can't go forward constantly considering that likelihood. If anything does happen, I promise to be honest and tell you about it. But I don't need to come every week."

"Okay. We'll make it every two weeks then. I hope everything works out well for you, Rhani."

Within the week, Rhani officially closed her office and sold the furniture to one of the Craig's list buyers. It had been one of the hardest things she'd ever done, and she worked through the pain of the separation with Alex.

The first weekend in September Greg moved Wil back to the dorms at City College. Rhani was concerned about what he would do during the upcoming holidays, but Greg insisted they would work something out. Right now, her brain couldn't take another problem.

She and Adanna had already had one video chat, and another in which his mother also participated. Rhani had also begun her online research into creating the specific kind of program she wanted to develop. His mother had stressed the importance of having all of the facts and figures in some kind of orderly format before she talked to the grant writer. Greg kept telling her how glad he was to see how much her mood had changed once she immersed herself in the project.

Her therapy with Alex continued, and being on the other side of the desk helped her to express her feelings in a way that hadn't been possible with her girlfriends or with Greg.

Before she put her things into storage, he asked her to come by and take a look at the changes he'd made. She hadn't been there in weeks and seeing the lengths he'd gone to in order to make room for her surprised and pleased her.

Her eyes took in how he had rearranged the furniture in the living room. "When did you do all this?"

"The day after the hearing."

"Where's your other bookcase?"

He took her hand. "Come here, let me show you." She followed him around the corner to the extra bedroom, stopped on the threshold and stared. "What is all this?"

"I thought you might need a work space where you can concentrate on your research and have somewhere private to sit when you have your girlfriends over—the girlfriends I haven't met yet." A smile lurked at one corner of his mouth.

"You'll meet them. Don't worry."

"If you have some furniture you want to bring here, we can find a spot for it."

"You didn't have to do this."

"Yes, I did. This is going to be *our* place, and I want it to feel like home to you, baby."

Rhani gazed up at him, hugged his waist and pressed her cheek to his chest. "You're a good man."

She released him and meandered into the kitchen. "I'm going to bring my pots and pans here, since your kitchen is utensil-challenged, and I'm going to start cooking dinner. Take-out is one of our biggest expenses, and since we're trying to save, you could bank the money instead. What do you think?"

"Can you cook?" he asked, sounding as though he was holding back a laugh.

Rhani stood with her hands on her hips "Yes, I can cook. I just didn't do it a lot, because I was always so busy. Now I have the time."

"I'm just checking. Charles' wedding is in a few weeks, and I want to be alive to stand up for him."

She punched his arm. "You'll be surprised at what I can do in the kitchen."

"As surprised as I am about what you can do in the bedroom?" He wriggled his eyebrows and squeezed her booty.

"You haven't even scratched the surface yet of what I can do in the bedroom, Mr. Stafford."

His eyes widened, and she could practically see the wheels turning in his head.

In the days that followed, they moved the items she decided not to take to his place into a storage unit and brought the rest to his apartment. After much shuffling and repositioning, they came to a mutually agreeable set-up. She had what she needed, and the apartment didn't feel cluttered. They had set up both laptops in the office/sitting room, along with the small file cabinet containing her personal papers which used to occupy a corner of her bedroom. Greg hooked up the shelf sound system from her office on the bookshelf and also installed the flat screen TV from her extra bedroom on the wall. After a visit to The Container

Store, they equipped the other wall with cubbyholes, hooks and shelves. She loved working in her first home office.

In the late afternoons, she stopped her research and prepared dinner so it would be ready by the time Greg got in from the studio. The meals weren't fancy, but he seemed quite pleased with the staples of most households—spaghetti and meatballs, baked chicken, and when she felt adventurous, chicken quesadillas or sweet and sour chicken with Asian noodles. There had been a couple of mishaps, and those were the nights they'd called for an emergency pizza.

Amazed at how much better she'd been sleeping, it didn't take long for Rhani to realize sleeping in the same bed with Greg was comforting. The first few nights, she'd woken up during the night disoriented about her surroundings until she felt the warmth of his body next to her. He had been cautious about initiating sex, and had left it up to her. By the third night in her new home, she met him at the door wearing nothing but her red satin robe when she heard his keys in the lock and surprised him with a pre-dinner romp.

Afterward, what he'd said about not meeting her friends weighed on her mind. Now that they were officially together, there was no logical reason why she shouldn't introduce him to Kat and Joie. Greg's intermittent, light snore told her he was taking a post-nookie nap. She eased out of the bed, shrugged into her robe and went into the living room to call Joie.

"Hey, girl," Rhani said when she answered. "What have you been up to?"

"Isn't that the question I should be asking you? I haven't heard from you in weeks."

"I've been really busy, but it's the reason I'm calling. What do you have planned for Saturday night?"

"Not much. Why?"

"I'd like you and Kat to come over for dinner. Nothing fancy. Let me give you my new address. Got a pen?"

"What new address? You moved and didn't even tell us? I don't believe this. Hold on a sec." She could hear the muffled sounds of her friend searching for something with which to write. "Go ahead."

"It's 1720 York Avenue not far from Lexington over by Gracie Mansion."

"You moved to the Upper East Side?"

"Yup. Is seven o'clock good?" she said, refusing to entertain her friend's questions.

"Perfect. You're really going to make me wait to find out why you moved all the way up there? You have a lot of explaining to do, Rhani."

"I know. Now let me go, so I can call Kat. See you Saturday."

Rhani handled the call to Kat the same way. She asked even more question than Joie had about the move, since Rhani had never mentioned her plans.

"So you finally decided to reveal me to your girls?" She turned around to see Greg standing totally naked next to the shoji screen separating the living room from the bedroom.

"You say it as if I've been hiding you or something."

He crossed his arms across his bare middle and grinned. "Well…"

"I haven't been trying to hide you. I just wanted to wait until things were a little more settled with us. You understand, right?"

He nodded. "We've eaten at home all week, so I think we can order in on Saturday. You know what they like."

"Yes, we have. That'll be our treat for the week."

"I'd really like my treat now," he said, closing his fist around his returning erection.

She couldn't rip her gaze from the raw, erotic sight, and it drew her back to the bedroom like a tractor beam.

♥♥♥

Rhani ordered Thai food from one restaurant and seafood from another on Saturday night. She'd spent the afternoon Swiffering the entire apartment. The shiny wood floors and black furniture in the living room was trendy and stylish, but it attracted dust like paperclips to a magnet. Greg adjusted the dimmers so the room appeared cozy but not dark. The food arrived early enough for her to transfer it into microwaveable dishes to be reheated later.

The buzzer sounded at seven, and Rhani chuckled. She knew her friends well enough to know they were together in the lobby watching the time on their phones until the time read seven on the nose. The night doorman announced them, and Rhani told him to send them up.

Greg finished selecting a playlist on his iPod while she opened the door.

"Girl, how did you luck up on a place with a doorman?" Joie asked from the hallway beside Kat who finished her thought as if they were twins. "Are you purposely trying to make us feel like poor stepchildren?"

Her friends came to an abrupt stop when Greg turned to face them and said, "Hello, ladies. I was just putting some music on." Both of them gawked at him then back at Rhani.

Their reactions were just what Rhani had expected. "Well, are you coming inside or do you just want to stand in the doorway?"

"Oh, we're definitely coming in," Joie breezed past giving her the side eye. She and Kat knew the routine from past visits to Rhani's old apartment. They removed their shoes and took a pair of sport socks from the basket beside the door.

"Greg, this is Joie Jarrett and Katandra Washington. Ladies, this is Greg Stafford."

"Come in. Have a seat," he said, indicating the sofas in the living room. "Can I get you a drink? We have red or white wine, beer, and I make the best screwdrivers on the East Side."

"I'll be the judge of that," Joie challenged him. "Screwdriver, please."

Kat blatantly studied him from head to toe, and Rhani wanted to laugh at the way Kat seemed to think she did it on the sly. "White wine for me, thanks."

The instant he left the room to go into the kitchen and fix their drinks, both of them bombarded her with a storm of whispered questions.

Kat pointed her finger in Rhani's face. "So *this* is why we haven't heard from you in almost a month. You two are *living* together?"

"Damn, that man is fine," Joie said with a hand splayed over her chest.

"You know it's a shame we had to find out what was going on with you from TMZ, Rhani."

Joie acted as though she didn't even hear Kat. "Does he have any brothers?"

Rhani burst out laughing. "He has five, but three are already married."

They tried to ask as many questions as they could before Greg returned carrying their drinks. Rhani watched as he proceeded to charm their white cotton socks off.

"I'm at a loss here," he said. "Since my business has been put all out in the street, you probably know more about me than I do about you. Tell me about yourself, Kat."

Kat gave him an abbreviated version of her bio. Joie went into elaborate detail about her business and love of fashion. When she finished, he flashed them one of his best on-camera smiles.

"I can see why the three of you are friends. You're very much the same."

"How's that?" Kat asked.

"You're all intelligent, beautiful and driven."

If Kat's complexion hadn't been such a rich, dark chocolate, Rhani knew she would've been blushing. Joie was used to compliments and didn't flatter easily.

Rhani marveled as Greg used his best interview skills and asked them questions which got both of her friends talking as though they were on The Scoop. When he seemed to sense that they were relaxed and comfortable, he took Rhani's hand and said, "Baby, let's get the food reheated so we can eat."

"We'll be right back. It'll only take a few minutes. We ordered Thai and seafood. If you want to look around, go ahead." She and Greg left the living room hand-in-hand. "They love you already," she said, once they were in the kitchen.

"I wasn't kidding. They're both a lot like you, so they're not hard to like." He gave her booty a playful swat.

"This is a great apartment," Joie, who lived in less than nine hundred square feet, said when they returned with the food. "I love the office. Wish I had room enough for one."

"I've had this place for a few years, but it was missing

something." He caressed Rhani's cheek. "Now it's perfect."

Rhani smiled at Joie's and Kat's expressions. They both looked as though they wanted to hug him. Dinner ended up being a happy, noisy conversation that ended with her knowing her two best friends approved.

For the next few weeks, Adanna and Mrs. Stafford helped her with the details of drafting a grant proposal and gave her the information she needed to contact a few different grant writers. This was just the beginning, and Rhani knew she had an incredible amount of work ahead, but she no longer spent valuable time mourning her practice. She finally told the girls at the center about all that had transpired and about her new plans. Their excitement gave her the added incentive she needed to forge ahead with the creation of Positive Future, Inc.

As October arrived, she and Greg made the trip to Atlanta for Charles and Adanna's wedding. The weather in New York had already turned chilly, but when they exited the terminal at Hartsfield-Jackson Airport it was sixty-five degrees, and it put an instant smile on her face. This time he'd booked a room at one of the hotels near the airport. They had become used to sleeping together, and didn't want to be separated for the entire weekend.

That night at the rehearsal dinner, Rhani got a chance to see the rest of the family including Vic and Mona who talked to everyone except each other. They didn't seem angry, just disinterested. The coolness between them was palpable, and Rhani wondered to herself if the couple were headed for the first divorce in the family.

The day of the wedding at Greg's parents' church

turned out to be a typical warm, sunny Atlanta October day. Since Greg was serving as the best man, Rhani sat with the family. The only one of the sisters-in-law in the wedding party was Gianne. When the groomsmen exited a side door in the sanctuary, Rhani whispered to Cydney, "Gianne wasn't kidding. This is the best looking wedding party I've ever seen." Cydney's shoulders shook in response. The men wore traditional black tuxedos accessorized with pillbox-style round hats and matching vests made from brightly-printed African fabric.

Once Mr. and Mrs. Stafford and Adanna's mother and brother had been seated, the rear doors of the sanctuary swung open, and the bridesmaids began their walk to the altar in traditional Nigerian dresses and head wraps that matched the men's accessories.

The music changed, and a beaming Adanna appeared in the doorway on her father's arm. She walked slowly toward the altar, a vision in a slinky, strapless snow white gown with a sheer, lace-trimmed cape which fell gracefully from her shoulder blades to the floor and contrasted against her ebony skin.

The brief ceremony was spiritual and humorous at once. The pastor, who had known Charles since he was young shared a couple of funny, candid anecdotes about him. Charles and Adanna repeated their vows and were introduced to the congregation as husband and wife. Since the groomsmen outnumbered the bridesmaids two to one, Marc and Vic escorted Gianne. Nick and Jesse accompanied Lezigha, Adanna's friend and former coworker. Greg walked Femi, the bride's best friend and maid of honor, out of the sanctuary.

Charles and Adanna had booked the Peachtree Club, an upscale venue on the 28th floor of one of the high-rise buildings in downtown Atlanta for the reception. Inside the Club, three decorated, adjoining rooms held the food and bar. The outdoor terrace, which offered a spectacular view of the city, featured the DJ and dancing. Naturally, Rhani and Greg left the guests who seemed content sitting around the tables chatting and joined the crowd working up a sweat in the cool breeze on the terrace. After they had danced until they worked up a thirst, he asked the bartender to fix them two strawberry-lemon mojitos then found an empty sofa away from the dance floor.

Even though the music was louder than he wished, Greg snuggled her against his side and spoke into her ear. "I've been waiting a while for the right time and place to do this. Ever since you agreed to move in with me, I knew I needed to step up." He moved from the seat to one knee in front of her and reached into the pocket of his tuxedo jacket. Rhani's hand flew to cover her open mouth, and she held her breath. "This may seem premature, but it feels right. I want to spend the rest of my life with you, Rhani. Will you marry me?"

Her lips trembled, and before she answered she noticed the music had stopped and everyone on the terrace was watching them. She took a deep breath and her words came out through a blissful smile. "You know I will."

She let out a small gasp when Greg slipped the ring on her finger, and she saw the beautiful pear-shaped solitaire. He swept her into a long, deep kiss while the crowd erupted in a shout so loud guests on the inside came out to see what the commotion was about. Charles and Adanna worked their way through the press and he asked, "What's going on over here?"

Greg looked up at the faces surrounding them with a proud grin. "She said yes!" The brothers embraced, and Rhani waved her hand back and forth so no one missed her beautiful ring.

Adanna squealed, "You're next!"

As the word reached the rest of the family, one-by-one they rushed out to the terrace to offer their best wishes. What touched her most were the heartfelt congratulations from Greg's parents.

"I knew it was serious when Gregory brought you home this summer," his mother said with moist eyes, "But I didn't want to get my hopes up and then be disappointed. You're the best thing to ever happen to him, Rhani. I'll be so proud to have you as one of my daughters."

"I agree," Mr. Stafford chimed in. "Just like his father, Greg has excellent taste. I just have to warn you, the engagement party is already working in my wife's brain." He laughed and placed a kiss on Rhani's cheek.

The rest of the night was a blur in Rhani's mind. Everything and everyone else seemed to fade into the background. She and Greg cuddled on the sofa and talked about their plans for the future. They agreed to a year-long engagement, and set a tentative wedding date for the following October.

Epilogue

Two years later…

He was in bed reading the profile of a future guest for *The Scoop* when she appeared in the doorway wearing a sheer teddy, the one he'd seen in the *Victoria's Secret* catalog.

"*What do you think?*" she asked with her arms outstretched on either side of the door frame.

He put down the file, eyed the lacy, red garment clinging to her curves and smiled. "*It's tantalizing.*"

She studied his expression for a few beats then sauntered into the bedroom and over to the dresser where she sprayed a spritz of perfume between her breasts and another between her thighs. He followed her every move as she came closer to the bed.

Her gaze locked with his while she crawled up beside him and took the file and his iPad and moved them to the night table. "*That show is going to be the death of us.*"

"*That show pays the mortgage on this lovely suburban house you just had to have.*"

She shimmied against his side as close as she could get and wedged her leg between his. "*You're so good to me, and you're so sexy.*"

Greg chuckled deep in his chest and pressed his lips to her neck. She smelled light and clean—a mixture of flowers and lemon, and he inhaled drawing her fragrance deep into his nostrils. When she put her hand between his legs, he closed his eyes, forgot about the profile and the interview and roughly pulled her body on top of his.

"*I want you so bad,*" she said in his ear, her hot breath fanning *his face as she pulled herself to her knees and straddled him. "But we have to hurry. We don't have much time."*

He loved when she initiated sex, and she did it often.

"Hurry! We don't have much time before she wakes up." He wanted to shout when she reached inside his lounge pants and took hold of him then pulled the crotch of her black teddy aside and guided him inside her. She leaned forward, kissed him long and deep then began a slow, measured ride that soon escalated into a frantic gallop. In two years' time, they had learned each other's bodies so well they could achieve simultaneous orgasm during a quickie.

When they eventually collapsed into the pillows, Greg thought about how he once scoffed at the idea of being in love. His heart had been so badly broken, and at the time, it had seemed like a ridiculous, far-fetched concept. He'd had countless women in his life, but now he only had two, and his world revolved around them—the sexy, wild-haired one who had become his wife, and the tiny six-month old who was the result of their love.

They had always done things their way, and their wedding had been no different. He and Rhani eloped to Maui, because other than Wil, she didn't really have any family she wanted to attend, and the idea of a huge Stafford wedding seemed like too overwhelming a project. They bought a ticket for Wil, and Charles and Adanna flew out to the island to stand up for them. Joie, Kat and Thad all attended the beach ceremony followed by a lavish dinner at the hotel he and Rhani had chosen for their honeymoon. Naturally, Mrs. Stafford was upset when she heard the news, but Greg pacified her by promising to let her give them a reception a few weeks after the fact.

At times he couldn't believe how his life had changed in three years' time. His wife was happy being a new mother. Lili, who they had named after his mother, had been a wonderful unplanned surprise. She was as beautiful and full of life as Rhani, who was again doing work she loved. She'd worked hard to secure funding for her non-profit corporation, found a suitable location, made a decent salary, and fulfilled her heart's desire to help underprivileged girls.

His return to The Scoop had catapulted the show into the number one spot in their time slot. He had even been asked to host a couple of specials for the network. After all the selfishness, the plays for attention, the mistakes, and the bad choices he'd made, he went to sleep at night with a smile, because he realized he was like his brothers after all.

Thank you for taking time to read *Don't Stop Till You Get Enough*.

If you enjoyed it, please consider telling your friends

or posting a short review.

Word of mouth is an author's best friend and much appreciated.

Chicki

A Preview of

It's Cheaper to Keep Her

Book Four in the Stafford Brothers series

Coming Summer 2015

Vic Stafford pulled into the circular driveway of his home at ten forty-five. Today had been the roughest day he'd ever had at the hospital, thanks to a horrific tour bus accident on Interstate 75. The fifty passengers on the bus and twelve occupants of other vehicles involved in the crash had been divided up between his hospital and Grady, since they were the only level one trauma centers in the Atlanta metropolitan area. According to the EMTs and State Patrol officers, the bus driver apparently mistook the exit lane at Northside Drive off I-75 as part of the carpool lane. He came up over Northside and continued over the side of the overpass. The bus traveled over a two-and-a-half foot tall concrete barrier, leaving it intact, and through the middle of the overpass, falling onto the Interstate below.

As chief of surgery, Vic had to pull in every staff member on call in order to handle the volume and even handled two of the surgeries himself, something he rarely did anymore. When he'd left for the night, six of the accident victims had expired, which in his opinion was a miracle. Five remained in critical condition, and twenty were being evaluated. Most had broken bones. The twenty were lucid and communicating.

Drained from the emotion and pace of the night, Vic needed to talk, but when he gazed up, every window in the sprawling eight-thousand-square-foot house was dark. Before he left in the morning, Mona had mentioned a meeting with one of her fundraising groups, but he hadn't really paid much attention, and he thought she'd surely be home by now.

Where were the boys? He drove around to the side of the house, hit the button for the garage door opener and went in through the kitchen. After he loosened his tie, he walked to the back of the house to the family room where he poured himself a scotch at the wet bar.

Ever since he'd been appointed chief, his hours had increased even though he wasn't performing as many surgeries as he once had. Now he dealt with a myriad of daily administrative issues. Every day he thought about stepping down and going back to just being a surgeon. But the position carried with it clout, some great perks he hadn't gotten as a staff doctor and a spectacular salary. When he was simply Dr. Stafford, he and Mona had a very nice, spacious home, but once he became *The Chief*, he let her talk him into upgrading to this house. This one contained three thousand more square feet, had an Olympic-size pool, wine cellar, home gym and a guest house where Maite, their live-in housekeeper, stayed.

It wasn't as though he didn't like the house, because he did, but after all the pleading and cajoling she had done, it seemed she never bothered to stay home to enjoy it. He'd ignored her behavior long enough. Tonight he'd confront her. She rarely parked her car in the garage, but preferred to leave it in the circular driveway in front of the house. When he'd explained why it was better for the car to keep it inside, she said she parked there because the Bentley convertible looked so good next to the fountain, and she wanted everyone to see it. Things like that made her happy, and as the saying went, *If mama ain't happy, then nobody's happy*. He loved giving her nice things, but recently it seemed as if she no longer got the same pleasure from her expensive wardrobe, top-of-the-line car or beautiful house.

His anger built as he sipped his drink. For the third time this month, Mona claimed to be at one of her charity meetings. He knew good and damn well the group of women who planned events to raise money for their favorite causes didn't hang out this late on a regular basis. If she wasn't asleep when he came in, she wasn't home at all. His boys had been spending too much time with Maite or at his parents' house.

Too tired to climb the stairs, he walked back to the foyer, removed his shoes and eased his weary body onto the uncomfortable decorative chair at the base of the double staircase to wait for her to come home. After he drained his glass and set it on the table next to the huge silk flower arrangement she'd insisted was the only thing that looked right in the foyer, he rested his head back against the wall and drifted off to sleep until the sound of keys in the front door woke him. Her heels clacked loudly on the marble.

"Where have you been?"

She jumped. "Oh, my God, Vic! You scared me half to death. What are you doing sitting here in the dark?"

"Where have you been?" he repeated, spacing his words.

She flicked the light switch on the wall which illuminated the chandelier hanging over the center of the twenty-foot ceiling. "I told you I had a meeting."

"Where are the boys?"

"At your mother's. She said they could spend the night, since I told her I'd probably be late. I gave Maite the night off. Why are you asking me all of these questions?"

He checked out her appearance. Mona had a lot of clothes, but he'd never seen the outfit she wore tonight—a low-cut number that hit her mid-thigh. Not exactly attire for a meeting with the wives of other doctors. "Was there anybody else I know at the meeting?"

She looked toward the ceiling a second then her voice grew louder. "Are you serious, Vic? You're really going to question me like I'm a teenager breaking curfew?" Jerky movements punctuated her words.

"Tell me who else was there," he insisted, his voice still calm.

"Why does it matter to you?" she shouted.

"Because you don't look like you've been to a meeting, Mona. And you don't smell like it either. What have you been drinking?"

"I'm not a child, Vic," she screamed. "Since when have you been interested in where I've been or what I'm doing?"

"You're my wife. I have a right to know where you've been hanging out."

"Hanging out? Please! You're not my father!" He ducked when her Hermes bag sailed past his head and hit the wall behind him. "I'm not going to stand here and be interrogated!" She flipped her long, thick hair over one shoulder and turned on her five-inch heels and stormed up the curved staircase.

He watched her long, shapely legs—very much exposed beneath the short dress. Even after ten years of marriage, she still had the power to excite him. Ramona Cox Stafford was the most beautiful woman he'd ever met. He would always remember the first time he saw. Twelve years ago they had been guests at a pool party given by one of the other interns. She walked into the back yard wearing a bikini with a sarong wrapped around her hips, looking like a Victoria's Secret model. As soon as they were introduced, a mutual spark ignited between them and had been burning ever since.

Until recently.

His brothers had always teased him about spoiling her, and he had. He loved her. She'd been a great wife and mother. Whatever request she made of him, he'd given her, because she deserved it. He bought her the Bentley for her last birthday. Trinkets made with chocolate diamonds filled her jewelry box, her favorite, and her closet overflowed with top designer ensembles. What more could she ask for? Sadly, he knew the answer, but he forced it to the recesses of his mind. Everybody wanted something from him, and he couldn't be all things to all people.

Vic eventually mustered enough strength to climb the stairs to the bedroom. How long had he been sitting there? Already in bed with a scarf tied around her head, Mona had her back turned away from the door. He knew she wasn't asleep already, but talking was out of the question, so he crossed the hall and entered one of the guest rooms.

♥♥♥

Ramona wasn't sleeping, but she didn't want Vic to think she cared enough to stay awake and wait for him to come upstairs. She had never been a crier, but right now tears dampened her pillow. Her emotions ran more toward verbal battle, but tonight she had no desire to get into another screaming match with her husband. How could such an intelligent man be so stupid?

Over the past three years, his interest in her had waned. He used to notice how she looked every day. Now, tonight he'd only noticed because he'd suddenly become suspicious. And he had good reason to be. After two years of begging him to spend more time with her and the boys, she'd made the decision that she would no longer come in second to his career. He had ignored her long enough, and thirty-seven was too young to become a medical widow.

When she and Vic got married, he'd only had eyes for her. Now his new love—his hospital—had taken her place. He nurtured her, protected her, spent endless hours thinking about how to make her better—the things he used to do for his wife. Nothing could be worse than having your husband obsessed with another love. Some women, like a few of her friends and even her own mother, thought she was nitpicking. After all, she had everything most women would die for. She tried to explain to them that she married Vic for love. She didn't have to work, and he left the daily finances up to her. He made the investment decisions, because he knew more about those things and always did so with the best of the family in mind. The money was wonderful, and he had always been extremely generous, but what these women didn't understand was that sharing money didn't take the place of sharing intimacy, whether it happened in or out of the bed.

Each time she tried to make him understand how she felt, he went into a long lecture about being under scrutiny as the first black and the youngest chief of surgery in the history of the largest medical center in Atlanta—in the South for that matter. It wasn't as though she didn't understand the importance of his job. In fact, she was wildly proud of his status, but most of the time she wished he could go back to being a surgeon. Surgeons were the elite of the medical community, but that hadn't been enough for him. Vic followed in his namesake's footsteps, and now he'd surpassed the professional status his father had reached. Sometimes his ambition actually frightened her. Where would it stop? Would he have to become Surgeon General of the United States before he was satisfied?

She yearned for the times Vic shared everything with her. During his time as a lowly intern, when they were dating, he told her all about his days doing the grunt work for the residents. At the same time, he'd been so excited and eager to learn everything he could about medicine first-hand. Often they stayed up late into the night talking on the phone, and he asked questions about her burgeoning modeling career. After the wedding, once they had their own apartment, she loved lying in bed listening to his amazing stories about the inner workings of the hospital. Now, if they talked at all, it was about mundane, necessary things before he drifted into a work-induced coma. When he was conscious, hospital business preoccupied Vic's mind. He traveled a lot to conferences, conventions and symposiums. His schedule didn't allow him to accompany her at fundraising events or sit with her in the bleachers at the boys' football games. He'd become little more than a ghost in their own home.

A few months ago at a masquerade ball to raise money for children with cancer, the idea came to her unbidden. The man had been watching her for about an hour. She had noticed his eyes following her before he made his way across the ballroom. From that distance she hadn't been able to tell his age, but as he got closer she realized he was young, probably only in his late twenties. And he was as different from Vic as he could possibly be—big, muscular, dark as a panther and quite good looking.

"How tall are you without the heels?"

"Five eight," she answered meeting him eye to eye. In her stilettos, she stood six-foot-two and towered over every other woman in the room.

Although he couldn't see her whole face due to her elaborate feather mask, he said, "You're stunning. What's your name?"

"Mona. Mona Stafford."

He extended his hand, and she marveled at its size and the stark contrast of their skin as it engulfed hers.

"DaQuan Patterson. Can I get you a drink?"

The way his gaze slowly traveled down her body sent a tingle simmering beneath her skin. It had been a long time since anyone looked at her that way. "A cosmopolitan, thank you."

"Don't move, Mona. I'll be right back."

She watched as he moved across the room and headed to the bar in what she could only think of as a glide. Even though he had to be at least six-foot-three, his movements were graceful, and his muscles flexed beneath his designer suit. She wondered what he did for a living.

DaQuan returned, placed the rosy cocktail into her hand and answered her unspoken question.

"This is my first big event since I relocated to Atlanta. I'm the new point guard for the Hawks," he said with a proud smile that seemed to glow against his smooth onyx skin.

"I should've known you were an athlete."

"Why?"

"You move like one. Point guard, huh? So you're the floor general, the play-maker."

His eyes widened. "You know basketball?"

"I cheered for my college basketball team all four years."

"I can see you doing that." He stared at the three-carat diamond and matching band on her left hand when she raised the glass to her lips. "You're married?"

"Yes, and I have two sons."

"That's a shame," he said, giving her yet another appreciative head-to-toe scan.

"Why?"

"I was hoping we could be friends."

"Married people can't have friends, DaQuan?" Her mind raced with all of the reasons why she shouldn't take this any further, but what harm could a little flirtation cause?

He grinned. "How can I get in touch with you?"

Mona opened her Marc Jacobs clutch and handed him the personal business card she gave to new acquaintances at networking events and social gatherings. "Call me."

Book List

Have You Seen Her?

Hot Fun in the Summertime

Hollywood Swinging

Ain't Nothing Like the Real Thing

I Can't Get Next to You

Ain't Too Proud to Beg

You Make Me Feel Brand New

A Woman's Worth – Book One in the Stafford Brothers Series

Till You Come Back to Me – Book Two in the Stafford Brothers Series

Don't Stop Till You Get Enough – Book Three in the Stafford Brothers Series

About the Author

Contemporary women's fiction/romance author Chicki Brown has published nine novels and one novella. Her books have been featured in USAToday. She was the 2014 B.R.A.B. (Building Relationships Around Books) Inspirational Fiction Author and the 2011 SORMAG (Shades of Romance Magazine) Author of the Year. Chicki was also a contributing author to the *Gumbo for the Soul: Men of Honor (Special Cancer Awareness Edition)*. She is currently working on the fourth book in her Stafford brothers series.

Nia Forrester, Beverly Jenkins, Eric Jerome Dickey, Lisa Kleypas, J.R. Ward and Suzanne Brockmann are among her favorite authors.

A transplanted New Jersey native who lives in Atlanta, Georgia, Brown still misses the Jersey shore.

Her many homes in cyberspace include:

Blog: http://sisterscribbler.blogspot.com
Twitter: http://twitter.com/@Chicki663
Facebook: http://www.facebook.com/chicki.brown
Pinterest: http://pinterest.com/chicki663/

Made in the USA
Columbia, SC
09 April 2021